that summer in paris

a novel

abha dawesar

NAN A. TALESE
Doubleday
New York   London   Toronto   Sydney   Auckland

PUBLISHED BY NAN A. TALESE
AN IMPRINT OF DOUBLEDAY

Published in the United States by Nan A. Talese, an imprint
of The Doubleday Broadway Publishing Group, a division of
Random House, Inc., New York.
www.nanatalese.com

DOUBLEDAY is a registered trademark of Random House, Inc.

Book design by Donna Sinisgalli

Library of Congress Cataloging-in-Publication Data
Dawesar, Abha.
    That summer in Paris : a novel / Abha Dawesar.—1st ed.
        p. cm.
    1. South Asians—France—Fiction. 2. Paris (France)—Fiction.
3. Young Women—Fiction. 4. Older men—Fiction.
5. Authors—Fiction. I. Title.

PS3554.A9423T47 2006
813' 54—dc22

                                                    2005052865

ISBN-13: 978-0-385-51749-2
ISBN-10: 0-385-51749-1

PRINTED IN THE UNITED STATES OF AMERICA

10 9 8 7 6 5 4 3 2 1
First Edition

To fellow writers and dear friends:

Claudette Buelow and Robert Steward

that summer in paris

part i

When you admire a writer you become curious.
You look for his secret. The clues to his puzzle.

—ZUCKERMAN TO LONOFF IN

PHILIP ROTH'S *THE GHOST WRITER*

Prem Rustum was tired. Seventy-five and tired. Thirty-odd books, countless awards, and a Nobel Prize later, he argued with Pascal over the phone that this was allowed. He regretted the conversation. Pascal hadn't won the prize yet, and it was not clear anymore that he would.

Pascal had taken the slight in his stride and pushed on. "It is the manner in which you write, my friend. You cannot stand at that tall table forever writing longhand. Move with the times, type on a computer, get online, buy your Viagra over the Internet. Prolong your youth. Learn to sit down."

Prem was already online; he just couldn't write fiction sitting down. He couldn't think of overarching themes and transcendental moments with his ass stuck to a seat, not with the same cleanliness as while standing up. He suspected that no one could. In fact, he was sure that his novels had an edge over Pascal's and Pedro's because he did it standing up. The foremost of the three Ps, he had been called.

Prem's ankles were stiff. There was a time not so long ago when he could go until noon without a break. He walked over to his bulletin board, where he had pinned the acupuncture chart that Homi had sent him from India. Prem traced his index finger over the drawing of the foot and its pressure points. Homi had sent a box of presents along with a card signed by Ratan that read *I miss you, Grandpa*. Ratan had probably chosen none of the items in the box other than the small G.I. Joe figure.

If the chart were to be believed, the stomach and spine regions of Prem's foot were causing trouble. But his stomach and spine felt fine—only his feet hurt like mad. Prem lowered himself into the tan leather couch in the corner of his studio. For a few minutes he looked at nothing in particular. Then his eyes settled upon the stack of hardback books piled in the corner, their spines all blue, his own name in italicized yellow in a speedy font. This jacket cover was different from all the ones before. His publishers had called him to the office instead of sending him a mock-up by mail.

"We've made the cover very sexy this time," Rudolf had declared at the meeting, when he had shown Prem the cover. Rudolf and Stern pretended that the jacket designer was caught up in a meeting and used an extra few minutes to praise the book cover before the sample arrived.

"The cover is fine," Prem said, dismissing it when it was presented. He had approved it because he knew instantly that this yellow was Ratan's favorite color. Ratan was still too young to read his books, but he would have an opinion on the jacket as soon as he saw it.

Rudolf and Stern had not been able to hide their collective relief. The designer—white, late twenties, nervous—seemed upset. On his way out Prem tugged at her elbow to pull her closer and whispered, "It's my last book. I'm glad you did such a good job with it."

In his studio, his eyes mildly out of focus as they stared at the blue and yellow tower labeled *Prem Rustum,* he was sure this was indeed his last. He had played with ideas for another novel, but they were going nowhere. Standing at the high lectern writing had become arduous. Prem felt his body getting slower and slower each day as if it were preparing for the full stop. Maybe it was time to move back to India and live with his family. In the absence of women, sex, and further mountains to scale, Ratan alone made Prem's life meaningful.

Prem rose from the couch and made his way to his desk. His

laptop was on. He hadn't touched the power button since Kenny had hooked it up. Sometimes when Kenny would drop in, he would shut off the laptop and come back a few hours later to turn it on. Prem peered from the bottom of his glasses at the screen. He clicked on his messenger icon to see if Ratan was online. He wasn't. Prem calculated the time in Delhi—it was late. He leaned over to his phone and called Kenny.

"Could you come over?"

"I thought we already made an appointment for noon."

"I mean now. If you're free, that is."

"You're not working, Mr. Rustum?"

"No."

"I'll be right over." Prem wondered if he should add that everything was okay. Of late it seemed that everyone had become more anxious about his health. A minor headache, and Mrs. Smith and Kenny would make a grand fuss.

Kenny was at the door in fifteen minutes.

"I just wanted to deal with the books," Prem said, pointing to the stack of *By the Thread,* which had been variously hailed, debated, and dismissed as an opus on old age, a self-congratulatory sensationalist sermon, and a pompous preposterous piece of mediocrity.

"Yes, Mr. Rustum. Do you want me to send them to the usual list?"

"Could you, Kenny?"

"Of course. Anything else?" Kenny looked at Prem's entire body as he asked the question, scanning Prem's face, heart, and knees for an answer.

"Oh! I don't know." Prem ran his hand over the surface of his laptop.

"How is the computer coming along?"

"The computer!" Prem chortled. That crazy day when Krishnan, his friend from Oxford, and Krishnan's colleague ran like rats in a maze over the blueprints of his manuscripts was etched in Prem's memory.

"Do you use it more?" Kenny asked. The old man had a tendency to lapse into a reverie at times, and Kenny had learned to keep the focus on his questions by asking them without pausing for too long.

"Not for my writing, but I send those messages to my grandson."

"Would you like to learn how to use a search engine, Mr. Rustum? You can do your research online."

Prem nodded. Kenny opened a browser window and started a demo. Prem squinted a little to see what Kenny was pointing to. He grunted once he had seen it.

"In this window type in whatever you want to find out about. Let's just put your name here." Kenny pointed to the screen, taking care not to touch it.

"My name?"

"Here we go—five hundred and sixty thousand articles."

Prem angled his head to read properly from the half-moon of his bifocals, his attention captured by a sentence in which the words *Rustum, bad,* and *sex* were in bold.

"Go here," Prem said pointing to the screen.

Of the three Ps Prem Rustum is by far the least articulate about sex. The Indian is no match for the Latin lovers! Rustum's words ring hollow when he attempts any description of sexual activity. To his credit, he doesn't do this often. Speculation about his private life in the past has linked him with ballerinas, actresses, and even two schoolgirls in France who were below the legal age in America. It is therefore hard to understand why Rustum is bad with sex. On this front, his archrival, the second P, Pascal Boutin, is Rustum's superior.

"Can I do a search in French too?"

"Yes. Would you like to try? You can put in multiple words separated by commas." Kenny slid away from the laptop. In the first months Prem had noted everything Kenny had said. But as he got more familiar with terms like *start key, escape,* and *control,* he stopped taking notes. Instead, in Kenny's presence, he fumbled to replicate what Kenny had done.

"Let me see, P-a-s-c-a-l space B-o-u-t-i-n comma c-r-i-t-i-q-u-e."

Prem moved his head closer to the screen and used his finger to read off each line that had appeared.

"Let's see. Yes. Good." Prem was already absorbed in the articles.

"Can I take the books and go now, Mr. Rustum?"

"Yes, that will be fine, Kenny. Thank you." Prem didn't turn his head.

Kenny thumbed some sheets on a side table in the studio for mailing labels, gathered a pile of books, and left.

The rest of the afternoon Prem experienced deep satisfaction from finding out that the majority of Pascal's compatriots thought that Prem Rustum was definitely the greatest of the three Ps even if he wasn't French. But even the French repeatedly poked fun at Prem's passage on drinking a lactating woman's milk in *Raga* and at the scene when Kochi sucks his young mistress's toe in *From Kerala to Karela.* Aside from these slight unflattering infractions, the rest was pure gold. Prem browsed through a myriad of French articles on Pascal, chuckling to himself at the things Pascal had failed to report to Prem on their biweekly phone conversations. There were even tongue-in-cheek references to Pascal's new engagement with youth after his article in defense of Viagra was published in *Le nouvel observateur.*

At six Mrs. Smith called Prem on his intercom to remind him that the car would soon pick him up to take him to dinner. Eddy Parma of Patriots Publishing was throwing a party in his house.

Prem reluctantly left his studio and went back to the house, where he changed into a fresh shirt and a rarely sported yellow tie. It bothered him, this near-universal view that he floundered when it came to sex. Prem had always been aware of the criticisms of his writing—after all, they were as old as his books—but on the screen, stacked one after another, they were like a litany of complaints. It seemed that none of the critics had understood that he wasn't really trying to write about sex at all. Maybe an essay was what was really called for. An essay on why sex should be done, not written about. Words, when written down, tampered with the reality of experience. Sex only worked, was only good, when it was fluid, but words were all about fixing. Moreover sex, unmediated by language and the morality necessarily innate in language, was the only way to have sex. The spoken word was more fluid than the written; it could be modified with new words and adapt itself to the situation. He still remembered the words he had used with Vedika. Were words the opposite of sex?

The drive from Prem's mansion in New Jersey to Eddy Parma's was an hour long. He let out a breath at having painlessly made the journey wrapped up in the past, musing between his books and memories of Meher and Vedika. Parma's invitation had suggested that it was to be a schmoozing party, but instead there were assigned seats, four courses of food, three courses of booze, and as many butlers. To Prem's left was Eddy's wife Sebi, and to his right Roger Johnson. Johnson was so awkward that Prem couldn't help pay him attention. There were no pretty young girls at the table, just the literary wives he had known for twenty years and an odd collection of dipsomaniac spinsters. Roger Johnson seemed more promising than anyone else. He was young, fresh blood. Maybe he was screwing someone and could be persuaded to talk about it. Prem could try writing about Roger's sex life the next day as an exercise.

"I have only written a couple of short stories, Mr. Rustum. As I was saying, I did a Ph.D. in literature before I started writing."

"What was your topic?"

"You." Roger Johnson lurched for his drink as soon as he said *you* and spilled the champagne on his tie as a result.

"Here," Prem said, handing him his napkin as he looked at the boy's face again. Twenty-six or twenty-seven.

"Excuse me," Johnson apologized nervously.

"Me? Is that what you said?"

"I had already read all your work by the time I went to college. I reread everything and did my undergraduate thesis on you. Your work is so rich and complex, Mr. Rustum, I decided to do my graduate work on you as well."

"Obviously not on 'the great P's treatment of sex,' " Prem quoted from one of the Web pages he had surfed earlier in the day.

Johnson gulped some more of his champagne.

"Look, tell me about yourself," Prem said, smiling graciously. The thrill of knowing how much he was adored by yet another stranger had dulled. And in America the praise he received could not hold a candle to the adulation, the adoration, and the sycophancy he got in India. But Johnson was still so green and naïve in his admiration that Prem felt soft. By the time Eddy's retinue of servants, as Prem called the catering staff, were serving chocolate ganaches with pepper ice cream and port, he and Roger had almost become friends.

"Listen, I just don't have the time to read most of the younger writers who approach me, but send me one of your stories and I'll tell you what I think."

"Mr. Rustum, thank you so much."

"You can send it by e-mail."

"Oh! I read somewhere that you didn't believe in computers."

"I don't write on one, but I'm wired just like the rest of you."

"My story is about online dating."

"One tip, young man. Never tell them what your story is about. Let them read it."

Prem returned home tired but invigorated.

Johnson came home equally invigorated, high from the port and the peppery Prem Rustum. He logged online to a dating site under his screen name, Plume, and met Maya.

Maya walked into the no-name diner a little after noon. The short run across the street from her apartment had left her cold.

The rain was coming down so hard that her gray sweater already smelled of wet dog.

"What are your soups today, Costas?"

"Chicken noodle, shrimp bisque, potato leek."

Maya ordered and sat at the counter. Mrs. Nonagenarian was seated two stools down. Maya nodded briefly and unzipped her sweater to retrieve the hardbound tome, weighing in at four pounds, she had carried inside to shield from the rain. She pulled her baseball cap farther over her head and settled down to read.

"Coffee shop/diner/coffee shop. Gotta think outside the box," Costas said emphatically as he tapped his pen on the napkin holder as if it were the box.

Mrs. Nonagenarian nodded.

"I'm a guy who thinks outside the box. Got to have a new menu. It's coming. It's all changing. Outside the box." He tapped the napkin holder again.

Mrs. Nona nodded again.

A customer walked in, her sharp high-heeled shoes clicking forcefully on the ground. Her leather skirt elicited a raised eyebrow from Costas as well as Mrs. Nona. She asked to see a menu at the cash register and remained standing.

"I'll just take three hamburgers to go," the leather skirt said, folding the menu closed.

Maya bit her lip as she read. At the beginning of the book she had been sure that the narrator just had a secret crush, a longing for his cousin Meher. But now he was suggesting that he had actually acted on it.

"Here's your potato leek. Try not to feed your book," Costas laughed as he placed the bowl in front of Maya.

Papa Beard walked in and tipped his hat to Mrs. Nona. Then he took the stool beside Maya.

"I'll have the same thing this beautiful lady is having," he said, pointing to her soup.

Maya acknowledged the compliment and placed her book facedown on her lap as she blew on a spoon of soup.

"Three hamburgers for under twelve dollars! And if you don't think that's the best bargain meal in Manhattan, you come take your money back tomorrow." Costas handed a brown bag to the leather skirt.

"I think you should serve relish with your hamburgers," said Mrs. Nona as soon as the leather skirt had stepped out of the diner.

"No one wants relish. No point having it." Costas raised his shoulders and dropped them as he spoke.

"Wouldn't you want relish with your hamburger?" Mrs. Nona canvassed Papa Beard.

"I don't eat no red meat. Not me. Not for eighteen years."

"You don't eat red meat?"

"I don't have no cholesterol. No red meat. No cholesterol. No medicine."

"No cholesterol! That's what I need so I can get off these pills." Mrs. Nona reached into her bag and pulled out a small pillbox.

After her soup Maya crossed back to her building and sneaked in a few more sentences of *Meher* in the elevator. The garlicky flavor of the potato leek soup had left her with a sugar craving. In the kitchen she stuck out her tongue and squeezed out a few drops of honey from the teddy bear.

Back in the rest of her apartment, which also doubled as writing studio, bedroom, and living room, Maya sat on the chair in front of her laptop and started work again. She was proofreading an article on two-photon fluorescence brain imaging. After a few hours she logged onto the new online dating site she had been trying out. Macho37 had written back. So had Writerlysoul.

Macho37:
Do you still let yourself feel the wet dew between your toes when it rains? What about just under your toenail? Can you feel under the nails of your toes? These are the kinds of

things I want to know about you. The rest, the books and
the literature and the art and the job life, those don't tell me
anything.

This had been going on with Macho37 for a week. Initially
Maya had been tantalized by the references to Hodgkin, Hockney,
and Bacon, but their e-mail exchanges had dwindled to pointless
questions. Maya deleted the message.

Writerlysoul had sent another unedited brain dump—a labo-
rious message excessive in detail and lacking in import. Maya was
irritated by insignificant detail from people unless they wrote like
Prem Rustum, with density in their prose and the power of transcendence, which they usually didn't. She wanted to meet a man,
see if she liked him, sleep with him, become a couple, and change
her life. Maya logged off the site.

She hated cooking for herself and usually ate a bowl of cold ce-
real for dinner. But she would read *Meher* tonight, and she enjoyed
eating with it. So she cooked small salmon-colored lentils. As they
simmered, she sliced an onion. It was always a race to see if she could
chop it up before it made her suffer. This one was small enough that
she succeeded. She threw a teaspoon of spices into a saucepan with
oil and put in the chopped onion when the spices sputtered. She re-
trieved *Meher* from her desk and stood reading it in the kitchen as she
periodically stirred. Once the lentils were cooked, she poured some
into a bowl and read another five pages waiting for it to cool. She distractedly ate her dinner and then stuck the bowl in the dishwasher.

Maya had been eating her meals in the kitchen within two
feet of the sink ever since Tom had dumped her. Tom had left
Maya with a gaping hole in the middle of her chest and an olfac-
tory deprivation that led her to order truffles, men's colognes, and
pheromones online in the hope of healing.

Maya had spent her yawningly free winter nights chatting online with Mr. Spinoza, an incorrigible Francophile like herself with endless things to say about French surrealism and the literature of Pascal Boutin. Eventually when she healed, it was not scrambled eggs with truffle butter that had done the trick but Mr. Spinoza's gift. When they finally met up at a bar one night, he showed up with a hardcover book by Prem Rustum.

"Have you already read this one?"

"I've never read anything by Rustum."

"I don't believe you. For a girl who has read everything by Pascal Boutin."

"I know, I know."

"This guy is the best of the three Ps. You will thank me for this one day." He handed her *The Smell of Wet Mud*.

Mr. Spinoza had unfortunately not started up a storm in Maya's insides. She never met him again after he gifted her the book that changed her life, though she did thank him in her head and sent a silent prayer his way a few times. As if to punish her for her crippling reliance on her brain's mysterious ways, Maya had gotten only idiotic one-liners from day traders with the attention span of fruitflies or from pedants enamored of their own voices. Internet dating was a lost cause and, luckily for Maya, was made unnecessary at the time by a trip to India.

Maya's father, ever ready to provide financing when it came to India, had helped generously, insisting she stay in the midrange options listed in *Lonely Planet* and feel free to use his credit card for something better should she feel her safety might be compromised. He had presented her with two more Rustum books, *From Kerala to Karela* and *Dharma*, his own favorite. On her flight she finished one of the two books her father had given her. She was determined to hit Pondicherry this time. Her parents had always pooh-pahed Goa and Pondy on their family vacations, saying they were not going all the way to India to see middle-aged white people stoned or speaking French. They had insisted on monuments of cultural importance, temples carved in stone, music and dance festivals, and hiking trips in the lower Himalayas. Goa was now notorious for young Israeli soldiers who had just finished their compulsory army service, and Maya decided to skip it. But Pondicherry, with its French colonial heritage and the Ashram, was a different story. Maya had finished reading the second half of *Dharma* on the road from Chennai to Pondicherry. Instead of filling her with a longing for her youth or awakening the desire for a world of great purity, it had put into her head the idea of meeting with and talking to Prem Rustum. In Pondicherry, between walks by the sea and bicycle trips to the gold-leafed hemispheric ashram, Maya had written and rewritten a letter to Rustum in her mind. As soon as she went back to New York, she would interview him and meet his beautiful head.

In the year she had spent working on her thesis on Pascal Boutin, Maya had not felt a similar compulsion. She had, of course, been curious about Pascal; he was clearly insouciant in matters of the heart and irreverent about sex. In his interviews and portraits he came across as the person who had written the books that he had, a man who believed he understood himself and therefore he understood you. In contrast, just two books by Rustum had impressed upon Maya that he was complex but also elusive. In the restrained and unapproachable way in which he talked about love, it was obvious that his heart was the ultimate prize for a woman. Boutin's books were clever, insightful, fluid. But Prem's were in altogether another league; the words themselves felt as if they were no longer the words of human beings but something more, words from prophets or gods. They felt as if they were made with lava that flowed straight out of his heart onto the page, and then when you read them, they liquefied and entered from your pupils into your soul. Reading Prem Rustum's books was like looking at one of Klimt's extravagant gold paintings like *Danaë*.

Still working on the first draft of her thirteen-page letter to Prem to ask for an appointment when she was back in New York, Maya had taken off from Pondy to the temple town of Thanjavur. At the train station in Thanjavur next to the Automatic Tea and Coffee Stall, a man was hawking some books. Hungry for more of

Rustum's voice, Maya bought *My Self in the West,* even though in her head she imagined her father telling her to read the India books when she was in India. On an overnight train a few days later Maya finished the book about Judith Q, the New York nutcase. She shuddered to see herself summarized in Rustum's words, which would likely be: Maya the guru-seeking yoga-breathing literature-loony. She ripped up her letter to Prem.

By the time she left India, Maya had read fifteen of Prem's books. She read the remainder in New York, steadily modulating the inflow of youthful contemporary literature by her cohort group with Rustum's masterworks. When she was almost finished with his body of work, she reread a stray one now and then. She had saved *Meher* for last and had embarked on it with trepidation because after *Meher* there would be no more books to read—she would have read them all.

Now halfway through *Meher,* Maya was in a different kind of panic than she had felt when Tom had left. Reading Rustum's pages at night had made up for countless otherwise fruitless days. Without new Rustum books to read and the company of a man, a lifetime of cold bowls of cereals was all Maya could see ahead of her. In preparation for Rustum's final unread book, Maya had decided to write up a new personal ad. She would not finish *Meher* until she got a real-life companion.

> Spiritual twenty-something aspiring novelist with hot buns and yoga body seeks another. Write like Prem Rustum, think like Prem Rustum, speak like Prem Rustum, be Prem Rustum. Worship at his altar like I do. Rank *Grinding India, Kerala,* and *Dharma.* Tell me what you would ask him if you met him. I'm reading *Meher,* don't tell me if he does it with her.

Within minutes Maya's laptop sounded a bing. Screen name Plume flashed.

Plume:	I just met him. I asked him to read my story. Do you have a pic?
Dogpose:	I don't believe you. Who is Homi? Who is Ratan? Your pic = my pic.
Plume:	Homi is Meher's son. Ratan is Homi's son.
Dogpose:	Is Meher real?
Plume:	Yes, Meher was his sister. In the book *Meher* she's real. But in *Dharma* she is only a fictional character. He likes to use the names of his family and friends in his books and fictionalize them.
Dogpose:	Okay, I believe you know his work. I still don't believe you know him.
Plume:	I did my Ph.D. on him. And I do, as of tonight, know him. I just got your pic! Wow! For real?
Dogpose:	I got yours. Nice smile! What did he tell you? Are you seeing him again?
Plume:	Who? PR?
Dogpose:	Yeah, who else?
Plume:	I'm e-mailing him my story.
Dogpose:	You're very lucky. To have HIM read your work. I'm jealous.
Plume:	Yes. It's my day. I met him and now you! Would you feel the same way if it were one of the other P's—Pascal Boutin or Pedro Nicolas?
Dogpose:	*Presque.* Almost. French?
Plume:	*Oui.* If you're nice to me I'll introduce you to him.
Dogpose:	You'll need to introduce yourself to me first!

Maya went to bed with a smile. Another writer! Someone else who lived for the words that these three old men turned into sentences, paragraphs, chapters, books, œuvres.

Prem sat in his studio reading Roger Johnson's short story for the second time. The first time he had been so caught up with the novelty of it that he had not been able to pay attention to the writing. The characters in the story seemed real only when they were in front of their screens. The rest of the time, as they rushed in and out of cabs, dates, dinners, drinks, and discos, Prem felt practically vertiginous. Was this also the pace of Pascal's life? He had never, in all their conversations, thought Pascal was different from him in any important way save all the sex he had been getting in the past ten years while Prem's own life had lain fallow. They wrote books at more or less the same pace and passed their books to Edward to sell.

Prem reached for his telephone and called Johnson.

"This is Prem Rustum calling. I've read your story. Do you want to come and have lunch here with me tomorrow?"

"It would be such an honor, sir."

"Listen, I have a question."

"Yes, Mr. Rustum."

"Are these online dating sites real? I mean, is this science fiction or fiction?"

"It's real all right. I've used real sites in the story. I might change the names later."

"See you tomorrow. I always eat a hamburger for lunch."

"Sorry, Mr. Rustum, I'm vegetarian."

"Oh! Mrs. Smith will manage something, I am sure."

Prem noted the websites listed in Johnson's story and went to his laptop. It took him several minutes to read all the options in minuscule font on citylovin.com and make a decision on where to click. Eventually Prem found a screen with several self-descriptions by (mostly young) men and women. The worst criticisms of his novel could have applied to these self-descriptions—self-congratulatory, sensationalist, pompous, preposterous. Before adjourning for the day, Prem tried out one last button on his screen: search. A complex grid with blank spaces and check boxes popped up. Prem squinted to read all the criteria. Then he went back a second time, checking only the box for gender. Under religion he typed P-a-r-s-i using his index finger. After considerable time with the hourglass he got a message: Sorry, no matches were found. Broaden your horizons!

Back in the house Mrs. Smith served Prem finger sandwiches with tea. He settled into the large recliner in his den and called Pascal.

"How are you, *mon vieux?*"

"I've discovered the world of online," Prem stopped abruptly. He twisted his head to look behind him. Mrs. Smith was dusting some books on the shelf.

"Mrs. Smith, do you think I could be alone?"

"Weren't you going to retire her as soon as I left?" Pascal laughed.

"Yes, but she doesn't want that." Prem heard the door click shut.

"Isn't she ancient?"

"Less ancient than I am. She's the same actually."

"*Alors*, which world did you discover?"

"Online dating."

Prem told Pascal about his meeting with Johnson, his short story, and the message asking him to broaden his horizons.

"But why search for Parsi? You've never even had a Parsi girlfriend."

"Meher."

"Not her again. Anyway, she was only as Parsi as you, which is to say not at all. Why are you doing this to yourself? We've got only a few more good years."

"What should I search for? Fifty years or older? Or do you think that too is unreasonable?"

"Fifty? That's too old. You know what I've been having?"

"What? Forty?"

"Thirty, even twenty-five."

"How do you do it?"

"I go to a dating site, and I do a search on my own name. I don't know what they call that in English—yes, keyword! I put *Boutin* in keyword and search for all the women's profiles with that keyword. It brings up the women who are listing me as their favorite author or referring to my books. Then I just send them a message."

"Do you say you're Pascal Boutin? What if they are looking for a thirty-year-old man or for someone with hair on the head? I saw that as a category! Can you believe that? And eye color! In our time you fell in love with the eye color of your lover."

"Ignore all that. The advertising *connards* who have designed these sites think they can deconstruct the human heart with their search fields. Let me tell you, the two of us, you and I, we understand love better than all the sterile analysis of these young dotcommers."

"How can one ignore all that? If a woman wants a man of forty, I can't pretend."

"I write and ask them something about myself, I mean about Boutin since they don't know I am him. If they say they are looking for someone like Bertrand from *Les marchés aux épices*, I ask why Bertrand and not Boutin himself? After all, the creator must encompass the creation. We exchange a few e-mails like that, and then I suggest that I might be Boutin."

"Do they believe you?"

"Not right away. But I let some private information slip in. When I have their attention, I tantalize them further, reminding them that I'm not a thirty-five-year-old who rollerblades around Paris on Friday nights but just might be Boutin himself. Once they choose my bald head over the *patins à roulettes,* we meet. All of them have chosen me."

"I hate to type. I'm slow."

"The only goal is to provoke them. You can do that with just one word."

"What do you say to a twenty-five-year-old girl?"

"Only serious readers write the names of authors and books in their profiles. I speak to them about books. I ask them about who else they have met online. It's easy once you start. I'll write about *l'amour cyber* one day."

"I won't be able to think of what to say."

"*Mon œil!* It's no different from meeting a twenty-five-year-old any other way. And with your Julie and Valérie episode, you demonstrated you know exactly how to talk to gamines. They were not even twenty, those two!"

"I was not seventy-five," Prem retorted.

"I am happy you are opening yourself to experience again, but let me tell you that for a teenage girl sixty-five is no different from seventy-five."

Roger Johnson arrived at Prem's door with a bottle of Glenmorangie 12 at the appointed hour. Prem vaguely remembered praising the label and the vintage in an interview to BBC4 in a more lighthearted moment after he had won the Booker. It was more than thirty years ago, before he had become an American citizen.

"Mr. Rustum, it's such an honor to be invited to your house."

"Let's not get into formalities, young man. Have a seat."

Mrs. Smith served them both a cold beer and appeared again only when it was time to ask them into the dining room. There were fresh-cut roses on the table. Prem noticed that Mrs. Smith had worn her beads. It had been far too long since they had entertained. Prem had not had anyone over for a meal since Pascal's last trip to the States in the fall.

"I read your story and made some notes in the margin. I think you should read certain books. I wrote those down too." Prem waved the brown envelope in his hand, which he then placed on one of the empty chairs.

"Thank you so much, Mr. Rustum."

"I hate it when people ask me if my stories are true. But you understand, when I ask you if it's true, I'm talking about something else. This whole Internet world is very new."

Mrs. Smith took away the salad plate from Johnson and served him a plate of grilled portobello mushrooms. Prem applied mustard to his bun as he watched her refill their empty beer glasses and leave.

"It's all true. Milli in my story, for example. She's true. She met seven people in one evening, after having lined them all up on an online dating service the same afternoon. And that fetishized encounter, that too. Linda said she was looking for two brothers who were willing to take her on, no questions asked. They exchanged photos and went all the way."

"Is your life like this? Full of instant gratification?"

"Not exactly. I've yet to meet anyone worthwhile this way, but that might have changed. I actually met her online after the dinner at Eddy Parma's."

"You mean the other day when we met?"

"Yes. And I'm meeting her later today."

"That's quick, isn't it?"

"We have a lot in common. We're both huge fans of yours, to begin with." Johnson fiddled nervously with his fork, scratching his plate with it as he spoke to Prem.

"How do you know she is a fan of mine?"

"She wrote it in her ad."

"On one of these sites?" Prem pointed to the envelope on the chair.

"Yes, sir." Johnson was blushing.

"How do you know she's not crazy? I've heard all kinds of things happen online."

"I don't know. She sounded fine. I mean, she has more to worry about than I do, given I'm the man."

"Did you exchange photos, like the people in your stories?"

"Yes, we did." A smile had edged its way to Johnson's mouth.

"And?"

"An exquisite beauty."

Johnson left after lunch thanking Prem profusely for the comments on his story. He had two bus rides and a transfer with a half-hour wait before he could meet Maya. She was the only person he had met online who had been willing to meet him right away after they had chatted. Usually it took weeks to convince a girl to meet him for real, and the attrition rate was over half. Prem's name had worked a miracle.

Prem lumbered across the garden to his writing studio to find this fan of his. One by one he went through the sites he had noted from Johnson's story, checking only the box for gender and typing R-u-s-t-u-m for keyword, as Pascal had suggested. After several brief mentions of himself, he came upon Dogpose.

> . . . hot buns . . . Write like Prem Rustum, . . . be Prem Rustum. Worship at his altar like I do . . . tell me what you would ask him if you met him . . .

Other than Vedika, no other woman had come to him on the strength of his words, though many had stayed because of it. Valérie had called his words venereal, and when he had objected, saying that he never wrote about sex, she had said that it was irrelevant, they contained a wisdom that included the erotic. His words were still having their impact, diffusing into this young woman's body honed by yoga. He wondered what she was like, this girl who called herself Dogpose. Did his words reach all the way into her groin or stop in her head? Did they give her a bellyache? The women from the past had, each one, reacted differently to his books.

Prem used to know Vedika and Harry when he was still with the anger monger, Angie, as he called her in his own mind. After Meher's marriage Prem found Angie and fancied he'd fallen in love and grown up too. But with Angie it turned out to be more and less than love at the same time. Prem dragged out their relationship for six years out of sheer fear of her temper. Prem and Angie had met the handsome Bedi couple at a party when Prem was writing *Raga*. He had two books behind him when the Bedis invited them for dinner to their Upper West Side apartment. There was an easy and instant bond between Harry—as Bedi was known to friends—and Prem. Prem just as easily adored Harry's wife, initially referring to her only as *bhabhi* or brother's wife. After he successfully disentangled himself from Angie's viselike grip and retreated to a monastic existence to focus on his elegy to Meher, the Bedis became some of the few people he frequented. And often, since Harry was away to perform specialized heart surgery in a hospital in Florida, Prem found himself taking afternoon walks with his *bhabhi*. He started calling her by the nickname he gave her as a joke one day.

"But why Vedika?"

"Someone who knows the Vedas. You're always telling me stories from the scriptures. You know all the stories that involve 'the good.' You are 'the good.' "

"Why must you mock me thus?"

"I'm not mocking you. If your goodness were less true, it would be banal."

What had started as admiration and adoration for she who was so good and pure, modest, Indian in her virtues, and Western in her openness, turned soon into an anxious longing.

A longing laden with sentiments he was unable to parse neatly or analyze with the help of his past; his past of two women: Meher and Angie. Meher, the sole recipient of his adolescent longing, sibling love, devotion, and in some of their moments together, the teacher, the adult, the protective older sister. Distinctions as other people learned them, between admiration and lust, platonic love and filial, teacher and student, older and younger, friend and sister, the absolute and the partial, had not existed for Prem. The universe he shared with Meher was organic, a living, breathing, entity that could be divided into these categories no less or more than a little puppy could be divided into its heart, brain, tongue, and tail. With Angie, Prem learned what lust and excitement meant when divorced from brotherly affection and awe. Images of Angie riding him, spreading her cheeks for him, acting obscene, never failed to agitate Prem's biology as if he were being lashed by a thunderstorm.

In his quest to understand the hollowness of his being when he did not see Vedika on a given day, Prem asked himself the obvious question, *Do I want to sleep with her?* He was unable to imagine Vedika exhibiting desire, wanting to be penetrated, wanting pleasure, giving pleasure in the forbidden ways that made him still feel ashamed of his manhood. And because he was unable to imagine it, he couldn't fantasize his way out of it. How was Harry—no matter how much he loved his wife—capable of making love to a woman as restrained in her sexuality as *bhabhi* and as incapable of frivolity as a mother?

Prem put aside all analysis of the problem and dealt instead with its symptoms. By following a strict routine of art, friends, cinema, and classical concerts on the days he did not see *bhabhi*, he could get through the day without feeling sick.

The writing of *Meher* was a self-evisceration in itself so complete and painful that it was hard to imagine that he could feel anything outside of its anguish. Yet the days without contact with *bhabhi* were so much worse that it seemed the very torment of writing fed the miserable longing for *bhabhi*. Seeing *bhabhi* assuaged the pain of his interior life and eased the effort of fictionalizing his life with Meher. Real life impinged on the emotional scars he was dredging up for his fiction, rubbing salt into his wounds.

Plying himself with excuses of every sort, Prem locked the set of unanswered questions pertaining to Vedika in a steel vault deep within himself. He bore the burden of friendliness and gentleman-liness with a smile for months.

He was ready for anything but the answer to his unasked questions. It came without any intervention from his will, like a breeze blowing through the quarters of a city, the city that was his brain. The answer in fact came as question: *does she shudder when she is in the throes of pleasure, and does she hide her shudder modestly?* No longer under pressure from Prem, his imagination had, on its own accord, gone ahead and freed itself.

The change in his sentiments for Vedika was like the change in the texture of egg white into meringue. The raw material of his feel-ings, the affection, the love, the caring stayed the same, but that day it hardened in his groin. He said a hasty goodbye after lunch. He still re-membered it clearly. Vedika had told him she had just come from buy-ing her spices. She had procured fresh curry leaves for a dish for Prem. There was only one store that sold Indian spices in Manhattan then, Kalustyans. In the scorching midsummer heat Vedika had taken the subway for thirty-five minutes each way to get a few stems of green.

Prem withdrew more into himself in Vedika's presence, rid-dled simultaneously by a sense of shame and a sense of desire. He had been dining in the Bedis' home several times a week as a mat-ter of course at this point and was welcomed and trusted like a brother. Declining Vedika's casual—why don't you come over tomorrow—invitations was not an option, especially with Harry in Florida overseeing the founding of a large heart center. She relied on him to do the manly things that needed to be done when Harry was not around, and Harry relied on his friend to take care of his wife. Vedika had never for a moment shown the slightest tear in the fabric of her love for Harry.

The change in the texture of his emotions went beyond the meringue in his pants. The constant hollowness he had been feeling now turned into a searing physical pain. His chest burned all the time. Harry's antacids did not help. Vedika plying him with yogurt did not help. Even Meher his sister and *Meher* his work receded into the background. Prem went to sleep believing that he could practically see a piece of hot metal passing through his throat and his chest, his stomach, and his cock, so great was the pain.

To drain out some of the misery, he let it leak on paper. He took the two hundred pages of *Meher* he had written already and injected them with the sap that was about to burst through his body. *I will make love to Vedika in my writing.* It was the only way to express what he absolutely had to have without causing harm to them all. The act of writing became the sex he had. *Meher* became a parallel stage where his transgressions were acted out. For a few liberated weeks he was back in control. Prem was young and still naïve about the power of literature and words, his words.

He gave the Meher in the book some of the characteristics of Vedika. When he took stock of his new draft and took stock of Vedika at lunch one day, he had the sinking realization that he had just managed to dig himself into a deeper hole. By reflecting on Vedika without the constraints of everyday life and politesse, he had put his foot on the gas pedal. Love was gushing at limitless speed through all the pistons and cylinders of his body. He broke down over lunch and asked her if she would read the draft of his novel. *If you will have this sex with me.* Full of fondness for Prem, Vedika inevitably said yes.

Vedika had been susceptible, no less than Prem, to the powerful universe he had created. On reading *Meher,* she saw herself but also someone not herself. She longed for the intensity of Prem's love to be directed to her. His imaginary universe heightened real life by giving it the power of transcendence possible only in art. Art that fitted ordinary people with the wings of Eros, Eros who was not just the god of love but the creative fluid pumping in every human breast.

Prem's language in the book, as in all his books, was constrained. The slight physical contact between the characters therefore left Vedika famished for more: a physical hunger that could be satisfied by only one person, the author.

Prem read the lines on the Internet posting again and then went to the bookshelf on the other side of his studio. He thumbed through Pascal's latest book and found the chapter titled "Tell me what you would ask him if you met him." He read the chapter standing up. In the story Pascal went from one provincial bookstore to another and hung around until he saw a woman leafing through one of his books. He'd then approach her and ask what she would ask the writer and proceed to answer the question for real. Prem chuckled.

He walked to his lectern and pulled out his fountain pen. He wrote several drafts of a possible e-mail to send the girl. They were all too long. Finally he just went back to his laptop to type in an answer directly. Hitting the reply button was not enough. The screen asked him to log in. The log-in button hurled another thirty questions in his direction, but Johnson's story had somehow demystified the process for Prem, who was determined not to call Kenny and expose himself to total ridicule. After an hour struggling with check boxes and providing information on his age, his address, his income, his sexual preference, and his favorite magazine subscriptions, Prem was finally congratulated on becoming a member and asked to choose a screen name. Impatient and no longer in a mood to agonize, he chose Indian Man of Letters as his screen name, and when an empty message tablet popped up for his message to the girl, he typed:

I don't worship at my own altar. What are you going to ask me?

Maya preened herself in the shower longer than usual. Even if there was no chemistry with Plume, she was sure that an engagement centered on a discussion of the three Ps could not be boring. He had promised her a story about Pascal Boutin. There were few people in her tiny circle of friends who read any fiction at all, and none had followed an author from first book to last. Scrubbing her back with a sponge in the shower, Maya recited some lines from Rimbaud. Water trickled into her mouth. She hummed happily and got ready.

They met in the fiction section of the bookstore at Lincoln Center. Plume was thumbing *From Kerala to Karela.* He turned it toward her, pointing to a page full of alliterations. They read it together in a whisper, "perverse, parsimonious, pedagogical, pedophilic, patronizing, parabolic, prevaricating, pensive, poisonous, pig-headed pagan."

Plume shut the book and looked at Maya.

"Nice to meet you," she said in a low voice.

"I'm Roger Johnson, by the way," he responded in an equally low voice.

"My name is Maya."

"Should we get something to eat?"

Maya's skin was white with an underlying hue, like a painting that was painted on straw linen and not on pure white gessoed canvas. Her eyebrows were perfect and symmetrical and, like her hair, were a darkish brown color.

Over dinner Maya and Roger excitedly recounted the circumstances under which they had read every Boutin and Rustum book and the plots, characters, and styles that found most favor with them. They had both been to the museum where Rustum's blueprints for his various novels were archived.

"It isn't the blueprints"—Johnson lifted his two hands to make quotation marks in the air around *blueprints*—"that make him brilliant. It's precisely that no hint of all the drudgery shows up in the final work that is amazing."

"His prose is electric. You can practically see a current running through his sentences page after page. A tautness and muscularity holding up the ideas."

"Your Internet posting asking for Prem was really quite unlike what I've seen before. Do you think you've mixed up the writer with the man?"

Maya paused by moving back in her seat. She had thought many times of meeting Prem—how could she not have? The very first paragraph of the very first Prem book Maya had read had caused every hair on her body to stand on end. Her mammary papillae had hardened, and the skin around her areolae had puckered.

"You tell me. Did he live up to your expectations in person, or were you disappointed by the man behind the writer?"

"I was nervous at the dinner where I met him. I think I said a few stupid things about other writers. But then I got less self-conscious and I could observe him. The way he was fit with what I had imagined. He was kind—that was surprising, I guess."

"You didn't think he'd be kind? He examines the world with such rapt attention, it's only possible if one is without barriers. One of my yoga instructors once said that 'love is attention giving.' "

"That's not too far off, actually. Prem looks at you, and you feel like your skin is melting away and he's penetrating you to the very core. You want to reveal yourself because you get this feeling you can reveal all of you. I hope I can be his friend. Actually, if I were a woman, I might even have been attracted to him. Seventy-five though he is."

"Does he smell like an old geezer?"

"I didn't get that close." Johnson came closer to Maya.

"You know what I mean. Haven't you taken an elevator with one?" Maya hovered tantalizingly in the space between them. She could smell Johnson, and he smelled of light cologne.

"No, he didn't smell. Can we stop talking about him now?" Johnson's face was all the way forward, inviting Maya for a kiss.

"You're the one who started it," she said with a smile.

"Surely we are not going to speak only about other writers," Johnson remarked.

"He's hardly another writer!"

"Why won't you talk about your work?"

"It'll be a novel, that's all I'll say."

"Do you want to come back to my place for a cup of tea?"

They returned to Roger Johnson's apartment and kissed to Miles Davis. Johnson's hands were soft, his breath sweet.

"Will you spend the night?"

"I'm not going to sleep with you even if I spend the night."

"That's fine. Let's get into bed and cuddle."

Cuddle. A childish word. Okay, forget it now. Maya got into his bed in her T-shirt.

Johnson held her all night running his smooth fingers over her forearms as Maya slept. The apartment was on the avenue, and by six-thirty it was already too loud to sleep. Maya got out of bed and put on her pants.

"You're going to leave so soon?"

"I have to get back and do some work."

"Will I see you again?"

"Yes, of course. You forgot to tell me your Boutin story. I'll call you."

Maya went back home and found a new message waiting from someone called Indian Man of Letters.

What are you going to ask me?

Almost certain it was a joke, she got to work on the article she was editing for a scientific magazine. She had to check all the foot-notes and make sure the citations were exact. At lunchtime she went to the diner across the street and ordered a feta omelet.

"No book today, miss?" Costas asked her as he put the omelet in front of her.

"It's impossible to read here!"

She ate watching the empty stool where Mrs. Nona sat. On solitary days Maya could identify with Mrs. Nona who, she was sure, was also feeling alone.

"You want an espresso on me?" Costas offered.

"No thanks, I don't drink espresso. She's not yet here today?"

"She'll come along for sure, unless she's dead," he said, laughing.

As Maya paid, Mrs. Nona walked in and sat down ignoring everyone's *hellos*. Would Rustum live as long as Mrs. Nona? She prayed he would produce books at the same rate for another ten or fifteen years. There was no chance *he* was Indian Man of Letters. Him/not him/him. And yet what harm could come from replying?

Under the subject heading Maya wrote:

I am asking you.

Then she typed her message:

Do you think desire can be totally arbitrary?

Simply writing the one line to Dogpose had put Prem in a good mood for the next morning. He woke up feeling energetic.

"Mrs. Smith, don't expect me for lunch. I'll be in the city for the day," he said when she served him his two toasts with marmalade.

"Mr. Rustum, did you ask for a car?" He shook his head. "Let me call the service. When should they pick you up?"

"As soon as possible."

Mrs. Smith went to the living room, and he heard her call the car. "The car will be here in ten minutes. You have Matthew today."

"Oh! Good."

Prem asked the driver to drop him in Chinatown and pick him up in an hour in the Village. He wandered past a frenzy of fish-loading activity before hitting the Chinese cake stalls that smelled like the bakery next to his house in Bombay sixty years ago. Rustum hummed and walked jauntily. He was wearing a blue shirt and a neatly folded silk scarf of a deeper blue. His thick silver-gray hair had a metallic sheen that wasn't very different from the steel buildings in Manhattan. The contrast against his brown skin was dramatic. If he had looked exotic and debonair when he was young, he now looked terribly striking. There were wrinkles on his face, but it was gaunt, its angular planes almost startling. His nose had always been his best feature. It was still proud, noble, Roman. All in all, a handsome man.

Prem chose his streets carefully. A block of little Italy, a few gentrified blocks with boutiques, Lafayette Street going north with its wide-angled fish-eye view, and then up on Broadway to take a quick look in the window of Shakespeare & Company. His book was still in the central position, where it had been since it got on the *New York Times* best-seller list twenty-five weeks ago, the week of its release. From there Prem walked into a diner on University Place. It was still early, and the place was almost empty. He ordered a coffee and looked at the girls on the sidewalk outside. It was a nippy day, and everyone was wearing coats and mufflers. Prem searched their faces for signs of an intelligent life or at least an interior life. He called his agent, Edward.

"I decided to come into the city. Are you free?"

"Lunch?"

"I want to go to someplace young."

"Let's meet downtown then." They agreed on the details and hung up.

Prem paid the cashier and got into his car, which was waiting in front. He asked Matthew to leave him on the western end of Bleecker Street and pick him up later in SoHo. He strolled around slowly, like a tourist—gaping at the tchotchkes on the sidewalk stalls, browsing books, smelling the appetizing mix of meat and turmeric at corner kiosks.

A bald woman in her sixties with a dog smiled at him. Sometimes people thought he was someone they knew but couldn't place. Prem brought his hand to his hat in a gesture of acknowledgment. He could not look at a bald woman without thinking of Meher's cancer and her death and, by extension, his own death. But today between his death and himself he wanted to put someone—say, Dogpose. Prem wondered what Dogpose looked like, whether her skin had the same ethereal luminescent quality of Valérie's or the olive hue of Meher's.

"I'm looking for an affair," he said to Edward as soon as they were seated at a lunch table at Babbo.

"After all this time?" Edward let out a short laugh.

"I'm dead serious."

Edward frowned.

"Pascal mentioned it in passing, and he's right. I need one."

"Well, when I was still in the market, I would tell women I was your agent. *That* was my selling point. So it shouldn't be hard for you—you are the sale himself! Anyway, there's always Judith Q."

"Judith Q the New York nutcase. Thank God I haven't heard from her in a while."

"I thought she wrote in the fall."

"She did. But not since then. The frequency of her letters has dropped. Oh! Let's talk about something more pleasant. Did Pascal ever tell you that he meets women online?"

"So did I, after Thalia and I divorced. Why do you think we've been telling you to get online all these years?"

"I found a fan online. I can feel spring. I am revitalized." Prem leaned forward as he spoke.

"You should be. The book has had sensational reviews. It's proven that winning the Nobel hasn't detracted from your writing. Have you started the next one?"

"Yesterday I was sure there would be no more. Today I am less sure."

"If having an affair is going to make the difference, then I'll find you someone."

"Aren't you representing any young women writers?"

"We're taking very few new novelists, but I got a fax from a guy today who said you had commented on his story. He quoted a line from your comment."

"Who?"

"Roger Johnson. He faxed the story on online dating. I think I'll take him on."

"I can't believe he quoted my comment. I wasn't crazy about the story at all."

"Come on! It was really good. He probably put the idea of an affair into your head more than Pascal."

"You're not going to take him on, Edward."

"Yes, I am."

"No, you're not. I am serious."

"I am too. You're telling me who I can take on now?" Edward laughed, opening his mouth wide open. The inside of his mouth was covered with silver fillings.

"Don't forget which side your bread is buttered on," Prem bristled.

"Don't forget who got you to where you are," Edward threw back lightly.

"My writing got me where I am."

"Aren't we forgetting a few things?"

"I think we are forgetting that I won *the* prize."

Edward could sense Prem's irritation—Prem was saying things he was normally loath to say. But Edward was irritated too and pressed on. "You're forgetting the time you threw the glass of water on Parma Senior's lap, and they almost called off the first big deal you ever got. You're forgetting who bailed you out when the entire publishing industry decided to boycott you after you had told Bobby, Bunty, and Barbara about the deals they each had offered you in confidence."

"So what? There was always the U.K."

"Where you had already antagonized the Clapham Seven as well as Charles, McCoy, and Reed. Where would you have gone? To Pastoral Press out of Cork?"

"I actually forgot about that. I think I've mellowed." Prem laughed, remembering.

"Or people have gotten used to the idea of the cantankerous Indian genius."

"And I'm not changing."

"I can see that. But what's your problem with Johnson?"

"He got your attention using my name without my permission. You know I hate that. Moreover, I gave him comments, but I didn't once praise the story, and whatever phrases he quoted in the letter he must have used out of context."

"He's just doing the best for himself. At the end of the day I'm choosing him for the story."

"His character development is flawed. The reader is left wondering if Milli is a gold-digger or an idealist, if she's bold or just insane. His narrative is fraught with substandard sentences."

"They are hardly substandard. There are a few flawed sentences."

"Enough to see he's not a born writer."

"I'd argue there's enough good in that story that he might yet become a great one."

"In that kind of stunted, stinted reportage voice of his? I think not."

"I've been an agent forty years, Prem. I think I can tell for myself."

"Edward, you'll lose me. My business and my friendship." Prem spoke evenly and touched Edward's hand when he spoke.

"You're blackmailing me!"

Edward had taken Prem onto his list when Prem had two very good books and an excellent one under his belt. He was in flight from his past and wrote books about music, love, and philosophy. Meher was lodged inside him—he could puncture himself anywhere, and she would flow out and appear on paper. This he could bear to do. But what he couldn't bear to do, until he went back to her bedside, was to look at the country he had left behind. Prem remained in India after she died, taking the train from Delhi to Calcutta to Benares. Then he came back to New York to produce an extraordinary tableau of India as she gained confidence in herself in her postindependence years. In the next decade he alternated his personal books with his big books—this was how Edward thought of them. The personal books were about the individual travails of the characters, their metaphysical truths and ontologies. The big books were about India and later about the United States. India struggling to maintain her integrity under the corrupting influences of a socialist economy. India turning into a dishonest woman, a loose woman, as she succumbed to the license raj, pimped by every small-time office *babu, chaprasi*, peon, bureaucrat, politician. India manipulated and demeaned, her democratic institutions ridiculed and finally denuded of her democracy like Draupadi, when her sari was unraveled in public. But in this real-life version, unlike in the *Mahabharata*, no godly Krishna came down to extend the sari. Instead a spineless president put his rubber stamp and declared Emergency, a suspension of all civil rights and personal liberties, leaving India to shiver in the cold, naked. Forced sterilizations, larger-scale corruption, mayhem, and tyranny followed. Prem's books were now, each one, about everything, the atavistic and the evolved, the blessed and the damned, the public, the political, and the personal.

At this time finally Prem's personal books and his social books came together in *Grinding India*. Those who had risen against the Emergency, risking their lives and the disappearance of their beloveds, were its heroines and heroes. Something had opened within Prem. He had once visited the dam on the Tungabhadra River, near Hospet, that held turbulent water in check with floodgates. The creative force of Prem in his forties was the force that water would have had if the floodgates had been lifted.

Edward had seen the furious wave that had the force of an ocean and the magnificent book it produced. He stayed up all night reading it and went back and read its best moments once more. Another kind of person would have stood in astonishment and gaped at Prem's manuscript, but Edward danced. In celebration he fucked his wife when she woke up in the morning and ate her pussy, he drove his kids to school, and he came to his office, closed the door, turned on an LP, and danced. Edward had always known how to live, he was a *liver*, and in moments of extreme joy he lived extremely. Prem would make himself and Edward a lot of money and win awards, but that was secondary. In his hands Edward had what could only be called greatness. And greatness was exactly what was missing in the impoverished culture of the leveling postmodern world. That day Edward found the one thing he had been searching for in his working life, a cause. He was elated that it came in a physical body, and that the body was that of a writer who was a client of his to boot.

Thereafter Edward did not peel his eyes off Prem and his creations. That mind, the few cubic inches of mush encased in Prem's skull, were going to restore Greatness with a capital G in the world through Literature. Grand themes came alive because they marched with microscopic detail. Grand without being grandiose. Profound without a moment of pomposity. Prem's interests became a priority in his mind—at moments above his own. Edward was, after all, serving an idea. And he intended to see that Prem served it too. When he got a whiff of the visit Prem's friend Krishnan had paid him, with an entourage of computer scientists, Edward had the foresight to realize that everything Prem touched was and would be invaluable. If he could have collected the microbes in Prem's sneezes, he might have done that too.

———————

Edward stared at the water in his glass. Then he looked into Prem's eyes. Prem raised his eyebrows for an answer.

"I'm not going to let you go after all this, you bastard."

"There's a personal reason too," Prem said.

"And what is that?"

"I'm trying to get a date with some girl this Johnson fellow went on a date with."

"Have you seen her?"

"No. But I get this feeling."

"I almost prefer your immoral libido to your hokey literary criticism."

"It's my last chance to live. You know what the last ten years have been for me."

"The death of the star. A star gets hotter and redder just before it dies."

"Don't scoff—you'll be in my shoes soon enough. Age gets everyone, as they say."

"Age gets everyone differently. In your case, you're going to run out of everything to burn, and your ego, big as it is, isn't the critical mass."

"Why this sudden devilish delight in my death?"

"No. In stars, and you're one. I've taken on another Nobel laureate. A physicist who wants to do a series of books explaining difficult concepts for the general public."

"What'll happen if my ego isn't the critical mass?"

"You're going to turn into a white dwarf as opposed to a black hole."

"And the physicist, your other star?"

"Obviously hopes to end up as a black hole, bending space-time."

"I hope to get some things to bend for me now while I'm still alive. Critical mass notwithstanding."

"The physicist wants to meet you, by the way. He says he's a big fan."

"Before my death I have time only for those who can bend into a yogic dogpose." Prem smiled to himself.

"Not an iota of sympathy from me for your old age or your impending death. You're going to die exactly the way you've lived: making people mostly miserable but sometimes immeasurably happy."

"Did you get the physicist because you were my agent?"

"Of course."

"So you're not going to take on Johnson?"

"Not until you're dead."

Prem returned to his house after lunch and went straight to his writing studio to log on. When he read the message from Dogpose, there was a simultaneous contraction in his chest and his scrotum on seeing the word *desire*. It was hard to sit and think in front of the laptop, and he was restless. He ambled in the garden looking at the new flowers Mrs. Smith had planted and thought about the conversation with Edward, his resentment of Johnson's youth, and his desire for a woman who had no reality in flesh and blood for him.

Maya finished up her work in the early afternoon to plan her upcoming trip to France. As the sole recipient of the Paris Fiction Fellowship, she would have enough money to live decently for three months and write. She wondered if Roger Johnson had applied and if she had won it over him. When should she tell him about it?

At the end of the evening Maya logged on to invite Johnson to dinner, and noticed that there was a message from Indian Man of Letters:

Not just arbitrary but even anonymous, as in this case.
Why me?

She went to her bookshelf and picked up *By the Thread* and looked at the photo on the back cover. She opened the book to a random page and scanned it. Paragraph after paragraph of long articulate sentences jumped out. Would the real Rustum type one-liners? She sighed and saw Prem's photo on the back again. Her internal organs lurched within her body cavity. She went back to her computer.

It was a general question about desire, and I didn't mean to imply that it was desire for you. I have only deep awe for PR. Anonymous desire for anyone is impossible in my view. But why PR is a question I can answer. I've given myself to Meher, Sara, Bertha, and everyone else who has come along with a promiscuity that even I find astonishing. I do understand you're not any of your characters. I don't purport to know you just because I have clutched your books on the Chennai-Pondicherry highway, through humiliating security checks in airports, and in ratty guesthouse beds all over India. I have tried to read your books honestly, allowing the narrative voice such full possession as to reduce myself to a tenant in my own house. It is rare to be so consumed by admiration, and its dictates forbid any veneer of coolness. For one year now, the yin and yang of my life, the pulls of occident and orient, have really been about whether to devour all your books swiftly—for the pleasure of the moment, or to abstain—so that a new one and its promises are always on the horizon. The real world with its humdrum routines and sporadic dramas alternates with this other one, one in which I can arrive like some sort of Vedantic mendicant to partake—without illusion or indifference—of the fruits of your literary tree. But I really don't believe this is you, Prem Rustum, who I am sending this message to.

Maya pulled out her suitcases from the back of the walk-in closet and made checklists of the items she needed to carry, the books, the notebooks from her Indian trips, the backup CDs of her previous writing, all the while pondering Johnson and the fact of her departure.

Roger Johnson showed up at her door with a bottle of Pomerol at seven-thirty. Maya stirred the mushroom risotto in the kitchen while Johnson filled two glasses of wine and told her about his day.

"You want to taste this and tell me if it's too al dente for you?" Maya offered a spoon of the risotto to Johnson after blowing on it.

"Perfect."

"Doesn't need more salt?"

"No."

"Let's go to the table. You owe me a Boutin story." Maya portioned equal halves from the pot into two bowls, and they sat down to eat.

Roger Johnson had ridden high his first few months at college. He had been the only member of the freshman class to be accepted on the board of *The Advocate,* Harvard's literary magazine. His Expository Writing professor was praising Johnson's work each week in class, holding it up as some of the best writing he had ever seen in his six years teaching the course. Nathan Zuckerman, Harvard's writer-in-residence for the year, had asked Johnson to apply for the spring session of his ten-person Creative Writing class, the most coveted class of the year, one usually restricted to upperclassmen except at the instructor's discretion.

It was no wonder then that at literary parties on campus Johnson was a regular invitee and a gregarious presence. His years as an outcast in high school, when he was regularly gutted as a bookworm, were finally over. He now had friends and acquaintances who were as familiar with Fitzgerald and Camus, Tolstoy and Rustum, Balzac and Boutin, as he was. He could speak in that wonderful music of writerspeak, where a single page in a book conveyed worldviews and mere references to possessive proper nouns like Bataille's Simone delivered hard-ons. These were people who had teethed on *The New Yorker,* people who had been shunned for the same reasons as he had right through their pizza-faced teenage years by peers deemed cooler. In the interiors of *The Advocate* and in the senior dorms where parties were thrown, Johnson was determined to redeem himself and seduce with precisely those charms and literary games that had been the cause of his pariah status less than one year before.

Pascal Boutin had a new book out on women: a book much like Boutin himself, who at fifty-something was still frank, sexual, and utterly unstoppable. Johnson had laughed his way through the first half of the book sitting on the can. Three bowel movements later Johnson had been persuaded by Boutin's narrative and went from total astonishment to complete belief in Boutin's project.

At *The Advocate* party held at an editor's senior suite in Eliot House, Johnson arrived in a dapper suit with a handkerchief sticking out of his pocket. The buzz of male conversation centered on words like *deconstruction, semiotics, syntax,* and that of female conversation on Stein, Woolf, and Morrison. Johnson found himself on a large comfortable forest-green sofa with three young women, one in particular.

"You're the genius freshman, aren't you?" she teased.

"Not really." Johnson was embarrassed by public declarations of his promise. The all-around intolerance of his high school had taught him to be proud and defiant in the face of adversity, leaving him with no tools for dealing with praise.

After two glasses of Madeira the conversation had taken a turn toward people on television shows and Harvard's array of provosts and deans.

"I'm in no mood to socialize. I don't know why I came," she said in his ear.

"Me neither. But I can think of something that would make me feel a lot better."

"What?"

"You really want to know?" he asked, arching up an eyebrow.

"Yes. By the way, I like your deep blue glasses. Very intellectual."

"Well, I'd feel a lot better if you fondled your breasts." Struck by the polemics of Boutin's latest novel, Johnson launched into an articulation of Boutin's theory. *You see, all women, whether they admit it or not . . .*

"What have you been drinking?" she asked when he was finished with a long-winded explanation of the thesis. Her startlingly white teeth came into view as her mouth stretched open in a broad smile.

"Same as you."

"And why should I fondle my breasts here? In plain English this time, please." She looked around the room as she spoke.

"You're going to enjoy it. You want to. The idea that it gives you pleasure will give me pleasure, and the idea that it gives me pleasure will give you pleasure."

"I may not enjoy it."

"You will by the end of this evening. Look, there's nothing else to do. Would you rather talk about Neil Rudenstine and David Letterman?"

"But what will people think?"

"No one cares. No one is looking. Look at C and D," he said as he pointed to the other two girls on the couch.

She was silent. She was trying to think this through.

"Look," he persisted, "you'll do a really good deed. I've been thinking about this for over twenty-four hours now."

"You didn't even know me before this party. And you didn't know I'd be here."

"No, not you specifically. Just a woman fondling her breasts in public. I haven't been able to get any work done. I even missed my French lit class this morning because I couldn't snap out of this."

"Does it really mean that much to you?" Her eyes had an innate kindness. Johnson felt they were changing color and softening as she contemplated what he had said—a lot like the reaction of the woman in Boutin's novel.

"I know making this suggestion to a stranger is not very acceptable. I hope you won't take me amiss," Roger said, feeling formal all of a sudden. He got quiet.

They sat in an awkward silence. Johnson pulled out the cushion from behind his back, laid it on his lap, and played with it. He stroked it, rubbing the tip of his finger over the raised red stitches on its surface. Soon he was running his whole hand over the cushion and caressing it as if it were human. The girl fixed her stare on his hands.

"Please stop that. It's driving me crazy," she finally said, breaking the silence.

He looked at her and smiled. "So you're thinking about what I told you?"

"Tell me what triggered it other than Boutin's new book."

"Maybe I miss my mother. But then again, my mother doesn't have breasts like yours." He looked at the mass of human comfort a few inches away from his chin.

"Thank you," she said, blushing.

"So what do you think?"

"I need some more alcohol in my system."

"You'll enjoy it," Roger said. "You'll see how much pleasure your fondling yourself will give me, and you'll enjoy it."

"I need more alcohol."

"You should try it sober—it'll be so much better. I'm getting myself a ginger ale. What should I get you?"

"Another glass of wine."

When Johnson came back from the corner of the living room where the host had set up the bar at his college desk, Breasts was talking to C and D.

"Here," he said, handing her the glass and sitting down.

"I was just telling them about what you said."

"No, you were not!" Roger remained standing.

"It's really fascinating," C said sarcastically.

"Amazing. We're where now? In the nineties? And you think

that a middle-aged French misogynist has the best pulse on a woman's inner sexual desires?" D had stood up and was poised with a hand on her hip, her knuckles digging into her body, accentuating the thin bony structure of her pelvis. No breasts.

"Maybe it doesn't work for you, but it might for others." Johnson looked at Breasts.

"You're making her uncomfortable," C screeched.

"I think she can speak for herself. No?" Johnson challenged. He looked at Breasts.

"I want to leave. Will you walk me to my dorm?" Breasts asked Johnson.

As they stepped out into the night, Johnson saw a shudder run through her.

"Are you cold?"

"No."

"I wish you hadn't told them. It makes me seem like a bigger schmuck than I am."

"I didn't think they'd react that way. Anyway, I've been thinking about it."

"And?"

"Why this stipulation to do it in public? I'll do it in private for you."

"No, this is about an extreme and complete display of one's sensuality. To revel in it, one has to exhibit not privately for one person—who can be seen as some sort of extension of oneself—but a group large enough to be a collective, to be other."

"I'll do it for you alone in my room," Breasts offered again, standing at the threshold of Winthrop House.

"I'd better be going."

Johnson planted a chaste kiss on the side of her cheek and came back home to have another look at Boutin's significantly more successful fictitious scene.

The next afternoon when Johnson went to the office of *The*

Advocate, White, one of the editors, told him he was in trouble. C and D had spent the rest of the night in an indignant fury claiming that it was guys like Johnson and girls like Breasts who were responsible for the patriarchal order that prevailed to this day.

"Dude, if I were you, I'd lie low."

Johnson slumped into an upholstered chair in the corner.

"*The Advocate* is having a board meeting to discuss this impropriety—that's what it's been deemed to be—and to decide if you get to stay on the board."

"You're kidding."

"Didn't they tell you about date rape and sexual harassment your freshman week, man?"

"But this was neither. It developed as a conversation. I didn't ask to touch her breasts, and even when she practically made an offer last night for me to come to her room, I didn't accept. And most of all I think she liked my suggestion."

"It's the other girls. They say that men like you make the space unsafe for women."

Johnson shook his head and stared at the floor mutely.

"Look, you better be going. One of us will call you and let you know."

"Let's take it up to Student Affairs. I am sure I will come out totally clean."

"We'd rather not do that."

Johnson was told that *The Advocate* had decided to wait for the noise to die down. C ran a militant feminist magazine on campus and had threatened to "out" *The Advocate,* as she put it. D said that she was sure she could convince Breasts to testify against Johnson for sexual harassment; a girl on two or three glasses of Madeira on a comfortable couch talking to an intellectual man two years her junior was hardly responsible for his wily seductions. White told Johnson that they had decided to postpone printing his name in the magazine until the spring issue, when the storm had blown over.

Johnson called Breasts to have a chat, but she never called him back. A month later Johnson saw a short story in *The Advocate* by C about touching her breasts in public and empowering herself. A woman's sexuality was her weapon against the phallic symbolism of every flagpole and belfry of New England; it was her way of telling men that her body was fundamentally a source of pleasure for herself and only then for men. The litcrits on campus were divided as to whether C's story was a takeoff on Pascal's novel, written from an internal point of view, or if it was a challenge to the patriarchal perspective that Boutin presented. After having failed to get on *The Advocate* her freshman and sophomore years, C was listed as a board member along with Johnson in the spring issue.

Soon every coed was fondling her breasts at keg parties, in the otherwise-uninspiring library stacks, while conducting acid-base titrations in the lab, and even at the public telescope at the Science Center that Harvard ran as a service for the local community. Far from enjoying this overweening display of female sexuality, Johnson, still reeling from the personal affront of that night early in the year, kept a low profile, turning out draft after solid draft about a boy intent on becoming an astronaut for Zuckerman's Creative Writing class.

It was not until he moved to New York City with a paralegal's job, money to spare, and a litclit-free (as he called the postmodern hyenas of the literature department) social milieu that he reclaimed his baser instincts. With a short-lived but spectacularly liberated girlfriend—and he did not use this word in its intellectual sense—Johnson was finally able to express his own sexuality. At a rooftop shindig teeming with investment bankers and hotshot lawyers, Johnson got to the edge of the railing and peed over Lafayette Street, screaming, "I piss on your tits."

Back in their apartment the same night, his compassionate girlfriend had lain in the tub and commanded Johnson to let his yellow stream flow over her mammaries, thus permanently erasing the trauma of Johnson's freshman year.

———

To show Johnson that she didn't judge him badly, Maya fed him dessert spoon by spoon and made out with him on the couch before taking him to her bed. She awoke early and remembered the e-mail she had sent to the guy pretending to be Prem. What if it was Johnson trying to have some fun? She logged on to her computer and saw another message waiting for her from Indian Man of Letters. The time stamp was during the night, when Johnson had been in her apartment. Maya heard the sheets rustle and logged off. Johnson was up.

"How about a walk together?" he asked after he had awakened with the strong cup of coffee she made for them. They headed out of Maya's building in their light jackets, keeping a brisk pace and talking very little, turning westward one more avenue whenever they had a don't-walk sign. In Central Park, against the dark black rocks carelessly jutting out of the earth, the yellow mimosas in full bloom looked dramatic. They meandered through a section of the bridle path and came upon the paved skating road. At that hour, instead of daredevil roller-skaters doing acrobatic routines to music, there were mothers pushing baby carriages.

"Look, their legs are up in the air," Maya pointed.

"I don't care if you bend your knee. I don't care how you do it. Lift your leg high!" the instructor, a stocky man in his late thirties, was yelling.

The women brought their legs down, switched the hands with which they were pushing their carriages, and kicked up with their right legs.

"Now, big step forward and lunge."

Everyone pushed their carriages a few feet and lunged.

"Right arm up all the way. Straight up, Michele. Good."

The women held their lunges for several seconds, their right arms swaying overhead, their left hands firmly on their baby carriages. Maya and Johnson watched.

"Now switch," the instructor barked.

"That's going into my next novel," Johnson said, looking at Maya.

"It's going into mine."

"We can't both have it."

"Whoever writes it first," Maya said, shrugging.

"I might have an agent very soon."

"For the novel you wrote in school?"

"No. I'm going to sell a collection of short stories first," Johnson said.

"I'm going to try to get my novel done this summer."

"In one summer?"

"Yes."

"I think I'll be getting to this story before you." Johnson pointed to the mothers, who were all bending toward their toes.

"Point your tailbones high up in the air. Hold, one, two . . . ," the instructor counted.

"Don't be so sure, mister," Maya said without looking at Johnson.

"Do you think it's fair for you to hoard the story when I might come out with it much sooner?"

"Not going to stop me from writing it."

"Do you have an agent yet?" he asked.

"No. Who is yours?"

"I approached Rustum's agent."

"Good for you."

"I don't want to fight about our future stories. If we do things together, we'll have common experiences."

"Why don't we take each step as it comes? I'm leaving for Paris pretty soon. You can have all your exclusives then."

"You are? For how long?"

"Three months."

"Are you going there to write?"

"Yes."

"That's great."

When they had crossed over to the other side of the park, Maya took the B train back to her apartment. An old Indian man in his late sixties got into her car at Columbus Circle. He removed his backpack from his shoulder once he sat down and fiddled with it. When he closed the backpack again, Maya saw that it said "Harry Potter" across the flap. She looked at him and smiled.

At Times Square three Hasidic men about the same age as the Indian got onto the car. They sat together on the side seats that faced the aisle. Maya noticed one of them was carrying a plastic packet labeled "Le Bon Ladies Underwear." The guy with the packet absentmindedly started to open it as he heatedly discussed something with the other two. Maya hoped he would open it before her stop so that she could see what was inside. Even as the train slowed to a halt, Maya debated staying on the train just to watch. The man reached inside and handed *Harry Potter and the Sorcerer's Stone* to one of the other men, who got off with Maya at her stop.

I am Prem, and there's only one way for you to verify. I propose the museum on Monday morning, when it's not open to the general public.

Men that age were grandfathers. Unselfconsciously grandfatherly. There was no chance of the real Prem Rustum—an Indian like the one on the train, a grandfather like the man in the black coat and top hat—turning up on citylovin.com! Maya jumped up from her chair and grabbed *By the Thread* again and looked at his photo on the back cover. A photo that had been used for his last three books. *It's not you, is it?* Maya tapped her finger on the nose of the photo. A Nobel laureate surfing the Internet to find a date! Maya laughed at her own gullibility and sat back at her computer.

I'll only meet you in a public place. The museum on an off day doesn't sound like it. How about a bookstore?

Notorious for shunning publicity and public appearances, Rustum was a mystery to the press. As he got older, he granted fewer and fewer interviews and mostly only in writing. He had allowed himself to be filmed only three times. Maya had tried procuring these tapes after she started reading Rustum. She accepted the impossibility of ever getting hold of a Delhi Doordarshan interview done in India in the seventies. She had written several times to *DD* on their website and even mailed the interviewer a letter to Doordarshan's offices in India. The second was a program commissioned by BBC4 on the occasion of Prem's Booker Prize. After repeated calls to BBC America and to Bush House in London, Maya had gathered that the tapes were available only on a broadcast basis to another commercial channel or for educational purposes. Maya had then tried to get the literary club at her old college to organize a screening, but the organization had become defunct following the expulsion of the club president due to a cocaine bust. Rustum's only other celluloid appearance was in a French documentary about Pascal Boutin, where he had been interviewed along with Pedro Nicolas about Pascal's work. Maya had already tried to procure a copy of this film in France her junior summer, when she was researching her undergraduate thesis on Boutin, to no avail. Maya searched for the tape again in her Rustum phase and quite by chance, surfing the website of the French paper *Libération*, noticed that the program was going to be rerun. Half a dozen long-distance phone calls later, Maya arranged for a friend's friend to tape the program and courier it to her. She had the tape converted to NTSC format for ten dollars in Little India and watched it. The documentary was eight years old, and at the time of its filming Rustum had been sixty-seven.

Maya's own grandfather had aged overnight. On his seventy-fifth birthday he had still been youthful, jogging five miles a day and standing upright. Within months he had rapidly transformed into a fragile man, a faded man. Maya wondered what the eight years since the filming in France had done to Prem Rustum. The day before their date she rewound and watched the sections where the camera focused on his face. She observed the deep lines where his face contorted, as he closed his eyes to think of the best French words for an answer. She rewound the tape again for the arc of his beautiful hands as they cut through the air in rapid movements as he explained a nuance in Pascal Boutin's work to the Canal+ interviewer.

At midnight Maya shut off the lights to sleep. In bed she told herself that she was going to meet some fat fifty-year-old loser who fancied he had the talent to write. Or thought he was like Rustum because he too was from India. Or hoped that by being twenty-five years younger than Rustum, he was thirty-three percent sexier than him. *But what if, but what if,* she had said all night to herself and as a result had slept little and woken up early.

Prem wondered if meeting an anonymous babe over the ether was such a bright idea. If all he had wanted was a fan, then there was no dearth of women who had filled his mailbox with snapshots and love letters. And then there was the small but not entirely improbable case that this woman was Judith Q herself. In some of her letters she had mentioned how hard she had tried to meet him, confessions that only succeeded in making her interest seem more sinister. Had he relied on Johnson's information too much? Kenny had told him, when he was showing him how to save articles from the Internet, that people could save photos too. Anyone's photo! But neither Pascal nor Edward had voiced misgivings about meeting women like this. As Prem saw Mrs. Smith set the table, he was conscious of watching a scene that had taken place almost daily for more than ten years. Prem felt like a bottle of juice entirely sedimented. Meeting this girl would shake things up a little. He might get a line or two for the next novel, which was refusing to take off. At any rate there was little to lose. If she wasn't delightful enough for him, he only had to signal the car and take off.

The first thing that Prem noticed was an ॐ symbol, set in a circle the size of a Susan B. Anthony dollar coin, emblazoned on Maya's T-shirt, in the middle of her chest, just to the right of where her heart was.

"It is you!" Maya's face exploded into a smile.

"A pleasure to meet you, miss," Prem said, formally putting out his hand to shake hers. Her grip was firm.

"My name is Maya. I didn't think there was any chance it would really be you." She had gone red.

"May I suggest a cup of coffee? There is a quiet French café not far from here," Prem said, showing her down the aisle with an after-you gesture.

"Great! It'll put me right in the mood for my trip."

"You're going to France?"

"Yes, I won a fellowship." Was she talking too soon? Showing off too much?

"Congratulations! Which one?"

"Oh! The Paris Fiction Fellowship." Without having to stare, Prem saw the flush that filled Maya's face, neck, and ears with crimson ink.

"Congrats! Do you speak French."

Maya nodded.

As they stepped out of the bookstore, the guard at the door tipped his hat to them.

"Such a coincidence. I'm likely to be in Paris all summer myself. I have a good friend there, and we try to catch up often."

Maya didn't want to ask if he meant Pascal Boutin and sound like a good student who had been doing all her reading for office hours with the professor. She was suddenly aware that her quadriceps and hamstrings, which shook only when she lunged and leaned in yoga, were full of tremors. They walked in silence for a block. At first Prem strolled comfortably but not slowly, taking in the presence of the petite girl beside him; beneath her snug T-shirt he could make out the shape of her back. After a block Prem slowed his pace. He had already noticed the mouth, the smile, the eyes, and the way they all conspired to make her face dance when she spoke. He wished to prolong the sweet agony of wanting to sit in front of her and treat himself to the sheer pleasure of watching beauty, trying to hold it in his thrall.

Maya's hands were shaking with nervousness, though she smiled her most charming smile and was sure her expressions were arranged gracefully on her face. At the don't-walk sign she teetered forward in nevousness. Prem reached out for her hand and tugged her.

There were no other customers that spring afternoon, and the waiter seated them right away on a small corner table and made himself scarce.

"I'm sorry to be less than articulate, Mr. Rustum. I was sure it was a prank." Maya looked at the table when she said his name but then looked up directly into his eyes.

"Why, I was sure it was a prank myself! I was sure I'd find myself captured on tape by some overzealous film students!"

"So you hoped to provoke the paparazzi by responding to my ad."

"Young lady, *you* were trying to provoke me. Me, an elderly heart patient with one foot in the grave and another perpetually in my mouth. You owe me some explanations." Prem tapped the table lightly when he said *owe*.

"I'm sorry, Mr. Rustum. I meant no disrespect," Maya said immediately. Her nervousness was now on top heat.

"I was teasing, dear."

Maya reached for her glass of cold water. The waiter had unobtrusively filled their glasses. The water cooled her down. She could feel her ears burning and wanted to touch the surface of the glass to them. Prem watched her silently; she was not yet at ease with him, but she was clearly bright. A bit on the reverential side, but to meet someone who wasn't, he'd have to go looking for a different type of woman, one who didn't read books.

"How did you find my ad, Mr. Rustum? I didn't think you surfed the Net."

"Not too many questions, young lady. Tell me what you'll work on in Paris."

"I'm writing a story about India. I don't know if it's possible to be an outsider like me and really write about India, but I'm going to try."

"Well, the bigger question is whether it's in your kismet, isn't it?" Rustum said, his eyes twinkling.

"The last time I checked in with a kismet spokesperson, he said I was going to get rich within the month."

"Are you sure he was competent? Where was this?"

"In the temple in Madurai. The soothsayer used a magnifying glass to read my lines."

"Fraud! Let me have a look." Rustum pulled out his glasses and put them on before bringing his left hand over the table, palm open. Taking his cue, Maya placed hers in front of him. He took it in his hand and used his right index finger to trace the lines of her palm.

In his somewhat Westernized pre-university days Prem had learned that this was the quickest, least sleazy, and most sensuous way of establishing body contact with a female without fear of recrimination. And unlike the other young men of his time, who used the palmistry trick to take hold of a fair hand and then deliver overtly dubious predictions, Prem had bothered to do his reading.

Without letting go of Maya's hand, he adjusted his bifocals with his right hand and rubbed his right palm over her open palm as if to smooth the creases. Flirting with this girl was coming so naturally to Prem, he wondered if he'd really been in hibernation for a decade. The memory of women, of sensuality, made its way to the forefront of his brain as if he'd never given it a break.

"Let's see, your Mount of Venus here. Hmm! Good. Creativity, some restlessness. Not bad for a writer, not bad at all." Maya's Mount of Venus was fleshy and soft. Prem let the flesh of his own fingertips run over it again.

"Peacock's Eye on your Mercury!" He furrowed his eyebrows to take a closer look.

In the squeeze of his hand and the soothing rub of his fingers, Maya felt herself relax. It was the same sensation as putting her head to one side after she had done a series of backbends. One of the yoga instructors at YogaNow! had said that backbends soothed the parasympathetic nervous system.

"Is the Peacock Eye winking?" she asked.

Prem looked up from Maya's hand. "Mademoiselle, this is serious business. We're talking about your future here."

"I am serious. Why haven't you ever written about palmistry in your books?"

"It's a hobby." Prem cleared his throat, then in a graver tone added, "The Peacock Eye shows an amalgamation of intensity and talent. And there is nothing better for a writer than to have it on the Mercury finger."

"Do you believe these lines really hold the truth?"

"Come now," Prem said, squeezing her hand before releasing it.

"But then why read palmistry books?" Maya was frowning at her hand, trying to see what Prem had seen.

"For aesthetic interest. I like hands." He grabbed her hand again across the table. "For instance, you have a waisted phalange here." He pinched the joint of her thumb between his index right finger and thumb.

"Does that mean something too?"

"A hand-reader will tell you that every whorl, loop, and mark means something. The angle your thumb makes where it joins your hand, for instance, points to musical harmony rather than manual dexterity." Rustum pressed into the soft pad of skin on Maya's palm with his thumb as he spoke.

"Your hands are more beautiful in real life than on TV."

"When did you see mine on TV?"

Maya told Prem about the Boutin documentary and about the letter she had almost written him from India.

"I am an unremitting admirer of yours, Mr. Rustum, and I would have been crushed to seem like a Judith Q to you."

"Judith Q does not have a Peacock Eye, and you can tell so from her letters."

"So she is based on a real person. A single real person?" Maya felt as if she were making an undignified demand on Rustum or asking him for a trade secret.

"Yes and no. The letters are not ones she wrote me."

Maya was afraid to inquire further after his injunction against *too many questions.* They bantered about their favorite haunts in Paris, the Maillol and Rodin Museums, and the merits of Pierre Hermé's *macarons* over those of La Durée.

"Maybe we can go to the museums together when we're both there. Pascal isn't usually up for it, and I don't like going alone."

"Yes, that would be lovely."

"How will I get in touch with you?"

"I'm staying for the first few days with a family friend. I'll give you that number."

"I'll give you mine, but you have to promise me that you'll keep it to yourself."

"Of course, Mr. Rustum. You can trust me."

"I don't just mean the number. I'm a very private person, and if you tell anyone about this meeting, I'm afraid . . ." he left his thought hanging.

"Mr. Rustum, I won't tell anyone about this if you don't want me to. I know my father would be thrilled if he knew that we had met, but I won't even tell him. It's a promise."

Rustum brought out a thick gold-nibbed fountain pen from the breast pocket of his jacket and unscrewed it. Maya shuffled in her bag for the small notepad she always carried around. Prem's hand moved rapidly, and Maya tried imagining the curvature of his Ss and the crossings of his Ts as she heard the sound of the nib on paper.

"I didn't know you were left-handed," she said, when he handed back her notebook. Prem had written in block letters, often joining several letters in haste, as if he hadn't lifted his pen up from the paper between letters.

"When are you getting there?" he asked.

"Next Wednesday."

"I believe I fly in on Friday," Rustum said, raising his arms in a would-you-believe-that gesture.

As soon as they stepped out on the sidewalk from the café, a black car drew up.

"Come, let me give you a ride."

"Thanks, but I can walk."

"Why this formality?"

"All right, then." Maya slid into the back of the sedan. At the next red light she and Rustum both stared at a department store window advertising suits for children. A photograph of two boys, one around seven and the other ten, was on display in the window. The photograph was several times the size of real boys that age. They were in seersucker pinstripe suits and bow ties.

"At that age I just loved Navroze the Parsi New Year because I got to wear my tie and suit. My father was excommunicated after he married my mother, a Hindu. We observed the day as a special day, and my father always wore his *dagli* that day, but my sister and I wore Western clothes."

"Did it make you feel important?"

"Did it! One of my first memories of life is of dressing up like this. My older sister Meher kissed me on my cheek that day and said I looked very handsome. It was the first time she was really nice to me."

Maya looked at Prem's face while he spoke, trying to pick out facts from the inflection of his voice but not succeeding.

"I'll get off on Forty-second," Maya said.

"In Paris then. *A bientôt.*"

Rustum removed his glasses carelessly with one hand before he reached to give Maya a goodbye kiss on each cheek. The driver waited till she was on the sidewalk and the car door firmly shut before he drove off. Prem's mouth wore a droopy half-smile for the entire ride back.

Back in her studio Maya proceeded to dance around the apartment. Johnson had invited her over to his house for an early dinner. Still dancing on her way to a quick shower, Maya removed her T-shirt and flung it across the room chanting "Prem Rustum is my friend." As she pulled down her pants and kicked off her shoes, she hopped to pick up *By the Thread* and turned it to see his photograph. After she'd seen Prem in real life, the photograph had come alive. *I've finally met you, I've finally met you.* Maya moved toward the bathroom jumping up and down in the nude.

"I've been thinking about your impending trip," Johnson said as he served her salad on his kitchen table.

"You have? What have you thought?"

"I can visit Paris for a week. Would that work?"

"I'd love to see you. I guess I'm not sure how my writing will be going."

"I promise I'll let you work. Three months just seem like such a long time."

"I'm not expecting you not to meet other women," Maya said.

"Maya, I've not felt so attracted to someone in ages. It's a shame we only just met."

"I know." Maya put her hand on Johnson's. She wanted to tell him about her meeting with Prem. She was bursting to tell him, tell anybody about it. But she remembered Prem saying that he didn't want her to talk about it and felt her body get tight—she was sure something bad would happen if she did. She withdrew her hand from Johnson's.

"What are you going to do over the summer?" Maya asked.

"I'll polish up my short stories and try to place some in magazines. I'll cultivate Prem Rustum." Johnson laughed.

"What's funny?"

"I just said that as if he were a plant or something. I used to despise all the social climbers at Harvard, but I just said I wanted to cultivate my all-time hero."

"One cultivates and fosters culture, art, friendship—it's not all that terrible." Maya tried changing the subject of their discussion.

"I'll introduce you to him when you come back."

Maya let the remark go.

"What's the matter? It's not like I just asked for a commission fee. Don't you want to meet him?" Johnson nudged Maya.

Maya shrugged. "I'm just tense about packing and leaving for three months."

"You need a massage."

After dinner Johnson pulled her to his bedroom and pushed her down at the shoulders so she was seated on his bed. He pulled off her T-shirt and shoes.

"Turn over onto your stomach."

As Johnson kneaded her shoulders, Maya relaxed. Lying face down with her eyes closed, she no longer needed to chain her mind, which wanted to be back with Rustum. It had been a sunny day with the first hint of warmth. Maya did not just remember but *felt* again exactly how she had felt in Prem's presence, like a very young flower receiving the first rays of the vernal sun and opening up to the world.

part ii

I preserved the solitude of those first books. I carried it with me. I've always carried my writing with me wherever I go. Paris. Trouville. New York.

—MARGUERITE DURAS, *WRITING*

Prem had taken two sleeping pills and fallen asleep on his comfortable bed in first class. The next thing he knew, the female flight attendant was shaking him. He heard his name.

"Mr. Rustum, welcome to Paris."

"Thank you, miss."

Prem sat up. Despite having slept like a log, he felt a bit gray.

"Are you all right, Mr. Rustum?" The attendant pulled up the backrest to vertical and the footrest too.

"I'm exhausted."

"Let me get you some water," she said, walking away.

"You must be dehydrated because you didn't drink anything all these hours on the flight," she said, returning a minute later with two glasses, one of orange juice and another of water.

"Thanks, you're kind." Prem took both glasses from her hands.

He drained them one after the other and then went to the restroom. His hair was disheveled, and he looked much older than he remembered ever having looked. He patted down his hair and went back to his seat.

At the airport exit the driver from the car service took over Prem's luggage cart and led him to the car.

"It's nice to be back in Paris," Prem said to the chauffeur.

"Not the worst summer! It's supposed to be fresh the next few days. Not too hot."

Prem acknowledged him with a sound from his throat and shut his eyes. He nodded off for a while. When he opened them again, they were already driving on the boulevard St-Germain-des-Prés.

"Can you drive past the church before turning to my street?"

"It's a diversion, but sure, why not?"

The driver continued straight instead of turning in at rue du Bac. Prem saw the Café de Flore and Les Deux Magots whiz past and then the church. The church never failed to remind him of his first visit to Paris. The visit to escape New York and Vedika. The driver had turned in at Odéon and was driving back to rue du Cherche-Midi. Soon they were at the discreet fully serviced apartment in an old Parisian building where Prem usually stayed on his trips. The driver brought Prem's bags up to the apartment, gave him a smart salute, and left.

The exhaustion from his trip had fallen away. The air was cool, and the sun felt good. Paris was perfect. It was the way he remembered it in his mind. Prem decided to wait for the evening to sleep so that he could adjust to the time difference. He freshened up before phoning Pascal, then walked to the Église St-Germain-des-Prés. It was dark inside and almost cold. Prem sat on a bench in the back. Vedika was everywhere.

The past was like a load that got heavier with each year. The burden of Meher, Angie, and Vedika had not reduced, but new weights had been added. The two French teenagers had affected him. The blue paint in the church with its benign vegetable-dye hue and small golden stars belonged to the realm where time stood still.

Like an old river at the end of its journey grown sluggish with accumulated debris, Prem's experience with women had clogged his memory. Yet despite the multitude of women who had come after Vedika, each filling his head with one more layer of experience, the Église St-Germain-des-Prés brought back the bitterness of Vedika as if she were just on the surface. He had come to Paris to get over his love for her and to avoid the Bedis without arousing Harry's suspicions. It was on this first trip that Pascal had become a real friend. They had met before in New York on two occasions, but no bond had formed there. Prem got up from the bench and left the church to meet Pascal at their usual café nearby.

"So tell me why this sudden trip? When I spoke to you a week ago, you said you were feeling too old even to be certain you would make it here this summer," Pascal asked kissing him on both cheeks.

"I followed your advice with the Internet, I found a twenty-five-year-old girl, I followed her to Paris. *C'est tout.*"

Pascal whistled. "You are back in action, *mon vieux.*"

"I don't know about that. She doesn't know that I had no concrete plan to come to Paris. I've only met her once in New York."

"But she knows you are here?"

"As soon as she told me she was coming here, I said I was too. I have to call her."

"What is she doing here? Is she French?"

"No, she's American. She won the Paris Fiction Fellowship. You were right about the Internet. I searched for someone looking for Prem Rustum, and there she was! Incredible!"

"See, I told you. Paris prize, not bad. So this girl has talent. What is her name?"

"Maya."

They sipped their *cafés* and looked at the women walking their poodles on the boulevard. Almost all the women were wearing skirts. Prem and Pascal looked away from each other every now and then when someone caught their eye. Prem felt as if Paris had taken a good ten years off his life—he felt physically energetic and mentally alive.

"I'm feeling nostalgic today. I thought of Vedika in the cab from Roissy."

"I spoke to my first wife. She's not well. She's got cancer," Pascal said in response.

"I'm sorry to hear that. I always liked Irène."

"It's getting nearer and nearer, this death business."

"I really want this girl or some girl like her," Prem said.

"There's no reason you won't get her. When you decide to se-duce, there is no stopping you. I saw you in action with Julie and Valérie."

"I didn't have to work too hard with them. But I really don't want to seduce Maya. I want honest love without calculation and without my fame playing a role."

"Your love won't be any less true just because your approach is intelligent."

"Yes, it will. I want, for once, the thing I never had except with Vedika and Meher."

"Those were both destructive for you."

"They went wrong, that's all."

"Even if you don't use your charms, your fame can hardly be ignored. Least of all by a young writer just starting out in life."

"I want her to come to me when she feels it. I want her to feel it strongly. I want to feel it strongly. And not because she's young and beautiful but because of something more. The beauty and the youth are a hurdle to knowing the interior, just as fame is a hurdle."

"A very sweet hurdle."

Prem came back to his apartment and called some friends to say he was in town.

On her arrival Maya made straight for boulevard St-Germain and sat with a first ritual coffee on the *terrasse* of Les Deux Magots to meditate on the novel she was there to write. Fifty years ago Parisian writers had sat around on the same block gestating their œuvres; today a group of Filipino tourists, scattered across the tables to her left, played musical chairs to snap pictures with the awning of the café as a backdrop.

Prem had told Maya he was going to be staying on rue du Cherche-Midi when he got into town. After her coffee Maya walked to the Carrefour de la Croix Rouge to check out his street. She slowed her steps as she walked past Poilâne. The breads and flaky pastries in the window beckoned her in.

"Je viens, je viens," she started. She had been engrossed in her own thoughts, and without enough concentration, her French had just unraveled.

"Yes, you come here. Now you are here. What would you like?" A young man who had been examining the flour section on the right side of the shop turned around and asked her. The lady at the cash register smiled at the man and then at Maya.

Maya ordered a *pain au chocolat,* recovering.

"I'll have the same thing," the man said to the attendant.

Before Maya could object, the man paid and grabbed both their *pains aux chocolats.*

"Why don't we get some coffee for these?" he said to Maya, striding out of the shop.

"Because I don't know you," Maya said mildly. She wasn't really objecting—he seemed charming enough.

"But you'll never know me if we don't talk."

He walked rapidly on the street, and Maya had to look up to see his face since he was very tall. She noticed that he was carrying a book under his arm, an English book.

"What are you reading?" she asked.

"*Carnovsky*. Do you know this book?"

Maya nodded.

"Are you American?" he asked.

"Yes. Are you from Paris?"

"No. I'm from Puy-de-Dôme."

"Ah! I think Georges Bataille is buried there, I'm not sure."

"Would you like to go on a pilgrimage to his grave?"

"Why don't we begin with Oscar Wilde at Père Lachaise?"

"Let's sit here and plan our itinerary," he said, choosing a café next to the Furla store.

"I'm here for three months," Maya said flirtatiously.

"Just the right amount of time to get to know someone, but not enough to get tired of them. I am Jean-Pierre, by the way."

"I am Maya."

"*Deux cafés, s'il vous plaît,*" he ordered when the waiter came to them.

"You could have asked me what I wanted," Maya said pleasantly.

"I am so sorry. What did you want?" he asked.

She wanted a decaf, and he went inside to change the order. Maya looked at his book. Jean-Pierre had used a ticket from the Rodin Museum to mark his page. Had Prem meant it when he had told her he would take her there? If he didn't call her in a week, she would ring him.

"What are you doing in Paris?" Jean-Pierre was back.

"I'm writing."

"I had this feeling that you were a writer," Jean-Pierre said, leaning forward.

"Why?"

"Who else walks around carrying a fountain pen poking out of the bag?"

Maya looked at her synthetic courier-style bag. She pushed the pen in farther.

"What do you write?" he asked.

"I am trying to write a novel about a white hippie in India. What do you do?"

"I am trying to write a screenplay."

"I assume the film will be in French."

"Yes. But India sounds much more interesting. Have you gone there many times?"

"My parents took me there often. They were both sort of hippies. They had real jobs, but when we would go to India for a few months, they would be hippies. Part-time hippies."

The waiter placed their drinks on the table. Jean-Pierre sipped his.

"You're not using that sugar?" Maya asked.

"Here." He passed her his packet.

Maya unwrapped the sugar cube and held it in her coffee, watching it turn brown as the coffee rose up its white crystalline structure. The sugar crumbled quickly.

"Are you alone in Paris?"

Maya nodded.

"So am I," he volunteered.

They sipped their coffee in silence for a few seconds.

"We almost forgot the *pains aux chocolats*," Jean-Pierre exclaimed, unwrapping one from its thin paper wrapping. Maya picked up the other.

"What is the story of your film?"

"There will be three short stories that will intersect. Each will feature a couple who are first very intensely involved and then leave each other. They never see each other again, but the influence of the other person is forever evident in their lives."

The waiter put their bill on the table.

Maya reached for her purse, saying, "I'm getting this." She rummaged for a few seconds for her small change purse and counted out her change. Jean-Pierre tore the bill in half and asked for her pen. He wrote his number on the back of one piece and handed it to her.

"Let me give you mine," she said, writing hers on the other.

Maya stood tapping her foot as she listened to the jazz quartet in front of the Église St-Germain-des-Prés. Prem had called her earlier in the week to fix the rendezvous.

"I am so delighted to hear from you, Mr. Rustum. How are you?"

"Just dandy. And yourself, mademoiselle?"

"*Très bien.*"

"Are you getting a lot of writing done?"

"Some. I haven't found an apartment yet, so that eats up a few hours every day."

"Will you let me distract you this weekend anyway?"

"Of course."

"There's a concert of Indian music on Saturday in the fourteenth."

Now the jazz quartet had finished playing and was trying to hawk a CD. Prem had been watching Maya for a few minutes. He hadn't wanted to interrupt her before the music stopped. He now approached her from behind, feeling stealthy.

"Are you waiting for someone?"

"Vous," she replied, smiling, as she planted kisses on his cheeks.

They hailed a taxi.

"What has been happening with you?"

"I found an apartment in Montmartre and moved. I've never met the *propriétaire*. We arranged the deal over our cell phones, and I got the key from a friend of hers."

Jean-Pierre had driven down in his rickety van that morning and helped transport her two bags and some books to the new flat.

"Is it a nice place?"

"It's full of light in the mornings and has a very pleasing view of the rooftops. I'll invite you to dinner one evening. I'd love to cook for you."

"I love to be cooked for."

"I think that cooking for someone is no different from listening to music or looking at art with someone. There is a moment when you are able to transcend the usual boundaries that are imposed by the fact that we are all separate human beings with separate bodies. I want to return a bit of the pleasure I've had from reading your books."

The cab had reached the beginning of the Villa Seurat, which was their destination.

"We'll continue this discussion some other time," Prem said, opening the door of the cab. Maya jumped out from her side. They found the address on Prem's invitation card and looked skeptically at the door.

"It looks like someone's house," Maya said.

"It probably is." Prem held the door open for her.

Two Frenchmen in Indian clothes welcomed them with a *bonjour.*

"Do we remove our shoes?" Prem asked.

"Yes, the seating inside is Indian style," one of the ushers replied.

Maya and Prem left their shoes at the entrance and walked into the room. Balinese puppets dotted the wall. In the center a small stage had been set up on a raised platform. Most of the audience were to sit on the floor on Indian cushions.

"I'm too old for that," Prem said, pointing to the carpet. He took one of the few chairs that lined the wall.

"Come here," he said, patting the chair next to his.

"I don't mind sitting on the floor," Maya said. There were seven people in the room already, most of them older than her. Maya didn't want to hog the chairs.

"Sit with me."

Maya sat beside him and looked around the room. A bookcase lined the far corner, several of its shelves taken with oversize art books. From where she sat she read off the spines: Balthus, Schiele, Utrillo, Guston, Pollock, and John Currin.

"Do you know Currin? He's quite young."

Prem shook his head. Maya walked over to the bookshelf and pulled at the book. Prem followed her and hunched over the book as she opened it.

"I saw his work at the Serpentine in London when I visited my brother."

"He's got his own distinct style down already," Prem said.

"Let me show you my favorite," Maya said, flipping to the index in the back of the book. She scanned the painting titles with a frown on her face.

"Here we go. *The Pink Tree*," she said, turning to the page.

"Can I flip through it?"

She handed the book to Prem.

"You might have chosen the one I would have picked."

"The point at which it diverges from reality is exactly where it becomes true. It's so strange. By being so unreal, it creates reality."

Prem nodded to Maya and traced the weak left calf and the stomach of the figure on the right with his finger before handing the book to Maya.

"That's true about books too, isn't it? I've always felt it when I write," Prem said.

Maya closed the book and looked at Prem questioningly. Since she met him, she had been wondering where the diversions occurred in his books. To know the man behind the writer, she needed to know just how far he had leaped.

"Let's take our seats," he said.

"There is no one in contemporary art who has achieved such form as far as figurative painting goes," Maya said, her tone impassioned.

"Have you heard of Lucien Freud?" Prem asked, raising an eyebrow.

"That eyebrow gives you away."

"What does it give away?"

"That you know just how patronizing you can be," she said, smiling.

"I concede you have a point about Currin."

Prem raised his head to examine the relatively low ceiling.

"This will be like listening to chamber music. I've never been to something so intimate," Maya said, looking up.

Several people who had walked in recognized Prem and folded their hands in *namaste* at him across the room. Prem made no move to speak to anyone. At exactly half past eight three musicians walked into the room, *namasted* the audience, and bowed their heads. They all wore stiffly starched, impeccably white dhotis and silk kurtas. After touching the base of the platform with their right hands and bringing this hand to their heads in a respectful gesture, they sat down cross-legged on the stage. From her seat Maya had a partial view of the vocalist and a full view of the mridangam player. The mridangam was wrapped in a magenta velvet cloth with a yellow satin border. The percussionist wound a blue blanket from his right ankle all the way to the middle of his calf before pulling the mridangam to rest on it.

The vocalist was the first to notice Prem once they had settled on the stage. He tapped the violinist on the knee and raised his eyebrows to the mridangam player before looking in Prem's direction. The musicians now folded their hands in *namaste* and smiled at Prem. Prem smiled back and raised his hand a little. The official acknowledgment from the stage caused a new set of heads to turn in their direction. Maya lowered her head a little.

"The first piece is in Raga Bhairavi," the vocalist announced.

"I hope you enjoy this. We can leave if you don't," Prem whispered to Maya, bringing his mouth close to her ear. Maya could immediately sense eyes looking at her. When she raised her head to look at the stage, women on the other side of the room smiled at her.

Prem closed his eyes when they started up. The chairs were arranged in a single row at an angle to the wall, and Maya could see his Adam's apple jutting out. The bones of his knees formed a visible outline under his pants. She closed her eyes, but with the complex vocalizations and the intermittent sound of the mridangam, she soon became too curious not to watch.

The vocalist slapped his right hand on his thigh to keep his beat. Sometimes he beat with the back of his hand, and sometimes used his palm. Maya tried to count at what interval he used the back of his hand, in order to decode the complex rhythm, but she couldn't keep pace. His left hand moved in front of his chest and in the space above his head continually as he yanked his voice backward and forward and bounced it up and down. Watching his hand move made the music easier to understand. The music was a river flowing in a rush as it curved along its course, a furious Seine turning under the Pont de l'Alma on a stormy night. At other times the music was like a kite flying over a large green meadow on a calm and sunny weekend morning, but then, with ease, the *chanteur* pulled it and pushed it away, only to cuff it again into a tight embrace. The violin played with the *chanteur* and sometimes trailed after him, like a puppy following a bouncing ball without letting it out of sight. The sounds coming out of the musician's mouth sounded like syllables. For over an hour the *chanteur* vocalized the syllables *Da da da ni dani da*. They stretched like elastic bands into unthinkable shapes and forms. They transformed into fluids of different viscosity, one moment as thick as honey, and then bubbly like champagne.

He ended the concert with two short pieces: songs sung in a super-express style, with foreign words pouring out of his lips quickly, the oscillations in his voice dampening. Some people in the audience were now slapping their own thighs, just like the *chanteur*, keeping beat as well. One or two even hummed with him.

Prem had thought about the opposite of music a long time ago when he had written his music book. What was the opposite of music? Silence. Noise. Disharmony. Cacophony. People talked about how music was like mathematics. At which point was it not mathematics? At the point when you took away the mathematics from the music or when you added to it? Music was the opposite of all these things, and yet it was other things, positive things. Prem wrote small, almost minute variations around each thing that was and was not like music, and then he enlarged these variations. Some chapters of the book had the incessant rhythm of a triple congo, and other chapters sounded like monophonic songs of South Indian classical music. His text was pegged to a sheet that resembled enormous diagrams of some machine. When he worked on *Raga*, he had charted every single beat in his paragraphs with such detail in a visual map that the blueprint itself was as thick as the manuscript. The sheets were laid out flat and glued to one another in the margins. It got hard to roll or fold the enormous collage of sheets. He started to leave it lying around in the study, but he had to move it to the living room when pages were added. It expanded so much that he could step into the living room only in his socks lest it tear.

Thereafter, every page of every book Prem had ever written was produced this way. Laboriously, with weeks of thought behind each idea. He chiseled individual sentences until they were fifty-seven facet diamonds. The end goal was simple, even simplistic: hide the labor. The musical tempos—largo, adagio, andante, allegretto, presto—disguised, the reader slid along the pages as if he were listening to Mozart and gliding on a well-polished wooden floor.

When fans said *your work changed my life,* Prem would ask, after overcoming his initial diffidence, how? He expected that readers had linked his ideas, disassembled his thoughts, somehow reconstructed the blueprint with which he had originally worked. But usually the reader spoke about a single book, sometimes even a chapter in a book. And Prem, disappointed, would nod. But then one day a fan quoted a single line and said, "That line changed my life." Prem remembered that line—it was the culmination of two different blueprints. The line, measured in terms of Prem's enormous graphing sheets, was a single dot reached and concluded through two series of ideas. The original blueprints were eighteen feet by twelve feet and fourteen by sixteen.

Once Prem had an idea, he couldn't let go of it until he had come at it from every direction and with all the different intentions possible. He would stay at it like a pharmacologist measuring a molecule in a test tube in ever-more-diluted solutions till there was just a trace left. Prem examined an idea at a hundred percent of its weight and then at less and less till it was just under half its weight. Did an idea still exist at half its weight, or did it disappear? Some ideas persisted even as they motored on dying batteries; others perished as soon as they had anything less than full thrust. Life plodded on, leaking and dripping away till it whittled to the very last drop. Perfection, on the other hand, diminished and ceased to be with the slightest flaw.

Soon after he had moved to the United States from England, he caught up with Krishnan, an old friend from Oxford. Prem visited the up-and-coming computer science department at Stanford, where

Krishnan invited Prem to sit in on a lecture, saying, "It's a pretty basic class, and you'll get a sense of what I'm doing with my life."

Krishnan proceeded in his thick South Indian accent—eating his Hs and barking his Os—to draw a simple flow chart. And then another more complex one. Prem mulled over the fact that there was a discipline based entirely on this approach to action and decision making. In ten years the novel would be dead, and so would thinking. A complex flow chart would plot all scenarios and code them, just as Prem plotted his novels before writing them. Shaken up after the lecture, he told Krishnan about his blueprints.

"Can I see one?"

"Yes. They're too big to carry around."

Krishnan flew back to New York with Prem just to see the chart. He trod reverentially barefoot in the cold, uncarpeted living room and examined each arrow, circle, and square, pink and blue, that Prem had put on paper.

"So you're color-coding according to probability—red for very likely, pink for maybe, and blue for unlikely?"

"Yes."

"Wait, and you have your binaries in black and white."

Prem nodded.

"And the arrows are dashed or solid depending on whether the movement from one step is necessarily linear or not. And then—" At this point Krishnan was shouting. *Loud!* is how Meher had dismissed their upstairs Tamilian neighbors in their childhood. *Even when they are not fighting, they shout. Are they all deaf?* Prem's eyes wandered.

"I asked why you have some of these in binaries when they aren't that obvious. Did you just decide as an author that you'd proceed on this premise?"

"No, that was the result of another chart, but basically in this case anything short of certainty would kick it into the opposite category."

"Why? It's not a binary. Do you have the flow chart behind this step?"

"I usually throw them away, but I kept this one. Let me find it."

Prem returned with a stack of some ten pages. Krishnan scratched his head.

"Do you want some tea?"

"Yes. I would love some."

Prem left Krishnan in his living room, relieved. His friend was going berserk. He remembered Krishnan on his worst days in Oxford as he was writing his mathematics thesis. Prem sighed and poured boiling water into a porcelain kettle. They were in for a long night.

"You're right—this is a winner-take-all." Krishnan had made his way to the kitchen and was less than four steps away, but he was speaking at the same volume as he would if he were addressing an auditorium of a hundred people without a microphone. The archetype of the brilliant Tamilian Brahmin. He grabbed Prem. "This is all the theory of programming. All of it."

"It's the way we all think, isn't it? Maybe we don't put it down on paper, but when we need to make a decision about something, we try examining it thoroughly and imagine various futures."

"Yes, but you've given them probabilistic outcomes."

"So? We weigh the likelihood of events."

"But this is very sophisticated. You've not missed a single beat, iteration, recursion—anything. You're looking at stochastic probabilities and root square regressions. You've pushed the boundaries of complexity theory in computation."

"Do you want more sugar in your tea?" Prem had already put one spoon in the cup.

"You don't get it! One needs mathematical tools for this. The more complex variations need mathematical tools." Krishnan's sentences rose and rose in volume. The last "mathematical tools" came out like a *Help! Fire!* call. Prem was reminded of a paragraph in his music book where he had tried to capture volume in his novel.

That was the hardest to do. Patterns, music, harmony, discordance, pitch, tone, repetition were all easier. But how to get a page to be louder? He had wanted some repetitions of his sentences to approach a crescendo and others to drop off into silence. This was one of the easier things to do with real music and the hardest to do with text. Eventually he'd settled on a solution he was still not sure had worked. To fade to silence, he started with consonance and ended with assonance, and to gain volume, he used alliterations.

"Did you use integral calculus?"

"You know I don't know any calculus. Don't you remember the number of times you tried explaining it to me at Oxford?"

"But how have you measured the cumulative effects of all these minute changes?"

Prem laughed.

"You came up with all this without algorithms? Without calculus? Impossible!"

Prem touched Krishnan's arm.

"Listen, *you* are the genius here. You're seeing mathematics here just as you saw it in Sanskrit verse and Yeats and Shakespeare."

"I am not talking about your language, Prem. I'm talking about your labor."

"My language is my labor. I have no other."

"Someone who studied these charts of yours can *derive* rules of calculus, the rules of programming, and then some."

"If you ask a child to walk you through one of these steps, which is just a simple life situation, he'd ask the same questions: *If this, then what? If that, then so.* That's all there is to it."

Two weeks later Prem got a call from Krishnan asking if he could come back to New York with a colleague called Metz. Prem, in the middle of making final editorial changes to *Dharma,* was irritated by the intrusion.

"You don't have a choice. This isn't about you. This is the future of the field." He had discussed Prem's blueprints in detail with Metz. They had a hunch.

"We think that the way computers think, and will increasingly think as the technology gets better, is like humans."

Had they flown across the vast American expanse to tell him *this?*

"Sure, this is how people think. And since people are designing the computers, they too will think like people."

Metz and Krishnan spent two days crawling on all fours examining Prem's flow charts. They then took his leave to rustle up a band of other wackos to discuss what they had seen. Wackos who went back pumped up to continue their work in artificial intelligence, cognitive science of mathematics, and neuroscience.

"Can we have your blueprint?" Metz asked over the phone a few days later.

"I'll ask my agent, Edward, to send his assistant to pick it up and mail it. I refuse to go to the post office. Edward's assistant does everything for me."

Edward told Prem that they were giving nothing away; his drafts and blueprints were potential archive material. Edward drew up a contract instead that allowed Metz's department to officially take the blueprint on *loan,* albeit for free, for five years. This free loan was then extended for another fifteen years.

Twenty-two years later at the annual meeting of the Meta Disciplinary Association for Scientists in Cognition (MDASC), Prem was honored with a medal. The keynote speech was delivered by Mario Scatz, who had written a biography of the science of the brain. It was the first popular science book on the subject to hit the imagination of the general public. Millions of dollars of research money came pouring in as a result of the book's popularity. Scatz had painstakingly documented Prem's role for posterity.

Edward Black negotiated a seven-hundred-thousand-dollar deal for the original blueprint that Krishnan and Metz had worked with. It now sat behind bulletproof glass at the Cognitive Science Museum that had opened in Washington, D.C.

"Who will want to shoot a hole in this?" Prem asked, looking at the glass, which despite its thickness was entirely nondistorting. His blueprint was by the main entrance.

"By paying that price, they put a value on it. Now it's artifact, jewelry, antique, just as anything valued at that price would be," Edward replied.

"I'm glad that people can buy the fruit of that ridiculous chart for just fifteen bucks in paperback."

Krishnan took Edward and Prem for lunch after showing them around the museum.

"I hate to say this for the thousandth time, but I still don't understand the fuss," Prem said.

"That day when Metz and I visited you, it became clear to us that the tools science has developed that made our field possible were somehow intrinsic to the human mind. Almost all minds work with rudimentary algorithms, we had never thought that more complex computation mechanisms were coded within the human brain, integral to it. And if we hadn't seen your diagrams, we still might not know, because *most* brains can't abstract on the fly to this degree of complexity. *My* brain can't. To see such a high level of computation applied to simple ideas—by that I mean nontechnical ideas—was a revelation. That computational capacity of the brain is just a generalized mechanism, like the movement of a limb, and can be applied widely by the mind, just as a limb can be moved."

"Forward, backward, up, down, sideways, rotated," Edward added. Was Edward in on this? Prem looked alarmed.

"Yes," Krishnan said, nodding in Edward's direction. "A finite number of movements can be applied to an infinite set of applications."

"I see."

"Who knows, you might have saved us five months to ten

years of work. There are times in science when you see a small sign and you go after it. This wasn't a small sign. Even someone who wasn't looking could have seen it."

"You were both buzzing with energy. If Metz and you had seen a street peddler doodling a shape on a scrap of paper, you would have had the same ideas."

"But no!" Edward said. "Imagine someone with a better nose than most people. Do you remember how my ex-wife Thalia could smell? A scientist observing her sense of smell would understand much more about the capacity for human smell than someone observing mine."

"He's right," Krishnan muttered. But then he stared at Edward uncomprehendingly. Edward had followed everything. This was exactly what Krishnan and Metz had argued with the medal committee about Prem having been intrinsic to the whole discovery. A lesser mind would not have ignited their sparkplugs.

"To think my writing has been working all these years because it's what a robot would have written," Prem said dismissively.

"Your writing works because you," Edward said, "work methodically, robotically, if you will, and this gives your ideas a rigor that is rare, almost extinct. Then you miraculously apply a layer of varnish over it. It's like a curve-building exercise on a graph—the original points have coordinates, but the emergent figure is smooth. Parabolic."

Edward caught Krishnan's expression.

"Why are you so surprised?" Edward asked him.

"I didn't know literary agents understood so much about cognition or parabolas."

"I got curious after Prem told me about your reaction to his blueprints. I've been reading about the field ever since."

"Edward represents other writers you know. I mean nonfiction writers. That guy who gave the annual lecture at your meeting is one of Edward's writers too."

"Prem means Mario Scatz," Edward explained.

Krishnan chewed over his meal so slowly, his mouth almost ground to a halt. How could he explain that the blueprint had been "on loan" and had never been given over to the museum until its *meaning* was established and *priced?* What the MDASC had understood and processed about the history of the various fields falling under its umbrella over a period of decades and only after much interest from the nonscientific community, this man Edward Black had *always* known. Had Prem's agent manipulated them all, strategically planting books that would focus on Prem as much as on the serendipity of the events that one weekend in the seventies?

"Did you ask Scatz to write what he did about Prem?" Krishnan asked. He was looking at Edward with a blind and blinding hostility.

Edward kept his cool.

"You and Metz told Scatz what to put in the book. It was the truth. Prem's mind is like no other."

Prem looked from one to the other. What was this now? He was over fifty years old with several books behind him that had gotten him a lot of recognition. He didn't need the idiotic blueprint or the accidental help he might have given Krishnan anywhere on his biographical note. This whole business had been merely an amusement from the start.

Krishnan shut his eyes. Prem knew that Krishnan was trying to recollect something. He opened his eyes again.

"You are right," he finally said, looking at Edward. The white pools of his vitreous humour relaxed like liquid that had just been allowed to flow.

Prem was glad the tension was easing up.

"It's another matter that I might have asked Scatz to come back and ask you some pointed questions if you hadn't told him the things you did. I had my own interests to keep in mind." Edward looked at Prem when he said *my own.*

Krishnan smiled. He watched out too for those on his team, the junior scientists and graduate students and technical departmental staff he worked with, and even the couple of mentors he looked up to. He did watch out for their interests after all.

"Fair enough," Krishnan said.

Prem was mobbed without warning after the concert. When the three-minute-long applause for the musicians came to a stop, various people arose simultaneously and moved toward Prem to shake his hand. As if expecting just that to happen, Prem stood up and put forth his hand. *Thank you. That's so kind of you. No, sorry, I'm not at all available these days. It's a pleasure to be in Paris as usual.*

The crowd of people abated. Prem rested a hand on Maya's shoulder.

"Let's go."

At the exit they found their shoes. Someone pulled a chair for Prem to sit on while he put his shoes back on. Maya slipped into her orange sneakers, lifting one foot and then the other to press on its Velcro straps.

"That was heavily classical. Sometimes they sing more popular *bhajans*, like the last two short numbers. Were you able to endure the evening?" Prem asked as they stepped out.

"Yes. I loved it! It reminded me of *Raga*. I felt I was inside the book and here at the same time."

"Which side did we come from?" Prem asked, looking at the board on the street that read:

Villa Seurat, voie privée.
Georges Seurat, Peintre 1859–1871

"That way," Maya said, looking at the board as well.

"We should go and see some Seurat at the Musée d'Orsay," Prem said.

"I was going to force you to endure my kind of music one of these days."

"We can do both, *n'est-ce pas?*"

Maya nodded.

"What is your kind of music?"

"Younger."

"These three guys were young," Prem said defensively.

"But the music is old. My musician is older than them, but the sound is young."

Maya wanted to tell him then that she had brought *Sisters in the Louvre* with her and ask if they could go to the Louvre instead, but he had ignored her comment on his music book. She decided she didn't know Prem well enough yet.

Prem was afraid he would manipulate his sentiments for Maya or hers for him. He did not want to love her as though she were a character in his book. After he had finished *Meher*, every affair of his life had been intricately connected with books he had been writing. Sometimes he took the initial sense he had of a woman and found himself investing similar or related characteristics to a woman in his fiction. Then he would fall in love with the woman in his fiction and transfer back some of his sentiments for the fictional character to the one in real life. What had happened innocently and accidentally with Vedika he had turned subsequently into a sort of formula. A formula different from Pascal's, better from the point of view of literature, but much worse from the point of view of personal life.

At one of their first meetings Pascal had discussed this with him. "You are not manipulating *la femme* in these cases, *mon vieux,* you are manipulating yourself."

"But I am aware of the manipulation, and I don't want it."

"You are still a victim of your own imagination. And as long as you work in it, it will capture you. Our work as writers is always bigger than we are. It's a huge hole into which we think we fit, but find that we lose ourselves. *C'est comme comme ça!"*

"How can you stand it?"

"There is nothing to do but embrace it. This is the nature of the *écrivain*. The essence of writerhood."

Ten years younger than Prem, Pascal seemed to have better self-knowledge. He instinctively understood what it meant to be a writer, the folly, *la souffrance*, the unbridled freedom contained in the pages of one's own work, and the war one had to constantly wage against oneself.

Prem had waged that war for the better part of his seventy-five years and produced work that had redeemed his suffering in many ways. He had used the prism of his fiction to negotiate his deepest spaces, exposing his fears to the constant scrutiny of anonymous readers all over the world and to his own scrutiny. It was not as if Prem had been writing thinly veiled memoirs or telling stories that resembled his private life; on the contrary, he had never let even the most painful emotional crises of his existence escape the net of his fiction. And in transforming them, he had to risk each time letting go of that thin cord of sanity that kept him from tumbling into the abyss. His fiction had threatened to balloon and swallow him whole. Writing was not just therapy, self-expression, creation for the heck of it, compulsion, intuition, the twisting of reality, the perversion of facts, the mere recording of reality, and even at times the anticipation of real life; it was a perpetual trap set up by Prem, the writer, to trap himself. Each book held a little piece of him that he had had to cut off and preserve in the work of art. And while Prem hoped fervently that the pieces of his soul were regenerative, there was no proof yet of their having grown back.

As a writer he did not know how to keep a distance from his writing without allowing the writing to keep a distance from himself. And he knew, as all real writers know instinctively, that the writing had to be close to the bone. Creating every day with the dark stuff of the soul, Prem risked each day never having a private life to return to at the end of the day's work. Each word tampered with his soul. For Pascal it seemed easy to play games with his writing and turn it into an instrument of seduction to get the better of it. Prem had envied him for that.

Pascal wrote about the raw and crude human stuff, his own, fearlessly. Prem took his raw and crude human stuff till he had absorbed it all and then wrote about other things using the poison in his body as the ink. Pascal didn't stake everything within. He didn't write dangerously or love dangerously. He merely exposed his demons, whereas Prem fed his demons with his own soul.

On his first long visit to Paris, recuperating from the loss of Vedika, Prem had so fallen in love with the city that he believed— by devoting himself to recording the light of its rooftops and the faces of its people—the city would become bigger than his imagination. But Paris, like Bombay, like New York, like London, was a city. It was not a self or a soul, even if the unbearable beauty of Paris suggested that Paris was *beau,* a man, or as in *une belle ville,* a woman. The flow of its river, the wide stone of its houses, the occasional raw exposed Haussmannian facade resplendent with magic, glowing luminous in the light of late May afternoons, seductively suggested a human consciousness. Its language plugged the holes in Prem's soul, a soul that he had scooped out like a melon for the sake of his own literature. French filled him with new words, words he had yet to dissect and master, words that reinvented his concepts of *l'amour* and of the self. Talking to Pascal over their first hundred coffees in bars around the Left Bank, Prem was renewed by ideas of *chez moi, soi-même, amour propre.* No doubt these ideas about existence were universal, but their flavor was French and could not be translated into English; it could not even be lived in English. The Francophone world saved Prem from completely emptying his insides of himself by replenishing him.

But in the end Paris—no doubt the most beautiful and special one in the world—was but a city. Even Prem's imagination could not make Paris a person, could not make it himself. He had to take his time after Vedika to move on to love affairs less *mystérieuses* but more *puissantes*. Prem divorced himself from his guilt. When he pursued the best friends of his ex-lovers, his Indian publisher's wife, or the barely legal French *filles*, he did so with the absolute conviction of a man who believes in the uses of sex for everyday life, in its necessity and in its amorality. With age, the large holes he drilled into himself with his fiction came to be about things even more intimate than sex and love, they involved his own fears and the universe that could not be shared with others.

Jean-Pierre called Maya, asking if she had settled in the apartment and offering her a tour of her new neighborhood.

When they crossed the boulevard de Clichy, he pointed to a freshly painted white building. "Do you know the famous Toulouse-Lautrec poster? This used to be the Divan Japonais in the early nineteen-hundreds."

"It's graduated from being Japonais to du Monde." Maya looked at the sign.

"Or regressed. Now everything is the same. Tokyo-Paris-New York. All one world."

" 'We are the world, we are the people,' " Maya sang.

"You're in good humor today, aren't you?" Jean-Pierre grabbed her hand as they climbed up the hill.

"I'm happy to be living here. I'm happy to be walking with you just now."

"Here," he said, pointing to the earth, and stooped down to kiss her. A quick kiss.

"Yes. Here. Now," she said releasing his mouth and pointing to the ground.

"Here"—he pointed to the earth again for emphasis with his free hand—"there was a convent. When Henri IV seized it, he corrupted the nuns and was linked with the woman he named the Abbesse. Rue Gabrielle is named after her.

"This way," Jean-Pierre said, pulling Maya's hand and her up a steep set of stairs. "This is one of my favorite cafés. It's very *sympa* and historic. Let's have a drink."

They sat at one of the tables on the sidewalk at Au Rendez-vous des Amis. The table had a colorful top that made it look like a van Gogh rendition of an Etruscan wall mosaic.

It was low key. Maya took a quick look into the darkened interior, where hundreds of photographs were tacked to the wooden beams running across the ceiling.

"Do you have a favorite café in New York?"

"There is a diner I go to, and there's an old woman who comes there everyday."

"You don't talk very much about your past. Your boyfriends, the loves in your life," Jean-Pierre said as he handed Maya his sugar.

"Nor do you."

"You haven't asked me." He smiled.

"And you haven't asked me!"

"I didn't want to pry."

"The last time I was in love was more than a year ago. And he said he left me because my mother was diagnosed with an illness that could be genetic. He said, 'With the medical history in your family, who knows?' "

"That is low. They have men like that in New York?"

"They have men like that everywhere. When was the last time you were in love?"

"Six month ago."

"*Months*. If it refers to more than one, it's plural. Do you want me to correct you?"

"Yes, I do. How long were you with him?"

"Two and a half years," Maya sighed. "It could have lasted

forever if he hadn't left. I think he used my mother's illness as an excuse. He had met someone else."

"Did he think the excuse would make it easier?"

"It destroyed my respect for him and made me question my judgment."

"Do you think he said it so that you could hate him?"

"He knew I wasn't that weak. I would have been upset by the truth, but I would have got over it. Now I keep thinking he must have meant what he said."

"Come, let's see the little museum nearby. There is a painting of this bar there," Jean-Pierre said, getting up from the table.

They walked to the Musée de Montmartre, where an authentic bar from before the war was preserved. It was made of metal. Above the bar hung a painting from 1920 of Madame Vaures, the manager of Au Rendez-vous des Amis. The fingers of her left hand were painted with a dark outline, each digit delineated to emphasize the beauty of her long fingers. If someone ever did a portrait of Prem, his hands deserved to be painted in the same kind of dark highlight.

"You like this painting?" Jean-Pierre asked.

"I like it very much."

"There is something else you should see. Let's go upstairs." He bounded up a flight of stairs. Maya climbed up, taking in the atmosphere of the old building in which the museum was located and the view from its various windows. Jean-Pierre was waiting for her by a maquette of Montmartre. She bent over the covered glass that protected it and tried to locate rue des Abbesses to orient herself.

"Look, this is where we walked up just now from my apartment. And this is the street where your apartment is located." Jean-Pierre pointed to the small street starting from the Place des Abbesses.

"You're right. That is in fact my building," Maya said excitedly. She recognized the independent *gîte* structure on the side of the building and its odd entrance. The miniature replica was so perfect that she could even see the windows of her apartment and the chimney that rose one floor above her bedroom.

Jean-Pierre pulled Maya toward one of the windows. A part of the estate around the museum was a vineyard. Maya could see row upon row of orderly vine trees.

"Do they make wine here?"

"Yes. And they sell it once a year. It's not the best wine. After all, it's the wine of Paris! What do you expect?" Jean-Pierre laughed.

They left the museum and continued walking.

"How is your novel coming along?"

"Not very well. I keep thinking of all the great novels that have been written in the past and wonder why I'm even trying to write. How is your screenplay?"

"The paralysis phase! I went through it too. Me, I really want to write about love. I want to lay it open directly like a book rather than talk about all these people and their daily lives that are merely touched by love on the side," he said. He pronounced *love* as if the *o* were round like an orange.

"Have you read Prem Rustum's books? Do you think he has been touched by love on the side, or has he been burned by it?"

"I like his work a lot. Writers are always burned, always scarred, aren't they?"

"I think I'm marked by his work. I feel like one of those cattle in a farm with a big number branded on the side. I don't know how to even think about writing without reference to his work."

"That's the second phase, the influence phase. You're afraid he will show up on every page you write."

"And what is the solution to that?"

"I spent last year watching films made by my three favorite directors. It's just like love. To get over it you have to get into it fully.

I was thinking that if I fell in love today, then I would do everything to realize that love, even if I knew she was going to go away in a week and I could never see her again. I don't think it would be futile or wasted."

As they descended rue Ravignan, Jean-Pierre tugged her hand and pointed his head in the direction of a second-floor window. A woman of indeterminate old age was standing in the window, her head covered tightly in a turban. She seemed to be speaking. A pigeon hovering in the window came and fed directly from the woman's mouth. Maya and Jean-Pierre stood still and watched. The pigeon flew away. The woman said something else, and another pigeon flew to her and fed directly from her mouth. They resumed their descent.

"She does this every day," Jean-Pierre said, then added, "I like talking to you. It makes me feel like writing."

"What am I supposed to do now that you've diagnosed my phases?"

"You'll find a solution. *Bon courage!*" Jean-Pierre kissed her on her lips and left.

Maya climbed up to her fourth-floor apartment and unrolled her yoga mat to practice. As she lunged back with her left foot—her arms folded in prayer behind her to stretch her tight writer's shoulders—the woman who lived on the floor below looked up into her window and waved at Maya with a *bon yoga!*

Later in her living room Maya tried to work. She wondered when it might be polite to hassle Prem for a date at the Musée d'Orsay. She envied Jean-Pierre his screenplay. Seeing him didn't put her in a mood to write. In fact, seeing him was an escape from writing. Going over her India notes, she could conjure up no descriptions of the country that had not already been mined, illuminated, exhumed, illustrated, violated, and exploded by Prem's pen.

part iii

It is the spectator, and not life, that art really mirrors.

—OSCAR WILDE, PREFACE TO *THE PICTURE OF DORIAN GRAY*

When Prem left the room with the Latours, he found Maya
staring at a painting in the next room. Her lips were parted, and she
stood in a kind of half turn, as if the painting had cast a spell on her.
Prem observed her from the corner of the room as she absorbed the
energy of the painting and pivoted on her feet to look at three workmen who were shaving and polishing the wooden floor of a typical
Parisian room. The pattern of light and dark on the floor under-
scored the strips that had already been shaved. In the far corner the
design of the metal balcony railing was visible, a pool of light collected over a rectangle section of raw, unpolished wood just to the
left center of the painting. The wiry upper bodies of the workmen
glowed in the light, and a wine bottle sat in the dark corner.

Having observed its details, Maya whipped around. Prem saw
her eyes scanning the room for him. He walked to her.

"Caillebotte. You like him?"

"I love this."

"They're young, dynamic men. It's natural that their energy
appeals to you."

"Look at all the browns, Prem. The two browns of the strips
of floor, the brown of their arms, the browns of the bags or whatever we don't see in the corner by the wall there." She pointed to
the upper right side. She had moved very close to it and was moving even closer. Prem stepped up to her swiftly and pulled her by
the arm.

"We'll have security upon us if you try to install yourself in the painting."

She stepped back, squeezed his hand tightly, and smiled. Her happiness was infectious and uncontainable; he felt she would jump up and do a pirouette like the Degas sculptures on the other side of the wall. Prem knew Orsay well enough, though he needed a map to find the *escaliers* and *ascenseurs*. Once he started seeing the art, one painting led to the anticipation of another. Rousseau's magnificent blades of grass in the forest made him anticipate Gauguin, whose Tahitian faces prepared him for Seurat's *Cirque* to diffuse the saturation of Gauguin. The memory of the paintings was integrated with the layout of the museum itself in Prem's mind. When a Gauguin exposition was held at the Met, he felt as if he had been cheated at the end. To finish without Seurat was like eating lunch without a *café* afterward.

"Don't you have a favorite? Show me something that you love," Maya said.

"Do you think anything I can show you could move you after those *Raboteurs?*"

"Yes, the colors in this room—the blue always touches me," Maya said. They were in front of *L'Église d'Auvers-sur-Oise:* the intense van Gogh sky reflected in the windows of the church, the shape of the building all wavy, dynamic, on the edge of madness. It was a small painting compared to the Caillebotte, and yet had a density and a force so completely different that there was no fruitful comparison to be made.

Maya was wearing a loose, full-sleeved white linen shirt that fell easily around her body, its shape hiding her petite frame, its transparency revealing just that. The light streaming in from the huge doors that led to the terrace lit up the golden down on the back of her neck. She was wearing lapis lazuli earrings set in silver.

"I'm suddenly impatient for Degas' pastels," Prem said.

They walked down the couple of steps into the darkened room where the pastels hung. Prem found *Le tub.* Maya came and stood beside him. He saw her on the edge of a small round basin, her back and neck exposed. Degas' gaze was intimate but nonintrusive, and Prem wanted Maya to see herself in the painting being watched by him in the same manner.

"Is this the one you wanted to see?" she asked.

Prem sensed the closeness of Maya's flesh as she stared at the pastel, but at the same time in his mind's eye he saw the pastel in its altered imaginary form. *It's the same problem when I create a character inspired by someone and then want the real-life person to be the character just as much as the other way round.*

"What do you think?" he asked her.

"I'm interested in it because it means something to you."

Prem sighed. He wasn't greedy—age had made him realistic. All he wanted was some period of time, however short, where his own state and that of someone else's matched. Exactly. It had never happened outside of sex, and even in intercourse rarely. He knew he had written things in books that elicited a kind of recognition from his readers. People sent him letters saying that something he had written had made them feel understood for the first time in their lives. It was his business to take readers to a certain emotional state with the aid of his stories and his words. Just the way every single painter who had been installed in the old Gare d'Orsay had painted a slice of time that could be tasted for eternity. Transcendence was possible, yes. But sharing, no. In his own calling the very act of fictionalizing—which made the transcendence possible—ensured that there would be no sharing. He couldn't feel what he made the readers feel, he could feel only its artifice.

He had discussed this too with Pascal who, resolutely practical, had refused to see his point of view. "You're inventing a concept that doesn't even exist. Consciousness is a function of the individual self, not the community, not even a community of two. The Marxist analysis of consciousness is useless for the appreciation of art and eros."

Maya had moved closer to the pastel. Prem looked at the

nuque de la femme and then at Maya's neck and brought his hand to the spot on Maya's cervical column corresponding to the spot in the pastel where he had imagined Degas' hand had focused; chalk in its grip. Maya's back tensed immediately. Prem kept his hand firmly on the spot looking from one to the other. Her neck slowly relaxed. A group of tourists walked into the room and made their way through the pastels at rapid speed until they reached Prem and Maya and clustered around them to see what they were looking at. Prem felt Maya exhale.

"I'm done with art. I can't take any more today," Prem said.

Maya didn't respond. She wanted to see Puvis de Chavannes, Bonnard, and the statues on the two terraces.

"Walk me to the sculptures. I'm going to sit down while you look at the rest."

They took the escalator to the level of the terraces, their bodies at a distance. Prem felt a force field emanating from Maya that resisted him and pulled him in at the same time. She was like a hot glowing metal about to melt.

"Where do you want to sit?" she asked in a quiet voice.

"By Maillol."

"Of course." She smiled distantly as they walked on the Lille Terrace.

"I'm going to be right here." Prem pointed to a bench. "Take your time."

Maya nodded and walked away without looking at him. As she gained distance from Prem, her heartbeat returned to normal. After he had let go of her neck, Maya had felt an irrational rejection, a separation from him. On the escalator when she had stood a step lower than him, it took all her will to resist the infantile desire to bury her face in his stomach.

In Salle 11 the monochromatic sepialike renditions of the back of a woman with a hot-air balloon and the front of a woman with a pigeon returned Maya to herself.

"But what happened just now? What am I feeling or not feeling?" she whispered aloud to the dark outlines of another Chavannes, a *panneau décoratif* of girls by the seaside. The outlines were dark, and the texture of the painting was gritty. *It would be easier to be the model of an aging artist who routinely sleeps with all his girls than this situation with Prem. What does he want? Do I know what I want?*

Maya was unable to hurry through the paintings. She needed time to face Prem again. She climbed back up to the pastels, careful to avoid Degas. She stood in front of the nocturnal scene of a park in Brussels in which the lamps between the trees looked like diffused moons that had descended into the blue-gray-green palette. As always, van Gogh pulled her back for one more view. She walked back rapidly going through the other rooms, blocking out all the American voices and the Japanese cameras.

Maya stood facing *La Chambre de van Gogh à Arles, 1889.* More than one hundred years later it had come in her dream when Thomas dumped her; it was in this room that Maya saw her life end up: austere, alone, and loveless. It was where her father's life had ended up. And her mother's. For several nights after the end of the relationship, Maya suffered from insomnia. She was no longer used to sleeping alone; the night without the sound of Tom's breath was like a coffin. She would come home as late as possible and fall asleep finally at four in the morning, only to dream of this lonely hermit's room and its bed for one. The painting took her back to the smell of her sheets after the breakup. Tom's scent was strong, and Maya had not done the laundry for weeks so that she could preserve his odor. The memory of Tom no longer hurt, but the painting was still a coffin. Prem was in that coffin. Hermetically sealed. Dying alone. Lonely. She rushed out of the room and flew down the escalators, practically running on the strange partial glass corridors that eventually opened onto the terrace.

Prem had been staring with unfocused eyes at one of Maillol's bathers without really seeing her. Years ago he had been in the Louvre, with the Goyas and Velázquezes, waiting for the downpour outside to end, so that he could join Pascal for a dinner party in the Marais. The long day in the museum had given him a backache, and he sat down in a bench in a small recess in the Spanish art section. It overlooked the end of the Tuileries. In the gray-white light of the thunderstorm, Prem saw the statues in the garden outside. The rain ruthlessly beat down on their bronze bodies, sending a shiver down his spine. It had been a cold summer; he had needed a coat and an umbrella most days. Prem wanted to run down and throw his gray tweed coat over *La douleur*, who rested her head resignedly on her hand. He got up from the bench and left the museum. Back outside he walked with his umbrella over his head past the Place du Carrousel, toward the hedges where the statues were placed. He found himself in front of *Flore* and the nymphs. These Maillol girls didn't need to be saved—they were strong and upright under the rain, their breasts rising in response to the cold, their stiff nipples causing an erection to press against Prem's pants. He rubbed his eyes to see if their breasts had really risen. They were still rising. He felt gooseflesh over his body, and his manhood stiff as iron.

As he made his way to the party exhilarated by the vision of the statues, the excitement that had been concentrated in his crotch diffused through his entire body, filling him with the sensation of flight. After he had removed his coat and given his umbrella to Cavalier, the host, he was introduced to the two goddaughters of the host: Julie and Valérie.

"Are you sisters?" he asked. They didn't look alike, but they laughed with ease and gave the impression of gliding past each other's intimate spaces like two Maillol statues gamboling together.

"No. Monsieur Cavalier is Valérie's godfather as well as mine." Julie answered in an almost impeccable English accent. "We have spent many vacations together in his house in Provence."

"I present the guest of honor, Mr. Prem Rustum," the host officially announced just before dinner. Pascal had tendered the invitation to Prem as a favor to Cavalier, a childhood friend. Prem had never met Cavalier before.

Prem was invited to sit on the other end of the table from the host. He asked the two girls to sit on either side. Pascal sat beside Julie, but he had just come out of an appendix operation a few days before and was not in good form. Over dessert Prem told the three of them about the statues by the hedges. The presence of the girls led him to gloss over the details of his excitement. As he spoke, his eyes turned inward, back to the moment in the Louvre when their force had assaulted him. Graced him.

"The Dina Verny Foundation supports a Maillol museum," Pascal said. "She was his muse. You can see the similarity between her face and the statues, his twentieth-century statues."

After dinner Julie jumped up and asked her godfather's permission to play music.

"Do as you wish, *ma petite,*" he said with an indulgent smile.

Julie skipped back and grabbed Valérie with one hand and Prem with the other.

"Non," Prem objected, resisting the soft pull of Julie's white alabaster arm, which reminded him of Bartolini's *Dircé* in the Louvre and not of Maillol's full curvy girls.

"Si, si," they cried out together as Valérie grabbed him from the other side.

"Mais vas-y!" Pascal said with a look that was at the same time jealous and incredulous.

Sixty-five-year-old Prem Rustum, in Paris that year to receive the Legion d'honneur from Mitterand, moved his still-energetic upright frame easily across the wooden dance floor. He held their hands above their heads and twirled the girls, first Julie, then Valérie, then both. He grabbed their waists and unfurled them as if they were rolls of satin. When he tired, he kissed their delicate hands and said, *"Merci, mademoiselles."*

Pascal watched the proceedings from a sofa in the corner of

the room. Prem came and threw himself onto the couch beside him after the dance.

"I need to go to the Maillol Museum. Will you take me?"

"Why do you want to see statues when you have these girls right here?"

"There's nothing here. They're just girls."

"I don't think so." Pascal almost hissed as he bared his teeth.

"What are you talking about? They've not even finished their *bac.*"

"*Et alors?*"

The two Ps said goodbye to the host and the other guests. Valérie and Julie stood by the door and kissed Pascal's cheeks. Then they turned to Prem. Julie, gathering her courage, asked him if they could see him again.

Prem looked uncomfortably toward the other guests, wondering who had heard.

"Listen, *petite,* we're going to the Musée Maillol tomorrow afternoon. Both of you can meet us there," Pascal responded rapidly without looking at Prem.

The girls got on tiptoes and planted two slightly wet kisses on Prem's cheeks.

Later, over a digestif in Pascal's apartment, the friends quarreled.

"But what is your problem when they are the ones interested? They're legal, they're old enough to make this decision, and you haven't been inappropriate."

"Legal? They're just sixteen."

"Here fifteen is legal."

"What is Cavalier going to think? He invites me to his house as guest of honor, and I make a pass at his goddaughters?"

"This is France. You keep forgetting this is France. I'm going to give you something to read tomorrow morning before the museum." Pascal handed Prem a yellowing old copy of Pierre Louÿs' *Manuel de civilité pour les petites filles à l'usage des maisons d'éducation.*

The next morning over his coffee Prem laughed at the dark sex-saturated humor of the book, even less sure than before about how he should comport himself with the girls in the afternoon. In his heart of hearts he knew that Pascal was encouraging him, because it just wasn't all that acceptable even in France.

The next day the girls were waiting for Prem and Pascal outside the museum. The girls and Prem made their way ahead of Pascal past the special exhibit on the ground floor to the paintings and sketches on the second. The girls walked quickly, and Prem followed them to a sunlit room with twelve statues. Julie and Valérie immediately positioned themselves next to a 1930s piece called *La nymphe*. They were almost the same size as the statue. Julie clasped the right hand of the statue and Valérie the left. They made a circle with their thumb and index fingers enclosing the statue's thumbs. Then Valérie, bored, walked away. Prem stared at Julie, who cupped the statue's hand within her own.

It all happened naturally. Julie and Valérie invited Prem to their godfather's house in the southern countryside. Cavalier had called too and extended a warm invitation to Prem to pass a few days in his villa near St. Tropez before the official award ceremony at the Élysée Palace. Prem accepted, relieved that there would be adults around, glad to be able to see the girls without risking any trouble.

On his arrival at the train station, the girls received him.

"Are you sure you have a driver's license?" he joked from his seat in the back.

Julie pushed her hand into Valérie's back pocket, and Valérie, who was driving, lifted her bum an inch off the driver's seat. Julie thumbed the wallet, found the license, and showed it to Prem.

They were prepared for all his questions: *Godfather Cavalier had a last-minute appointment but would arrive the next day with his family. There would be a dinner party on Saturday. Prem had an independent cottage to the side of the old mansion. The girls had their own rooms in the house.*

Julie showed Prem his cottage, and Valérie carried his bags.

"We will be right by the swimming pool when you want to join us," Julie said.

"We will be *in* the swimming pool," Valérie modified.

A brand-new pair of swimming trunks with the label intact had been placed on his bed. He was told that lunch would be served, in the gazebo by the pool, whenever he felt hungry.

It was almost noon, and the heat had mounted. A splash in the cold pool followed by an afternoon of Flaubert by the poolside sounded marvelous. Prem changed into his trunks and walked over to the pool. The girls were splashing violently at each other, generating so much foam and swimming-pool fizz that he couldn't even tell them apart. He settled on a pool chair under an umbrella. They stopped and waved, their small bare breasts making minor arcs in the water. For a second he felt he was seeing Meher. Then he waved back to them and settled into *Madame Bovary*. He was attempting it in French for the first time.

Sometime later they waded to the shallow side of the pool. Their bare breasts emerged from the water, followed by their torsos, and then their behinds—encased in small girls' bikini bottoms, a modest red schoolgirl design—slid out into the sun. Prem could not help but look at them. Meher at eleven had had that body, before she had got her period.

One day, without an exchange of words, Prem felt something change with Meher. A strange kind of fear grew in him all evening. Meher had been in consultation again and again with their mother; the two of them had whispered and locked themselves repeatedly in the master bedroom. Prem's father sat reading his newspaper in the living room as if life were as usual. Prem sensed that his father knew what was happening but was pretending otherwise for Prem's benefit. It was obvious that the person they were trying to keep in the dark was him. Prem therefore couldn't bring himself to ask his father what the matter was. At night Meher was very silent when she shut off the light. Usually she touched his head and asked, "My Premi Prem, are you sleepy sleepy?"

Prem apprehensively edged closer to her in bed and then reached out his hand blindly in her direction. He felt her stomach.

"No. We can't anymore," she whispered.

The sound of her voice, its familiarity, infused him with courage. "Why?"

"I've grown up."

"Are you having your period?"

"Who told you about that?" She grabbed his wrist authoritatively and pushed it away.

"I know."

"It's over. Our childhood is over. My childhood is over," Meher said in a dazed voice, as if she were repeating something her mother had said.

Prem brought his hand over her mouth to shush her and came closer. He didn't insist on touching her stomach—he was squeamish too. Blood everywhere, he thought, feeling faint. Then he hugged her and fell asleep.

The next day Prem begged and whined all day. "But it was you who always said that we would never hide anything from each other. You said we would never have secrets."

Meher finally acquiesced to changing her pad in front of Prem.

"I'm warning you again, it stinks." She pulled her thick cotton underwear down.

Prem made a face and pinched his nostrils.

"I told you it was awful."

Meher's period only lasted three days, and when it ended, she triumphantly stated, "Over."

As though the end of the war had been declared, they rolled jubilantly toward each other, reaching under her flimsy nightie and his small T-shirt. Prem put his hand over the small mound of her underwear, feeling as if a precious possession had been returned to him. Whatever this fearful, grown-up bleeding business was, it was thankfully temporary and had left her unmarked and intact.

"Some melon?" Julie was squatting beside his beach chair with slices that were a deep orange color. Her accent had slipped, and she'd pronounced *melon* the French way, the *n* light and nasal.

"That looks good." Prem reached out for a slice. Julie grabbed one and sat carelessly on the Flaubert that he'd placed face down. Prem looked down at the spot where her ass touched the book. It was a small round ass.

"You remind me of my sister when she was young." He did not avert his eyes from her bare breasts, and he did not stare. His glance was equanimous. Grandfatherly.

"Is she like you?" Julie bit into the melon, holding it in both hands.

"Was. She died a long time ago." Suddenly he was overcome. Tears welled up.

Julie licked her fingers and dried them on her thigh before wiping the tears from the corner of Prem's eyes.

"I'm sorry it makes you sad to think about her," she said.

"I'm just nostalgic." Prem laughed self-consciously. He had forgotten she was sixteen. He hadn't even spoken this way to his wisest mistresses in recent years.

"We'll cheer you up today." Julie looked beyond him in the direction of the gazebo.

"We'll make you feel young," Valérie said, walking toward them with a plate full of apricots. She laughed nervously, her voice huskier and deeper than Julie's.

Prem finished his slice of melon and ducked his head to see the sky beyond the umbrella. "It's beautiful here."

A sudden breeze blew across the swimming pool, causing Prem's thick graying hair to whip about his face. His long, curly salt-and-pepper strands fell over his eyes. Julie brushed aside the hair from his face.

"Your hair is so thick. I have thin hair," she pouted.

Yes, fine and blond.

"*Mes minettes,* go play in the water. I'm reading," he said aloud.

"I'll let you read after you taste this apricot. It's so good." Julie brought an apricot to his mouth. Prem obediently opened it and bit the fruit in half. Some juice unexpectedly squirted on the side of his lips. Julie looked at Valérie, who was hovering around the head of Prem's beach chair. She covered his eyes with her hands from behind him.

"My eyes are fine," Prem laughed. He felt a tongue on the side of his lips licking what he imagined was a smear of apricot. The tongue withdrew, and the weight pressing his book down lifted. The hand was removed from his eyes. The two girls ran at top speed and jumped into the pool. Prem covered his sudden erection with Flaubert and popped the remainder of the apricot that had been left on the plate into his mouth. He sucked the pit, rolling it many times between his tongue and cheeks, till there was no more flesh on it. Then he spat it out carelessly and eased himself into a supine position, waiting for the erection under *Madame Bovary* to ebb away. He fell asleep.

He woke up to the sensations of soft palms on his belly and chest.

"We're hungry, we want to eat," Julie said.

"Come." Valérie gave him her hand. He grabbed it and sat up.

To his shock, there was a maid in the gazebo hidden behind all the plants arranging the table for lunch. They ate in their swimming suits. The girls had put on their bikini tops for the formal banquet: *entrée, plat, fromage, dessert.*

Prem let out a small burp of satisfaction after they were finished. He ran his hand on his bare belly.

"You need to swim after this or you'll get fat," Valérie said.

"I'm going to sleep. *Faire la sieste.*" Prem smiled at the maid, a woman of peasant stock in her forties.

"You will sleep and you will swim," Julie declared haughtily.

The girls spent most of the afternoon in the swimming pool, their small breasts taking in the heat from the sun. Ever so often they stepped out and lay down on the chaise longue beside Prem to spread sunscreen over each other.

By five in the evening the temperature had dropped, and Prem stepped out from under his umbrella to walk around. Julie and Valérie were back in the water, Julie on Valérie's shoulders, her knees hiding Valérie's shoulder blades and squeezing into Valérie's chest. To keep her balance, Julie had hooked her feet behind Valérie's back, and Valérie was gripping Julie's thighs. Julie waved excitedly to Prem as if she were seeing him for the first time. Her breasts looked like fluid gold skimming off a Klimt painting.

"Are you having fun?"

"*Rejoignez-nous,*" Valérie said, wading in a big circle carrying Julie on her shoulder.

"I'm going for a walk to see your godfather's olive groves."

"One second," said Julie, impatiently kicking Valérie's back with her foot to free Valérie's hold on her thighs.

"You're hurting me," Valérie said as Julie plunged into the water.

Prem didn't want them to fight—he felt responsible for the girls in Cavalier's absence. Julie was at the edge of the pool and placed her palms flat on the stone to pull herself up.

"Ouch, it's hot." She shook out her palms as if they had burned.

"Are you okay?" Prem took her hands in his and turned the palms up to examine them. He looked up at her face. She looked terribly serious and mute.

"*Ça va?*" he asked again, more concerned this time.

In a flash she pushed into him with all her weight and threw him into the pool. Through the rush of water in his ears, he could hear the girls laughing. Julie was already beside him pulling at one leg. Valérie pulled at the other.

He came up gasping for breath.

"I'm too old for this. I'll have a heart attack."

"*Laisse!*" Valérie said to Julie. They both let go of his legs. He felt the bottom of the pool under his feet. Julie tried to climb onto his shoulders the way she had been riding on Valérie's earlier.

"Wait." Prem planted his feet firmly on the tiles.

"Okay." He brought his hands to her legs and lightly gripped the outside of her thighs so that she wouldn't fall off his shoulder.

"Now march in the pool," Julie ordered.

Prem walked deeper into the water until it came up to the middle of his torso.

"Now off you go," he said.

Julie slid off.

"My turn," Valérie said. She had been watching from the shallow end and started swimming toward them. Julie looked at Prem and slid her hand up his inner thigh. His heart started beating fast.

She continued to look at him without blinking but addressed Valérie, "*Attends.*" Then she slid her palm all the way to his crotch and touched the enormous snake threatening to unleash itself from his trunks.

"Julie, stop," Prem whispered.

She let her hand go.

"*Viens,*" she said, looking at Valérie who was a few feet away.

Valérie made straight for Prem's shoulder and climbed on. Afraid of letting his lower body out of the water in this state, Prem walked deeper into the water and then walked across the breadth of the pool, keeping his waist submerged.

Valérie dismounted, and they all three stood by the edge of

the pool. The maid came out of the house and walked across the garden to offer them snacks. The girls asked for some ice cream from the freezer in the gazebo.

"We'll take it in the pool," Julie said, giving Prem a sympathetic look.

Prem licked at a chocolate-covered vanilla stick as the tent that had formed in his swimming trunks slowly collapsed.

"So Maillol's girls or us?" Valérie asked him.

"Vous," he said, looking away from them both.

After dinner at the gazebo Prem retired to read. After a couple of hours he felt restless cooped up in the small cottage. He could be outside, in the breeze blowing in from the Mediterranean. He walked out of the cottage, waiting for his eyes to adjust to the darkness. The dogs in the house barked as he walked.

"Shh," Prem said.

"You are still awake?" It was Valérie's husky voice. She walked to him with a flashlight.

"We were watching the lights of St. Tropez. Come see them with us," Julie said. She held his hand and guided him in the dark. Valérie turned the beam of light in front of Prem's feet so that he could see the path. Julie clutched his hand and didn't let go. They stood at the edge of Cavalier's olive plantation and looked at the tiny lights flickering below them.

"Close your eyes now, *tous,"* Julie commanded.

"I've closed them," Prem said.

"Moi aussi," Valérie said.

"Let us all imagine the sea," Julie said.

"It's black," Prem said. "We are in darkness, and the black waves are rolling. Sometimes they catch the flicker of the stars."

"And the edges of the black waves are frothy and white from the light of the stars," Julie continued.

"And the waves roll and roll because the sea rolls and the earth rolls and the moon rolls. The moon is pulling the sea, and the earth is pulling the sea," Valérie almost sang.

"Venus pulled herself out of the sea," Julie said.

"Out of a seashell," said Valérie.

"Girls, I'm going to kiss you both and go back."

"Attends." Valérie skipped away from him. She had addressed him in the familiar person for the first time.

Julie ran her hand on Prem's forearm and said, "I am so glad I met you. You're different from the other adults."

"I am? How?"

"You don't act superior with us."

Valérie returned with an extra flashlight and handed it to him.

"Bonne nuit, mes belles." Prem kissed them both on their cheeks. He picked his way down to the cottage, flashing the light over the stone steps and the gravel so as not to lose his balance. The sound of the girls' steps grew faint behind him as if they had gone to the other side of the house.

Prem removed his dressing gown and made his way to the bed by the light of the table lamp. As he pulled his feet up on the bed, he sensed the pleasure that comes from lying down after an exhausting day. When he reached out to switch off the table lamp, he was completely startled by two high-pitched squeals of "Surprise!" It took his heart a good minute to slow down.

"I already said be careful. I'll have a *crise cardiaque* at this rate," he said irritably.

Julie's face fell a little. Prem regretted his crabbiness immediately.

"What do you want now?" he asked smiling.

"Move to the middle of the bed," Julie said, getting in on his left side. He felt Valérie sliding in from the right.

"Valérie, à poil!" Julie started pulling off her own T-shirt.

"There is no question of it," Prem said firmly. He was not going to sleep between two naked gamines all night.

"But you're only wearing this *caleçon,"* Valérie complained, pulling at his boxers. The bed was hot, and Prem didn't want to get up and put on the only pajamas he had with him, a blue flannel set.

"*Garde ta culotte!*" Julie ordered Valérie.

"Are you girls still wearing your bathing suit bottoms?" Prem asked.

"Yes," they replied in a chorus.

"Look, I really don't think this is a good idea. I'm old enough to be your grandfather." He felt himself torn between what he thought should be his demeanor toward them and what felt natural. Absurdly, everything that had happened felt utterly natural.

"My grandfather was no prude," Julie said.

"Your parrain, Cavalier, will not appreciate this. I have to be a responsible guest."

"Our parrain had an affair with one of our classmates himself," Valérie said.

"Look, we're not children. Please don't talk to us as if you're responsible for us."

"But, Julie, I feel responsible for you. You're young, how can I not?"

In response, she brought her hand down on the buttons of his boxer and started moving it up and down.

"Julie, *non!*"

"But what do you think? We were raised on eclectic soirees by our godfather. *Les soirées parfois laïques parfois lubriques,*" Valérie said in an eminently reasonable voice. Secular soirees and lecherous ones.

"What are you trying to say?"

"She is telling the truth. We've heard our *parrain* and his guests discuss the nature of French secularism and the eroticism of Bataille and Sade. We were always allowed to listen," Julie said softly, continuing to rub his crotch.

He pulled her hand away and laid it on his navel. Her touch was like Meher's. The memory of being seventeen was fresh in his mind. Weeks before Meher's marriage, tasting her, penetrating her, making love to her against the wall, in the bed, in the bathroom, and crying, crying, crying whenever there was a pause in their love-making—that was what it had been like as a teenager. He had been no less an adult then. *But now I am sixty-five.* There was no way he was going to put his aged *braguette* inside their tender French *fentes.*

"No intercourse. *Tous sauf pénétration,*" he said aloud.

Julie agreed to the compromise with a jubilant *d'accord.*

The night was delicious and delicate. Prem fell asleep in the early morning hours to the regular breathing of his two *minettes.* If he never woke up from his sleep, his life would have been full, satisfying, beautiful.

He found himself alone on waking up. He showered and dressed slowly, looking at his watch only after he had put on his khaki pants. It was already nine. It was a bright and blinding day outside the cottage. A woman he didn't recognize was sunning herself in a bikini by the pool. He heard laughter and voices from the gazebo beyond. Up the steps and behind the orgy of plants and creepers that were growing everywhere were Cavalier, his wife, his two kids, and the girls.

"*Coucou.*" Julie ran to him and planted a quick kiss on his lips. He smelled hot chocolate on her mouth.

Valérie kissed him on the cheek. "*Bonjour!* Did you sleep well?"

Prem walked to Cavalier and shook his hand warmly.

"Did my goddaughters take enough care of you? They can be a handful sometimes."

"They were impeccable hostesses," Prem said, smiling at the girls before greeting Madame Cavalier on the cheeks and then the kids. A boy and a girl. Both a few years younger than Valérie and Julie.

Cavalier brewed some coffee for Prem.

"What would you like for breakfast?" Madame Cavalier asked.

"*Pain au chocolat?*" One of the Cavalier kids waved to the basket on the table.

"No, nothing that heavy," Prem answered, running his hand on his stomach.

"Eat some fruit," Julie said.

"Would you like some fruit?" Madame Cavalier asked.

"Marraine, laisse-moi le faire." Julie jumped before Madame Cavalier could get up.

The woman who had been sunning herself joined them, and Cavalier introduced her as Mrs. Werner. She had moved from Germany with her husband to run a guesthouse for German nudists in the Côte d'Azur and had continued living in the South of France after her husband died. Prem was sure she had been brought in for him. People inevitably invited a single woman to come to parties where he was invited. He nodded politely at her.

Madame Cavalier went into the house to unpack and organize for the party. Prem sipped his coffee as Cavalier asked him about the traffic on the drive up.

"I'm going to go in and help Madame Cavalier," Mrs. Werner said shortly.

"Be careful, or Marraine will really put you to work," Julie said cheerfully, placing a plate of peaches and apricots in front of Prem.

"That's too much," he protested.

"I'm going to eat some too." She climbed and sat on the table right by the plate and picked up a peach. Its juice ran over her fingers and all the way down to her elbows as soon as she broke its skin. Prem grabbed a napkin and placed it under her elbow while continuing to talk to Cavalier.

"Attention, petite, don't let the juice drip on Mr. Rustum's clothes," Cavalier said.

"It's okay." Prem picked up a peach himself. It was the sweetest fruit he ever remembered eating in his life, and so juicy he had to hold his hand over the plate so that he wouldn't get himself dirty. Cavalier laughed and handed Prem a napkin.

Prem took up Cavalier's offer to go to the farmer's market with him in the next village. They spoke easily and frankly. Cavalier had read all of Prem's books.

"Boutin is a very good writer. We're proud of him in France. He's a major export for us. But you're different. It's all that Eastern wisdom you bring to your writing. Boutin is just one of us. Even if he can rise above us, he's still a product of modern Parisian society."

"And I'm exotic?"

"No, I didn't mean that. India is old and has integrated other cultures for thousands of years. You're a product of that world. The fact that you've lived in New York and London and traveled a lot gives you the ability to talk to us in a language that we in the Western world can understand, but your knowledge is from that other world. We French love your country."

"You're kind. I sometimes don't find much knowledge in my writing."

"But that's also natural for a writer. You may not see it, but we do. I teach a set of your books in my class on world urban sociology. I want you to give a lecture when the university is back in session."

"Sure. I'll be around in September."

In the afternoon Prem retired for a short siesta in his cottage. Within five minutes the door opened without warning, and Julie walked in. She locked the door, which had hitherto been unlocked behind her.

"No way," Prem said from where he was lying down.

"Don't say no," she whispered, coming close to Prem's face and lifting her skirt. *Sans culotte.*

He held her loosely by the waist as she brought her leg over the bed and started to slide down toward his stomach.

"No, come here," Prem said, pulling her all the way up to his mouth.

"Ah!" she moaned.

"Shh!" He put his hand over her mouth. She was like the peach he had eaten for breakfast.

"Your turn," she said.

"No. Leave. Please, Julie," he said.

"Okay." She kissed his forehead and left the cottage.

Before falling asleep, Prem remembered Vedika quoting from the *Chandogya Upanishad* to him one day: "One should not reject any woman; that should be the vow."

Prem slept deeply, waking up only when Valérie knocked on the door. She carried a tray in her hand.

"My godfather said that Indians like to have tea in the afternoon, just like the English. I made you some." She placed the tray on the table beside his bed.

"Thank you, Valérie."

She sat down on the edge of the bed, somewhat awkward and shy in the absence of Julie. Then she stared at her thigh and pulled up her skirt. The door to the cottage was still open, and light streamed in from the five-inch crack. Prem put his hand on the part of her thigh she had exposed, tapped it to get her attention, and pointed to the door. Valérie got up and locked the door.

"It's such a hot and humid afternoon. You did well to sleep," she said as she came back to the bed. It sounded like something Julie had asked her to say.

"Where's Julie?"

"She went with Parrain and Marraine to La Motte."

Prem laughed.

"No, it's really the name of the village nearby." Valérie brought his hand down and placed it on her thigh. He let it rest. She pulled it farther up.

"Lie down, get comfortable," he told her. He turned to his side, resting his body on his elbow and his head in his palm. With his free hand he touched her face and her eyes, her chest under her T-shirt, and her *motte*. Her skin was like Meher's. He closed his eyes and let himself caress her slowly, trying to remember everything Meher had loved at that age. Valérie was groaning softly. More softly than Julie. After he brought her to climax, he gave her a kiss on the forehead.

"Prem, we didn't believe it, but Parrain was right—older men are gentler."

"What did Cavalier say about me?"

"Nothing. At one of his soirees the adults discussed their youth and the affairs they had with older people. The women said that older men are less selfish, and Parrain agreed."

"So you're testing out this theory with me?"

"No, Julie and I were—how do you say it?—*on en avait marre.*"

"You're too young to be fed up. What have you been reading?"

"I've started reading *Platon. Le banquet.*"

"Plato and *The Symposium* in English. Do you like it?"

"It's difficult, but I want to finish it. I've read four of your books. But all in French."

"Which ones? The French translations are good. I'm satisfied with most of them."

"*Grinding India* because it's the one Parrain makes everyone read first. He calls it your *chef d'œuvre.* Then I read *Meher* and *Pondy in My Cherry.* Now I'm reading *L'odeur de la boue humide.*"

"Which do you like the most?"

"It's hard to have a favorite. After we met at Parrain's house in Paris, I went back and read my favorite chapter from *Meher,* and suddenly you were no longer only the old man I had met but also at the same time the young man in the book. I kept thinking of myself as Meher, and you as the cousin she falls in love with."

"It's fiction, Valérie. I slept with my sister, but the story of *Meher* is not true. The man she loves in the book is nothing like Meher's real husband, but he has all the outer characteristics of that man because I didn't want the book to destroy her personal life. Do you think now, while you read *L'odeur de la boue humide,* that

I am the depressed New Yorker on the verge of finding wisdom in my motherland?"

"Yes. I see you in every page I read now because you're here in front of me and they are your words. I hear them as if you wrote them for me."

"Have you ever tried writing a story?"

"I want to write a story. I'm trying to write about Julie."

"Are you in love with her?"

"No. But we've had boyfriends at the same time and grown up at the same time in"—she struggled for the word—"in spurts. We wanted to experience something together."

She pointed to Prem with her finger as if he were an object in the room.

"This is your common experience?" He pointed to himself.

"Yes."

"But why me? Why not Cavalier? Or one of his friends?"

"Our parrain is our parrain. We've known him since we were children."

"When did you both choose me?"

"We talked that night after the dinner in Paris. Julie, who doesn't like reading, started one of your books that night. She loves sculpture. When we were smaller, we could always get nearer to the objects in museums because we were children. One day she fell at the feet of *St. Jean le Baptiste,* you know the large one at the Musée Rodin, and started weeping over his toe. When she heard you speak about those Maillols, she said she had met her *âme-sœur.* How do you say that?"

"Soul mate."

"Julie's English is better than mine, but I'm going to improve mine. I'm going to read *Meher* in English. I want to read your words directly from your mouth." She touched his lips with her thin fingers.

They heard the sound of a car pull into the estate.

"Everyone is here. I'm going to tell them I just gave you your tea."

Prem nodded.

"Julie and I will take care of you tonight, okay?"

"I'm well taken care of already. I don't need anything more."

"I need something more," Valérie said. She brought her mouth close to his and kissed him gently on the lips. Prem closed his eyes to receive them and kept them closed until she had left and closed the door behind her. There were moments when Meher had transformed from a young girl into an ardent woman, giving him glimpses at the ages of thirteen, fourteen, and fifteen, what it was to respond to a real woman, what it was to be a real man. Valérie had transformed in the moment of the kiss into a woman. He sat up and had his tea, though it was tepid.

Prem walked to the gazebo, where he found Mrs. Werner still cooking in the sun. She had burned to an unsightly red color that made her look like a large rash.

"You got some sun," he said.

"And you didn't get any," she accused.

Prem smiled as pleasantly as he could and made a turn behind the foliage by the gazebo to find his host. Cavalier and Prem took a long walk around the vineyards and spoke about André Breton and Antonin Artaud. When they returned to the gazebo, it was already time for aperitifs. Madame Cavalier had prepared melon with ham, and the girls were setting the table. The Cavalier kids had just fought over the music for the party and were both sulking. After dinner Prem had a tisane and retired to his cottage. Mysteriously, the girls timed their appearance to perfection. Exactly when he was finished with his last page of Flaubert for the night, they opened his door and glided to his bed. As soon as the mattress pressed down on either side of him, he shut off the light.

"It's your turn now," Julie ordered.

"If it's my turn, then do I get to choose what I really want?" Prem asked.

"Yes," Valérie answered.

"I want you to run your hands on my back."

"No," Julie whined.

"Why won't you let us give you what you have given us?" Valérie asked.

"This will give me more than what you have given me," Prem said.

"You don't want us," Julie accused, then added, "Would you have preferred Mrs. Werner with her *gros seins?*"

Prem ignored the comment on Mrs. Werner. He was in her boat, and he didn't want to forget he was older and only a little more attractive than she. "Today I just want this. I let you do what you wanted yesterday."

"But that was yesterday."

"I think we should do what he wants." Valérie, the voice of reason.

Prem turned on his stomach and felt their light touches and fell asleep for the first time in over forty years without missing Meher.

The party the next day was an array of France's *intellos* who were holidaying in St. Tropez, Nice, and Monaco. Julie and Valérie were dressed in glittering silver dresses and were the center of attention of Cavalier's dirty old friends. Prem spoke to a young couple struggling to make it as artists in Cassis. They had moved to the South for the light, but it was hard to sell their paintings here except to American tourists in the summer. Now they were thinking of splitting their time in Lille in the winter months to teach at an art school.

"You have to persevere. Since there's no set path for the artist to take, the ability to hold your horses counts for the greatest part of success."

"Monsieur Boutin bought one of our paintings," the woman said to Prem.

"Is it in his house? Which one?"

"The long narrow one with the violet candy pattern and the woman's silhouette. She painted that one," the husband said.

"I love that one. It reminds me a little of Klimt."

"I was in a Klimt phase," she said.

"Maybe I can see your paintings."

"We're around for the next few days since there's a big artists' exposition in the village nearby."

"I'll come with Cavalier."

After dinner Valérie turned on the music at top volume. Cavalier's son had helped her install a strobe light in the gazebo, and they had cleared out some of the plants. Julie grabbed Prem's hand and led him under the strobe. He followed, trying not to think of all the people who would look at him. He swayed a little, with the energy level appropriate for a man of sixty and not like the sixteen-year-old he was feeling inside, and made a hasty exit after the first song. Twenty minutes later he was back. Cavalier and his wife were shaking their behinds vigorously. Many of the guests had got into the groove too; Mrs. Werner was waltzing in her flowing dress with a balding French actor in his forties who reminded Prem of a younger Pascal. He found the girls in a corner and gave them a spin.

The party went on until two in the morning. Except for a few people who were spending the night in Cavalier's mansion, almost everyone had an hour's drive ahead.

"I'm wiped out," Prem said. He kissed Madame Cavalier, the two kids, Mrs. Werner who was spending the night, Julie and Valérie, and even Cavalier.

"I'll take you to the cottage," Valérie said to Prem.

The garden and the poolside were well lit, but when they got to the gravel path near the house, Prem had trouble seeing and was grateful for Valérie's slow steps and steady hand.

When she'd deposited him in the cottage, she said, "It might be difficult for us to slip out today with a full house, but leave the door open."

"Okay."

Prem removed his clothes and fell asleep as soon as he put his head on the pillow. He heard the door open and woke up with a start.

"Shh." It didn't sound like either Julie or Valérie. His eyes could make out the vague silhouette of a larger person.

"*C'est qui?*" he asked loudly.

"Mrs. Werner."

Prem turned on his bedside lamp and instinctively shut his eyes from the brightness. She was still in the long white robe she had worn while dancing. He rubbed his eyes and looked at his watch. It was almost three in the morning.

"Mrs. Werner?"

"Can I join you?"

"Now?"

"We are both here. We are both alone. *Je me suis demandée pourquoi pas?*" Her French accent was much better than his. She was walking closer to the bed.

"Mrs. Werner, I don't think so," Prem said, getting out of bed. He stood in his boxers.

"Why not? Cavalier won't mind."

"I'm sorry, Madame, it's not possible." Prem walked to the door and held it open wide. She made no move to exit. He stepped out of the threshold barefoot onto the gravel, his chest cold.

"You are cruel, Mr. Rustum. Am I too old for you? *C'est ça?*"

"Mrs. Werner, please don't make a scene," he said coldly.

She walked past him, and he could see tears in the corners of her eyes.

"One day someone will do this to you," she said bitterly as she stepped out.

"I'm sorry, Mrs. Werner, but I can't help my feelings," he said regretfully. He knew someone would do it to him and he would suffer. *Tant pis.*

Back in the cottage Prem rubbed his feet on the towel by the shower in the bathroom before getting back into bed. Five minutes after he had shut off the light, the door opened again. This time it was the girls.

"We saw that," Valérie said.

"We waited for her to get back in the house," Julie said.

"Was it difficult?" Valérie asked. A question less than innocent, full of the arrogance of youth.

"Vieille vache," Julie laughed.

Prem sat in bed, his back resting on a pillow. His heart thick with guilt for the fat cow because he'd rejected her. If Meher were alive, she would be his age. Would he reject her too in favor of the milky skin and downy hair and erect upright tits of these lovely young maidens?

"You look sad," Valérie said.

"I'm one of her, one of them, the old cows," he said.

"You are a great writer. You have been invited by Monsieur le Président de la France to accept the Légion d'honneur," Julie said, running her hands over his chest.

"Nonetheless, I'm old and decrepit."

"Decrepit? What is that?" Julie asked.

"Usé, brisé."

Valérie had ducked under the duvet and placed her head on his thigh. She was running her hands up and down his legs. *Do you think Mrs. Werner would hesitate if a sexy young bull were by her bedside? This is a gift—accept it graciously. You may never again have this in your life.*

Julie licked little circles on his nipples. Prem let his sensations take over. He felt both their hands reach down into his *caleçon* at the same moment and cup his *couilles* with such tenderness that love flooded his heart before gushing to engorge him.

The girls had already left when Prem woke up. At breakfast he learned that Mrs. Werner had driven away without saying goodbye to anyone.

Sunday was relaxing. In the morning Cavalier took Prem to the village exposition to see the young painters' work. Prem bought one and asked for it to be shipped to his address in Paris. Bathed in light and outlining two youthful figures, it reminded him of the weekend he had just spent with the girls.

When they got back to the mansion, Prem splashed in the pool all afternoon. The Cavalier kids were in the pool too, and Julie and Valérie played with them. Monday passed the same way. The idyllic warm weather and the light breeze from the seaside inspired Prem to look for hours at the blue sky. Cavalier's wife pampered them all by baking fresh olive bread. They left on Tuesday. Valérie and Julie took the train with Prem while the Cavaliers drove back. Prem was to receive his medal on Friday. By the end of the long train ride the girls had convinced him to make all the phone calls necessary to have them invited to the presidential ceremony.

After the ceremony and the banquet the press got wind of the girls. Prem had invited Pascal to sit at the table beside him for the function. The girls had another table farther away from Prem. After Prem had been pinned and photographed, the girls made their way to him shyly through the crowd. Elated to see them, he had held out his arms and taken their kisses naturally. White flashbulbs had gone off around them. Later the girls had gotten into his limo and come home with him. Julie grabbed his medal and placed it on her stomach. She slowly pulled it down and pushed it inside her underwear.

"*Fais pas ça,*" Valérie said looking worriedly at Prem.

"Oh, I don't care!" Prem was delighted at how much delight it seemed to give Julie. The outline of the medal and its spokes were visible through her underwear. Prem rotated it slowly so that the ten beadlike nodes brushed past her sensitive spots one after the other. She moaned. Valérie watched enthralled. Julie pulled it out from her panties and placed it on Valérie's triangle.

In the morning Prem was the first to wake up. He went down to Poilâne to buy croissants for them all. They would start school on Monday, they would go back to their friends and their lives. His heart felt heavy. They had talked about visiting him in New York for a weekend in the fall. The idea cheered him.

"*Petit déj, mes filles.*" He stood at the edge of the bed, watching their bodies move up and down as they breathed. He woke the girls and showered with them.

After eating two croissants each, they left. Later, when Prem bought his newspaper and sat over his lunch at a restaurant, he saw the photos of the girls. He bought some other newspapers and tabloids. They all carried the pictures, two of them on the front page. A few days later the weeklies carried the same. He thought he would hear from Cavalier, but Cavalier never commented, not even when he called Prem to set a date for Prem's lecture. Nor did the parents of the girls. With each passing day he dreaded the worst.

After two and a half weeks he got a short note from Valérie saying she would drop by one afternoon after school. He paced up and down the apartment all day, anxious as to the news she would bring.

"Julie barely acknowledges me in school. She said she never wants to talk about what happened."

"Did your parents say anything?"

"No. My father started to say something, but my mother told him I was old enough."

"Do you think her parents have forbidden her to talk to you?"

"No. She said it has nothing to do with anybody else. Not even us. I see her with a young guy all the time. He's in his first year at Sciences Po."

Jealousy pierced Prem.

"I love her, I miss her," Valérie said, and started crying.

Prem sat beside her and ran his fingers through her hair. He could smell the scent of her apple shampoo. The jealousy passed.

"I don't want that guy of hers. I just want to be close to her again."

"Do you think she thinks you want her guy?"

"After we shared you, maybe she does. We had planned it with you. We were both tired of our experiences. I had one boyfriend who was twenty and one who was my age, and neither was any good. And she had the same."

"Why didn't you contact me earlier if you were so unhappy?"

"My boyfriend didn't want me to. We had a short fling before the vacation, and when we came back to school, he said he was still attached to me. He got madly jealous of all the photos in the magazines and said that if I ever saw you again, he would kill himself."

"And now?"

"I broke up with him. I changed in the summer. He's too young for me. I read *Meher* in English when I couldn't see you. I was scared that you would go to New York and never come back."

"I have to come back to Paris. I have to finish the novel I am writing."

"Is it about Paris? What is it called?"

"Paris a Halfway House."

"When will you finish it?"

"I don't know. I'd written most of it when I met you, but since then I haven't been able to write."

Valérie giggled.

"What's funny?"

"That we managed to distract you."

"You've distracted me a lot."

Valérie moved to Prem's lap and played with the buttons of his shirt as she talked. She told him everything that had happened since she had last seen him. Her English class was fun, but her French literature class was a drag, they had a new puppy at home, the boyfriend she had dumped could not understand even the first page of *The Symposium* but she had read the whole thing. She had written a twenty-page story about Prem.

She opened all the buttons of his shirt and placed her cheek on his chest. He could feel her light breath on his nipple.

"Can I read the story?" Prem asked, touching the skin under her panties.

"Yes, but not now. Your hands are like magic. I wrote about your hands, how you write books with your hands. When I think of your hands touching me, it becomes hard to control myself. I feel I am drowning in a flood. I haven't been able to control myself."

She pulled his hand and slid it inside her underwear and guided it to the flood.

"Oh, Valérie!"

They kissed for a long time.

"Come," she said, finally rising from his lap and leading him to the bedroom.

When Valérie could not take the long languorous touch of Prem's fingers any longer, she whispered, "I want more. I want you."

Lost in the moment and completely her slave, Prem lay down and pulled her over him. She slid and glided like a river, a silk scarf, a feather, like the young girl she really was. Then she started moaning like a woman, she churned faster and faster. The transition from river to sea, from feather to rope, from girl to woman, was so extreme that Prem too changed from being the teenager he had been with Meher to the virile man he had been with Vedika. Under the light weight and white skin of Valérie's body, his own muscular darker one now moved with a force and will of its own.

"*Tu peux jouir?*" she asked, her eyes closed in a grimace.

"*Avec toi,*" he replied, grabbing her shoulders and then her breasts.

"*A dix. Un, deux, trois, quartre, cinq, six, sept, huit, neuf.*"

"*Dix,*" they both said. Prem exploded inside her. Valérie fell over his chest.

"It was the first time in my life," Valérie said.

"The third in mine," Prem said.

"*Non, c'est pas vrai!*"

"*Si.* It's only in the movies that people come together all the time."

Valérie promised to pass by after school again that week. She arrived with her story and some bonbons to go with his afternoon tea. They made a different kind of love, wiser. After she had left, he read her story about him. It was in French. It began:

Since antiquity the likes of Alcibiades have hankered after Socrates . . .

In Valérie's story the main character was called Raj. He was a man made of words. She wrote that she had been seduced in the best possible way by him. He, the *séducteur,* had played no role in the seduction. She had described his body—the signs of age on his person, his wrinkles, the lines on his face—without shyness. Everything aged except words and art. The Venus de Milo and the words of Plato remained young. Inside his aging flesh, because Raj was made of sentences, he remained young. When they made love, the heroine felt it was his words and his hands that made love. And his hands, even wrinkled and old, had the knowledge of touch, an ageless knowledge. He was capable of loving a woman in the way in which she most needed to be loved.

Valérie didn't call or come over the weekend. Prem read the story several times and went to bed in tears on Sunday. He was falling in love with Valérie. He was already in love with Julie. He didn't know if he would ever see her again. He cried because he could not imagine any sixty-five-year-old man in the world who could have been happier than him and because like everything else this too would end, change, move on.

Midway through the week he got a phone call from Valérie saying that she and Julie would both come. He bought a box of *macarons* from La Durée and listened to a Ravi Shankar record to hold his impatience at bay.

They graciously accepted the tea he brewed and smacked their lips after popping in the first *macarons.*

"Julie, are you doing okay?"

"I wanted to say *au revoir* before you left. I can't see you again." She seemed sad.

"I don't know when I'm leaving. Are you angry about the press? I'm sorry. I should have anticipated it and been more careful."

"It's not because of the *publicité.*"

"Then what is it?"

She looked away from him at the window, her eyes distant, betraying nothing.

"It is sad to see death. The death of love," she said.

"Julie." He came toward her painfully, struggling to push away what he had learned. He touched her upper arm. She put her hand on his for a second and then removed his hand.

"*Désolée je ne t'aime plus.*" There were tears in her eyes, but she blinked them away.

Feeling old and befuddled, Prem looked at Valérie. She averted her eyes.

"*Et toi?*" he asked, stepping toward her though he knew the answer already.

"I killed it. This weekend." Tears were streaming down her cheeks. She sniffed.

"*On se casse,*" Julie said, rapidly grabbing Valérie's hand. She looked afraid, as if she would love him again if she stayed.

"Please stay and talk to me. Let Julie go if she has to," Prem said, imploring Valérie.

"I'm going with her, Prem," Valérie said, wiping her tears.

At the door Julie turned around and said softly, "I'll keep some beautiful memories."

Prem heard the door shut and watched from the window as they left the building. Then he went to his dining table, which looked ridiculous with its ornate wooden legs, its polished silver tea set, its china, and its box of lurid-colored *macarons*. He tugged ferociously at the tablecloth till it all came crashing down.

"Mais moi, je vous aime toujours!" he screamed.

A few minutes later he called the housekeeper for the building, saying he probably owed her one thousand francs for some damage in the dining room. Could she send someone to clean the mess? Then he went to meet Pascal.

"I'm brokenhearted. I'm heartbroken. My heart is broken."

"I'm sorry. It was them?"

"Yes. I'm going back to New York tomorrow if I can. I have to get out of this pain."

"You will."

"Not soon enough."

"Do you remember when you first came to Paris? You were worse than this. You left New York to escape Vedika."

"Now I am leaving Paris to escape Julie and Valérie. Valérie and Julie."

"At least you had the chance and good health to enjoy them," Pascal said. "You haven't been cut open for the removal of an inflamed vestigial organ."

"Sorry. You've been a true friend." If Pascal had flirted with one of the girls, everything might have ended differently.

"No. I've been jealous. But I never wished that you didn't have them."

Prem laughed. The love that women gave was there in art. But that of friendship was only in Pascal. A hundred visits to the Maillol Museum could not replace his friend.

For the next ten years it was Pascal who roped in the girls. Without his appendix restraining him, Pascal was like a satyr, he was Pan. Prem finished *Paris a Halfway House* in New York. Then he used the fragments of his heart to write *Sisters in the Louvre*. He insisted that Patriots publish the painting featuring Gabrielle d'Estrées and her sister on the cover. It was the tragedy of two sisters who loved the same man and were unable ever to enjoy him. Eros divided them repeatedly until there was nothing left; the small pieces of love had become thinner than dust mites, flimsy, weightless.

Prem received a letter from Valérie when *Paris a Halfway House* was released. She loved the book. She had stopped writing and was going to apply to Sciences Po. A year later he got an invitation to attend Julie's wedding. He sent a polite response saying that he was indisposed due to the release of his new book. When *Sisters in the Louvre* came out, Cavalier told him that Valérie too was married. Pascal saw Julie on a street near Place des Vosges once and told Prem on the phone that her skin looked all the worse for the sun it had been getting on the Côte d'Azur. Would he even recognize them if he saw them?

The Maillol girl on the Lille Terrace at which Prem had been staring was only a little older than Julie or Valérie had been when he met them, but her youthfulness was preserved. Valérie's story was right—everything aged except words and art. Love both aged and died.

"Did you miss me?" Maya asked, coming close and sitting on the ground beside him. She was at ease again and looked up into his face.

"Please don't look at me like that," Prem said.

"I'm sorry you look troubled," Maya said, getting up immediately. She refused to be upset by Prem bristling.

Prem pointed diagonally to the floor below them. "I want to see the Courbets in that open hall."

"Let's see them then."

Prem went to *L'origine du monde*, hanging at eye level, and stared at the dark pubic hair in the painting and the crack that reached all the way into the sheets.

Maya frowned. "That's odd."

"What?"

"I've always remembered this painting as being huge. I thought it was the same scale as one of these immense Courbets." Maya pointed to a wall-sized Courbet hanging nearby.

"Are you sure you were thinking of this painting?"

"I remember it exactly. Exactly. Down to the last detail," Maya said. Tom had told her that when he went down on her, he often thought of this painting.

"Did you see everything else you wanted to see?"

"No. I want to see paintings from Manet's pre-Impressionist phase on this floor, but I can come back."

"Go see it. I'll wait."

"Are you sure?"

"Yes. You'll tell me about the one you like best."

"In that case, I'll be back soon."

Maya walked rapidly, stopping only a few times for any length. Manet's portrait of Émile Zola from 1868 hung beside a Manet from 1863, *Olympia*, which featured a black woman holding a bouquet for her naked mistress on the bed. The mistress was modestly painted with barely visible nipples and a hand covering the entirety of her sex. In the Zola painting, his desk was scattered with books: the most prominent was titled *Manet*. A black and white painting was tacked above Zola's desk. The painting within the painting above Zola's desk was a black and white rendition of Manet's *Olympia*. The one hanging just beside the Zola in the museum. She walked back to the hall with Courbets. This time Prem did not look lost in his own world. In fact, he walked to her as soon as he saw her.

"You have to see one thing here," she said excitedly. "Manet paints Zola looking at another Manet, and in front of a book titled *Manet*. Manet as a painter of writers and of paintings within paintings."

They crossed the corridor. Maya pointed to the portrait of Zola.

"Zola defended *Olympia* when it caused a scandal." Prem pointed to the book titled *Manet* that sat beside Zola in the portrait. "Zola claimed in there that *Olympia* was effectively the flesh and blood of the painter and that he could read Manet's personality in it."

"You've read the book in the painting?"

Prem nodded. "According to Zola, Manet decided not to lie, he made us know *Olympia*. He gave us a girl from the times, one we might see on a Parisian sidewalk."

"I even like the black and white *Olympia* in Zola's portrait."

"It's distilled, a little like looking at a love affair after it's over. You have a different perspective and what was important and what was noise becomes much clearer."

"Were you thinking of a love affair that's over when you snapped at me on the *terrasse?*" Maya asked.

"Did I snap at you? I'm sorry."

"You said, 'Don't look at me that way.' "

"The last person to look at me that way was sixteen when she seduced me."

"One of the underage French girls? You were all over the press with that one."

"No one got the story right. They were the ones who discarded me."

"I wasn't being critical."

"Let's leave."

Outside the Seine was gleaming white in the brilliant sunshine. They shielded their eyes and walked in the other direction to a café on St-Germain-des-Prés.

Maya ordered a chèvre salad and Prem a steak, rare.

"I'm depressed. Orsay made me exuberant at moments, then very depressed."

"Me too. I spent an hour moping about those teenagers."

"Was I gone that long?" she asked.

"Why were you depressed?"

"Painful memories."

"You *could* talk to me a bit more openly."

Prem brought a smile to Maya's face with his remark.

"I associate some of those paintings with my past. Actually I had a moment in the room with van Gogh that made me feel that two epochs of my life had just collided. Some time ago, when I was very miserable, one painting haunted me. It symbolized my utter wretchedness. And at that same time reading your book tided me over possibly the worst crisis I have ever experienced."

"Which painting?"

"The one of van Gogh's room in Arles."

"Which book of mine?"

"The Smell of Wet Mud."

"I'm glad, Maya."

"Huh?"

"I'm glad something I wrote served as a palliative."

Maya was silent.

"Are you thinking about it still?"

She shook her head.

"I have to do this once. May I?"

"Do what?"

"Gush."

"Gush away," Prem said, easing back into his chair.

"It still feels strange sometimes to be beside you in person. I mean, for the past year your books have meant everything to me. After it ended with Tom, I discovered that as long as I was reading your books, I didn't miss other human contact, life felt complete. Sometimes I thought to myself that it couldn't be very healthy."

"It isn't."

"I know. I know. But it was, it is, so agreeable."

"Is it less agreeable now that you're not reading me but are talking to me instead?"

"Of course not. But the full force of that hit me in the museum. You see, there I was looking at one of my most painful memories, and the person who had healed me was right there. But, and please don't hold it against me for saying this, I thought that you weren't the person who had healed me. You are now a person I know. But what healed me was the unknown writer. And the real you is as vulnerable as the real me." She thought of how she had come running for Prem.

"Why should I hold it against you?"

"I can't cope!" Maya pressed her fork into the wooden table with violence.

"Now, now, Miss Maya."

"Sorry."

"You alarmed me there for a second."

"I'm having trouble with my writing. I can't separate anything from anything anymore. I'm here in Paris to write, and I can't write a word." She groaned.

Prem reached his hand for hers on the table and stroked it.

"Talk to me from the beginning. I'm not sure I'm following too well."

"Writing is *so* impossible. I've read so much of you to the exclusion of all else that on that simple plane I'm worried about your influence showing up. Then there's the much larger problem that I'm trying to write about India without any connection to the country. My efforts are doomed. But worse still, my last trip to India, my notes, my memories, the *details*—those excruciating simple details that breathe life into a novel—are completely overrun with memories of your books. I was reading your books the entire time I was there, and I can't begin to separate the experience of a place from what I was internally experiencing because of what I was reading!"

"Since when have you been having such a hard time?"

"Since I got to Paris. In New York I told myself it was hard to write while working, and so I applied for this fellowship. I have no excuses anymore. But it all just hit me, the role of your writing and now your presence."

"Zola said that when he posed for the portrait he had the sense that Manet no longer knew that Zola was there; he drew him like he would have any other human, with an artistic attention he had never before seen. Once you put yourself to work, Maya, even my presence will not get in your way."

"I don't know. It's one thing to see Vuillard take from Bonnard's palette and Bonnard paint Vuillard's portrait. They were friends, their influence on each other mutual. And Manet and Zola were not both writers. I'm truly stuck with you, Prem."

"This is the life of a reader. And most writers are readers too. It happens to everyone."

"Not like this. I look at my notebooks from India. Next to the date, the place, and the name of the guesthouse, I always noted the name of the book I was reading."

"And you were reading nothing but me?"

"Correct."

"People have gushed before, but this is a torrent," Prem laughed lightly.

"That's because you've corrupted me, your armies have invaded," Maya retorted.

The waiter put their plates in front of them and refilled their glasses.

"Seriously, don't worry so much. I've gone through my own literary obsessions: Tolstoy, Dostoevsky, Hardy, to name a few."

"But they were dead!"

"So?"

Maya pushed her salad to the side and brought her palm to her forehead. It made a sound. Prem pulled her hand away.

"The real problem is that I know you now. I haven't adjusted to that. I wonder sometimes if it's not your writing that is threatening to eclipse my style but that you are threatening to eclipse your writing in my mind."

"I knew it," Prem said, tapping the bloody steak on his plate with his knife. "I knew that the writer Prem Rustum would always win over me. I'm too real."

"The opposite. You're still not real enough for me. I feel like I'm in some dream. Anyway, tell me about your teenagers."

"I felt like I relived the saga. It had the freshness of a raw wound."

Prem looked at the meat oozing blood in his plate. It was dead, but it was still alive because it was vibrant, it had color. Love was like that. It died. It just switched off, as it had for Julie. *I don't love you anymore.* But its death left bloodstains everywhere. He pointed to the steak in his plate still oozing blood. "To love is to bleed. But to bleed is a sign of life. Even if I am seventy-five, in some way, it consoles me to bleed."

Maya stared at Prem's steak. She was jealous of the girls. She wanted to be an Olympia painted from Prem's flesh and blood or a Manet painting Zola, so absorbed in his art that he forgot the subject.

"I stopped bleeding for Tom very quickly. It makes me wonder if it was real love. Can't love die a natural death?"

"If love dies without taking me with it one more time, I'll join the living dead. I want to die while I am totally alive."

"Please, let's talk about something else. Let's talk about the Louvre, about *Sisters in the Louvre.*"

"I don't want to answer questions about those gamines."

"I don't care if you deflowered them in the Presidential Palace, as the rumors had it. It's the only book of yours I brought to Paris. I think of it as a guide to art, to the Louvre."

"I need to buy you some art books in that case!"

"It's so personal. When I first read it a few months ago, I knew that I wanted to be in Paris reading it. I wanted to read the whole book while sitting in the Louvre."

Judith Q had written that she had bought his book and flown to Paris to read the book *in situ.* She had read it from start to finish in the Louvre and even written him the letter from there. She had written that all these decades after his first book he had not lost his magic. To that letter he had almost been tempted to reply, but then he let it go.

"Somebody did that once."

"A fan?"

"Yes a fan."

"So I guess it won't be a very original experience."

"Come now, Maya. Since when have you started thinking this way?"

part iv

Be drunk, always. Nothing else matters; this is our sole concern. To ease the pain as Time's burden weighs down upon your shoulders and crushes you to earth, you must be drunk without respite. Drunk with what? With wine, with poetry, or with virtue, as you please. But be drunk.

—CHARLES BAUDELAIRE, *ENIVREZ-VOUS*

Accomplishments pleasant days horror nights
Vegetations Couplings eternal music
Motions Adorations divine regret
Worlds self-mirroring mirroring us
I have drunk you without being slaked

—GUILLAUME APOLLINAIRE, *VENDÉMIAIRE*

Maya stood outside Le Grenier à Pain on rue des Abbesses to buy herself a croissant. It was Sunday morning, and the entire neighborhood was in the line ahead of her. Behind her an old Arab looked at the plant by the door and touched a little plastic bird perched on it.

"*C'est mignon,*" he said, smiling with genuine happiness, his eyes gathering in wrinkles. The plastic bird had blue and yellow wings, which the old man stroked. Then he remarked, "*Il a des fruits.*" He examined the tiny fruits, real ones, hanging everywhere from the plant. It seemed like some kind of an orange tree, possibly kumquat.

The patisserie windows were replete with a range of specialty cakes and tarts to provide for the high flow of customers on Sunday. The colors of the pear and rhubarb pies and the golden ribbons decorating the cakes took Maya back to the pastels in the Musée d'Orsay. Everything in the store was glistening, soft, jellylike, moist, rich, and luscious—the old man behind her was Prem—and the *mille-feuille vanille* (never called a napoleon in France), with its layers of crisp flaky pastry and sublime yellow vanilla-infused cream, was dying for a lick.

The woman at the counter looked expectantly at Maya.

Maya ordered a croissant and paid with a series of niceties: *merci, bonne journée, au revoir.* She exited the shop feeling light-headed, wanting to share a dessert with Prem, and then threw a last rapacious, lascivious look at the window display from outside. The smooth-brushed texture of custard sat in harmony with the wrinkled skins of baked figs and *mirabelles;* each *gâteau* had perfectly serrated sides to complement the frictionless surface of its face.

Maya punched the code to her heavy building door. As she crossed the courtyard, she touched the back of her neck, at first unselfconsciously and then a second time, aware that Prem had touched her there in front of the Degas. Had he cast a spell on her? She was hypnotized by him, by life, by the city of Paris itself. Intoxicated. Every corner of the city was criminally beautiful. How would she ever leave?

Maya worked through the afternoon until Jean-Pierre called suggesting a picnic at La Villette, a movie under the open sky. He picked her up from her apartment, and they went to the nearby Champion to pick up olives, bread, and cheese.

The grass in the park was moist, and the sky did not fade into darkness till ten-thirty. The film began only at eleven. Jean-Pierre rubbed Maya's back and hugged her close as the night got cold. When they took the metro to Pigalle, he climbed up the hill with her.

"Thank you for walking me back," Maya said. She was standing on the second of her building steps and from that height could look him directly in the eye for a change.

He reached forward and kissed her lips. His lips were soft, and his kisses tender. They stood at the threshold of her building for five minutes, kissing.

"I should let you go to sleep," he said finally, releasing her.

Maya and Jean-Pierre saw each other every night for the next few nights. And each night he made his way closer to her. The very next day he spent the night in her flat. The one after that he spent the night again, and this time only in his *caleçon.* The third night, as they were getting into bed, Jean-Pierre glanced into the window on the floor below and stared. Maya pulled herself higher on her bed to see what he was looking at. From Maya's window two sets of depilated legs were visible, and a red lamp glowed in the room.

"They are two girls," Jean-Pierre whispered.

"Seems like it," Maya said. The girl who had wished Maya *bon yoga* lived in that apartment.

Even as Maya and Jean-Pierre watched, the limbs on the bed started to move, and the bodies drew close. They were grinding against each other.

"Enough. It's not right," Maya said, pulling Jean-Pierre back to her bed with her hand. He joined her and came close to her himself. Aroused.

"No, not yet," Maya said, turning her back on him and drawing his arms over her.

They woke up to a clear blue sky. Jean-Pierre left after a quick coffee. Maya surveyed her living room. She felt at ease in the apartment. Anne's apartment. She had never met Anne and wondered sometimes about her, what Anne did for a living, whether Anne had a boyfriend, if Anne was pretty. Maya liked the round dining table—it was large enough for two people to sit and eat comfortably. The kitchen was fully equipped. She called Prem.

"I want to have you over for dinner to thank you for taking me to the museum."

It was the season for asparagus. She would cook him her father's special recipe for risotto with asparagus.

Prem arrived in the evening with a bouquet of burnt pink orchids. When Maya spotted him in the courtyard below, she went down the stairs to greet him and carried them. He was out of breath by the time they were on the second landing, but he insisted they keep climbing up.

From the kitchen Maya had ferreted out decent china, wineglasses, side plates, white metal dessert spoons, flatware, and real cloth napkins. She served them both melon and some Martini Blanc to start.

"This apartment is quite charming. Very Parisian." Prem looked around. The apartment across the courtyard was illuminated and, like Maya's, had no curtains. Beyond the green plants by the windows he could make out an old couple sitting in white clothes. He felt he was looking into a *chawl* in Bombay in the evening, when husbands had just returned from work and drank cups of tea while sitting around in their white *banians*.

"Do you know anyone living in this building? Do you have friends in Paris?"

"I'll tell you over the risotto, which is delicate and must be eaten soon."

Maya cleared the table and brought out the main course. Cutting the asparagus stalks on her plate in two, she told him, "I picked up a boy in the bakery on the very street where you live just the day you landed in Paris."

"Tell me more."

She recounted everything in that special Maya way, her eyes lighting up, her lips dancing in half-smiles, her hands flying everywhere. Prem stopped listening and concentrated on the aesthetic spectacle of Mayaspeak, trying not to hear the actual words.

"I've been speaking for so long. I got carried away," she finally said.

"I like hearing you talk." Prem finished dinner and put his fork and knife neatly to the side.

"I feel so close to you. It is truly absurd, our friendship."

"What's so absurd?"

"I remember how famous you are, and it feels strange. I haven't told anyone about you, but I know that Jean-Pierre would love to meet you. He sang your praise before when we were talking about writers."

"Is he a writer too?" *First Johnson and then this guy J-P. What is with the J's?*

"He's trying to write a screenplay."

Prem nodded.

"Are we ready for dessert?" Maya removed the fork and knife from her plate as she put his plate on top of hers.

Prem looked outside the window carelessly and noticed the old man in the window across staring at them. *He's probably my age.*

"Are we turning salty today?" Maya looked quizzically at Prem for his failure to respond with his usual enthusiasm for sugar.

"What's for dessert?" He could not manage a smile.

"*Panna cotta* with a light dash of limoncello."

"Bring it on."

"What's the matter? You don't seem yourself. *Ça va pas?*"

"*Si,*" Prem protested.

Prem collected himself while Maya took a few minutes to organize dessert. He paced about the living room and looked outside distractedly. He had lured devoted mothers and wives from their duties in his time. He had to think strategically. But right now all he could feel was a dullness in his chest.

"Tan-ta-tan," Maya pronounced a drumroll as she walked into the room with a tray.

There were webs of crisp caramel over the scoop of *panna cotta.*

"Wow!" At least this effort was for him alone.

"*Voilà!* I hope you like it." She placed a plate in front of him with a small spoon and one in front of herself.

"So when do I get to see your *garçon?*"

"*Mon gars?* Is it okay for him to come to the concert with us later this week?"

"Your young concert to which you want to take me?"

"Yes."

"Can he still get a ticket? Otherwise you can take him instead of me."

"No way! I want you to hear this guy's music."

"Why?"

"The same reason you wanted me to see Degas and I wanted to cook risotto."

"Is it the same reason your dessert looks so scintillating?"

"I was in the patisserie on Sunday, when the orgy of dessert left me euphoric. I wanted so much for you to see everything in the display and sort of experienced it for you since you weren't there. I wanted to try to recast the experience for you, though it's not the same because you only get one small dessert."

Prem smiled.

"Why are you giving me such a smirk?"

"I'm not smirking, I'm touched. Though the enterprise is flawed. It was a mistake to show you Degas. As Pascal says, experience and consciousness are entirely subjective. Look at the evidence. We could both put the same jalapeño pepper in our mouths, and the result could be completely different: anguish for you and joy for me."

On the spot Maya was unable to come up with a counter-example that ran deeper, but she was sure he was wrong. Or else all experience was totally imaginary, subjective, interpretive—and there was no difference between thinking of Prem at the patisserie and having him here beside her. *Did he not intend to hypnotize me in front of the Degas? And the burning awareness running through me for entire minutes in the museum—was that, too, imagined?*

Maya cleared the table, and Prem looked outside the window again.

"Have you met the old couple who lives across from you?"

"No. Would you like a tisane?"

"Yes."

"You can also look into another girl's bedroom if you go to my bedroom. She doesn't have curtains, and she might be in bed with another woman."

"Do you look often?"

"I try to give her some privacy. But she's one floor below and sleeps on a mattress on the floor, so I can see everything except her head from my bed."

Prem opened the door to her bedroom and looked at the window. A dark-skinned girl was sprawled on the mattress in her boxer shorts. She had a remote control in her hand, and from the ambient glow in the room he could tell the television was on.

"She's watching TV," he reported back to Maya.

"If you open my window, I bet you'll hear it too. She usually has her window open."

Prem walked back to the dining room, and Maya followed him with two cups.

"Dinner was delicious. Thank you."

"You're welcome. I wanted you to see where I live even though it's not much compared to your lodgings."

"No, it's nice. And this way, when you talk, I can immediately imagine your surroundings." *Instead of imagining you about to step into a bathtub in a Degas.*

In bed that night Prem spent a few seconds being the old *voisin* in his white underthings as he watched Maya brush her teeth and hair. Prem had let his hand slide against the satin pajamas on her bed when he had been in her room. To his surprise they had the same gleam as the crisp strands of caramel she had used to garnish the dessert.

"Voilà, here we go!" Maya said to Prem as the musicians came onto the stage. Café de la Danse resounded with applause.

V. Guru's vocalist was covered in a long shiny *dupatta* the likes of which Prem had long associated with Hindi films. It looked like a silver bedspread and reflected all the spotlights on the ceiling. As soon as the music started up, Maya looked with concern at Prem's face. She was afraid he would find it too loud, too rhythmic, unintelligent. She leaned into his ear just as the lighting in the hall went dimmer and said, "Tell me if you hate it."

Prem nodded. Then he removed his glasses, folded them, and put them in his pocket. Maya was sitting between Prem and Jean-Pierre.

Prem listened to the Bangladeshi singer onstage. She had opened her mouth so wide, he thought it would tear. She sang from her throat, her chest, her stomach, with the wisdom of a fifty-year-old woman though she could have been no more than twenty-five. Her sounds were so deep that they flushed Prem's distress. Jean-Pierre was really just the boy next door. Prem assumed girls found him good looking. His face was symmetrical, without any flaws, without any character. He had spoken to Pascal earlier in the day about it.

"If you want, I am sure you'll be able to lay him open in ten minutes as someone less than you in every way. Don't do it. Girls don't like that. Be nice to him. She'll see his flaws herself," Pascal had said.

But Pascal had failed to remind him of the ways of the French and the ways of youth everywhere. When Prem cracked open his eyes, he could feel movement in the corner without having to turn. Jean-Pierre was running those hands all over the inside of her wrists and her forearms. *Why didn't I make a pass at her before it was too late?*

Just put the idea in her head—she'll do the rest, Pascal had said. But Prem's age and the numerals seven and five came into his mind. Jean-Pierre in this poetically cruel karmic world was bound to be twenty-five—one-third his age. Prem turned himself slightly so as not to have to see Jean-Pierre's hands.

The Bengali girl had gone offstage, and V. Guru was dazzling the audience with his ambidextrous playing, arms crossed at the elbows in an X—the right hand playing a tabla on his left side, the left hand banging a drum on his right. Onomatopoeia gurgled out of his throat into a mike that was fixed to his head.

Prem looked to see if the music had captivated Maya. Jean-Pierre was banging his fingers on Maya's knee to keep the beat.

Maya noticed Prem and lurched to whisper, "Are you liking it?"

Her hand hung in the air in front of him like a question.

Without thinking, Prem grabbed it in his and replied, "It's great. So energetic!" Then he let the hand go.

He couldn't be sure, but he thought he saw Maya bring her head down for a second as if closing herself in before returning her attention to Jean-Pierre.

Maya watched the concert with a focus that only rhythm could induce; an immediate vortex of sound pulled her in its churn; she was reduced to a small particle, acted upon by the force of the beat. She felt as if she were all rhythm in that theater with its sides painted black and a Parisian wall serving as the backdrop of the stage. The singers and their instruments, their faces, the play of the spotlights on their shiny clothes, the patches of sweat where V. Guru's oversize kurta stuck to his body, and the yellow exposed brick wall were all part of the rhythm. Jean-Pierre's tapping on her knee, her collarbone, and her hands brought the stage wall and the music close to her and put it right inside her body. As if making love, Jean-Pierre put all of that music and the rhythm inside her with his tapping.

The concert ended, and the audience brought the roof down, thumping their feet on the wooden floor to the resounding chant of *Encore! Encore!*

Maya looked at Prem's knee and saw it bouncing too. She put her hand lightly on it to see if he was actually tapping the floor like the rambunctious young audience.

"You liked it that much, eh?"

"Yes, his music is rather young, but I'm in my second child-hood myself."

The musicians filed back onstage.

"This encore piece is the jewel of the evening, if it is what I think it is," Maya said to Prem. Then she leaned away, no doubt telling Jean-Pierre that and some other things.

The Bangladeshi belle in her glittering silver *dupatta* was even more endearing than before. Prem was getting quite fond of her. She told the audience to *la la la* after her, provoking them with a come-hither flick of her hand and *très bien* when they got it right. People lit their lighters and swayed. V. Guru interrupted this mesmerizing communal experience with humorous instructions on how to follow the complex beats he was going to throw out to the audience. He said he would scat with the usual Indian sounds of *ta ta dha dha* mixed with some French ones. When he got off the mike and gave back the stage to the girl, she continued as if nothing had happened, the audience putty in her hands. Maybe I should go talk to her after the show, Prem thought to himself.

But when the concert ended, Prem followed Maya out and proposed dinner. He wanted to prolong the moments with her and to reduce the amount of time Jean-Pierre would have to get up to mischief.

After dinner Jean-Pierre took Maya back home. As they lay on the couch in his living room, he caressed her ass as if all of her were her ass. His light touch was almost ticklish but felt increasingly sensual as it was repeated. Maya felt her body melt away. He made love to her greedily and with a force that she had not thought him capable of when he had been caressing her. In the morning he fetched croissants for breakfast.

"You know, you are lucky to be friends with someone in your métier whom you admire so much. I think he is very fond of you."

"I adore Prem. I don't find his fame disconcerting anymore."

"It was amazing to dine with a guy who is nothing short of a legend for me."

"He's surprisingly well known here, I think because of his friendship with Boutin."

"Oh, come on! Boutin can't hold a candle to Rustum. Boutin's writing is all about the big screw. He's narcissistic. Rustum is a world great."

"I saw an interesting film on Boutin in which Prem was interviewed."

"Yes, I've seen it too. If Boutin was your friend, I wouldn't trust him with you at all."

Maya laughed. "You think Pascal Boutin with his large belly and reddish dome is my taste?"

"Jean-Pierre, Jean-Pierre. So ordinary I can't believe I'm forced to spend time thinking of him! A rival! A rival, goddammit!" Prem said, raising both his hands up toward the sky.

"What happened after the concert?" Pascal asked.

"Nothing. I invited them to dinner, and we sat outside. They sat on one side of the table, and I sat on the other. He kept touching her under the table."

"And Maya?"

"She was conscious of my presence. She kept her elbows on the table. He grabbed the back of her neck when we stood up to leave. I think my feelings showed on my face then, but they didn't really seem to notice."

"*La jalousie.* Not your friend."

"I am afraid I am turning into some kind of father figure for her."

"It's your fault. I've been telling you all along not to have these intellectual conversations walking *au bord de la Seine.* Pay her compliments about her dress."

"I do! I did! She blushes! She blushed!"

"Why didn't you kiss her then?"

"Look at me." Prem pointed both hands inward to himself.

"You look like you."

"*Mon visage.* I am an old man. My face is old," Prem lamented.

"It's the face of a man who has lived life. Do you think this girl will actually choose some Jean-Pierre who works in a bureau in the *banlieue* over a Nobel Prize–winner if she had a choice?" Pascal was obsessed with Prem's Nobel. Prem was sure that if Pascal won it, he would go on a world tour to screw every model, starlet, and *jeune fille* he could find.

"It's too late now. She introduced him as her boyfriend."

"Stop calling her. Stop meeting her. She'll get the idea."

"I can't do that."

"Why? Because you feel obliged to take her out to dinner and that sod of hers too?"

"It's not his fault. He was nice actually and pretty intelligent."

"There you go!" Pascal pointed his finger to the air. *"That* is the right attitude. You must separate the idea of this man from the idea of her to win effectively."

"She addresses me less formally now—*on se tutoie.*"

"Was the concert any good?"

"V. Guru played well. He's a real performer. He made some self-deprecatory remarks, and a woman in the audience screamed *But you are so beautiful.* It made his day."

Pascal chuckled.

"Some guys just know how to get the girls. You're one," Prem said.

"You really want someone to tell you the same thing? I can get up and ask." Pascal looked around. "This is my friend Prem. Do you think he is still beautiful?"

"Stop it." Prem didn't put it past Pascal to embarrass him in public. It had happened on several occasions already. A woman at the table behind Pascal turned.

Oh no! Prem sat still, hoping she would look away, but instead she turned fully and took a long look at him. Late forties, he guessed.

Pascal saw the look on Prem's face and understood. He grinned.

She got up without averting her eyes from Prem. She was tall, around five eight, wearing a skirt and high-heeled shoes. She took the two steps to their table and said, *"Monsieur Rustum, vous êtes très beau. J'adore vos cheveux, ils sont magnifiques."*

"Merci, madame." Prem felt compelled to rise from his chair and kiss her hand.

"I have read all your books, Mr. Rustum. You're a great writer."

"You're too kind," Prem mumbled.

"My friend Judith introduced me to your books." She said *Judith* as if Prem were supposed to know. He looked at Pascal. Did he know a Judith? Pascal grimaced.

"Judith Q, the New York nutcase," she enunciated slowly.

"Ah!" Rustum said.

Pascal paid for their coffees hurriedly, in case they needed to beat a hasty retreat.

"I wish you had responded to her letters. She is really not crazy, and she was hurt by that book, though it hasn't changed how she feels about you."

"I was never beautiful, was I?" Prem said, looking the woman in her eyes. They were a dark honey color. Her voice was smooth like that *lait entier* yogurt they had in France.

"If you ever meet her, ask her to show you her tattoos. She carries the titles of all your books on her body."

"Mon vieux, we are late," Pascal said, getting up and taking Prem firmly by the elbow.

"Pascal Boutin," he said, formally putting out his hand to shake hers.

"Marie-Louise Lefevre. *Enchantée."*

"We have to go," Pascal said.

"Je vous laisse." She smiled and stepped back to her table.

Once outside the men walked to rue de Buci and turned on to rue de la Seine.

"Do you feel more reassured that you too are beautiful?" Pascal said scornfully.

"I learned my lesson for that, didn't I? Judith Q!"

"This woman seemed sane enough, but I didn't think we should take a chance."

"I thought you were going to get her number. She was stunning."

"Someone who comes licking your ass. Never!"

Prem laughed.

Rustum was Judith Q's. And she was getting impatient that he had not yet found her. He was the man she was destined for. She had truly understood every word he had ever written in his novels, she knew him like no one else, and she could no longer bear the wait.

Judith Q had been trying unsuccessfully to stalk Prem since she read *Dharma, Raga,* and *Grinding India* in the course of a month. *I have to meet this man. I have to have this man.* Such thoughts fired at her brain from the moment she woke up to the time she slept. She clipped his rare interviews in newspapers, his essays in *The New Republic,* his photographs as he aged and succeeded some more. She looked for him with single-minded determination in the Upper West Side, where he was rumored to be conducting a torrid affair with a singer called Lilia, and she drove once a week to suburban New Jersey to scour the roads for the grand mansion where he lived and entertained.

She reread his books like a detective seeking source material and concluded that at least as long as his affair with Lilia lasted, they would take long walks on Sunday through the park, past the Ramble and the Reservoir. Judith even concluded from Prem's books that he was a sentimental type and was likely to keep up the same walk after Lilia was cast aside. He was said to spend the winters in India to find material for his novels, so she went to India one winter in the hope of finding him. He spent part of the summer in Paris to hang out with Pascal Boutin, so she went to Paris for a weekend or two each summer. Several times a week Judith took time out from her work as the leading salesperson for a currency hedge fund and caught a cab to Columbus Circle. From there she would take a path through the park to the Museum of Natural History—*just in case he was taking a walk.* On days when the financial markets were going berserk, Judith found the stamina to wake up an hour earlier than usual for a stroll at six in the morning. Rustum, after all, had once told *The Village Voice* that he was an early riser. When Judith heard he was moving to Paris on the wings of love for a French gamine, not quite eighteen, she started interviewing with French banks.

Her enormous obsession, tempered by nothing, grew and grew until it became the backbone of Judith's identity. *My sexuality is Rustumian, my nationality is Rustumian, my religion is Rustumian, my identity is Rustumian,* she would say while laughing over a cigarette. She wrote letters to him—in the beginning one every week—that went unanswered. She had written almost daily after that and even thought about hiring a private detective, but it seemed, at the same time, too creepy and too ordinary. A true labor of love it had to be. The worse the weather, the greater the windchill, the more fervently Judith staked out his neighborhood. One day she even took the New Jersey Transit bus during a blizzard and had to rent a hotel room for the night in New Jersey. *I'm going to see him tonight. That's why I came so far.* But it wasn't that night. And it wasn't any other night.

Having accepted a job for Banque Paribas and having called the movers, Judith read in a gossip column that Rustum had moved back permanently to the States. He had been involved with not one gamine but two!

"I changed my mind," she told the movers. She faxed in a letter of resignation to the Paribas manager in Paris and returned the signing bonus she had already cashed.

I can't take it one more day, she would tell herself when she woke up, and yet she would take it another week, a month, a year, a lifetime. As long as Rustum lived, she would take it and suffer. It was six years into the obsession that on her Rustum Run, as she called it, she thought she saw him. It was an ordinary spring Sunday in Central Park. Families of all races and tourists toting guides in every language had flocked in. Judith sat on a bench not far from the Ramble, sure that Rustum would never be caught dead in such a frenzy of activity. *I should have gone looking for him in New Jersey. What was I thinking?* Judith moaned. She made her way to Central Park West, looking at the traffic on the avenue, wondering what next to do with herself, when she saw a cab fleeting by—though she couldn't be sure—with him inside. She frenetically waved in the middle of the incoming traffic to hail another cab to follow him, but none stopped for several minutes. Those minutes, in the fast-moving traffic, made the difference between the fulfillment of a lifelong desire and its frustration. Forever.

Then Patriots announced a new book by Prem Rustum. It was billed as a deviation from his usual work, set for once in the occidental universe, deeply personal, raw, and remarkable in the balance it struck between the false and the hyperreal. As soon as the first bound galley was dumped in the Strand, Judith bought it and read it overnight.

Between panegyrics to Lilia's mellifluous voice, the book was engorged with spite for Judith Q, the New York nutcase. The stalker, the Rustum-chaser, the vile witch who wanted to suck him dry of his creativity and aggress his life in ways that normally only men aggressed women. And in the prose of the novel itself, in the meat of its chapters and its parts, distorted versions of her letters to him, the most personal offerings of information, were twisted till they were entirely foul anecdotes.

She had been his biggest advocate for years, gifting her colleagues, her clients, and her friends his books, speaking freely of his genius, speaking diarrhetically about her own fixation for him, participating at reader forums in local Ys and libraries, championing him every single minute of her life. And then to be rewarded with this? Without ever having met her or replying to her letters, he had used everything as material. And with such cleverness he could not even be accused of plagiarism. He had reversed her letters, inverted them, perverted them, liberated them, whittled them, rearranged them, and produced a narrative of extraordinary madness without once acknowledging her and without once looking bad. For a full year after that book was published, Judith kept a low profile. She took some time off. Everyone at work assumed she was off at the loony bin or in some esoteric retreat in the Berkshires, a total vacuum—where people couldn't talk to each other or write or signal their feelings with hand gestures. She had often spoken about going off to some place to exorcise Rustum. Most people thought she was finally doing it.

Judith returned to work one November morning, somber and businesslike. She spoke less frequently of Rustum, but wherever there were Rustum symposia so was Judith. Rustum himself never came to these things, but often some good writers got together and spoke about him. Thanks to her evangelism more than half her office was turned on to him, so they often went in groups to book events. They were a bit worried about bringing up his name in front of her, but after he had another book out, they got careless. And they were surprised to find Judith reveal the same enthusiasm for his work as before. One of the young interns in the firm tried to push it one evening at drinks and asked her about *My Self in the West*.

"That one I don't talk about," she said.

No one understood how she had dealt with it until Cheever, the office secretary, came by her house one day when she was down with the flu. She had brought home some files the previous day that were urgently needed back in the office. Cheever approximated that in her house there were easily eighty photographs of Rustum (sometimes just cheap photocopies of photographs) and dozens of copies of every book he had ever written—in hardback, in paperback, and in foreign-language editions that read from top to bottom, left to right, and front to back. Reviews from magazines were tacked onto bulletin boards in the hallway, or framed on the walls, and since Cheever had to take a leak, he discovered that some reviews encased in photo frames were even poised atop the toilet tank.

Cheever reported back to the office: *It's a fucking shrine, man, a fucking shrine. She's totally insane.* Everyone knew this within minutes of Cheever's return to the office. People piled out of their cubicles and offices to congregate around his desk. The CEO had to herd them into the largest conference room on the floor for a company-wide meeting so that Cheever could answer all the questions in one go.

"The cushions on the sofa had imprints of Rustum's face. She must have paid a fortune to have his photographs transferred to fabric and then stitched into cushion covers."

The company was strongly divided into two camps: *He drove her nuts with that book. No, she was nuts from the start.* The Rustum fans and the Judith sympathizers fought and argued until they were shaking fists at one another.

"There is only one way to know—to see her letters!" someone from the Judith camp shouted.

"Regardless, even if they are sane and he made it up, he's no less a writer and she's no less a madcap," the Rustum camp countered.

"We've got to ask her to bring her letters."

"She's already nuts. Who knows what she'll do next? Maybe she'll kill herself."

"She's never talked about killing herself."

The CEO, trying to hide his own bias and restore some order, planted his behind on the conference room table and clapped his hands.

"People! As her manager, I can say that she's never shown any signs of insanity since she got back to work. And it's my duty to protect her from this kind of talk. We're not asking any of you how you conduct your private relationships. Are we?" He stared menacingly at the more vocal members from each camp.

"She's doing a great job as usual and she's certainly not exposing us to any risks. We owe Judith the same privacy we all feel we are entitled to. This discussion is no longer appropriate. I request you all to come to work tomorrow having put this behind you. This hasn't happened! It could hurt Judith a lot to know how we talked about her."

"And we might drive her nuts if that old creep hasn't already," one of the Judith campers said, determined to have the last word.

The office dispersed, grumbling. Judith returned to work after the flu and continued to live too much in her own head to notice any possible silences that befell the coffee room or the water cooler area near Cheever's desk when she passed by. And she continued hopping on cabs to Columbus Circle and walking on the streets of the Upper West Side on daily Rustum Runs. She knew the wind eddies on Broadway intimately. As the winds changed from westerly to northerly, she knew which side of the street to walk on and never once lost an umbrella from the ferocious April showers that made Manhattan feel like February.

Prem and Pascal had reached the statue by La Palette. Venus de Milo sliced vertically in three parts, parts interspersed with the transverses of a more African face. From her left stuck out the skeleton of a cello and the section of a photo frame. Prem and Pascal circled it together and peered under her dress. Prem counted the twelve small books that were sculpted underneath. He did this every time they were there.

"Toujours douze," Pascal laughed.

They hovered around the sculpture for a few minutes before continuing their walk past the Académie Française and over the Pont des Arts. They did not walk fast. Pascal's gait was somewhat portly, and Prem always thought of him as Balzac in the making.

"Do you remember you took me to an excellent *fromagerie* last time I was here?"

"Yes. Do you want to go there again?" Pascal asked.

"I was thinking of taking her there."

"Your *jeune écrivain?*"

"Yes. She cooked a very good dinner for me."

"That *fromager* is the only person who possibly understands eroticism as well as we do. Are you sure he won't steal her from right under your nose with his lecture on the palate, *les papilles gus-tatives*, and the qualities of cheese?"

"I'll take my chances."

"Careful, my friend. She will climax between the third and fourth course."

"It was truly good, that meal," Prem said, remembering.

"Sometimes I go along and admire his following of girls who come by themselves on Friday night to submit to whatever progression of cheeses he wants to subject them to. I've picked up two girls there. There's an erotic intelligence to the experience of food."

"You say that even though you don't think two people ever experience the same stimulus in the same way."

"This emphasis on sameness is very Platonic. There is no one experience. Intimacy is about watching the other person climax in front of you, possibly being a direct or indirect instrument for her pleasure. After all, when you go down on a woman, you don't have the foggiest idea what she's feeling, and yet it's so profound."

Pascal and Prem were opposites in many ways. Their physiques would have suggested contrary personalities. Pascal, short, round, and bald, was savvy and confident with women. Prem, tall, handsome, and regal, was still in his core in constant need of reassurance about everything except his writing. His looks, his sexuality, his desirability he carried as complexes on his sleeve. He remembered a different him only before Meher had married. Her decision to marry had left him permanently damaged. The hundreds of women who had kept his bed warm in his lifetime had not made a difference.

"You're my little brother. I have to have a man." That was how Meher had squelched his innermost self effectively and, it was beginning to seem certain now, forever. By the time of her death, he had known she had said this only to help him get over her, in the hope that he would hate her. But it was too late. The psychic damage had already burned his ego to a crisp. At seventy-five, with Meher long dead, he had not yet recovered. When Meher had died, after the months of initial grief he had thought he would be liberated. He was liberated only from the angst of knowing she was there and he couldn't have her. The person he was had already been formed—or deformed, he thought correcting himself.

Maya had awakened in the morning and found only dark gray clouds in the sky. The light had been so flat that from the window it was impossible to tell the time of day. When she turned to her side to look at the table clock, she found her neighbor from the floor below looking up at her. They smiled and then waved to each other. Maya got out of bed and threw open her window. The neighbor stretched herself in bed and pushed open hers. As she extended her arm, her cover fell off and revealed her breasts.

"*Coucou,*" the neighbor said.

"*Un café?*" Maya offered.

"*Volontiers.*" The girl disappeared from the window.

Maya got the coffee going in the kitchen and brushed her teeth. As she rinsed her mouth, the bell rang. They greeted each other with a kiss.

"I'm Nadine," the neighbor said.

Nadine spoke rapidly and posed a thousand questions. Maya answered them as she poured coffee for them in the kitchen. She felt she could tell Nadine anything: *Yes, the boy with her from time to time was French. No, she wasn't in love. In fact, she might break up soon. She couldn't stop thinking about a writer in his seventies but didn't know what to do. She was so paralyzed she couldn't even write. Her fellowship was going to go to waste. Did Nadine want some milk in the coffee?*

"*Noir.*"

Nadine said she wasn't a lesbian. Not yet. Her white girlfriend was the first woman she had ever slept with, and it was too early to say if they were in love. Nadine was a contemporary dancer. Sometimes she worked in clubs as a hostess. There were all kinds of exercises that dancers did to get ready for the stage. Maya needed an exercise for her writing.

"Jean-Pierre said that after the paralysis and the influence, there comes a stage when I need approval. He thinks if I can get the old writer's approval, I will be free to write again."

"I am reading the memoir of a love affair between a young woman and an old woman. The two women wrote it together. You need to do something like that with your old writer."

"I don't know him well enough to suggest something like that. I wouldn't be able to write a word in front of him anyway."

"It doesn't have to be writing. You need to create something with him. What do you do in New York? I mean for a living."

"I freelance as an editor and translator for two scientific magazines."

"Do you like the work?"

"Yes. Sometimes I find myself thinking in scientific terms about my life. It's the opposite of the way writers think. I keep thinking that Prem has inseminated my brain. That my book will be a baby and he is the father. Everyone says that about books, but I think of it in a very technical way. You know they've created mice for the laboratory that have human cells inside them?"

"I don't think you should think about mice. But the baby idea is good."

"I want to show him a part of Paris that he hasn't seen. I'm doing a photo project on the streets—maybe I can involve him in that."

"I have to go now, but we should meet again."

Maya handed Nadine a pen and paper to write the name of the lovechild of the two women, Élula Perrin and Louna Borca, the *lovebook*.

Prem and Maya strolled through the back streets of the quartier after they'd finished with the two private galleries on rue de la Seine that they had agreed to see.

"I have to stop at La Hune for a minute, and then I must take the metro back home."

"I'll come with you. I'd like to browse around myself. What are you looking for?"

"I finally spoke to the woman on the floor below me, and she recommended this book to me to help me get over my writer's block."

Prem and Maya walked into the bookstore. Prem veered to the section on the left, while Maya went to the information desk to ask after the book.

"Mon vieux, what are you doing here?"

Prem greeted Pascal and raised his eyebrows in Maya's direction. Her back was toward them. Pascal stared at her.

"Stop looking like that."

"Only if we can get a drink. All of us."

"We have to ask her. I don't think she's free."

"Irène just came back from the doctor. The tests are showing the worst now."

"I'm sorry."

"I'm going to quickly buy this new edition of Artaud. Will you wait?"

Prem nodded. Maya was pulling something out from one of the shelves. He walked to the cashier's desk as she headed there with the book.

"What's this book called?" Prem asked.

"Un amour, deux femmes."

"Clever wordplay! By the way, Pascal is here. He wants to have a drink with us."

Maya handed the book to the cashier and pulled out her purse. Jean-Pierre had called earlier to say he had bought tickets to a show at a theater near the Place des Abbesses.

"Unfortunately, I have to go."

Pascal lined up behind Maya.

The cashier put the book in a plastic bag for Maya and then turned to Pascal.

"Bonjour, Monsieur Boutin."

"You didn't recognize Monsieur Rustum? You have his books everywhere."

The cashier immediately looked at Rustum and smiled. "I'm so sorry. I know your books, but I've never seen your photo."

Rustum nodded pleasantly. As they all stepped out, he hissed in a low voice so that Maya ahead of them could not hear, "That was totally unnecessary."

"I have to put up with it all the time."

"That doesn't mean I should."

Pascal stepped up near Maya and said, *"Alors,* where should we go?"

Prem introduced them to each other. Pascal gave Maya a kiss on each cheek.

"I am so sorry I have to leave. I would have loved to have a drink."

"Next time then!" Pascal said.

The men raised their hands to wave as she walked away in the direction of the metro.

"Le Vieux Colombier? I haven't gone there in a while," Pascal suggested.

They crossed the boulevard St-Germain and headed down rue de Rennes.

"She is cute. And hot."

"I guess so."

"You guess so! *Mon œil!* You followed her all the way to Paris."

"There are a lot of pretty babes around. We've become friends."

"Friends? Friendship happens between you and me. Between old men. Between young men. Between women who are sick of their stupid husbands. Between women who are no longer beautiful and men who are no longer young like Irène and me. Friendship doesn't happen between geriatric authors and aspiring ones."

"What are you trying to say?"

"She's going to make a lousy friend but a great lover. Friendship requires equals. A woman who is one-third your age cannot be your equal."

"And what am I going to give her as a lover? She has that insipid Adonis already."

"You're going to give her the same thing you give her in conversation—your wisdom, your experience, your comfort with this world, which you understand much better than she does because you've lived here fifty years longer."

"We'll see. What did Irène's doctor say?"

"Irène is sick. Very sick."

Roger Johnson lay awake in his bed, unable to sleep. He was feeling at an all-time low about his work. Prem's agent had said no. He needed reassurance. He wanted a true friend in this treacherous literary life, where one's future was uncertain until someone decided you were worth betting on. But there had been no news from Maya for several days. Today he had gone through the short e-mails she had sent him from Paris, each hinting at the increasing gulf between them. It could only mean that she had found someone.

Apart from a few stray episodes at parties, Johnson had had a dry run for a year. Maya, when she arrived, had been perfect, from what he'd seen. He liked her body. He liked her brain. And now she had disappeared. He didn't want her to break all ties. At the moment he was lonely in every sense, desperate for a friend. He found a story he had written that was different in style from the story he had sent Prem's agent. He sent it to Maya, asking her what she thought. Did someone like him stand a chance in hell in a universe of Boutins and Rustums?

Homi called Prem early in the morning. The election results had been out for a few days, and there was pandemonium. A couple of stray voices from the ousted party had said they would resign their memberships in the upper house of parliament if Sonia Gandhi became the prime minister.

"And what is the nation saying?" Prem asked.

"The media says these people are fascist and racist."

Prem laughed. He had distanced himself from Indian politics after *Grinding India*. But Homi was passionate about it and launched into a diatribe on the phone.

"Out of one billion people we cannot find even one of our own capable of holding the premier office of our land? We need an Italian? It's shameful!" Homi railed.

"What does Ratan think?"

"He asked me whether the Italians would let an Indian woman become the prime minister of their country."

"Can I talk to him?"

"Sure, I'll put him on."

"Hello, Grandpa."

"Ratan, my young man, how are you doing?"

"I'm fine. I found out a lot of things today."

"You did? What did you find out?"

"It has to do with the elections in India."

"Tell me." Prem pictured Ratan on the phone, his small hand gripping the receiver.

"Grandpa, do you think an Indian-born *naturized* citizen of America can become the American president." Ratan let out the word *naturized* after some trouble.

"You have to be born in America, according to their constitution."

"That's correct. And what about England? No. And Germany? No. And France? No. And Iceland? No. And Pakistan? No."

"Is this what you learned?"

"Yes. Daddy says that these elections have even taught *him.*"

"What have they taught him?"

"He says the media is *opportunic.*" Media! Opportunistic! Prem tried to remember what he had been doing and thinking at Ratan's age. He and Meher shared the same bed, and she would ask him to run his small palms over her bare body till she fell asleep. She insisted they not get out of their clothes until their parents had shut off the light and left them alone.

"Grandpa, can you hear me?" Ratan was screeching.

"Yes, yes. Why is the media opportunistic?"

"The media is *opportunic* because they show news which is not important in place of news that is very important just because of the money their sponsors give them." Ratan enunciated each word as if he were in a declamation contest at school reciting a poem.

"What news have they been showing?" An image of Meher was still dancing close to Prem's consciousness. He pressed the receiver to his ear.

"Yesterday I counted that they showed Laloo Yadav fourteen times in the news during the day saying the same thing again and again. Do you know why?"

"Why?"

"Because Laloo Yadav is the darling of the media. He brings in advertisements."

Ratan's *darling* evoked an image of Meher just weeks before her marriage. *You'll always be my darling. My darling brother,* she'd said.

"What was he saying?" Prem asked, trying to come back to the conversation.

"He wants to teach a lesson to the last government. He wants revenge."

"What do you think about all this, Ratan?"

"I am going to become Prime Minister of India and set everything right."

"Can I speak to Daddy?"

Homi came back on the phone.

"What are you telling the kid?" Prem demanded.

"I didn't say anything, I promise. He asked question after question, and you know how he is. He won't let slipshod answers go by unnoticed."

"You've indoctrinated him."

"Even Ratan can see from all the testimonials for Laloo on TV that well-respected members of the intelligentsia are now kow-towing to a thug convicted for corruption."

"That's democracy for you. It *is* the government of the masses."

"But he hasn't done anything for his masses in Bihar. It remains lawless and utterly benighted. I don't understand why they support him."

"He's one of them—that's why they support him."

"And the media!"

"What has the media done now?"

"The media shows Laloo making his inane comments all day long every half-hour. Ratan was not making that up—he actually counted the number of times that clip was shown during the day, and we only had the TV on for a few hours."

"So the media is unimaginative and lazy, they repeat the same clips all day long. And the politicians are still choosing their bedfellows based on psephology, not philosophy. What's new? It's not worth getting your blood pressure up."

"It's vicious. When the president of India speaks, they don't show him for more than a second. For once we have someone truly dignified saying things that make sense, but the media prefers to show a convict talking about revenge in that crude way of his."

"Homi, you're getting too worked up. Do I need to remind you that it's no good for your health?"

"I'm raising my son here. If he were listening to President Abdul Kalam's speeches, he would grow up with a deep belief in education and with high ideals."

"Shut off the TV."

"It's not just the TV. Even the papers don't publish his speeches. We should really move to America. Ratan will soon lose faith in the process, but it isn't too late yet."

"You know you can always come. But I must clear up one

misperception. Nothing is any different there. You'll be moving to a nation that was much more interested in getting to the truth about Clinton's cigar and where Monica put it than about Bush's decision to go to war with two countries."

Homi groaned audibly on the phone.

"What should I do?"

"Cultivate his interest in other things, like that Meccano set you so loved as a child."

"You're right. But enough of this! When do we see you?"

"You know India is too hot for me in the summer."

"Will you spend the winter with us?"

"I think so. There are some personal things—" Prem ended his sentence abruptly. He had never really spoken to Homi about his personal life, and Homi had never asked.

"You simply have to come."

"I wanted to say that you should consider coming to Paris for a short holiday."

"Ratan would love to see you. He says good morning to your photo every day. I don't think I can get a lot of time off work at the moment. I'll try to take a week off."

"He should outgrow that," Prem mumbled, his voice cracking.

"Here, say 'bye to him."

"Grandpa, I love you."

"Me too, darling. I love you."

"I want to become more famous than you when I grow up."

"You will. Now promise me you won't watch more than one hour of TV and you'll read one book every week."

"Is that how you became famous?"

"No, but without it I wouldn't have become famous."

"I promise. Only one hour of TV and one book a week." Prem imagined Ratan speaking into the phone with his eyes shut tight so that he would remember.

" 'Bye. Now give it back to Daddy."

"Deepika says hello to you," Homi said.

"Deepika will fall in love with this city."

Homi listed all the pills that Prem was supposed to take one by one and put down the phone only after Prem had answered in the affirmative to each one.

As Prem dressed for his rendezvous with Maya, he wondered if he should have been the one checking on Homi's health instead. Homi had married only at the age of forty-six and was now fifty-six, diabetic, and not in the best of shape.

Maya had insisted on a sightseeing trip to certain parts of Paris—the seventeenth, the nineteenth, the twentieth—that Prem had never explored in any depth.

"I am not interested in lining up with the tourists. I'm too old for it."

"We're not lining up anywhere. We are just going to take a cab to the nineteenth and walk around for half an hour and then get a coffee somewhere. I want to photograph some of the street signs there."

"Are you still on to the street names? What's with you and the streets?"

"They are all interesting even if they are not all achingly beautiful. Where else do you find rue de Bellechasse: street of the beautiful hunt, or rue des Blancs-Manteaux: street of the white coats? Which other city has streets named Nijinski, Freud, and García Lorca?"

"I still don't know why we aren't going to see the new Godard film instead or to the Musée Guimet, which we have spoken about many times now."

"Because it's a beautiful day and the sun is shining."

"You lead, I follow."

Maya grabbed Prem's hand in response and, hailing a cab, lightly pushed him in.

"Les Buttes Chaumont, s'il vous plaît," she said, getting in after him.

The traffic was flowing fast. Maya was in a summery maroon dress with thin delicate straps that lay over the hollow of her clavicles. She was in good form.

"Prenez à gauche," Maya instructed the taxi driver when he turned onto rue Manin and the park. She directed him to rue Michel Hidalgo, and then they got off.

"What's the matter? You're very quiet," Maya asked as they stood on the sidewalk.

"I spoke to my nephew and my grandson. It felt momentarily like being in India."

"What did you speak about?"

"The elections."

"How do you feel?"

"Less strongly than my nephew."

"Can I ask you something?"

"You can ask me anything." Prem looked at Maya and smiled. He could not see her eyes too well behind her dark glasses.

"It's a bit personal."

"Vas-y."

"You always refer to your nephew and your grandson. Do you mean your nephew Homi and his son?"

"Yes. Did I tell you his name?"

"No. I saw the dedication in *Meher.*"

"That's right, it's him. My sister died when Homi was ten, and her husband died when he was twenty, so I've been as close as a parent to him."

Maya brought out her *Plan de Paris* and looked.

"Where are we going?" Prem looked up and down rue Michel Hidalgo.

"We're going to go there," she said, pointing east.

They walked along briskly. Prem was glad he had let himself get talked into this. Sitting by himself all morning thinking about

Indian politics and missing Ratan would have been too depressing. They walked in and out of the shadow cast by the trees.

"You hardly talk about India, given how many times you've been," Prem said.

"With my parents the trips were great. Then I went on that trip I told you about. I got so hassled by the guys because I was traveling alone."

"That's because you're white and exotic."

"Do you like white women like all the other Indians?"

"Sure. But I like dark ones too."

"I would read the newspapers when I was there, and I found the matrimonial columns with their demands for fair domesticated brides very interesting."

"Fair is the measure of beauty."

"But everyone is so dark."

"Exactly."

"In *Pondy in My Cherry* one of your characters says that Indians love fair skin because they were ruled for so long by white skin. The British were light skinned and before that the Mughals were light because they had come from Central Asia."

"Yes, Professor Bala says that."

"Do you agree with Professor Bala's reasoning?" Maya asked. *"Évidemment."*

Maya pulled out her small digital camera and took a photo. Prem looked at the sign on the street, rue de la Liberté. They walked for a short time before she pulled out her camera again for rue de la Fraternité.

"Let me guess, we are headed to rue de l'Égalité next?"

"You get just no marks for that one."

"Even if I can prove that there is no equality? *Nada. L'égalité n'existe pas.*"

"There are equal rights for people, that's just a fact." Maya took a quick photo of the sign and tugged at Prem's hand.

"And now, miss?"

"Villas. There are a large number of Parisian villas in this area for some reason."

"You mean their kind of villa, with a cobbled pedestrian road and often a dead end?"

They had walked back to rue Miguel Hidalgo.

"*Voilà!* Villa Monet," Maya exclaimed, taking out her camera again.

"Why are you shooting these signs?"

"I don't know. Maybe I'll write about them."

"Come, let's walk to the end."

At the Villa Paul Verlaine Maya took two photos.

The next one was Rimbaud.

"That's cute—they put the two lovers next to each other," Prem said.

"I am mad about Paris because they love their poets," she said. "The most beautiful villa is named after the most beautiful poet."

There was a creeper growing beside a lamppost. The cobbled lane was so narrow the creeper had crossed to the other side, forming a natural bough. Sun filtered through its branches and formed a pattern on the ground.

"*Je suis de race inférieure de toute éternité,*" Maya recited from *A Season in Hell.*

Prem thought of the rest of Rimbaud's lines in the same section. To tan in a warm climate and to return seeming to be of a darker, stronger race was the opposite of what Homi and he had been talking about. Rimbaud's theory was the opposite of Bala's.

"There is a difference between Bala and me. Professor Bala thinks that Indians have a permanent inferiority complex about their race because the political hierarchy has always been arranged from fair to dark. I think he may have a point, but I'm too optimistic to think it's a permanent complex."

Sometimes Prem thought that he had managed to escape the colonial complex only because of Meher. When India was getting on its feet, he had been absorbed in his sister. And when he'd left for Oxford, he'd been so smarting from the turn of events in his personal life that entirely burying himself in Dostoevsky had been the only possible escape, outside of the politics of race, outside of the struggles of a newly born nation.

"Why give an extreme version of your views to your characters?" Maya wanted to take her question back as soon as she had asked it. When their conversation moved from the personal to the professional realm, Maya felt uncomfortable. When they discussed literature, books, and India, she was acutely aware of her shortcomings.

"Drama, opposition, black and white."

Maya was quiet.

Prem continued, "You forget that *Pondy in My Cherry* also had Bala's wife, a bleeding heart. A soft-headed, well-intentioned idealist. Well, she represented my rather nonsystematic and mishmash views on Indian politics. There you have it. Make fun of me if you will." Prem tapped his walking stick on the ground. An expedition to the nineteenth had seemed so far away to him that he had felt they were going outside Paris, so he had brought his walking stick along.

Maya laughed at Prem's admission. He had never confessed to holding the views of his characters in the press interviews she had read.

"Should we get something to drink?" she asked.

"Yes. Where should we go?"

"Let's go to the Place Armand Carrel, in front of the town hall. Then afterward we can walk inside the park for a while."

"You planned it all out, didn't you?"

"You're talking as if we were on an excursion to Giverny."

She was right. He made less of a fuss going from his suburban New Jersey residence to Manhattan. They were just a few miles from his quartier on the Left Bank.

"I told Pascal we might go to the nineteenth today, and he was hysterical. He told me to carry my hat and a bottle of water if it got too hot."

"We still have to walk for a few minutes. You're not tired, are you?" Maya asked with genuine concern, suddenly aware that he was an old man.

"I'm fine. I'm almost as energetic as you at this time in the morning."

Maya had asked the cab to stop at one of the higher parts of Buttes Chaumonts so that Prem would not have to walk uphill for any distance. The walk now was a steep downhill. Prem put his walking stick down with each step as if he were afraid of putting too much pressure on his knees. Maya wanted to hold his hand as they walked but stopped herself.

"Now that we've come tumbling down this hill, I am thirsty," Prem complained.

"It isn't a hill. It is just rue Compans. We'll be there in ten minutes." Maya could not stop herself from sounding out the names of all the streets she passed. She would walk around in her neighborhood to buy her baguette and read off rue des Trois-frères, rue la Vieuville, rue Garreaux, as if the street names were like *shlokas* from some ancient Vedic text that would illuminate the truth about life. In her yoga class the Indian teacher would often chant a mantra in Sanskrit and then explain its meaning. For Maya the streets of Paris sounded like the building blocks of an epic love poem, the scriptures of a religion called Art.

"*Mademoiselle des rues*. Peripatetic Maya," Prem said.

"Isn't it unfair that in English the word refers to Aristotle and the philosophers who walked and talked, but in French the feminine form *péripatéticienne* refers just to a whore? You're right—there is no equality, not of the sexes."

"A woman of loose character. Anyway, I used the English masculine word for you because that's how you seem as we take this promenade."

"You make fun of my love for this city, but you told me you've come back here every year since your first trip."

"And often for months at a time."

"An even greater malady than mine."

"I was here for the girls, not the streets."

"But you're not here for girls anymore, so what's your excuse now? May I remind you that you are here for an aging fellow writer whom you claim as your evil twin and for this yellow stone that you love as much as I do? You are a patient like me. *Le mal de Paris.*"

Prem caught his breath. Did she really think he was here for Pascal? Had he actually mumbled that at some point? He could no longer remember anything very well and certainly not the small white lies he had told Maya.

They sat at a corner café by the square in front of the town hall.

"Un café, s'il vous plaît," Prem ordered the waiter.

"The same," Maya added.

"Alors, deux cafés," the waiter said, walking away with a smile.

A middle-aged man from another table looked up at them and stared.

"What's the matter? Something happening behind me I should know," Maya asked.

"That guy is staring at us. He thinks I'm too old for you."

Maya felt her pulse race at Rustum's comment. Did he intend the obvious implication? In her nervousness she turned around indiscreetly.

"That is your book in his hand."

"You have hawk eyes. Which book? Is it in English or in translation?"

"L'odeur de la boue humide."

"I don't feel like talking to anyone," Prem said warily.

"I can pretend to be your bodyguard."

"A woman came up to me when I was with Pascal the other day and said she knew Judith Q, the New York nutcase."

"You are giving away your trade secrets. You're really Mrs. Chitra Bala with a Pondy in *your* cherry, and you spend as much time thinking about your stalker Judith Q as she does thinking about you."

"More time than she ever did."

"Why do that to yourself? Why write about something that's already unpleasant enough to live?"

"I made most of it up. But you're right. I've always done that, taken the most gut-wrenching *merde* in my head and fed it with my own self until I have a novel."

"Art from angst," Maya summed up. Prem felt slighted.

"*Café, café,*" the waiter announced, placing the two cups on the table.

"Whatever," Prem said.

"You're angry," Maya said.

"It was gut-wrenching *merde*. *Meher* was."

"I didn't mean to make light of it."

Prem had never looked so exposed. Even in their lighter moments together Maya felt that he was very much a superior both because of his age and his stature. Now he seemed just like any other person, a hurt person. She had glimpsed the possibility of this in Orsay, but it hit her now as if for the first time. As she stirred the two small sugar cubes on her plate into her coffee, she couldn't help but wonder if he had indeed loved Meher in *that* way. Was he the young boy who had been hurt by the sister who was the love of his life? In *Meher* the male characters had all seemed like foils—the narrator who was the brother and the cousin who was the lover. But the love felt real. And when Prem uttered Meher's name in real life, Maya had the feeling that the love in the book was real. She suddenly hated their calling as writers. If only what was fact and what fiction could be really clear for this moment. Was she with a Nobel laureate who had the reputation of a Rasputin or with a boy who had felt abandoned by his sister?

Maya removed her dark glasses. Prem was staring away from her at the bus stop in front of the town hall.

"Prem, please look at me."

He turned to look at her, still cross.

"I am sorry."

"Pascal was right. A friendship with someone fifty years younger is impossible."

"Don't say that, please."

Maya could think of no arguments. It had been impossible to imagine spending so much time with a famous man who had reached the acme of success in a métier she had just started out in. She felt as if she were still in kindergarten. What did she know about angst or writing books? All she had were a few stories published in decent literary journals and a jury of four people behind her who had decided to give her money one summer to go to Paris.

They sipped their coffees silently. Usually Prem gave his sugar to Maya. But today he didn't offer it, and she no longer felt as if she could just pick it up. The espresso was bitter.

She saw Prem looking beyond her. Then the young man was upon their table, holding out his hand to Prem.

"Mr. Rustum, I am a big big fan."

"Merci!" said Prem offhandedly, shaking the hand with a loose grip.

"Mr. Rustum, this book is just so beautiful."

Prem shrugged at the compliment.

"What inspired the title, can I ask?"

"Go to India in the rainy season, and smell the earth after the rain." Prem looked away from the man as if dismissing him.

"Yes. I leave you alone. Thank you." He walked away.

"I want to go back home," Prem said to Maya. She wanted to take him to the park. She had saved the view of Sacré-Coeur from Le Parc des Buttes Chaumonts, its *grotte,* and its stunning *jardin à l'anglais* for the end. But she felt defeated, sunk.

"Yes, of course," she said, going into the café to pay for their coffees. When she came back out, Prem was on his feet looking around for a taxi stand.

They got into a cab and rode in silence. At Prem's apartment Maya got off as well.

"Well, *au revoir,*" Prem said coldly.

Maya watched him go past his big, heavy *porte.* Then she crossed the Seine and walked up past the Place Madeleine and the Opéra, cutting across the ninth to the Place des Abbesses.

Le malheur à Paris. For the next several hours Maya understood the complete significance of being miserable in a beautiful city. The external world receded. An uncertainty from within took its place. She ignored two messages from Jean-Pierre before calling him back, only to say she couldn't meet for dinner, she was in a funk.

"A funk? What is a funk?"

"J'ai le blues. J'ai le cafard."

"Maybe I can help you."

"No, you can't."

"What happened? What can be so bad?"

"Prem is not talking to me anymore."

"Are you in love with him?"

"T'es fou?"

"Please don't isolate yourself like this from everyone else."

"I already have."

She spent the rest of the day staring at the light from her window as it faded. When she felt cold, she got up once to close the window and then turned away from the darkness to sit in the light of a dim lamp. She wanted to call Johnson in New York and tell him what had happened. He didn't even know that she knew Rustum, but she felt he was the only person who would understand.

Maya stepped into the bathroom and reached for a pair of scissors. She gathered a clump of hair and cut it. Then another. Soon she was no longer looking at the mirror while doing it. The left hand was grabbing randomly at whatever tuft of hair it could, and the right was snipping. Snipping. Snipping. The bathroom floor was a mess. Maya dusted her shoulders, her T-shirt, and her face. Then she found the vacuum cleaner and sucked up the fallen hair as best as she could. Her face had been transformed—without the slightly wavy, always shining brown halo, she looked stark. No one would notice her on the streets now.

Do I matter even in the least bit to him? I don't know why he ever responded to my ad, and now maybe I'll never know. Why did he touch me like that in front of the Degas? She wanted to know everything about his life, about the Degas woman stepping into the bath, about the French *filles* he had been linked to, about Meher. She wanted to drink up on Rustum, satiate herself with his company for all the years in her future when he would no longer be around.

When he had been upset, he had looked like Maya's grandfather just before he had died. Old, feeble. She wanted to have every minute that she could with Prem—there wouldn't be enough. Thoughts of his imminent death came into her mind, and they displaced all the other questions and the coldness with which he had said goodbye to her. In the emptiness of her apartment Maya found her eyes fixed on the telephone. She wanted to call Prem and apologize, but she was afraid that this would anger him further. She had to wait till tomorrow. How she would pass a whole night without calling him, she didn't know. She went down to the Internet café and found Johnson's e-mail. She was too scattered to comprehend it, even though she clicked it open and stared at it a few minutes.

She felt her nose twitch and a large lump form once again in her throat. Maya logged out of the computer and asked the man running the kiosk for an international calling card. Then she enclosed herself in a booth to call her father at home.

Her mother picked up.

"Maya here, Mom. How are you?"

"Okay."

"I am in Paris. It is beautiful here."

No response.

"Is Dad there?"

"No."

"Do you know when he'll be back?"

"No."

"Will you tell him I called?"

"Yes."

"Are you sure you won't forget?"

"No."

"I'll try later. Take care."

She hung up. She put the plastic card in her pocket and walked down from the the the top of the hill on Abbesses through the ninth. Then she walked past the Bourse to the river and on the quais of the Seine. Her mother's flat, toneless voice had unhinged her. Her mother's disease had distanced Maya from the entire world. As the link with her mother had broken, so Maya's own connection with society had become tenuous. If something so basic as a parental bond could be so fragile, then where was the chance of anything permanent and lasting with a stranger who had met her at seventy-five?

She couldn't understand how her father lived with it. She couldn't understand how her brother managed to call each week and keep up a cheerful monologue on everything that had happened in his life in London. And she couldn't begin to understand how she herself had become so entirely graceless and loveless when her mother showed no signs of recovering from the acute depression that had taken over a few years ago. In the beginning Maya had been like her father and brother—she had done everything to keep her spirits up and theirs. But when it became obvious that nothing was going to change, she suggested one night at Christmas, when she and her brother were both home, that their father hospitalize her and set himself free. Her brother had accused her of betrayal and regarded her with a slight suspicion ever since. Her father had understood her motive, her love for him, her wish to see him have a normal life. But he shook his head sadly and said he wouldn't do it.

Father and daughter stayed up by the fire in the living room late into the night. Maya pressed on and on until he eventually said, "I can't do it because she wouldn't have done it if it happened to me."

"It wouldn't ever happen to you."

"You know it's not true. You were there when the doctor told us. Impossible to predict. Never any signs beforehand."

"But you have to live too. How long can you go on like this?"

"Forever. I make time for myself. I play golf. I see Roger and Samantha once a week. I dine with Leif on Mondays."

"You always lived so intensely. I can't bear it."

"This is life, Maya. I have to be a man. I couldn't respect myself if I didn't."

Her father continued without complaining. Maya visited two or three times a year and did her best in front of her mother. But she couldn't handle the phone. Her mother never recalled the phone calls, but they perturbed Maya. Her father realized this and started to call her. But with the time difference from Paris, their routine had been derailed.

Maya was still walking and had reached Pont de Sully. She must have been walking for well over an hour. The sky was getting dark. She looked at her watch. It was ten. She crossed over the bridge and walked back on the quai on the other side. Suddenly she was aware of being alone. She picked up speed. In the shadows by the side she saw two men lurking.

"Mademoiselle, venez dîner avec nous."

She walked faster till she reached the quai by the next bridge, where people were still picnicking. She had broken into a sweat. Her tall blond father had a muscular energy; its mere presence made an area safe. He was the kind of man every girl and woman wanted around. You could take him to the devil and be sure he would give his life fighting for you. She missed that man. He had withdrawn into himself and diminished after her mother's illness.

And now Maya felt it was her turn to protect him the way he had protected her. It was the same protectiveness she felt for Prem, but Prem could be fiercely distant when he was most in need of comfort. Prem had lodged himself right beside her father in that chaotic swamp within where emotions held forth, in that mute, blind, deaf zone of feeling that was utterly unencumbered by reason.

At Notre Dame Maya climbed up the steps and left the quai. She walked through the back streets of the quartiers St. Michel and St. Germain to Prem's building. She pressed the door code and entered the main courtyard, where she sat on the steps outside Prem's entryway, sure deep down in herself that she shouldn't ring his bell. She looked at the time. It was now midnight. The walk had exhausted her, and she got very cold. She left reluctantly and took a cab back home.

In the morning she tried calling Prem but got no response. She went to the Internet café and read Johnson's e-mail. He sounded very upset. Prem's agent had responded with a curt note saying the agency could not handle him. He had attached a story to his e-mail. The story pulled Maya into its world, provided her with a brief interlude from her own sorrow. She passed it to a mentor from her college days who was in publishing, suggesting Johnson e-mail the lady for advice.

She also wrote:

I'm depressed about my writing too. I saw a Fantin-Latour in the Orsay the other day, a painting of writers and thinkers including Rimbaud. At my age he had already produced all his best work.

I thought of you last night. I was deeply unhappy about something that happened and I felt as if you were the only person in the world who would understand me. I almost called you. I do have a boyfriend of sorts in Paris. But it's just a summer fling. I was upset due to someone else. An unrequited love I cannot fully understand at this point. And I don't want to talk about it. The fact that I thought of you last night when I was suffering and not of my other friends in New York or Paris told me something. I feel a complicity with you, Johnson. Only a writer can understand another writer's loneliness. I am distraught by something that has taken a hold of me and is more powerful than me or my will. Thanks for your story—it took me away from this.

Maya tried calling Prem again. There was still no response. Her tears had run dry, but her chest felt like lead.

It was foolish to try to re-create his first love. Meher had happened to him before his ego had been formed. How can I ever love anyone again more than I love myself? Why am I even trying to do this? There can be no such thing as total submersion. And I am not even having an affair with this girl. What am I doing here?

In the late afternoon Prem called Pascal.

"I need to change my ticket. What is your travel agent's number?"

"What happened? Are you leaving earlier or later?"

"I'm leaving tomorrow if I can, or the day after."

"*Qu'est-ce qu'il y a?*"

"It's over with that girl."

Pascal whistled and then said, "I am having a *café* at Mabillon. Come by."

Prem was agitated as he crossed the boulevard St-Germain. He felt even more irritated when he saw that Pascal was not alone.

"Prem Rustum," he said, kissing the woman briskly on both cheeks.

"She's just leaving," Pascal said.

Prem continued to stand as if waiting for her to leave. He had never seen her before.

"*Mon vieux*, sit down." Pascal pulled a chair from the next table.

Prem looked around, reluctant to get drawn into the conversation. He noticed she had pulled out a cigarette, but to his relief she got up from her chair after Pascal had lit it.

"It was nice meeting you," the woman said before leaving.

"*Une amie,*" Pascal said in her direction by way of explanation. Prem nodded.

"Why this sudden detachment from your enchantress?"

"You were right—the age gap is too much."

"For what? I can't even remember saying that. I only remember telling you to avoid the fifty-year-olds in favor of the twenty-year-olds."

"For any true friendship."

"What nonsense! You are supposed to love her. You are supposed to fuck her. All this friendship crap is too American. It doesn't suit you at all. *Pas du tout,*" Pascal declared.

"I am not you."

"What is that supposed to mean?"

"I'm looking for more than a fuck."

"So you have a higher morality now?"

"Yes," Prem said. He was angry with Pascal too. He was angry with the world.

"Ooh la la! Mathilde, Liz, Catherine, Lilia, Tamar, Rhonda, Claire, Vedika, Angie, Mishka, Laetitia, Julie, Valérie—those were more than just a fuck?" Pascal said, listing the few names he remembered.

"Vedika was not just a fuck."

"The exception that proves the rule."

"Nor Julie and Valérie."

"You were not in love with them."

"Let's forget about them now. I don't want to just fuck. Not at seventy-five. I don't even know if I *can* fuck. I haven't in over ten years."

"That's a minor detail modern medicine can solve. But tell me why not just fuck? It's worked for us all our lives."

"Because in the end it hasn't worked."

"Well, I am sure this girl will be eager to have more than a fuck. At this age you can get the fuck only if you are giving her much more," Pascal said cruelly.

"I don't think she can ever love me."

"What happened? I told you not to go to the nineteenth."

Prem burst out laughing.

"At least you can laugh."

"She said my art comes from angst." It sounded ridiculous said aloud like that.

"But it does. You've said so yourself so many times."

"It sounded like a glib advertising slogan."

"What does this have to do with whether or not she can love you?"

"What does she know about my angst? What does she know about losing love when you are a teenager, just when you should be beginning?"

"Are you talking about your sister again?" Pascal always made light of Meher.

"I'm saying I have to stop looking for that love," Prem said.

"And you should certainly not tell the poor girl you're after her because you want to re-create your incestuous relationship."

"Pascal," Prem said in a threatening tone.

"I'll stop, but at least admit to your double standard. You go on about your angst, but when Maya says the same thing, then it's a betrayal. You go on about Meher, but when I call it by its name, you can't take it."

"Fine. You are right."

"Your ego was hurt, *mon vieux*. This girl saw you for a moment as a fellow artist whose art she could understand, and it hurt your pride to not be seen all the time as a myth."

"I don't think that's it," Prem muttered.

"What you need is to let it rest for a few days. Let's go away from Paris. Irène's sister is here to look after her this week, and I really need a break."

"Hmm." Prem was listening to Pascal only remotely.

"I need to get out. Come with me." Pascal placed a hand on Prem's shoulder to emphasize himself.

"I don't know."

"When we're back, you can take her to dinner. Even if I make fun of it, I don't want you to lose something you don't realize you have."

"I don't have her. She's *not* mine." Prem spoke with his teeth clenched.

"You have your sentiments. Even if it doesn't fulfill the idealistic standards you've set for the last love affair of your life, it is still something very genuine and precious. I can see that she has done something rare to you. I admire you for exposing yourself like that."

"Stop mocking me."

"But I am not." Pascal looked at Prem quizzically.

Maybe he wasn't mocking him.

"What a day! First my grandson went on about Laloo Yadav over the phone, and then I had this scene with Maya. I'm exhausted."

"Who is Lah-loo Yada Yada?"

"A politician. *Un con. Pas très important.* I can't believe I'm talking about him. Anyway, where do you want to go?"

"A place with no memories of my past with Irène. Brittany or Normandy."

"I've never been to either."

"You haven't seen Mont-Saint-Michel?"

"No."

"You have to. It's our Taj Mahal. I have to show it to you."
Pascal rose from the table as if the decision had been made.

"Where are we going now?" Prem said, getting up after
Pascal.

"Let's eat, and I'll come pick you up tomorrow around
eleven. I want a head start on the lunchtime traffic."

"Is it a long trip?"

"Four to five hours if we're lucky. It's the middle of the week
after all."

Prem lagged a step behind Pascal as they walked to the
Marché Mabillon. Pascal seemed undecided between two restaurants but eventually chose one, mumbling to himself. Prem followed and sat at the bistro table Pascal had chosen.

"I'm too old for this."

"For what? The road trip?"

"That too. I meant pursuing Maya."

"Your problem is that you're not pursuing her. You want her
to land in your lap."

"I want to be sure she's interested in the real me. Not in all
the feathers in my cap."

"You talk as if someone other than you won that prize."

The waiter bustled around them. A man with a pitted face
and a strong nose. Prem vaguely recalled the face and recalled sitting at the same bistro table. He had a moment of déjà vu. The
serveur looked at Prem and asked, *"Et pour vous?"* Pascal had apparently already ordered.

Prem tried to look at the menu in his lap.

"Just order the *coquilles Saint-Jacques* like me. It's what's good."

"Deux, monsieur," Prem said to the *serveur* without arguing.

"You won't regret it. They have a good white to go with it."

It was pointless explaining that even if the dish wasn't great,
he wouldn't regret it. Couldn't regret it. Whenever he felt a malaise
about the world, Prem didn't really relish food.

The waiter had poured some wine for Pascal, who lifted the glass to his nose. He turned the wine around in the glass and let it slosh on the sides before inhaling more deeply. Prem watched. Finally Pascal sipped it and then, a dramatic pause later, nodded.

The waiter poured their glasses. Prem, despite himself, brought the glass to his nose and sniffed it. He kept his nose in it for a long time. Could he discern the bouquet in it if he tried? The aroma of his lovers from the past?

"There's a hint of mint in it."

"And the smell of a young woman who has just hit puberty," Prem offered wisely.

"See, you're doing better already."

Prem laughed.

"I, on the other hand, really need to escape."

"*Quelque chose ne va pas?*"

"I picked up a woman yesterday. I've met her a few times at literary soirees."

Prem listened carefully. Pascal had rarely exhibited such grimness.

"I finally got her to bed. But I couldn't."

"For the first time?"

Pascal nodded.

"You are the one who wrote that Viagra article for *Le nouvel observateur.*"

"It wasn't that. I was preoccupied with Irène and her sickness. I kept thinking she's going to die, and I'm fucking."

"But she and you have not had that kind of relationship for a long time. Or have you?"

"No. But it's like a sister dying."

Prem was quiet.

"I didn't mean to remind you of Meher. Irène and I have become like siblings."

"I know."

When their food arrived, Pascal attacked the shells and their slithery insides with single-minded determination, almost as if he had given himself a mission. Prem could sense Pascal's fear of his own death. Irène's impending death had thrown him off entirely.

Prem went back to his apartment and took two sleeping pills that knocked him out. On the drugged sleep from the pills he dreamed of Angie. Angie, the sexy beast of his passage into virility. Angie, the *salope*, the whore, the cunt, the big-breasted, perpetually slick-pussied, cock-hungry bitch. In his dreams she found him lying naked in a prison cell and got on all fours over him, her heavy breasts hanging over his mouth, her crotch gyrating over his penis. She took him till she fulfilled herself and then disappeared through the grilled entrance just as mysteriously as she had entered. *Why is she haunting me after fifty years?* Prem felt stuck in a permanent time machine where his age advanced but his feelings remained static.

After a shower Prem walked to get a newspaper and have his coffee. He stared at the front page without registering much, then looked at the early-to-work Parisians and the traffic on the street. A few odd people were cycling to work—men in suits, women in skirts and formal jackets. They compromised nothing even on their bicycles, their heels pointed and long, their purses stylish, their hairdos spectacular.

Two American women came and sat down at the table beside his.

"What is this *invalid* thing here?" one of them asked the other.

"Let's see. Army museum, Napoleon's grave, used to be a hospital for the soldiers."

"*The* Napoleon?"

"This guide doesn't have too much."

"I loved the movie in which Brando played Napoleon."

"We should go just as a homage to Brando. Let's do that first."

Prem picked up his paper again. In India the Italian woman had refused to take on the prime ministership. Opinion was divided as to whether it was a strategic move or a great sacrifice. Some sycophants in the Congress were comparing her to Mahatma Gandhi.

"Missyou, can we get the addition, please," the American ladies asked the waiter.

They left. The ensuing silence pulled Prem back into his past. Women hung heavily on his conscience. Every woman he had dumped had taken it badly. *But I thought you loved me. In fact, I know you love me. You're afraid of how much you love me—that's why you're leaving me.* This had pretty much been the refrain. And Prem, who had never once made a false promise or used the word *love*, would ask, quite naturally, why they thought so.

You're so sensitive. The way you make love, the way you touch. It's impossible to be that way with a woman unless you are in love.

Prem's hands were the culprits. He touched women the way Meher had taught him to touch. But he did not feel for them the way he had felt when he touched Meher. And so Prem fucked them, not the way he had made love to Meher, but the way he had fucked Angie, in the early days when they were still fucking. He fucked almost as if it were a kind of revenge, a ruthless taking back of what had been stolen. The women mistook this for an insatiable greed for their bodies and therefore their souls. If there was ever any doubt in their mind, it was banished by the gentle postcoital caresses that he showered on them by habit.

For the first eight months of their relationship Prem had been in love with Angie. And in those months he had found himself confounded with emotions of which he had no previous experience: forms of love and bestial desire that had not existed in the Meher universe. The only expression of these new passions lay in sex. Angie had responded like a charm. Each day he had pushed the envelope with her, slapping her, humiliating himself, humiliating her, saying things pertaining to her sexual abuse as a child and using it as an aphrodisiac. In an environment of love and trust Prem believed they would both heal. But unfortunately for them Angie's furious temper and Prem's nonconfrontational style were so incompatible that steadily but irrevocably they began to despise each other. Their sexual life, rooted no longer in love but in habit, headed steeply in the direction of perversity for its own sake. After four years Prem unilaterally made the decision that even if they were unable to get rid of each other, he would not have sex with her again. Angie begged him, wept, pleaded, and on occasion jumped on him in his sleep, but apart from three instances in two years, Prem kept his promise.

Finally they split.

Prem's agent before Edward, a mincing, effeminate man called Cole—who Prem was sure was gay—fell in love with Angie and took her. He left Prem in the capable hands of Edward. Looking back, Prem thought of this as a masterstroke—he got rid of a girlfriend and won a world-class agent.

Angie, however, continued to loom in his subconscious. She had left her imprint on the nerves leading from his dick that reported back to his brain. One day after he and Vedika had started their secret liaison, he found himself saying things to Vedika that he had learned from Angie, things that could be positively injurious to their relationship, if not utterly lethal for the struggling morality of a good woman cheating on her husband. To his shock, he found that Vedika had so given up any control of herself that even Prem's incorporation of Harry Bedi into their lovemaking process was not salacious enough for her to pull away and slap him. Their trysts continued, day after day, in an abandoned and wanton celebration of their deception of the man whom Vedika called her husband and Prem his brother. Once Prem made her act out a Hindi film scenario where she, as a typical self-sacrificing wife, was raped by her brother-in-law and eventually turned into a whore. He had been talking dirty to her for weeks, but at this point when Vedika looked into his eyes pleadingly, he thought she would say it was time to stop. Instead she begged: in Hindi. And he had commenced with the few crude words available to a half-Parsi boy raised in Bombay speaking English.

Vedika revived Prem's hope in life, in love, and in women. Where the relationship with Angie had filled him with disgust and the one with Meher with incredible loss, the one with Vedika had reinvented the very idea of eros. A man and woman so totally naked to each other, so intimate that they were able even to fuse their culpability and their conscience. After their first six months together, from spring to late autumn, Prem decided it was time to ask her to marry him. It was obvious to them both that Harry would sooner or later find out and Vedika said she could never again make love to Harry. Or to anyone else.

"I want to be with you forever," Vedika had said in response to his proposal.

She would go to India for a month and announce her decision just before her return.

"It'll be easiest for him that way if I give him a break from me."

"That's a good idea. You can move in with me when you arrive."

Three weeks after her departure it was Prem who received a letter telling him that he had to forget her and move on. She knew he would never betray her by telling Harry or any of their friends about what had passed between them. In a profoundly religious moment in her parents' home, Vedika had seen Prem and herself teetering on the edge of an abyss. They shared an intimacy of degradation, based on their inner fears, their base desires, their dark sides. *But no! We share both that and the other side, the nobler side. Have you forgotten the hundreds of hours before we became lovers?* Prem wanted to protest while reading her letter. But Vedika believed that they had suffered from an illusion that they could be saved by each other. Being in India had convinced her that the right path lay in fulfilling the promise she had already made to see her husband through his life, to be by his side. The individualistic self-aggrandizing life of sensation with Prem was not for her.

Prem was broken.

Prem called Harry to say he was off to Paris and to give his love to Bhabhi when she got back. He left North America with the hope that he would regain the stability and the balance to come back to New York in some months. He let his writing drown him like never before and forced himself to stand at the very edge of the cliff that so terrified Vedika. Prem determinedly looked at the precipice without a lifeline to protect him in case he lost his balance. Since then writing had been primary, he himself secondary.

part v

I lifted her chemise and found marble.

—ARISTIDE MAILLOL TO PAUL GAUGUIN

ON CLOTILDE NARCISSE

The two men hit the autoroute to Dreux. Pascal had a new toy for the trip: a sleek white box that he claimed contained hundreds of symphonies. He connected it to the car and fiddled with a dial till Bach came on.

"Feel free to change it," he said to Prem, smiling.

"Yeah, right! I was barely ever competent with the radio dial or the car stereo, and now you have to go get something that all the kiddywinks play with." Prem peered at the display, afraid to press any of the buttons.

"Turn the dial—you'll see the choices."

Prem tried turning the dial, but the LCD flashed the same thing again and again. He placed the little box by the gearbox. Outside the car the trees were a leafy green. Paris seemed far away. It had been a while since Prem had experienced this anticipation of a new place. He knew practically nothing about where they were headed. He had very few images and a few faded lines from Maupassant to feed his imagination.

"New things to discover even at this age!"

"That's right, *mon vieux!*" Pascal was wearing his dark glasses and steadily accelerating. Prem threw a sideways glance at the speedometer.

They saw her at the same time: the hallucinatory blonde in black clothes sitting on a chair at the edge of the forest as if she were waiting for Luis Buñuel to step out and direct her. Prem undid his seatbelt to turn around fully and look. She smiled.

"Did you see that?" His heart was thudding.

"Yes, wasn't it amazing?"

"What do you think she was doing there on the edge of the highway, sitting like that with a cigarette in her mouth?"

"What do you think she was doing?"

"Come on—no one can stop here to pick up a whore."

"No? We almost did."

"But there's still no exit! No place to pull off. I think she was there for a surrealistic photo shoot."

"That must be the edge of a park. People probably have access from inside."

Prem put his hand on his chest. It was still beating fast.

"Are you okay?"

"Yes. It was just so unexpected."

"Makes one want to fuck. I didn't feel anything like that with the woman who came home with me the other night."

"The setting was sensational. Whoever saw a woman sitting like that on a desk chair without a table? Smoking in a black skirt. In the middle of the day!"

"This calls for Wagner."

"Oh, no!" Prem groaned.

"Just a few minutes, I promise." Pascal reached for his white toy and tried to manipulate it, one hand on the steering wheel.

"Can we please pull over and do this?"

At the next exit Pascal pulled to the side and with a few efficient turns of the dial turned on Wagner. Some ten minutes later Prem couldn't bear any more.

"Can we move on to Mahler? Or even Strauss?"

"Ha! You'll have to learn to operate the new technology. *Bon courage!*"

"Damn you."

Pascal explained how Prem could move back and forth with

the dial, choose an artist or a song, and then change what was playing on the car stereo.

"Not that hard, see."

"No. Homi would love this. I should buy one for him."

They fell silent to *Symphonie fantastique*. Prem remembered his
last road trip. It was twenty years ago with Lilia the singer. Prem
had felt that it was time for him to write about America. A big
American saga. The Emergency in India was over, and Prem felt
finished with Indian politics. But America was huge and unknown,
even though he had been living in New York for several years. Lilia
suggested a cross-country drive. Coffee at Dunkin' Donuts every
morning, motels, motels, more motels at night. Lilia beside him as
he drove, choosing the radio, fighting over the music. Tapes, talk
shows, diners, and a lot of eggs and waffles. And then Lilia sitting
on his face, Lilia fucking him, him fucking Lilia. At night before
sleeping. In the morning while getting up. Lilia, the only easy relationship. Without love but with understanding. If he didn't want to
talk, she'd let him be. She was the only person who never assumed
he loved her. And she didn't insist on more than he could give. Lilia
with whom he never felt culpable.

Pascal pulled into the main parking lot of a village for lunch.
"We've made good time. We're already in St-Hilaire. But we
should've stopped earlier. It's hard to get a meal in some of these
small towns except between noon and two."

The two brasseries turned them down.

"We can get a sandwich at the *boulangerie*, no?"

"I want a meal," Pascal carped.

"It's not going to kill you to eat light for a day."

Pascal glared at Prem. Prem ignored him and walked to the
boulangerie, the glass doors opened automatically. He ordered himself a small quiche. Pascal ordered the same.

They stepped out and found a bench where they ate in silence. Pascal looked unhappy.

"Should we get a beer at the bar there?" Prem suggested.

"Yes."

Seated at the stools on the bar, they both watched the girl who was busy cleaning the floors and tables. The television on top of the bar was on.

"I can't believe you grew up in a small town like this," Prem said.

"I knew I had to leave. I didn't even do my *classe préparatoire* there. I just fled."

"I was thinking about Lilia earlier. The sex with her was so uncomplicated."

"You can have it again now if you really wanted. I can introduce you to women."

"I can't do it. I couldn't do it then. Somehow she got through the net."

"I'm getting laid tonight. I have to."

"Do it. It starts to fade fast after seventy."

"That's why I want the prize now. It's no use getting it when you can no longer get it up."

Prem was quiet. He hadn't told Pascal whether or not he could still get it up. But Pascal's comment wasn't about Prem's virility, it was about that seething ambition that swam inside him and occasionally bubbled to the surface, throwing a wedge into their friendship.

"You don't think they'll pass me up totally, do you? That's not possible, is it?"

His friend looked lost for a moment. Afraid. This was why he needed Irène, the woman who had always calmed him, given him a mothering kind of love. Prem ran his hand through Pascal's hair and imagined for a moment he was Ratan. Pascal calmed down.

"*On y va,*" he said firmly to Pascal, putting down money for their beers.

They walked back out in the sun and found the car.

"They probably thought we were gay," Pascal said as he put on his seatbelt.

"Je m'en fous."

"I think we'll be there in another hour if the traffic stays light."

Pascal seemed to have a new determination as they drove. His teeth were mildly clenched and his foot somewhat aggressive on the gas pedal. Prem played with the new toy he had just learned to manipulate and saw them through Saint-Saëns' *Le carnaval des animaux* and Ravel's *Daphnis et Chloé.*

The first sight of Mont-Saint-Michel was unexpected and spectacular. It stood up high against all the surrounding marshlands. The long straight approach road was only a few kilometers, but somehow time itself seemed to flatten around the edges of the edifice, lending a profound longitudinal effect. A few large drops of rain fell on the car.

"We've had such splendid weather. Why is it raining now?" Pascal hissed as he pulled into the parking lot. A woman directed them to a free spot. Rain hit the windshield harder and with increased frequency.

"We'd better wait in here. I don't want to send an old man like you to his death," Pascal said. A satanic grin played at the edge of his mouth.

"No, then they'll never give you the prize," Prem said.

Pascal glared at him.

Prem moved the dial on the toy and chose Mozart's *Jupiter Symphony.* Pascal started whistling. The rain was beating down hard now, and the entire *îlot* and its dramatic monastery were invisible. Even the cars in the parking lot were barely discernible. Pascal and Prem were isolated, a universe of two. Apart from the women he had loved, if Prem had to choose anyone to be in this situation with, it would be Pascal. He wanted to tell him that. But Pascal was still whistling to his favorite music. His stubble was reddish and unruly. He had probably not shaved in the morning.

Almost as abruptly as it had started, the rain stopped. The skies cleared in cracks, and a pink light peeped out. Pascal's eyes were closed. Prem shook him.

"Wow."

"I wish Maya could see this. She loves the play of light and color."

"I've been here two times before, and it was different each time. It really transforms with the changing colors of the brooding gray sky so typical of Normandy."

"Should we get out?"

"Be careful—it's going to be slushy."

"Don't worry, I'll keep the cane."

Prem pulled out his cane from the backseat and placed it on the road after he opened his door. He tested it for a second while still seated in the car, then hauled himself out. His shoes caused water to splash on to the cuff of his pants.

"We're actually staying at a hotel inside. We'll need to climb a little"

"I can climb. I'm just slow."

"I'm worried about myself," Pascal said. Both of his hands were supporting his paunch.

They walked to the narrow wooden bridgelike contraption that led to the main gates of the medieval city. A busload of French kids on a school excursion came running toward them. Pascal and Prem waited against the side of the wooden bar, letting them pass.

"The other hotel was even higher up, so I chose this one," Pascal huffed as they continued on the incline leading up to the hotel.

"Nonetheless, we'll have to climb up all the way to see the monastery."

"We don't have to. We can go halfway and take in the atmosphere and the view."

"We've come a long way for this. If we give it time, we'll make the top tomorrow."

They checked into the hotel, and Pascal handed his car keys to the reception desk with instructions for their bags.

"I'm going to take a siesta. Should we meet here in an hour?"

"Yes. I need to lie down and straighten my back," Prem said.

In his room Prem threw open the curtains and lay down, looking at the pale palette of the sky through the window. He couldn't remember why he had been so upset by Maya's remark. It didn't seem all that bad in retrospect. What seemed amazing, however, was that he had followed her all the way to Paris. Of course he'd told himself he would have gone anyway to see Pascal, and if things hadn't worked out with her, it was a good excuse to spend time with his friend. He hadn't skipped more than one or two summers in two decades. Prem had moved away from most of his friends and acquaintances; apart from Pascal, the only other person he felt close to was Edward. But there were intrinsic limits to his relationship with Edward: while one of immense confidence, it remained professional. After Julie and Valérie he had not opened to any woman or even been tempted to. He couldn't help feeling as if events had conspired to lead him to Maya. Pascal had mentioned meeting girls on the Internet, and he'd met the boy who had sent him those stories and come to lunch. He'd found Maya just the way Pascal had said he would find her.

Maya made him feel young even though he was never as aware of his age as when he was around her. For example, today he had had little doubt that had she come with them on this trip, both Pascal and he would have been more enthusiastic and basked in the glow of youth that she cast with her sunniness.

He awoke to the sound of the phone in his room.

"I overslept, but it seems like you did too."

"Yes, I was asleep. What time is it?"

"Six. We were knocked out. Should we meet in the lobby in ten minutes?"

Prem washed his face and changed his shirt. The nap had done him good. He thought he should call Maya and tell her that he wasn't upset anymore with her. But when he looked at the watch, ten minutes were already up. He swung his cane in his hand and made his way to the lobby.

"Are we ready for a climb?" Pascal asked.

"Yes. I feel new."

They left the hotel and took the main path that led up to the steps of the monastery. The ramp was steep, and they walked slowly. The sky was still light, and birds were twittering about. There was no handlebar, and Prem had to place some of his weight on his cane. Soon the ramp turned into a steep stairway. After some seven stairs Pascal sat down on the steps.

"I don't think I can go much longer," he said breathlessly.

"Yes, you can. If I can, you can. We'll take it slow."

Prem envied Pascal his sixty-five years. Despite all his weight problems, he could sit easily on the steps. Prem knew that if he sat down, he would have trouble getting back up. A minute later they continued. They reached a landing with a vista and walked to the edge. The circular rampart suggested that it was an old watchtower. They had a view of all the surrounding land and the marshes.

"When the sea comes in, everything gets covered and this place becomes an island." Pascal moved his hand, sweeping a wide arc.

"What about the road on which we came? It's higher, on an embankment."

"That *digue* is the only way of getting to the island, but the parking lot gets covered so everyone has to walk a mile to get here. I saw it like that once."

"How often does that happen?"

"I don't know. We can ask someone." Pascal shrugged.

They walked farther up. There was no one on the path. It seemed like a ghost town. They crept up to the steps of the abbey, which was closed in the evening. Pascal sat down on the steps once more. This time Prem sat down as well. A small stone archway framed a piece of deep blue sky. It was the same blue that had stopped Maya's breath in the van Gogh painting.

"She's right, everything is beautiful. Maya loves France in the way American girls often do. But in the end it's true."

"I had an American girlfriend once, and she would go crazy for things like this." Pascal pointed to a couple of yellow and white wildflowers growing out of the gray stone. "I don't know if you noticed on the drive, the sky was very dark on one side and blue on the other."

"I remember. There was a small hill with a field of yellow flowers on the dark side where the clouds were almost black. The contrast was dazzling."

"I should have rolled down the window so you could smell the air. They're calzo flowers, and the air is sweet around them. I loved them as a kid."

Prem wondered if Pascal had been serious about getting laid. The prospects here in the deserted closed-off islet didn't look too promising.

"It seems awfully quiet around here."

"Everyone's eating, and we should be too. We should get dinner in the town."

"There's a town?"

"Just the small strip of restaurants we passed while driving up. Most people stay there since the accommodation is a whole lot cheaper than within Mont-Saint-Michel."

On the descent the ten years between them were more obvious to Prem than they had been in the car when Pascal was explaining his music machine. Prem could still learn and get his head around new technology, but his body was a different matter. His sense of balance had diminished, and he was perpetually afraid of slipping and falling. There was nothing to hold on to, and his cane seemed fancy and inadequate. Pascal saw Prem's hesitation, grabbed his free hand, and stepped down just a little ahead of him, assuring him wordlessly that he wouldn't fall except on Pascal himself.

"Look at us both—we're getting on," Pascal said, laughing.

Prem felt grateful for the remark. He was getting on a lot more than Pascal.

In the specialty seafood restaurant that Pascal had chosen for them, Prem excused himself to take a leak. When he came back, he found that Pascal had moved them to another table and invited a woman to join them.

"This is Cary, and this is Prem," Pascal introduced them.

"I'm just such a huge fan of yours, Mr. Rustum." Cary was American, enthusiastic, two volumes louder than anyone else in the restaurant, and definitely not a city kid.

"What are you doing all alone here?" Prem asked.

"Cary's spending her senior year in Paris, and since none of her friends wanted to make the trip, she decided to do it alone," Pascal said.

Pascal kept up the conversation for most of the evening. Cary didn't know much about French literature and had only a vague idea of Pascal. Prem heard Pascal mention the three Ps a couple of times, to cast his lot with Prem's. Every now and then Prem interjected, without paying much attention to what they were talking about, to say something about one of Pascal's books. After dinner, when Pascal suggested they go to the bar in the hotel for a drink, Prem said he was tired and wouldn't be joining them. Back in his hotel room he found himself calling Maya. Her voice sounded subdued, dampened.

"I thought I'd never hear from you again."

"How have you been doing?"

"First I was upset, but then I was really worried because I tried your number several times today and there was no response."

"I'm in Mont-Saint-Michel with Pascal, who's trying to put the make on a lady in the bar. You would like it here. The colors of the sky are muted, a bit pastel, but extreme."

"Pastel like Degas?"

"Not quite. Have you been thinking of Degas?"

"I've been thinking of you. I know I shouldn't be saying this because our interaction has been so restrained, but I can't be restrained anymore. I don't feel even remotely sane around you, and yet I force myself to act sane all the time."

"Now now, Maya. You're being dramatic. You feel perfectly sane around me. Our little tiff just upset you."

"It brought home the truth."

"What did it bring home, dear?"

"You're a big man. I'm just some young chick who keeps you amused when your friend is busy chasing girls or doesn't want to go to the museum."

"You know that's not true."

"Of course it is. It has to be. You're larger than life for me. I imbibed you for so long through your books, I never questioned we could be friends. I was stupid enough to think we were friends. But there's an intrinsic *déséquilibre* between writer and reader, famous and unknown, old and young."

"There's no imbalance. We *are* friends. I'm calling you. I miss you. I saw things that reminded me of you, and I wished you were here. What did you do?"

"I cried. I tried calling my father when I couldn't reach you on the phone. But I got my mother. She's crazy. Depressed. Like a dead person. It frightened me that I'd turn out like her. The world seemed so far and inaccessible without you."

"Maya, you never told me."

"I wanted to have only happy moments with you. Moments that would make you want to keep seeing me again."

"Do you think I'm so fickle that a little unhappiness would send me away?"

"I'm ashamed of how I feel about my mother."

"You never, ever should feel ashamed with me."

"If you talk like that, I'll not have any control over my feelings anymore."

"Stop being silly. Can we meet for dinner when I get back? You'll see nothing has changed."

"When do you get back?"

"Not sure. Another day or two, I'd guess."

"Thank you for calling. I was afraid I had lost you."

"I don't make friends easily anymore, so I intend to keep you."

Prem went to bed replaying what Maya had said. With Julie and Valérie it had been different, he had given his heart, but he had never thought it could last and he'd wanted nothing from them. Usually at the first sign that a woman was opening up to him, Prem made for the exit, but with Maya he felt a desperate desire to grab her tight and hang on for dear life. To ask her her woes and share his.

The next morning Jean-Pierre called Maya to suggest they take a walk in the Bois de Boulogne. He picked his way with care.

"No, this way. Trust me," he said when she veered off the path he had chosen.

They were circling the lake. As soon as Maya caught sight of the island in the lake, she scanned the lake for a bridge over which they could cross it. As they walked on, she realized there were two islands, not one. Between the thick vegetation and the curves of the land, it was not evident if the bridge between the two small islands also connected with the main park. Jean-Pierre watched her intently.

Her eyes came to rest on the statue of a couple that sent a shiver through her legs. Four legs, four thighs. Legs with an immense muscular energy that electrified her own legs and transmitted the energy all the way across the rippling water to where she was standing. A man and woman were embracing. They were lightly touching each other and embracing. Was this a single statue? Or was it two statues? She wanted to ask Prem if they were two or one. It was important what he thought. She had to get on

the island and see the statues from up close so that she could examine whether and how they were connected to each other.

"I love them. I wanted you to see them," Jean-Pierre said. He
had a deeply satisfied air about him. He clasped her hand.

"Can we go across?"

"I will take you there, but you must be patient."

Maya walked to where the path curved so that they could
loop back up and across over the bridge. Jean-Pierre with his long
legs usually walked faster than Maya, but today she was propelled
by the kinetic energy running in the legs of the statues. At the end
of the curved path she ran down a few steps, sure that the bridge
was hidden behind, only to discover a bench for sitting and staring
at the lake.

"Just a little longer," Jean-Pierre said.

Several minutes later they arrived at a small platform where
a boat was standing.

"There's no bridge—we have to take this."

Maya hopped onto the boat, but then immediately hopped off.

"What's the matter? Are you afraid of the water?"

She shook her head. *What to tell him?*

"I don't want to cross and see the statues immediately. I'm not
ready for it."

He smiled.

"Where did you get your hair cut?" he asked, running his
hand through her hair.

"I cut it."

"It's very messy, but it looks good on you. It highlights your
jawline, which is very arresting, and your elegant neck."

He ran his finger on the edge of her jaw and then caressed
her neck. Her skin there was sensitive, and his touch made her
shiver. She pulled away.

"Can we go back? The breeze is getting chilly."

On the metro Maya was in her own world. After riding for

several stops in silence, Jean-Pierre asked her, "What happened? Still worried about your old man?"

"I spoke to you about my father?" Maya said, startled.

"You told me Prem wasn't speaking to you."

"He called me. He's not in Paris at the moment."

"What did you think I was talking about?"

"My family. My mother's nuts. My father has turned into a full-time mental health official." She spoke flippantly, not wanting to engage in a real conversation but needing the weight off her chest. The load had somehow magnified after the misunderstanding with Prem. Prem and her parents had become intertwined.

"I'm sorry. Is this what you referred to when you said your boyfriend left you?"

"Yes. But he knew about my mother's illness long before he left me."

When they got out at Pigalle, which was equidistant from both their apartments, Jean-Pierre invited her to dinner.

"No, I need to go home. I want to contact my father today."

Prem's call and the statues had given her a new lease on life. She wanted to reach her father while she could still be the daughter giving love and not the daughter in need of love.

The next morning Prem found Pascal sitting alone at breakfast in the restaurant.

"Et alors?"

"She's getting ready. I promised her we'd take her to the castle at Fougères if we manage to see the monastery here before noon."

"Are you feeling better?"

"Infiniment."

Prem laughed.

"One fuck is all it takes, huh?"

"Don't disdain a fuck. In the end that's what makes life real. You think a book is real? Sure it's real, but never, never as real as flesh. The humidity of a woman's cunt, that's what's real."

"While it lasts. And it doesn't last forever."

"Sure. You want to say that our books will last forever, I understand that. But even if the books are eternal, we are not. The only difference between me dead and me alive is that me alive eats and fucks and pisses and shits. I'm sixty-five. I know I won't live forever, and I don't want to forget the basic things ever again. The superfluous and the redundant are the luxuries of youth. I'm living the rest of my life on a timer."

"Did Cary give you this idea? What did she do to you?" Prem asked, amused as he sipped his *café*.

"She sucked me. She let me fuck her and screamed her head off."

"Cool it. She'll walk in here, and I'll feel uneasy if you tell me anything more."

"Mon vieux, when did you become a prude?"

"When I stopped having sex," Prem said drily.

"I think I should have a chat with Maya. You're behaving like an adolescent trying to woo a woman for the first time."

Cary arrived. She wore a strong floral scent that made Prem recoil. He worried about how he'd sit in the car as they drove around the countryside all day.

"A hot chocolate for me and a croissant," she ordered. She pronounced the *t* in *croissant*. She wolfed both down when the waiter placed them in front of her. Prem groaned inwardly as he observed her remotely. Damn Pascal for saying those things.

"We're slow, so if you want to see things by yourself this morning, we can just meet you at noon," Pascal suggested.

Cary disappeared with her guidebook. Prem ordered a decaf, and Pascal smoked.

"I haven't seen you light one of these in a long time."

"I bummed it from her."

"Should we start our slow-motion geriatric ascent upward?"

"We better, or we won't be back in time."

They left the hotel and made their way up to the ramparts where they had been at night. The place was now milling with tourists.

"I'm glad we came here when no one was around," Pascal remarked. After a five-minute break at the vista, they climbed up to the entrance, where a small line of tourists were waiting ahead of them.

Someone recognized Pascal and said *bonjour*. In a few minutes a security guard with a badge arrived and led them through a side entrance. He handed them two tickets. Pascal dug into his pocket for money.

"No, the city of Mont-Saint-Michel is honored to have you," he said, and disappeared.

Prem slapped Pascal's shoulder. "Always useful to know a famous man."

Pascal glowed. It had made his day. With renewed enthusiasm he led them both up the ramp and inside the abbey. They walked around in a somewhat desultory fashion, stopping and looking at maquettes of the abbey from earlier times and reading the descriptions posted in its various rooms. The increasing number of tourists around them was making Prem mildly claustrophobic. He focused on the woman ahead of him with thin, twiglike ankles carrying a baby. She was of some sort of Asian origin, and the baby looked twice her size. He imagined how easily her ankles could snap and break as she climbed up a step, the fragility of the connection between her body and this earth.

"Let's go left—there's a terrace where we can breathe in some air," Pascal said, grabbing Prem's hand in the crowd.

Prem followed him out and felt a blast of air hit his lungs. In the mild morning light the marshes surrounding Mont-Saint-Michel seemed calm. There was almost no wind. There were different kinds of light and dark clouds in the sky. It was hard at times to discern stray patches of water from the marsh, but if Prem concentrated, he could see the reflection of the sky in the water broken up wherever the marsh interrupted the water.

"I'm not inclined to finish. I think we saw what we had to last night. We got a real flavor of the place then."

"I'm in agreement. We should find a pleasant *terrasse* in a corner somewhere for a coffee and then head out with your girl."

It took them half an hour to make their way out and plant themselves at a table overlooking the marshes.

"I spoke to Maya. She said she'd been upset. I'm glad I called."

"You were upset too. Why do you always have to act as if you have no feelings for these women?"

"What do you mean?"

"If you showed them just half the love you show me . . ."

"When did I act as if I had no feelings for Julie or Valérie?"

"Forget them. Or Vedika. I'm talking about the real women. The ones you almost lived with. The ones who were around when you had the flu or had your surgery or needed physical therapy. The ones who drove you around and cooked dinner for your twenty friends. The ones who washed your socks and filed your fan letters."

"I didn't have all that much feeling for most of them."

"You're full of horseshit. You treated them well. We went on vacations with them. Irène and me and you in the beginning. And after my divorce, Ghislaine and me and you. And then when I was living with Kobiko, it was her and me and you and your *minette* of the day. Do you really think you never had any feelings for any of them? Stop being a fool."

"I didn't say no feelings. Just not enough. Not as much as I needed to have."

"How much do you need to have?"

"The person has to become a lifeline, an anchor. Otherwise she's not essential."

"But you weren't drowning! You were in the prime of your life writing a book a year and winning every award there was. You had friends and looks and fantastic reviews. Always fantastic reviews."

"I wasn't drowning *because* I was writing. These women always came after the book. That was the problem. And I usually lost interest after a few books."

"But they weren't in the books."

"Not obviously. But some bit of the relationship was allowed to germinate inside the book, and usually it didn't go beyond one book. I don't know how else to explain it. Maybe that is making it too complicated. In truth we all have only so much love to give. I ran out of the little I had left after Vedika. She was the last one."

"What exactly are you hoping for with Maya? How are you even sure she can deliver what none of these other women managed to deliver?"

"I'm different. I'm not trying to write any books. If I write one, then I'll write one. I think the choice is between life and literature, and I'm tired and I'm going to choose life."

"You'd be better off choosing someone who is not a writer then, *n'est-ce pas?*"

"You think she'll do to me what I've been doing to everyone?"

"No. You're a special case. I doubt she's so warped. But you'd do well to remember that she came to you through your writing. She was first a fan and then a friend."

"Exactly what I've been worrying about. For her I'm probably first a world-class writer and then me."

"Oh! That idiotic choice again between you and you. If we condensed you to your basic, what will be left, my friend? Not the lover, certainly not. But the writer. *Voilà!*"

"Even our own friendship is based on this. On our writing."

"Of course. It always has been. As a writer, one is on the exterior of experience, one is watching. And that's what we have in common. It gives us an honesty that is contrary to a certain kind of living because it demands falsification. Even when we falsify and fictionalize, we're perpetually doing it in service of some truth."

"With age even my relativistic French friend has started talking about truth."

"I said some truth, not *the* truth."

"Nonetheless a greater admission than before. I've been keeping track."

"Is that what got you the prize? The truth?"

"Possibly."

"Do you really think your writing is better than mine? Put your hand on your heart and say it," Pascal said passionately.

"It's so different. We don't write alike."

"Cut that out. Tell me what you really think."

Prem was silent. He knew the answer. Many people knew the answer, including Edward. He felt mildly irritated at Edward for not having done his job as Pascal's agent.

"Do you realize you were scared witless about Irène and about yourself in Paris when you said you needed to make this trip?"

"I was pretty scared."

"It wasn't about sex—you realize that."

"Of course I do. But the answer lay in sex. In face of terror all one can do is affirm, and sex is a form of affirmation."

"And writing is affirmation, and all art is affirmation."

"Your point being?" Pascal asked.

"Next time don't fuck. Write."

"What are you getting at?"

"Face the terror—that's the only way."

Pascal was quiet. Reflective. He turned over the spoon in his empty coffee cup.

"Bastard. You really think you deserved it and I don't?"

"I'm not talking about the prize. We all know it's a crapshoot. There are mixed motivations, luck—it depends on the year. I'm talking about something much more profound: your writing.

"You still haven't written the best book within you. It's crouching inside, hiding from all the terror. The day you write it, you will surpass anything anyone has ever expected. I know this because I know you better than most people, and I see that fear, and I see that your talent has never been applied to it. You've written from the surfaces, from where it's pleasant. You've challenged yourself intellectually, no one can deny that. But you haven't let the beast inside go uncaged. Even if a fraction of that primordial fuel were harnessed into your writing, you will stun yourself with the result."

"Are you making this up to make me feel better?"

"You know it's true. Why are you asking me?"

"Does anyone else think so too?"

"Edward possibly. But you should do it fast. It gets hard to sustain a novel as one gets older. You don't have infinite time left. And in any case if you write it, I want to be around to read it. It would be stupid if I was gone."

"It's very odd you said that. I've thought once or twice that I really want to win the prize while Irène and you are still around. I wanted Pedro around too. And I don't think it's sheer rivalry, my wanting to show you that I too can win it."

"You want the people who count, the ones in your life, to know. I thought of Meher and wished she could have known. I thought of my parents. One realizes how old one has become when most of the people who matter are gone."

"If we continue this discussion, Cary will have to suck me off before our afternoon trip. Let's go find her and save ourselves from this old-man depression."

"I hope her scent has worn off."

"You didn't like that floral bouquet? I gave it to her as a present."

"It's way too strong. I'll sneeze to death in the car."

"Don't worry, I'll tell her not to use it again."

They found Cary at the hotel and drove to the château at

Fougères. The soothing dark gray stone structure was surrounded by a moat. After a walk around the château, they ate galettes and crêpes with a jug of cider, then headed for a tour of the small town with its twisty streets. Pascal spoke to Cary about the major French writers from Chateaubriand to Balzac and Hugo who had passed through Fougères. She took notes. Prem ambled along, lost in his own world, reading the plaques the city had put up quoting various literary greats.

They headed back to Mont-Saint-Michel for dinner. The next morning when Prem came down to the lobby for his coffee, Pascal told him that Cary was staying on for the *grosse marée* over the weekend, when the Mont would turn into an island again. He was relieved. He had been half afraid they would end up driving the rest of their trip with her. In another day and age he wouldn't have minded, but time with Pascal suddenly felt precious. Who knew when they would have this time again? One slip in the bathroom, and he could be bedridden for months. Or something could happen to Pascal. Those arteries had been working overtime for years through several extra millimeters of grease.

The small country roads going east were pretty. Every village they passed looked straight out of a Rohmer film. Prem severely regretted not having asked Maya to come along, almost forgetting that their tiff was what prompted him to make the trip.

As they passed through a small town, Prem noticed a poster for an exhibition.

"A flower show in this fairy-tale town!"

"You like flowers, don't you?"

"Yes. I just don't like flower scents."

"Let's check it out." Pascal swung the car into the parking lot of the Naturoscope and dropped Prem off at the entrance by the glass doors.

"Just orchids?" Prem asked the woman at the ticket counter.

She nodded and smiled, saying, "You speak perfect French, Mr. Rustum. I wouldn't have guessed."

Pascal followed him in.

"Why, we have two celebrities here! What a big day for us!"

Within a few seconds someone had arrived with a digital camera. Prem and Pascal found themselves posing with the woman at the front desk.

"We also have a tropical forest here for a butterfly exhibit. Would you mind coming inside and letting us take a few pictures? That way it can go into the newspaper tomorrow and get us some visitors for the weekend."

They humored her. Pascal broke into an effusive sweat in the tropical forest. Prem felt a bit warm himself. They stood still and smiled. Butterflies came and sat on them. Pascal was about to brush one off.

"Don't—it's more authentic," Prem whispered. Despite himself, he was enjoying this.

The orchids were at their normal temperatures. They were the only ones in the room.

Prem took a long time with each plant. The exquisite vulvas of the flowers were enchanting, astonishing. Pascal was rooted in front of an odd plant with a deep Venus flytrap–like mouth. Prem came up to him and examined it too.

"You found the gem," Prem observed.

"Everything, she's got everything. *Vagin, bouton, poils!*" Pascal took his little finger and stuck it inside the pregnant mouth of the flower. Prem glanced around the room quickly. He felt he was abetting in the rape of a minor. There was an indecency to Pascal's gesture that was worse than the usual public display of affection one saw between young couples.

"Are you finished yet? We're going to get caught," he whispered.

"It's just a flower."

"Not for you. Not for me."

"Touch it—it's remarkable," Pascal said, removing his finger.

Prem let his finger slide over the bulging pregnant cup, a receptacle. On each side it had a leaf that fell down like a curly ribbon. The superior petal was perfectly symmetrical and small, and the clitoris of the orchid was glistening, pointed in that round way that a woman's clitoris does when in a state of excitation. The flower sent a jolt through Prem. Things that were extremely delicate and beautiful had always aroused a tumultuous desire in him: a tumult from which a desire for life seemed to gush out unrestrained.

"Let's get out of here, please."

"Are you trembling?" Pascal asked, laughing.

"No, but I will if we keep this up."

They stepped out of the exhibit room. The lady at the cash register gave them each a copy of the photo taken earlier and asked them to autograph another one she had printed on glossy paper. She stuck the signed photo with tape on the glass door of the main entrance.

"I hope that exhibition room is not under surveillance," Pascal said as they drove away.

"You've got a reputation as a sick fuck already, but what about me? Everyone thinks I'm so decent because I don't write about cocks and cunts."

They burst out laughing.

"Finally, the sexiest moments on this trip had nothing to do with my getting laid. That woman we saw on the highway and these flowers were the erotic highlights."

"Poor Cary. I feel bad for her."

"I feel sorrier for your girls!"

"That was a long time ago. That chapter closed some fifteen years back."

"The mere passage of time has undone your sins, has it?"

"The word *mere* would be better applied to my sins than to the passage of time."

"I think we should drive by Étretat. It's not too far from here. And you'll see what the passage of time can do to the surface of the earth."

"I've seen what it's done to my surfaces."

"You've not been there, have you?"

"No."

"I leave you no choice. *Les falaises sont magnifiques.*"

They went back to the car.

"You're driving—what choice do I have? As long as we are back in Paris by tomorrow and I can take my Maya to dinner."

"We'll be back tonight by nine, even if the traffic is bad."

At Étretat, Pascal and Prem walked on the pebbly beach and looked at the giant rock formations of the alabaster coast. People were walking up the cliffs, and Prem could make out their silhouettes from below.

"That climb is not for us. There is no question of trying," Pascal said when he saw Prem look up.

"Actually I can still feel all the exercise from yesterday in my bones."

Prem scanned the sea. It was a gray-blue color that matched Pascal's eyes. The pebbles in various shades of pale and dark gray, matched his eyes as well. It gave Prem an idea. He used his walking stick to move the pebbles on the shore around and to examine the shells that had washed up. Finally he found what he had been looking for: a flat light-brown piece of marine life, possibly the well-eroded half of an oyster shell. He picked it up and examined it. It seemed to be of the same light-brown tinge as Maya's eyes, and it even had occasional green flecks, as her eyes did on sunny days. He wasn't sure the green on the shell would remain after a thorough wash—it could be just an encrusted piece of seaweed— but he put it in his pocket and followed Pascal to the café by the seawall.

"I just wanted you to see the two elephant tusks dipping into the bay that have inspired Gide, Monet, Maupassant, and Courbet, to name only a few of our greats."

"There are two Monets of this scene in the Orsay. Frankly I didn't care much for them. Courbet's painting of Étretat after the storm is the one that captures its true spirit."

"I went to Orsay with Irène after a long time. I was surprised by how much I enjoyed it. At the end of the afternoon I finally figured out that she had suggested it because she knew it would cheer *me* up. And she used the fact that now she could ask me to do anything and I would do it."

"You're still stubbornly committed to only seeing *art naïf?*"

"Was. Irène made me realize I couldn't undo what I was educated with. My tastes have changed since the last time I was in Orsay. I found myself drawn to genre paintings—artist in his atelier, artist and his model, portraits of artists by other artists."

"Maya was excited by Manet's portrait of Zola."

"Have you seen the *portraits réciproques* that Bazille and Renoir did of each other? Renoir's shows Bazille at work, while Bazille captures Renoir in a reflective mood."

"*Les portraits réciproques.* One showing the other how he sees him."

"More than that, he shows him who he really is. Friendship is what makes the painful truths about oneself tolerable." Pascal's bulbous nose had turned color, a sentimental color.

"The acceptance of a fellow artist. Your friendship, my friend. Yours."

They sipped their coffees in silence together, watching the majestic cliffs on either side that bordered the semicircular bay. Then they hit the autoroute and drove all the way to Paris listening to Beethoven.

Maya took the metro to the thirteenth and walked the long stretch of road toward the *Bibliothèque Nationale*, where the restaurant was located. Prem was already seated inside. He looked at Maya's brutally chopped hair and kissed her on her cheeks.

"Is this a new fashion?"

"I know I butchered it."

The waitress had given him a table beside the large collection of *tommes*. Maya leaned on the glass window that separated her from a huge chunk of Tomme de Savoie.

"Are you ready for this?" Prem asked Maya.

"I haven't yet heard such unfettered praise from you about anything. I hope I haven't been set up for a disappointment."

Prem had asked Pascal to call the *fromager* to make a booking on his behalf and to ensure that Maya and he got the most of his time. After taking them through their choice of vertical or horizontal sampling, Chérif proceeded to recommend a plate of Corsican cheese. Both Maya and Prem chose Chérif's vertical Corsican plate, which promised a progression of sensations from the very mild to the very strong. Chérif recommended a complementary Corsican wine from Calvi—sometimes masculine, and sometimes feminine, always untamed, was how he described the wine.

A young woman, possibly no more than twenty-two, walked in and sat down by herself at a table in direct view of Prem. She spoke in low tones to the waitress who served her. Prem was beginning to see Pascal's point: to see a girl walk in alone for a gastronomic experience was no less exciting than seeing one on the bus reading a book.

Chérif presented them their plates and lectured in high French about the numerous papillae in the mouth that allow for the exhaustive possibilities of taste.

"The wine should be sipped slowly so that the oxygen of your breath can air it for you. The antipasti on your plate will absorb the richness of the cheese. The confiture will reduce the acidity of the stronger cheeses when they reach your stomach."

Maya listened to Chérif without taking her eyes off him. He spoke flawlessly and fluently, as if he had reflected his whole life on the philosophy of cheese. Prem looked at Maya and then at Chérif; when Chérif spoke, it was with the zeal of an evangelist.

"Cut each cheese in half, and commence with the mildest cheese." Chérif pointed to the mild goat cheese. "Then move on to this aged cheese, made with a mix of cow and sheep's milk. This one covered with herbs from the bush should follow it. Always end with the most intense one."

"So I should begin at the six'o'clock position and continue counterclockwise?"

"Yes. At some point you will reach a state where words are no longer needed or sufficient. You will be in pure experience. That is the goal. A moment of gastronomic orgasm."

Maya smiled.

"And what should I do?" Prem asked, looking at his plate.

"The same. Everything I told her is true for you too. Food sets into motion a complex biochemical process that is common to all humanity, though it remains intensely personal."

Maya regarded her plate with concentration.

Prem raised his glass and held it. Maya raised hers.

"To you," Prem said.

"*Tchin.*" Maya clinked her glass with Prem's.

"*Bon appétit.* I'm diving in." Maya cut a piece of the mild chèvre and popped it into her mouth with her knife.

Prem watched her. He had not brought her here hoping to share the same digestive process but rather to look at her face and the expressions that flickered over it. He had brought her to the Maître Fromager to watch her in a moment of profound enjoyment or possibly ecstasy that he had previously not seen.

When he removed his eyes from Maya and put a slice of the same cheese in his mouth, Prem forgot her for an instant. He felt the fluid spread of the white substance on his tongue. When he returned to his surroundings, she was staring at him intently.

"You weren't here. I could see."

"No, I wasn't."

"We could never be on the same page so precisely with a book."

Prem reached for his three o'clock cheese. Maya picked at her antipasti.

"Hmm," Prem sighed.

Maya leaned forward into her plate and carefully cut a thin slice of the cheese.

"It's perfect after the last one," Prem remarked.

Maya was eating with her eyes closed. Prem reached for his glass. The fruitiness of the wine strongly contrasted with the cheese and hit him.

"A form of transcendence open to all," Maya declared.

"Since food is such an intimate matter for you, can I ask why you wanted to cook for me? Why do you want to share this kind of intimacy with me? After all, we're not lovers." Corsica had unleashed its strong sensuality in Prem; its wine and cheese emboldened him.

"Intimacy isn't merely about romantic love. I feel close to you, and I wanted to implicate myself with you in some way."

"And Jean-Pierre? Do you want to implicate yourself with him too?"

"I know the limits of that intimacy. On the other hand, the friendship with you I want to keep forever."

"There is no forever. I'm going to die soon," Prem said.

"I've thought about that."

Maya returned to her plate without expanding further.

Prem looked at the midnight number on their plates. A strong white cheese covered with herbs. Maya was putting it into her mouth. It was his midnight. It was her noon.

"*C'est sublime!*" Maya exclaimed aloud, and looked around the room for Chérif. He was standing just behind the glassed cheeses on the other side from them. Chérif looked at Prem and said, "She said it's sublime."

"What have you thought about my death?" Prem cut a piece of his own midnight as soon as he posed the question.

"A world without you. Without your books. When I hadn't known you, I thought about your death already. I felt sad that one day there would be no new books to anticipate. You're already immortal in a way because your books are immortal, but now you, Prem, are much more important to me than the writer Prem Rustum. Paris without you is unthinkable. I associate even the colors of Degas' and van Gogh's palettes with you. I'm sorry, I've never spoken to anyone about his or her death. It feels like a transgression."

It was a transgression. It was like splitting open his flesh and pushing her finger in. It was like knowing that the piece of cheese in his mouth was stimulating parts of his epithelium as they had hers. It was like taking away something that was his and making it her own. Is this what women felt when men fucked them? Is this what he had done to all the women he had penetrated?

"I have not written for far too long," Prem said.

"Why did you think of that?" Maya asked.

"To live always meant to write, but now I feel more alive than I have since adolescence, and I'm not writing at all."

"Do you wish you were writing?"

Listening to Maya speak about his death had released a certain kind of desire inside him that went hand in hand with violence. The violence of pushing past an acceptable boundary. The erotic and romantic equivalent of writing. Writing was a constant violation.

"I want to write something for myself for a change. I will start tonight." *I will take you exactly the way I want to.* This thought had more force than the bestial Corsican wine from Chérif's cave. Prem felt such a brutal desire for living that it made him feel young.

"Who do you usually write for?"

"I usually write for art. For the artist in myself. Now I will write for the other me."

"Do you know why there is an opposition? I too think of you as two people. And I think of myself too as two."

"I know you do. When we had lunch after Orsay, I thought it was driving you nuts."

"It was. But today I am a slave to real life. You are Prem. This is cheese. And this cheese is more real than what I'm trying to write. There's no struggle between the real world and this one," she said, tapping the side of her head with her index finger.

"I want you to have a sip of the wine to cleanse your palate of the herbs and then to put that strong cheese in your mouth." Prem startled himself with his tone. Prem and Maya had vanished, they were two stomachs.

Maya had a sip of wine and then neatly cleaved the buttery nine o'clock cheese with her knife and put it in her mouth. The jewel in the crown. The climax.

"Vous êtes un génie!"

Chérif, no doubt cognizant that such a moment happens at a certain point in the meal, was already hovering near the table. Trying his best to hide his triumph, he smiled sheepishly and said, "It's the cheese, not me."

"Your progressions are like music, and you know it," Prem said, smiling.

Maya was picking on a speck of jam. Prem, suddenly feeling greedy and impatient, dove into his nine o'clock as well. This time he kept his eyes open and stared at Maya.

"You look as if you just saw the dark side of the moon. S-T-A-R-T-L-E-D." Maya laughed.

"He is a genius," Prem said, reaching for his confiture as well.

"See, we are each of us exactly the same. Our oral sensations compel us to reach for jam after that last cheese. This is my final proof of the possibility of true shared experience. It's rooted in absolute but common subjectivity."

"A second ago you were even doubting the existence of a single you."

"The body is what unites the two people, the writer and the person."

Your body. Can love or desire be so great that both of us could take pleasure from just one body? Yours? Prem looked away from Maya and reached for his wine. With Vedika he could have believed that that kind of love was possible. He wanted intimacy without power—not the power of sex, that would always be there, but the power of fame, accolades, stardom—at this late stage of ripeness. He wanted to love someone with immoderation and without pride, despite whatever risks of laceration it brought with it. He looked through the glass at all the cheese near them. There were small round cheeses with rinds so rancid and green, they could not possibly be fit for human consumption, and yet they had takers. Palates refined enough to appreciate an aged cheese came to Chérif's, justifying the storage space.

"I am like that St. Marcellin."

Maya smiled. "I happen to love that."

"It stinks."

"*L'odeur est profonde.* The French turn of phrase is so much more accurate."

Chérif returned to them.

"Now you will start again in the same order and finish the rest of your antipasti and your wine. You will see that this second time around the experience is different, deeper."

Maya raised her glass to Chérif. So did Prem. He bowed and left them.

"So you already know that I am going to die," Prem said.

This time Maya turned red. She was ashamed. She was going to go on living. When she had spoken to him a few minutes before so frankly, it was because she had not been able to imagine the world without him.

"*L'égalité!*" Prem said aloud, bitterly: as if the taste of a *chèvre crèmeux* could be the same in the mouth of someone with one foot in the grave as in the mouth of a woman still waiting for a lifetime of fame and seduction.

"Please don't." Maya reached across the table and removed the knife from Prem's hand. He put his fork down, and she took both his hands.

"For God's sake, don't feel sorry for me now."

"I've thought morbidly about your death. I've no right to have thought of it."

Prem pulled away from her.

"You *don't* have a right. You don't."

"When you think of making love to a woman, do you think you have the right?"

"Did I ever say I thought of making love to you?" Prem challenged. *For me this is it. My very last chance. There is no retreat.*

Maya sat still. Then she let out in a mumble, "You must have."

"And why must I have? Because you are so young and beautiful and I am so corrupt and old? Because you are a *chèvre doux* and I am a *vieille vache?*" Prem pointed to the window of cheeses.

Maya dropped her gaze. She reached for her glass and drank a sip. Then she stared at her plate and deliberately broke Chérif's order and reached for the *fromage plus fort.*

"Why must I have?" Prem persisted.

"Because *I* have."

He laughed. Suddenly it was all too ridiculous. A man who couldn't brush his teeth in the bathroom sink anymore without getting his toothpaste on his undershirt. And this poor young admirer had suddenly not just made the personal acquaintance of a literary hero but been thrown into an intimate travel partnership with him in a foreign city where he knew people. She had even driven herself, in her awe, to think of being screwed by the older, powerful, established male writer. Wasn't that what he had not wanted?

"That is even less appropriate than thinking about my death."

"How so?"

"At this age death would be a natural occurrence for me,

whereas screwing a young girl like you would be bizarre." Prem laughed loudly.

"Well, both thoughts were equally transgressive when they came to me, if you would like to know," Maya said, shaking her shoulders.

"Your *belle tête* can't even begin to imagine the rancid taste and smell of age."

"You are so wrong." Maya looked with renewed vigor at her plate and decided to attack the remainder of the cheeses in the prescribed order.

"I am touched by your saying you imagined it even if you didn't."

"Why would I lie?"

They were silent for a few minutes. Prem tackled his cheese without interruption, his mind devoid of reflection. When they had done justice to the food, they both looked up.

"What more can I do for you, Monsieur Rustum?" Chérif said, coming to their table.

"Please open your strongest cheese. Your most difficult cheese, and let us smell it."

"I have just the thing for you." Chérif smiled knowingly at them both.

Maya's eyes followed him as he went behind the counter and got out a packed round cheese from the display.

"It's a *Corse fermier* made with raw milk," Chérif announced, coming back with the cheese on a plate. He fished out a knife from his apron and cut the plastic packing. Then he brought the plate close to Rustum's nose. Prem smelled and nodded.

Chérif held the plate for Maya. She inhaled it and then asked, *"On peut le goûter?"*

The *maître* cut a little of the cheese and placed it on the finger that Maya proffered to him. Prem put his right index forward as well.

"C'est super," Maya said.

"All the cheeses that are classified as erotic are put into that category because they usually correspond with some part of the human body. When people don't like a certain kind of cheese, it's usually connected to some real condition in that corresponding part of their body," Chérif explained.

"Are you suggesting this cheese is classified as an erotic cheese?" Prem asked.

"That's right."

New customers walked into the store, and Chérif excused himself.

Prem smelled his finger after swallowing the cheese. The finger smelled stronger than the plate had smelled when the packet had just been opened.

"You still haven't told me if you ever imagined it," Maya said.

"Maya, *you* cannot possibly have imagined it. This is what an old man smells like." He stuck his finger under her nose.

" 'U. Niolu. Fromage de Brebis.' Carries the name of the valley in the center of the island of Corsica. Smells like the anus. An old man smells like St. Marcellin. There's a difference. I happen to know the difference."

"I haven't imagined anything with you." Prem had thought of the idea and had wanted to imagine the act. He had come close to imagining the act. But it had seemed unreal, and he didn't even have a draft of the act in his mind. By abstaining from his pen, he had even avoided thinking indirectly about it. And now as he tried to imagine it, he could only think of the loose pajamas he wore to bed, the number of times he got up at night to go to the bathroom, and how old he felt at these times. It was impossible to imagine the energy of thrust and penetration.

"I can't believe I am more perverted than you!" Maya said lightly.

"You simply have a richer imagination, dear. Not to mention a better sense of smell."

"Desserts?" Chérif was back at their table, one eyebrow arched questioningly.

"What are your recommendations?" Prem asked.

"Fontainebleau with mango coulis."

"Two." Prem ordered.

After dinner they walked out of the restaurant and looked for a taxi. There was little traffic whizzing in from across the Seine over the Pont Tolbiac.

"We'd better call for a cab," Prem said, his eyes scanning the horizon.

"No, there's one coming now. And I think there's another one at the red light."

"Well, hop in. I'll wait for the next one."

"Are you sure? I can drop you off and go on. It won't be out of the way," Maya said.

The taxi drew up. Maya opened the door.

"No, it's fine. I'll wait."

"Prem, I wanted to ask you for something." Maya hesitated. The cab driver turned his head back and looked at her impatiently. Prem saw his face.

"What is it?"

"Can I get a hug? I need to hug you."

"Sure. Of course." Prem hugged her a little awkwardly but squeezed her tightly to make up for his awkwardness.

That night, more restless and sleepless than usual, reflecting on the conversation with Maya, Prem got out of bed and looked out of his window. It was the height of midsummer. The Parisian sky was a deep bluish black, the silhouettes of the nearby buildings visible. Prem slowly loosened the tie of his pajamas and pulled out his member. It was turgid, strong, and hot. He imagined it with Maya. The roving overhead light of the Eiffel Tower swept through his room, periodically illuminating his cock as he moved it up and down.

Prem could no longer put it off. It had been in his head since he had finished writing the last paragraph of *By the Thread*. The book had been published, released, sold, and reviewed, and he had yet to pick up the notebook, which was fresh, empty, and white, with its orange front and thin fine sheets waiting to be filled.

Make a list. A death list.

What would go on that list? He had no idea. In the beginning it was obvious it should be a list of the people to see and talk to before he died. How was Vedika doing? The last time he'd seen her was at a party to celebrate his National Book Award eight years ago. They had spoken warmly. Harry was ill and hadn't made it. How was Harry doing? And Angie? Did he even want to know anything more about Angie? Since he was in Paris, maybe he should call Julie and Valérie. Valérie in the least. Why a list of people? Why not a list of the moods and the music that he associated with his life? Why not a list of feelings? Why a list that looked backward? What better way to go on living than to make a list of the things he still hadn't experienced and the places he had yet to see? He'd never been to Japan. Traveling tired him, but the idea of Tokyo was a bit like the Eiffel Tower: all scintillant, writhing in a pattern for fifteen minutes each hour, effervescent, energetic. Buy tickets for Homi, Ratan, and Deepika, and go to Tokyo for two weeks! Accept, as any old Indian man would have long ago accepted: your place is with your family. Ratan's daily life, his ups and downs, his curiosity, affection, and excitement, were reasons to live. Ratan—Homi's son. Homi—Meher's son. Meher—his Love. With the capital L.

Usually Meher and Prem looked forward immensely to their summer vacation with their cousins. Every two years they visited their cousins in Delhi. Their cousins came to Bombay for a return visit the intervening years.

Prem vividly remembered the summer it all changed, the unbearable ride marking the beginning of the change. It was the first time Meher and he were allowed on the train without their parents. Prem was deemed old enough and responsible enough and strong enough to take care of his sister for the thirty-six-hour ride. For those thirty-six hours they were unable to have physical contact with each other. Meher's berth was in a ladies' coupé, and Prem had a sleeper just next to hers, separated by a metal sheet that went up as high as the last inch of the ceiling. A strong metal net made up the very last inch. They lay with their fingers wound around the metal wire, squeezing each other's thumbs and index fingers, trying to summon all the needs of their bodies to the little inch of space where they made contact.

Their uncle picked them up at the railway station and brought them home. Prem carried their heavy bags up to the third-floor flat, while Meher carried her bedroll and purse. Their aunt showed Prem his room. Of course they were to be in separate rooms! What had he been thinking? Meher reached up, huffing. One look at Prem, and she understood. She unconsciously brought up her hand to count the number of days they were staying.

On their last trip their uncle had lived in a smaller flat. The four kids had slept in the same room. Prem and his cousin Sattu were given the double bed; two cots had been placed on either side for Meher and Rinku. Prem systematically kicked Sattu through the night, and Meher was asked to take the double bed next to her brother. Their cousins would fall asleep quickly. Meher and Prem, used to staying awake past their parents' bedtime, would come close, cuddle, and caress before going to sleep.

The next year it was their cousins' turn to visit Bombay. Prem and Meher had skillfully suggested it best to leave their living arrangements unchanged and continued in the room they shared. Rinku, still small, was made to sleep on a cot in their room. Sattu had to take the living-room couch.

In their normal school year they parted from each other at school just long enough to look forward to getting home and having time in bed together, the curtains drawn tight, the lights off, the sheets on Meher's bed soaking up the humid Bombay weather.

In Delhi, day after day passed without them having a moment alone. It was this summer, when he was thirteen going on fourteen, that Prem and Meher felt their first real aches of longing. He wanted to feel his chest spoon her bare back from behind and grab her in his arms. He wanted to caress her belly and her small breasts and plant small kisses where the fine strands of body hair mixed with her long braid. When he kissed her there, she shivered.

His little cousin Rinku, whom Prem had adored second only to Meher, was now simply an impediment. By nightfall Prem found himself resenting everyone because they were obstructing his natural path to Meher, separating her from him, and him from her, one more agonizing night. Meher tried to keep her spirits up, but she was not used to sleeping without her brother's touch and started to look more and more sullen as the vacation went by.

The days passed torturously for Prem and his sister. One afternoon their aunt decided to visit a relative, leaving the kids by themselves. Rinku wanted to play with Meher. Sattu wanted to watch an adult film. Prem and Meher recognized the desperation on each other's faces. It was now or never. Prem picked up his book in Sattu's room and feigned deep concentration. Meher feigned a headache. Their cousins, unable to entertain themselves, fell asleep. Meher tiptoed out of the room on hearing Rinku's first snore. Prem stole off to the kitchen where, he was sure, Meher was headed. Meher put on a saucepan of water to boil in case anyone should walk in. Then she fell into Prem's chest.

"I thought we'd never be able to hold each other." Meher's hands trembled.

"I can't take any more. Let's go back home."

"We have two more weeks. We won't come again. We'll find an excuse next time."

"I can't do it, Meher." Prem let go of his tight grip on her and fell to his knees burying his face in her stomach. She ran her fingers through his hair, tugging at his curls. He looked up into her face, his eyes imploring her for something he did not understand himself. She stroked his face and his eyes that burned from lack of sleep. Her cool fingertips in the summer heat felt like ice. She cradled his chin and then pulled him up by his shoulders till he was standing. They were painfully aware of their bodies in a way that had never happened before the ten-day separation. Meher moved Prem's torso till he was leaning against the kitchen shelves and pulled his face toward her own to kiss his lips.

"What is so unbearable, Prem? You're suffering."

"Not being able to hold you. To touch you."

"To touch me where?" she said.

All of Prem's love for his sister and the yearning that had had his heart beating so hard for ten days moved itself in a concentrated motion southward. The lump in his throat pushed into his chest, swelling his heart, and then farther down to his belly, which clenched like never before into his pants. He closed his eyes.

Meher slid her body down past his. Her face grazed past the buttons of his shirt and her forehead came to rest on his belt.

"I'm going to die," he whispered.

"No, sweetheart, I would never let you." She unzipped his pants and took his adolescent anatomy in the soothing skin of her hands.

That night Prem risked going to Meher's room at night. She

slept on the top bunk of Rinku's bed. Prem moved close to the bed and put his finger on Meher's lip to shush her. Standing with his feet rooted to the ground, he pulled up her nightie and stroked the skin of her shoulders, her breasts, her sex. He let his thumb rest there momentarily before starting to stroke the sensitive skin on the inside of her thighs. He had known then, as he had always since, exactly when she could take no more.

"We need to go back to Bombay," Prem declared over breakfast the next morning.

Meher almost choked on her tea. She wished she could retract what he had spoken. The tone of his voice made his motives sound highly suspect.

"But your return ticket is not for another two weeks," their aunt said.

"I've decided to build a helicopter for my physics project. I have to go back."

"In that case Meher can stay and you can go back," Sattu said.

Meher saw the murderous look on Prem's face and was sure they had been exposed.

"I'm going to go back with him," she said firmly.

"Well, I'll look into changing the tickets," their uncle said.

"We have to ask your parents first," their aunt said. "In any case, Meher, you should stay here for the full time. Sattu is right."

"Yes. Sattu can take the train back to Bombay with Meher. She won't have to return alone." Their uncle looked at Sattu, who seemed more than willing to do so.

"I will only go back with Prem." Meher's voice was hard and low.

"Let's place a call to your parents tonight from the post office," their aunt said.

"I might as well change the tickets first so that we don't have to call them again and again. When do you want to leave?" their uncle asked.

"As soon as possible. Thank you, Uncle."

In two days they were on the train to Bombay. Their parents were told that the kids were just a bit strange. The brief separation they had suffered made them more mercenary of their time together. Almost no day passed when they did not find a tactile expression for their love or a release for the tension in their young bodies. What they had done only with their hands they now started to do routinely with their lips, their tongues, and the hollows of their mouths. Any outside observer watching the four people in the Rustum household would have been sure that Meher and Prem Rustum were a young couple happily in love at the pinnacle of their harmonious lives together.

When Meher was doing her premedical, the parents revealed that they had received a proposal for her marriage.

"Did you ask her if she wants to get married?" Prem shouted, getting up from the dinner table.

"Calm down. You're not the only one who loves Meher!" his father shouted back.

"I can't eat," Meher said, pushing her plate aside, complete misery washing over her.

"I told you they would never agree," Meher's mother said, looking at her father.

"She's already twenty—this is an excellent match," the father said, his voice calmer.

"At least meet him," their mother pleaded.

"I guess you're not even going to ask her if she wants to go to medical school and become a doctor first," Prem said, his voice quivering. "What happened to you, Ma? All your education and your modernity. We were always so proud to say we had a working mother."

"He wants Meher to study further. He promises she can study as long as she likes," the mother said, then added, "In any case, I would never have made it to nursing school without your dad. I did it for him and only with his support."

Meher stood up and carried her plate and Prem's to the kitchen.

"Are you going to throw away everything I cooked?" the mother called after her.

They heard her dumping the half-eaten rotis in the garbage can and rinsing the dishes.

"I am going for a walk," Prem said, getting up.

"I am going to go with you," Meher said, hurrying out of the kitchen and wiping her hands on her pants.

"No, Meher, you're not going anywhere," the mother said.

"I am coming with you, son," the father said. He pushed away his plate.

"You're not going to eat more either?" the mother asked.

"Later," he said, rising to the sink in the corner to wash his hands.

For the next few weeks the parents worked on their children relentlessly. *Life has to go on. You can't just live here forever with your parents and brother. Why don't you want what's best for your sister? You will be off in another year or two to pursue your own dreams and then what will happen to her?*

The lectures left them in different moods. For a few nights they continued to seek each other out, but eventually the things they heard from their parents made them unsure. Prem was hurt but angry, sure at times that Meher really wanted to go off with this eligible bachelor their parents had chosen. Meher told herself that it would be best *for Prem* if she went away. *Why should I be a burden on him when he has his full life ahead of him?*

In the afternoons when they got back from school, they kept out of each other's way. On one or two occasions they found themselves in terrible pain at the same time, his anger and her resignation having evaporated in the face of their mutual desire. At such moments Prem would turn totally rigid and Meher, longing for her brother, would reach out to him. She would stroke his face and neck for as long as it took to draw him out. And then, all of a sudden, they would be in each other's arms, kissing and clinging. As the date of the marriage got closer, this happened with increasing frequency. Their physical appetite for each other was like a burning fire. It spread from Prem's heart to his groin. Meher felt her insides turn hollow. They had sex.

Several months later, in Oxford for his education, Prem received a letter from his mother. Meher was expecting. Prem wrote Meher immediately. He would put through a trunk call for her in three weeks at such-and-such time.

"Are you sure it's not mine?" he whispered across Europe, Afghanistan, Pakistan, and divided Punjab, where the blood had not yet dried, all the way to Meher's ear.

"Yes."

"Certain. You wouldn't lie to me?"

"Never."

Much later, when Meher was dying, he had asked again. Repeatedly. The answer was still no.

"But how can you be so certain?"

"I counted, Prem."

"I've counted too."

"You're a week off."

DNA tests could now answer the question without a fragment of doubt: *Do I, Prem Rustum, want to die not knowing whether he, Homi, is my son? Of my flesh and blood?* Wasn't that uncertainty the sentiment he needed to evacuate most from his insides before dying? But what difference could it make? Would he love Homi more? He already loved him as much as he would a son. He loved him as Meher's son. Meher, Meher, Meher. At least he could join her when he died.

And Homi—so normal, happy, adjusted, having unquestioningly accepted all of Prem's books as products of genius—did he want to throw him into turmoil at this late age?

Prem's mind was churning before he even got out of bed. Were these early-morning reminiscences a sign that death was closer? Or was this the price a man his age had to pay for having meditated on Maya's vulva as he abused himself? Was it like an orchid? An iris? A tulip? A carnation? A lily? Her juices thick? Creamy? Milky? Her taste acidic? Feral? Her lips closed in, modest, like those of Manet's *Olympia*, hidden from view by her hand? Or more like O'Keeffe's oriental poppies? The clitoris—stiff as a sheath, its ten hidden centimeters so erect that the tip was like that of a fountain pen with a gold nib? Or a slippery button, the size of a tiny diamond, that one could never locate for more than a moment here and there? Under his blue-and-white-striped flannel pajamas, he had a boner. He couldn't begin to remember when that had last happened.

Prem undid the tie of his pajamas and pulled them down his hips. He opened the buttons on the front of his pajama top and brushed his left hand over his chest thinking of Valérie, of Julie, of the swimming pool in Provence where the two girls had come running to his beach chair and drawn sensuous circles over his nipples. Angie was gyrating suggestively an inch above his cock as the pungent odor of her insides filled the room. Vedika was telling him she loved him so much that he had taken up all her mind and soul. Without him she was empty, and she would die if he didn't fill every space in her body with his semen, his cock, his fingers, his toes, his tongue, his words, his words, his words.

"I'm filling you," he shouted senselessly as he came.

He recovered his senses soon enough. *Meher, do you think I'm going crazy? Was it like this for you when you were dying? I thought I shared it with you. I thought it was about sadness, grief, occasionally a determination to fight against it tooth and nail. Am I not dying? Is that my problem? Seventy-five and jerking off before bed and on waking up. What am I going to do with Maya? I can't go through one more manufactured feeling. I want to love so much that just the loving hurts. I think she has the potential to rouse that in me. But if I'm not allowed to seduce her, how to go about it? Am I going to write another book before I join you, Meher?*

Prem went through his morning as usual. A shit, a shave, a

shower, a *café* at the bar by the carrefour with the morning news-paper, a few niceties with the waiter, a shot of Paris in his veins. The day was brisk and clean. The sunlight warmed his legs where it fell from the side of the table. Prem ordered a second coffee and opened his blank notebook. He caressed the whiteness of its sheets and pulled out his pen. *Why not tell Maya's vulva what I think?*

The day had begun well. On waking up Maya had gone straight to her yoga mat and practiced for an hour. Then she took two of her notebooks from her trip to India, to find a way of weaving a story around the pages, and headed to find a café. When she was down in the courtyard, she heard her name being called and looked up.

"Where are you off to?"

"Au Rendez-vous des Amis for a coffee. Do you want to come?"

"Go ahead, I'll join you soon," Nadine said.

A few rays of sun were hitting the corner table outside. The waiter brought Maya a coffee. A few minutes later a woman took the next table, brought out her sewing, and started to stitch what looked like a skirt. Apart from the occasional tourist walking uphill past them, the street was empty. Maya thought of the audacious things she had said to Rustum, but with the sun falling on her shoulders and her body in a state of post-yogic calm, it didn't seem all that grave. It was all true. And how could one regret having spoken the truth?

"Are you sure I'm not disturbing your work?" Nadine asked, sitting down beside her.

"No, not at all. I'm in paralysis, remember."

Nadine ordered a coffee for herself and played with one of Maya's notebooks.

"Can I look, or is it private?"

"Go ahead."

Nadine opened a page from the middle and read for a few

minutes. She seemed to have trouble with Maya's handwriting. Then she turned a page and frowned.

"What is this?"

"This is the problem I was talking about. The influence problem. I saw my trip to India through the lens of the old writer's writing."

"Did you do your photo project with him?"

"It didn't go well, and I was afraid I wouldn't see him again, but then it worked out."

Nadine was already engrossed in Maya's notes again.

"But you have your solution right here, Maya."

"What do you mean? I can't find a way of separating any of the interesting observations from his books and characters."

"Precisely. You shouldn't. Just write it as it is. Keep his lens, use it like a filter as you would while taking photos. I promise it will free you."

"Free myself by putting myself in chains?"

"Try it once. Tell me, what happened with him?"

"I told him I'd already imagined sleeping with him. A mistake?"

"It's good. You have to make the first move. Have you been with an older man before?"

"No. I never thought about it. But now I look at all the men in the street who look his age just to see if it's only him or the whole category that I've fallen for."

"I was in love with an old man, a choreographer. He was only sixty, but he wasn't in good health."

"And what did you do?"

"I hung around the cafés where people had seen him and went to shows by his students. I saw him once at a party but didn't talk to him there. Then something happened."

"Did he influence your dance?"

"Yes, it was like the problem you are having. He got AIDS. I knew he was gay, but I still should have approached him when he was in good health."

"What happened? Did you manage to meet him?"

"I will tell you that story, but only after you try the formula I just gave you."

"I should never have complained to you. Now you've found an effective way to stop me from whining in the future."

"You can complain all you want, but only if you try out the solution."

"Fair enough."

Maya went back to her apartment and, despite every contrary instinct in her body, pulled out the first of her India notebooks and sat down to type. She embellished the facts, enlarged the scenes, and provided context, but not once did she cheat on Nadine's suggestion. Prem Rustum's books and his characters intertwined unedited with her experience of India. It was exhilarating to see words on the screen and to hit page preview and find ten pages by the time the afternoon sky had turned ominous. A few minutes later it started to pour.

Maya had been reading *Paris a Halfway House* in Delhi, where she stayed for a week with one of her college friends. The two of them had been drenched in a thunderstorm. When they got home, her friend's mother had greeted them with what seemed a strange welcome: "It's the perfect weather for *pakoras* and some strong tea. What timing!"

Maya had wanted to curl up with *Paris,* but instead, after she and her friend dried themselves, they sat in the covered front porch watching the rain fall as they ate hot *pakoras* and drank tea. In her notebook Maya had written that her friend's mother's remark had made total sense.

The rain now in Paris reminded her of the rain in India. The sight of the black Parisian sky emptying itself out in the absence of *pakoras* made Maya restless. She felt like munching something salty. There was nothing in the kitchen. Pulling on her cargo pants, she left her apartment, umbrella in hand. Rain was coming down furiously, horizontally. The streets had cleared out. Clumps of people were huddled together under the awnings of shops waiting for the storm to abate. Maya's umbrella swayed in the wind, and rain invaded from the front. She went into the local Arab's and bought a packet of chips. She walked back home knowing that chips would not suffice for her restlessness. The meteorological turbulence had pulled it out from inside her and brought it to the surface. She wondered if it was having the same effect on Prem. She wished she were sitting in Prem's plush apartment in the sixth sipping a cup of hot Indian tea. She called him.

"It's Maya. How are you?" Her blood felt thick and congealed. Her internal inquietude belonged to the same domain as sex, melancholy, and doom.

"How are you doing, miss?" Prem's mood was different. His voice was light.

"I was just thinking of you."

"And what were you thinking of me?"

"It's pouring where I am, and I was wondering if thunderstorms make you feel restless. If they make you crave hot tea and *pakoras.*"

"I can't organize *pakoras,* but if you make it here, I'll figure out something for the hot tea. Maybe a *croque-monsieur?*"

"*J'arrive,*" Maya said, hanging up. In four economical movements she let her cargo pants fall and pulled on a skirt. Paris made her want to dress pretty, like a Parisian. She slipped into her delicate white sandals and made for the mirror to have a last look. Her hair was sticking up as though electric impulses were running through it. Maya found a taxi almost immediately at Place des Abbesses.

"I've brewed some tea. The café is sending *croques.*" Prem was sprightly.

"I didn't know they delivered."

"They don't. But I'm there every day and I said something about my health, so they're doing the favor this one time."

"I want to watch the rain."

"Let us." Prem went to the window and threw it open. Fury had given way to a patter. They stood together and looked at the sky. The clouds directly overhead were still dark, but the edges of the horizon were almost white.

"I wanted to see the rain with you," Maya said, taking his hand in hers for a second. She let it go almost immediately.

"I wanted to see you, despite your plucked chicken look," Prem said, putting his hand on her shoulder. He let it stay.

Maya didn't trust herself to speak. She wanted only to feel the weight and warmth of the hand on her shoulder.

"Did you write today? I wrote," Prem said.

"I did too. What did you write?"

The doorbell rang.

"I'm finished with fiction. I started a journal." Prem walked away to answer the ring.

"They're here." Prem took them to the kitchen to find plates. Maya followed him in. As he unwrapped them from the tinfoil, Maya tore one off with her hand and ate a bite.

"I hope you don't mind my using my hands."

"No." Prem tore off a piece as well and then put the tea-kettle on to boil. They remained in the kitchen eating over the tin-foil. When the water boiled, Prem brewed some tea.

"This is really rich. I can't eat anymore," Maya said.

"Let's go back to the living room with the tea."

Prem sat down at an armchair, his cup of tea beside him. The living room was large and felt less intimate than the kitchen.

Maya took another chair. *We are separated by the sides of the armchairs (velvet), the floor (wooden, slatted, almost Caillebotte), several cubic meters of space.*

"What are you thinking?"

"That you are suddenly very far from me."

"I'm two feet away," Prem said matter-of-factly. *It was a good idea to write about all the things I wanted from her. If I hadn't, I'd be sitting here with a phallus the size of the Eiffel Tower.*

"And what are you thinking?" Maya asked, smiling wickedly.

"Absolutely not something I can share with you."

"I've become friends with the girl on the floor below. Her name is Nadine."

"I remember the old couple across the courtyard from you. They were both sitting around in white underthings while we ate dinner."

"They stare into my apartment all the time. And they've become pretty shameless about it too now."

The conversation came to an abrupt end. Prem was Maya's neighbor again. First he watched her as she lay in bed, and then he transformed into the man from across the courtyard standing in the window and jerking off. Any second now he was afraid his anatomy would embarrass him.

Maya couldn't think of how to start a new conversation. Prem seemed somehow stiff and distant. She looked around the room, caught sight of a stack of CDs, went over, and squatted by the pile. It was mostly Indian classical music, the people on the cover all resembling the young men Prem and she had heard at the Villa Seurat.

"You don't have anything less heavy? Like Bollywood."

"There's something in a pile in the drawer just behind there," Prem said, pointing.

"Hmm. Let's see. Not bad. Ah. Okay." Maya kept up her commentary as she pushed AR Rehman into the CD player.

"Turn it up, let's dance," Prem said, all of a sudden rising up.

Maya turned up the music and stood standing by the stereo.

"Come on, girlie," Prem said, grabbing her hand.

Think Valérie. Think Julie. You could do it then, you can do it now. It's just a dance.

Prem moved rhythmically but slower than the music, at half its speed. Now and then he held Maya's hand to give her a twirl. Then he let go of her as she danced beside him.

" 'Mustafa, Mustafa,' " she was mouthing with the music.

"You know this?"

"I heard it everywhere in India when I was there. It played in every bus and train station. In the marriages on the street. When I was in Delhi, there were fourteen thousand marriages on one single day!"

"The stars were aligned correctly."

The next song was slower. Prem came closer and held her, swayed with her. She rested her head comfortably on his shoulder and touched his arm with her hand. They stayed like that for the whole duration of the song.

"My tea is going to be frozen," Maya said.

"I can make you another cup."

"No, no, don't." She gulped it down as if she didn't want to miss the next song. Prem watched her head as she threw it back. The muscles of her throat moved as the fluid went down her throat. Maya brushed the back of her hand over her mouth to dry it and started dancing again to the fast, catchy tune that was playing.

She grabbed Prem this time and spun him. She passed under his arm. She made them both spin simultaneously. Prem was soon tired and stood by one side of the room. She moved faster as the song reached a crescendo, coming to a stop only when the song ended.

The sky had cleared, and the late afternoon sun was drowning the city in its glow.

"We should go for a walk," Maya said, leaning out the window.

"I have to go to dinner, but I'll take a short walk with you."

"Let's go." Maya carried the teacups and plates to the kitchen.

"Leave them. The maid will do them in the morning," Prem called after her.

"Before we leave, I have something for you."

"And I have something for you," Prem replied, going to his study, where he had put the flat brown shell from Étretat.

Maya handed him an envelope.

"Here. All the way from Étretat. It goes with your eyes. Let me see." He pressed the shell against her neck, where it would sit if it were hung from a necklace.

Maya blushed. Prem had never said anything about her eyes before. She put her hand over his for a second and pressed it into her collarbone before taking the shell from it.

They left his apartment and walked out onto rue du Cherche-Midi. Maya skipped a little, then looped her arm through Prem's. She whistled.

"You seem happy."

"I am. I'm the happiest." She turned to him and kissed his cheek.

"That's nice," he said, smiling, feeling his own heart filling with her high spirits.

Prem walked Maya to the metro at rue du Bac and took a cab to Pascal's.

"You look happy, *mon vieux,*" Pascal said as he opened the door in his apron and kissed Prem on the cheeks. His slight stubble tickled Prem.

Ella Fitzgerald was slithering out of the stereo in Pascal's living room. Prem grabbed Pascal's hand and danced toward the living room, crooning, "I'm the happiest."

Prem fell into the plush leather sofa pulling Pascal into it with him.

"You're going to be even happier when you put what I've made in there." Pascal pressed his hand onto Prem's stomach and then his own.

"What is it?"

"Lamb with truffles to go with the nineteen eighty-two Château La Tour Haut-Brion I just acquired."

"I just ate half a *croque,* but I'm hungry again," Prem said.

"*Hop!* I have to finish in the kitchen. Stay here." Pascal pushed his right arm into the sofa armrest to use his legs and arms to carry the weight of his stomach.

"I'll come with you." Prem was swiftly on his feet.

Pascal's kitchen was fragrant with the smell of lavender.

"Did you bring it from the countryside?" Prem pointed to a bush that sat in a gigantic glass vase.

"Yes. I brought home-pressed olive oil from Cavalier's estate, *mirabelles* and fresh mint from Irène's, jam from my cousin's house—and a change of ideas for myself."

"All in a day?"

"I told you, life on a timer."

"What kind of change?"

"I'm going to address the critics and take them head-on in my next book."

"Go on." Prem was curious. Usually any mention of *critic, criticism, critical, critique,* the Latin *criticus,* or the Greek root *kirtikos* put Pascal in the foulest of moods.

"For the last fifteen years they've accused me of writing similar books that treat the same subject, yet not one of them steps up to analyze why each book outsells the other. If I'm merely repeating myself, I wouldn't be so enormously successful. They focus on finding a formula for my work; they treat it like genre fiction, except the genre is *Pascalien.*"

Prem nodded. He was familiar with this train of thought.

"Well, I'm going to take the bull by its horns. I'm going to address the question the critics don't ask and can't answer. I'm going to apply the full logic of their critique to my work and turn it around to present it as my critique of theirs!"

"How are you planning to do this? Essays?"

Pascal pulled the lamb from the oven and tested it with a knife.

"A novel. And just like the rest of my novels, it will be about a famous writer, me. I'm going to use elements of the plot I already used in the other novels but recast them."

"If I follow, you're going to pull out sections of previous work and build a new story with the same scenes."

"Yes!"

"The same pages?"

"No. The same scenes, but I'll rewrite them, keeping only the essentials. Pedro would've loved this idea."

"I haven't spoken to Laura for two months. Do you know how she is doing?"

"I spoke to her yesterday when I was with Irène. I can't believe she's still living in that dismal gray city that she complained about every day when he was alive."

"She doesn't want to leave the house where they lived. She doesn't want to leave him just because he's dead. That's what she told me," Prem said sadly. He had had an irrational desire to stay on in the house where Meher had died, even though it was her husband's house.

"He's dead! He's free! He'll move to Granada with her. That's what Irène and I tried to tell her yesterday."

"I'll call her this week. I've neglected Laura."

"The only one of us three who had a real family life, a wife, kids, is the one who dies the earliest. If I were dead, really very few people would miss me," Pascal said.

"*Arrête!* Is that lamb ready yet?"

"The wine has respired for an hour. Do you want to pour two glasses? I'm just going to toss a tomato salad."

Prem poured out two glasses from the vintage Bordeaux, whistling.

"You haven't told me what happened to make you so cheerful."

"Nothing has happened. I don't know if it ever will. But right now I don't need anything."

"I was thinking about what you said about loving someone without the element of artifice that seduction introduces. I've been thinking a lot about love because of Irène. I don't want Irène to die, but I think my reasons are selfish. She loves me. She's the only woman who really loved me, not for my fame, not for this *hôtel particulier,* not because I seduced her, but for me. And I don't want her to die because I don't want to lose the only person who has loved me so totally. My motive has nothing to do with my loving her. I love that she loves me. The knowledge of this egoism is too much sometimes."

Pascal was tossing the small quartered tomatoes with olive oil. Prem brought his hand just above the tie of Pascal's apron and squeezed his thick red neck.

"You're being harsh on yourself," he said. Then he wore Pascal's kitchen gloves and carried the lamb to the dining table.

Pascal followed him with the tomato salad. In his other hand he carried a side of truffle sauce. He served them the salad before sitting down.

"Why not start?"

Prem picked up his fork.

"Oh! I forgot the apron." Pascal got up, untying the apron as he walked toward the kitchen. Prem waited, holding the fork and knife in his hand.

Pascal walked back and took his seat. *"Bon appétit!* I want to make Irène feel better. She's afraid, and I am too."

"How much time have the doctors given her?"

"They think they can extend it out for several months, maybe even a year. But the diagnosis changes every few days."

"When I went to see Meher toward the end, they had given her one month. If one discounted the hours she would spend sleeping, she had less than five hundred hours to live. I've never been so greedy about time. I counted every second of the five hundred hours. I still remember that is one-point-eight million seconds. One-point-eight million seconds too few, they were. I put all my energy in trying to live those five hundred hours fully with her, to make her live them."

"If I slept again with Irène, I think it would give her a lot of pleasure."

"Do it."

"I can't. I don't love her enough."

"Since when has that stopped you?"

Prem cut into the lamb and poured some of the sauce over it. Pascal's talent in the kitchen was extraordinary. He wanted Maya and Pascal to eat each other's food.

"You're misunderstanding me. I don't have any physical desire for her, and I don't love her enough to be able to overcome the hurdle."

Could one ever think of loss unselfishly? If Maya had thought of his death, it was because he put her in a good mood, he was an instrument no more or less than Irène was for Pascal. For that matter, when he had lost Meher, hadn't he suffered because someone who mattered to *him* had gone?

"You're silent. You won't react to that?"

"It's called a mercy fuck back in America."

Pascal laughed. They ate quietly for a few minutes, each in silent conversation with their dead and dying.

"This is really good."

"Have some more."

"I'll have some more of the tomato salad. It smells heavenly."

"Cavalier's olive oil is superb. I ate lunch with him when I went to pick it up. Valérie was there with her kids, and I told her you were in town. She said she'd like to see you. Are you tempted?"

"Yes, I'm tempted. I was thinking of her the other day. How does she look?"

"Very good. She has two kids now, but she's still got her youth."

"I think all the time of the past. I'm drowning in my memories. Maya has triggered something in me."

"That's never happened to me." Pascal frowned. He helped himself to some more lamb.

"When you fall in love, you never think of all the other times you were in love?"

"No. Do you always compare like this?"

"I don't compare them. I just remember the range of feelings from the past."

"Maya has to be every woman you already loved in order to fulfill you. Poor girl."

"She doesn't have to be anyone."

"Of course she does. She has to be more than just Meher or just Vedika. Your mind has mixed them all together and distilled all your love sentiments into a single essence."

Love sentiments into a single essence! Where had Pascal learned such English? From the first time they had met, he had presented such jewels on a regular basis. Pedro had been even more excessive. After Pedro had moved to the English-speaking world, even though he continued writing in Spanish, his language had taken off. Every verb and gerund was perfumed with the scent of Spanish. When Pedro had died three years ago, Prem's first thought, preceding the sadness, was *Thank God it's not Pascal. I'm much closer to Pascal.*

"I'm afraid I'm just turning into a sentimental old man."

"Write something unsentimental to get out of it. Sentimentality is the worst disease."

"I am writing!"

"You are? You told me you weren't writing."

"That was before your day in the countryside. I'm also responding to my critics."

"Which critics?"

Prem ignored the sardonic nature of the comment.

"The usual criticism that I don't write about sex. This is only sex. Pure sex."

Pascal whistled. "I can't wait to read it."

"It's not for publication. It's my journal. After fifty years of writing, I am finally keeping a journal. Writing only for myself."

"And you're writing about sex in your journal? "Pascal roared with laughter.

"What's so funny?"

"We use sex to sell everything now, but you're making it deliciously private. It's the ultimate subversive act. No one even knows of your subversion!"

"That's a flattering idea, but it's just my daily dose of Viagra."

Pascal roared with laughter again, slapping the table with his hand. "You're really writing for your dick?"

"I don't know if I'm writing for it, but it's certainly grateful to me."

"I don't know what is more marvelously sick—your libido being a slave to your literature or your literature retiring to entertain you privately in the pages of your diary."

"None of it is sick if it can give me what I want."

"And what is your agenda, Mister I-don't-believe-in-manipulation?"

"All the artifice in the world colluding to take me to a point beyond artifice. I want something with Maya that is beyond all my past experiences with love, beyond my fame and success. Just pure feeling. I want us to be pure stomachs eating cheese!"

"Chérif has seduced *you,* and there I was afraid he would snatch her away from under your nose. But you're being naïf. What is pure feeling? She's a hot little number who doesn't just read but also writes."

"I'm not denying that. I just want to step out of myself and experience her totally."

"Before this weekend with Irène, I wouldn't have understood that. I think I have a vague idea of what you are saying. It's a naïve idea."

"If I can't be naïf now, when will I start?"

Prem went home and opened the envelope Maya had given him. There was a rough sketch of two people kissing.

I saw these two figures yesterday placed on an island in the Bois de Boulogne. Even from across the lake I could see that the energy in their bodies was very extreme. Somehow I felt that it was a single sculpture even though it was not a single piece. The island is inaccessible by foot, but when I had the chance to hop across it on a boat I couldn't. I knew I wanted to see it with you.

He opened his journal and this time addressed it directly to Maya instead of her vulva. He couldn't escape the women of his past, not even Angie. But he didn't need to put Maya through his past. He wanted the five hundred hours in whatever shape or form they came. With or without art. With or without food. With books. Without books. Without language. With French or without English.

Maya emerged from the metro at Abbesses to a message from Jean-Pierre on her cell phone. He had bought some girolles in the market and was cooking. They ate and watched a Claude Chabrol film on video before going to bed. Maya was almost glad for the contact with Jean-Pierre. Gentle, considerate enough, it soothed something in the middle of her chest that hurt when she said good-bye to Prem.

Her relationship with Prem had remained cerebral, and Maya often had the sensation of floating in and out of pages and words when she was with him. Of being a cloud. With Jean-Pierre she had little doubt she was flesh. She was only flesh. They had sex, and he discharged with a moan, yelling *I am going to finish.* Maya lay awake thinking of Prem. But what could a man of seventy-five give her by way of his body? More important, what could he take from hers? He had probably risen above needs of the flesh by now. Jean-Pierre turned in his sleep and embraced her. His armpits smelled like the humid towels in his bathroom. Maya turned her back to his body.

In the morning Jean-Pierre had his head to the side, the hair under his arm glistening with sweat. His porous white skin and muscles were the texture of gravel. The idea of further physical contact with him was abhorrent. The room was hot and stifling, her throat parched. Maya washed her face.

"You're leaving so soon?" Jean-Pierre stretched in bed, waking up.

"Yes, I have to. See you later."

Maya left abruptly and ran down the one flight of stairs to the ground floor, slowing only once she was on the street. The upslope of the road between his house and hers felt sharper than usual. The breeze blowing on rue des Martyrs gave her gooseflesh on the arms.

Jean-Pierre, who had been a pleasant distraction, was now a burden. The conversations were turning tedious, the phone calls to say hello were a terrible chore. Maya could anticipate the dread these simple acts would cause her, were in fact already causing her. She hadn't and couldn't imagine the graphic act of sex with Prem. But she imagined routinely that they were close, naked—metaphorically speaking. And that kind of closeness forcibly implied sex. She just couldn't go on as if the idea hadn't crossed her mind, even if he said it hadn't crossed his.

Back home she showered and stared out at the common courtyard she shared with the rest of the inhabitants of the building. A black cat with green eyes purred on the ledge of one of the apartments. Her phone rang.

"Am I disturbing you?" It was Prem.

"No. You couldn't disturb me if you tried."

"I'm thinking of going to the Rodin Museum. Want to come?"

"I can be there in half an hour."

The ride on the metro passed as if someone else were making the journey. Maya jumped out at Solferino and walked to the museum. The government buildings along the way stilled her restlessness. There was no better antidote to the tremulous longings of the breast than the State and its evident presence everywhere. The first time she visited the Rodin Museum with a friend, she'd insisted they also go to the Invalides since it was so close.

"But you can't mix the two. It's criminal," he objected.

With her arguments—limited time, leaving Paris in a week, Napoleon too is France—Maya prevailed, only to her immediate regret. The militaristic statues dotting the inside of the Invalides, the gargantuan tombs of war heroes in over the top black-, white-, and pink-veined marble, the hideous gold leaf superimposed over *n'importe quoi*, were suffocating. Everything delicate, precise, and profoundly individual that had been evoked within her by the works of Rodin and Camille Claudel was assaulted just five hundred meters later by the grand vision of empire: a vision where the State and not the nation (a nation of people, a nation of Rodins) was paramount.

Prem was waiting at the entrance on rue de Varenne. He had a red silk scarf around his neck. He had written another five pages about the possibilities inherent in Maya's anatomy, fusing the images easily from the previous ones in his life. It had made him miss her. He could transport himself into the world of his memories at the snap of a finger, but these memories didn't come with her voice. He wanted to observe her closely, so that when she wasn't there, he could re-create her with greater accuracy and fullness in his mind.

"You're looking very handsome," Maya said, kissing him.

"So are you." It was a tongue-in-cheek comment on the male cargo pants she was wearing. His phone call had rendered her so impatient that she had left without changing out of her work pants. She usually wrote in her cargo pants because she could carry her sharpener, pencils, and small notebook in its pockets to the café.

They took in the rooms on the ground floor. Maya circled Camille Claudel's jade sculptures, her lips quivering. Prem and Maya hovered over different statues, deliberated over different angles, but moved at the same pace from one room to the next. Prem sat for a few minutes after they were finished with the ground floor.

The rooms upstairs were priceless for Prem. *Is she going to feel the same tactile need I do for the toes and asses, hands and spines, necks and spinal columns of the statues?*

Prems reflections were short lived. Even before he was finished with the first room, he felt his body covered with a peculiar sensation. If it had been stronger and less pleasant, it would have been an itch. In the next room, at the first glimpse of the naked woman holding one foot in her hand, her *origine du monde* open to the world, Prem's sex in his pants was less fleshy than the bronze statues in the room. Maya was closely observing an old woman titled *La misère*. It was hard to focus on her and not on his own condition.

"Look, her body is sagging. Such sheer genius to use a substance as hard as metal to convey the softness of old flesh folding over itself like this." Prem looked at Maya's hand as she pointed through the glass cabinet at the woman beyond. He wanted the hand to move toward him and discharge him as a lightning rod takes the electricity from the sky.

"What do you think?" Maya's hand was really moving, and he could see it would come to rest on his shoulder. He stepped aside to another statue. If she touched him, he was sure he would come in his pants.

Prem maintained a good deal of distance from Maya. Had Pascal crushed some slow-release Viagra tablets into the truffle sauce? Neither the colossal head of Balzac nor the staid Victor Hugo alleviated Prem's condition. Rodin's Balzacs got fatter and fatter from one statue to the next. Prem thought alarmingly of Pascal; he should have said something when Pascal served himself a third helping of the lamb. As they moved past the room of public monuments and went to the marbles and plasters, Prem could anticipate he was in for worse. There it was, the bearded old man kissing the young gamine, *L'homme et sa pensée*. Prem felt a new surge of testosterone. The glass case was thoroughly insufficient in protecting him from whatever emanated from the work in plaster. He was at maximum tumescence.

Prem, priapus, *pensée,* penis, pastel, patisserie, *panna cotta,* palate, *papille,* peach, pool, petal, poppy, pajama, pillow, pen, palette, paint, paper, priapic, prem. *I should really excuse myself to the bathroom and take care of this.*

"We still have to see the rooms on the ground floor to the side."

Prem nodded. They walked down the stairs and into the rooms they had missed. When they were finished with the inside, they walked around the neatly groomed garden. Prem was sure everyone could see his erection through his pants, everyone but Maya, who he had been careful to keep to his side all the time.

They walked around the statue of Ugolino, reflected in the still water beneath it. Past the hedge that provided the statue with a backdrop was a garden with easy chairs. Maya stretched herself on one and tapped the one beside her for Prem to come sit. From her low perspective he would be compromised. He maneuvered himself and stood behind her easy chair. Luckily the sun disappeared behind clouds, and it got cold.

"Brr."

"Why don't we go back to my place?" Prem suggested.

"Yes, some hot tea." Maya sprang up from the chair.

In front of the museum someone dismounted from a taxi. Prem directed Maya in and followed. He folded his arms and leaned forward, giving instructions to the driver.

"Are you okay? Do you have a stomachache?" Maya asked, concerned.

"I'm fine."

The seven-minute ride was interminable. *Is something wrong with me? I need to call a doctor.*

In the apartment he excused himself immediately. In the bathroom he pulled down his pants. There it was, accusing him, pointing straight up to the ceiling. Prem closed his eyes and tried to think of Maya. He could tell it wasn't going to work. Even the image of Angie turning herself into a whore for a multitude of lowlifes was going to do nothing.

Please God! One by one they came streaming in, *St. Jean-Baptiste, Sisyphus, La misère, Vertumne et Pomone, Eve, La fatigue,* and eventually as the molten metal from his insides poured out, *Le penseur.*

Relieved, human again, laughing at the absurdity of his life at seventy-five, Prem removed the silk scarf around his neck and washed his face before joining Maya in the living room. She had put on some music and was staring out the window.

"You're not in a mood to dance? *Ça va pas?*"

"I'm feeling moody."

"And what is your caprice today, my young lady?"

"I don't want you to misunderstand me. It's difficult. I feel strange saying this."

Prem inclined his head in Maya's direction. "Out with it."

"Can I hug you? That night after dinner was just not enough." Maya smiled so that she didn't seem too serious.

"Of course." He stepped forward, determined to be less awkward this time.

She rose from her chair and, holding him by the hand, led him to the loveseat in the corner and sat down. They hugged while sitting. He stroked her hair. He had to twist himself a little to do it. He was afraid he couldn't remain in that position for much longer.

"Are you uncomfortable? We can go to your bed. I promise not to molest you," Maya said.

Prem laughed.

"I'm serious. I'm not trying to get into your pants."

"That's what's so sad," Prem joked, getting up.

He led her to his room by the hand. She kicked off her shoes and got onto the bed. It took Prem a minute to unlace his shoes and lie down. He held her tightly at first, but then his grip relaxed and they lay side to side, his left arm hooked under her neck and his hand gently caressing the top of her arm.

"Thank you," Maya said.

"There is nothing to thank me for."

"I wanted to be nearer you. I need some form of physical contact with you."

Prem was quiet. But his hands were talking, and he knew that Maya could not have any doubt that he wanted to touch her.

Maya clasped Prem's right hand in her left and raised them both up into the air.

"Your hands are beautiful. Just so, so beautiful. When you read my hand in New York, I felt like grabbing your hands and not letting them go."

"Gosh! It feels like long ago."

"We've crossed the ocean and time zones. We've climbed over the mountain of time, over weeks and months. But now I want to pause it. I don't want my momentum with my writing to change. I don't want this feeling with you to change."

"It's almost time for you to go back, isn't it?"

"Yes, another few weeks."

"What will you do with Jean-Pierre? He doesn't want to follow you to New York?"

"It's over, but I haven't told him yet. I can't sleep with him. It's too false."

"You weren't so tentative about him earlier. At least you didn't sound it."

"I wasn't. I woke up and didn't want to be there. I saw him and wanted to leave."

"Are you always so cold? Do you just switch on and off?" Prem put his hand in the air and moved it up and down as if he was turning a light on and off.

"Well, it's happened before—change, I mean. Sudden change."

"Your love stops dead in its tracks?"

"No. It wasn't love. It isn't love. I never thought it was love."

"I think it's time to get you out of this bed if I don't want to be seduced."

"I'm going to the *Bibliothèque Nationale* to watch some tapes. Do you need anything?"

"No. What are you watching?"

"An old Jean Renoir film called *La fleuve*. He shot it in India."

"I saw it a few years after it was released. I saw it with Vedika."

"Who is Vedika?"

"An ex-lover."

Maya slipped her shoes on. She left Prem's building skipping. She was still skipping after she turned off to rue d'Assas.

Prem called his *médecin* for an appointment to find out if it was normal for a septuagenarian to turn into an erotoman.

Maya wanted to hear Nadine's story about her old man.

"Nadine, Nadine, *t'es là?*" she called, aware that all the apartments around the courtyard could probably hear her.

Nadine opened her window and waved.

"Come up," Maya said.

Nadine was dressed in very high-cut denim shorts that barely covered her bum. Maya would never have been able to get away with wearing them.

"You're looking drop-dead gorgeous."

"A lifetime of training in ballet," Nadine said as she stood on the tips of her toes.

"Your formula works! I wrote ten pages. Now you have to tell me about your man."

"Did you see yours again?"

The phone rang.

"Yes, I did," Maya said to Nadine as she picked up her phone.

"You're not alone?" It was Jean-Pierre.

Maya mouthed *mon petit ami* to Nadine.

"The neighbor came up."

"The girl?" Jean-Pierre's voice was excited.

"Yes."

"What are you doing?"

"We're drinking coffee."

"I'm coming to have coffee with you," he said, hanging up. He used the plural *vous*.

"Jean-Pierre is on his way. I don't want to deal with him. He thinks we're doing it."

Nadine laughed. "I'm going to leave before he arrives."

"But what am I going to do with him?" Maya sank into her chair and put her head in her hand.

"Tell him the truth if you don't want him. It's always the easiest thing to do."

"He won't believe me."

"When he sees your eyes talking about the old writer, he'll believe you. Come to my apartment after he's finished if you want to talk." Nadine rose and kissed Maya goodbye.

Maya took a quick shower and washed the used coffee cups.

"Where's your neighbor?" Jean-Pierre asked as soon as he walked in.

"She left."

"Did you sleep with her last night?"

"No."

Despite her negative reply Jean-Pierre moved in closer. She stepped away.

"What's the matter?" He was aroused.

"I can't be with you anymore."

"What happened? What did I do?"

"You didn't do anything. I'm in love with Prem."

Jean-Pierre laughed. "You're not serious. Do you want to sleep with him?"

"I don't know. But there's only one logical conclusion to this kind of longing." Maya pressed her belly to show what kind of longing.

"He doesn't bother me. I thought we had something together. Don't we have something together?" He grabbed her hands.

"I'm sorry, I don't feel that way."

"Did you ever?"

"I didn't rule it out when I met you," Maya sighed.

"When did you rule it out?"

"That day in Bois de Boulogne maybe." She winced.

"When you didn't want to get on the boat? You wanted to go with him? *C'est ça?*" He spat out the *C'est ça*.

"Sorry."

"Did you go with him already?"

"Not yet."

"If I tell you not to? Never to?"

"I'm sorry, they are beautiful."

"But I took you there because they are special to *me.*"

"But it's art. You can't own it. Or my reaction to it."

"*Je ne le crois pas.*" He got up and left her apartment, letting the door slam. She heard him noisily go down the stairs and then saw him emerge in the courtyard below her and exit the building without throwing his head up for a last glance at her window as he usually did.

Maya went down to Nadine's apartment.

"I broke up. I was mean, but I don't know how I could have done it better. There is no right way, I guess."

"No, there's never a right way when desires diverge."

"You didn't tell me if you ever met your old choreographer."

"I met him once. It was after he had been admitted to the hospital."

"What did you say to him?"

Nadine had said nothing to the old man. She had danced for him instead. From the time she had watched his choreography performed onstage, she had known she had to choreograph and to dance what he had choreographed. But she was unable to. His work was perfect, and all the dancers in the world who could ever execute his choreography were his for the picking. Nadine too had been paralyzed and then had given in to the influence of his work.

"It's gray outside, it's perfect. I'll show you something," Nadine said as she pulled down a screen by the wall on one side of her bare living room and turned on a projector. Images of dancers came on the screen.

Maya looked at the dancers and wondered how she would watch Nadine at the same time. It was clear Nadine was getting ready to perform.

"Don't worry, your eye will look at what is important, but I have to move you."

Nadine moved the solitary chair in the room to a specific spot and asked Maya to sit. She danced. At moments Maya noticed the couple on the screen behind and Nadine's own body juxtaposed against the screen. But mostly she noticed Nadine. It was a short piece set to Ravel's *Pavane pour une infante défunte.* When Nadine was finished, she drew a collapsible chair from the stack against the wall and sat down.

"I danced that for him in his hospital room."

"What did he say?"

"You see, I wanted to choreograph something that was not simply a copy of his work, or full of impressive moves. I needed something that would convey the nature of my feelings for him, his importance in my life. Anyway, that's what I was thinking when I was trying to work on it, and my problem was that I could never get past the piece you saw on the screen. So I decided to incorporate the whole piece in my piece by having it run in the background. That's why I suggested the same formula to you yesterday."

"I may go and remove my references later, but it did help me start writing."

"He was entirely bedridden in the hospital when I asked him if I could dance for him. I danced and he watched, and I knew that he understood what I had done. For me it was like showing the baby to the father."

"Did he understand that?"

"No, he understood more than I had understood. I sat beside him after I danced, and we looked at each other. He was quite weak, and I didn't want to tire him with words. After I had been looking at him for some time, he said that I had given him the only experience he had never had before in his life. He told me that as a lover he had been both the man and the woman, but he had never in his life been a muse. Someone else was always the muse. I had made him a muse."

Maya smiled.

"He used to be handsome when he was young. In his time he had slept with every beautiful dancer in the world. But AIDS had entirely ravaged his body. He was very thin, and some of his teeth had fallen out. The wrinkles around his face made him look ninety."

Maya nodded. She had a vision of Prem in a hospital bed. And then she had a real flashback of her grandfather when he had been dying. She could just imagine Nadine's man with feeding tubes and catheters weaving between his limbs.

"I didn't want him to tire, so after I held his hand for some time, I went near him to give him a goodbye kiss. He whispered in my ear."

"What did he say?"

Nadine was fighting back tears.

"I'm sorry," Maya said.

Nadine wiped her eyes.

"He said, 'I was never so beautiful in my life. Thank you.' "

part vi

What I am after, above all, is expression.

—HENRI MATISSE, *NOTES D'UN PEINTRE*

Pascal arranged lunch with Valérie at the Place du Marché Ste. Catherine and called Prem. Prem said he would make it as soon as his doctor's appointment was over. The clinic was in the Marais as well.

"Is everything okay with you?" Pascal asked.

"I'm not so sure. That's why I want to just run it by him."

The appointment was shorter than Prem had anticipated. His blood pressure and pulse were normal. His last EKG and blood test from just two months ago had been perfectly normal.

"You're very lucky. It seems that everything from bronze statues to flowers release nitric oxide in the corpus cavernosum of your penis. I don't have any theories for this sudden development except that these events might be precipitated by your new style of writing, based on what you've said."

"Even I wouldn't have thought the pen had the power of the penis," Prem said.

"You are the only one in a position to treat yourself, Monsieur Rustum. That is, if you want to. I can only give you my heartiest congratulations."

"But statues? Even male ones? I'm afraid of what's happening."

"A writer should be used to this. All you creative types have a sense of sexuality that is a bit *décalé*. How do you say it in English?"

"You don't, Monsieur le Médecin. The concept does not exist in the Anglo-Saxon world. That's why I've always been attracted to your country." Prem got up and shook his hand.

In the half-hour Prem had to spare before lunch, he went to the bookstore on rue Pavée. Several hardcover books of interviews with Rodin were arranged prominently on the sculpture shelf, which Prem was afraid to touch lest the word *Rodin* induce an immediate hard-on due to associative connections that had formed in his brain the previous day. A rare book on Maillol's work printed for an exposition in the thirties sat beside the Rodin. Maillol's sketches anticipating his sculptures were printed in the book. The reproductions were not of great quality, but some of the naked nymphs displayed the energy and the characteristic style of the sculptures in the Tuileries. He bought it and made his way to lunch. The others were already seated at a *terrasse* in the square. His heart skipped a beat when he saw Valérie. She stood up on seeing him.

"Such a pleasure," he said, kissing her on both cheeks. She was a woman now.

Then he greeted Irène, who looked gaunt and ill. He wouldn't give her more than a few months.

"Is everything all right?" Pascal asked.

Prem nodded. He didn't want to talk about his perfect health. It seemed obscene in Irène's presence.

"Tiens." Prem handed the book to Valérie. She put it in her bag without looking at it but kissed him again to acknowledge the gift.

They ordered lunch and chatted easily. *Paris was empty this August. The weather was miserable. Jeu de Paume had finally reopened. Not a lot of good movies were out. Six hundred books were being published for this year's* rentrée.

"How many children do you have? What are you doing?" Prem asked Valérie over the *café* at the end of the meal, his face turned away from Pascal, who was sitting beside him.

"I've got two kids. My husband is doing a building project

with an American company, so he is away frequently. I don't work, I'm just raising the kids."

"Are you writing?"

"I'm writing a children's book."

"Your English is very good now."

"I read a lot in English now. Look!" Valérie pulled out *By the Thread* from her bag.

"That's the American edition. Where did you buy it?"

"My husband picked it up for me. Will you sign it?"

"Sure." Prem pulled out his pen from his shirt pocket and wrote in it.

Pascal grabbed the book from him before he could pass it to Valérie and read aloud, *"Un, deux, trois . . ."*

Valérie blushed.

Prem grabbed the book back and passed it to Valérie saying, "Sorry."

"Where are you staying?" Valérie asked.

"The same place."

"I'm going to bring my children to Musée Zadkine in the next few weeks. It's close to your place. Maybe we can meet. You can see them that way."

"Let's be in touch," Prem said as he kissed her warmly.

Prem strolled with Pascal and Irène around the Marais and then went back home. His phone was ringing. Homi was calling from Delhi.

"I managed to get leave and was thinking we could come and visit you in Paris."

"Great! When do you plan to come?"

"Tentatively mid–next week. We can probably spend around ten days."

"I'll send a car to the airport."

"Ratan is really excited. Here, talk to him."

"Grandpa, we're coming to Paris."

"I can't wait to see you, darling. What do you want to do?"

"I want to see the Eiffel Tower. Will you take me?"

"You can see it from my window. It lights up every hour with a squiggly light."

"I already started reading *The Little Prince.*"

"That's very good."

"Do you need anything? Mommy says you can't get good mangoes there."

"I don't need anything except you."

"Talk to Daddy," Ratan said, passing the phone back to Homi.

Prem hung up on his family feeling a momentary release from the emptiness he almost always carried unless he was writing. The news of their arrival shortened the distance he maintained from the world. He went to his stereo and turned on the radio. "La Bamba" was playing. He shook his ass for a minute and heard the phone ring again.

"I've been trying to reach you," Maya said.

"Are you all right?"

"I just need to see you."

"Come over—let's have a cup of tea."

"*Tout de suite.*"

Maya got into the metro reciting: *Mr. Rustum, I love you. Prem, I'm crazy about you. Prem Rustum, I've fallen for you.* She rode all the way to Sèvres-Babylone with her fists clenched tight and her left foot tapping impatiently. She had to tell him regardless of the outcome.

The door to Prem's flat was open. She let herself in and found him in the kitchen.

"Hi. How was your day?"

"It was good. I met someone from the past. And yours?"

"I broke up with Jean-Pierre."

"Do you feel free?"

"One is only free when one expresses oneself."

"And you haven't?"

"Not yet."

"And why not?"

"Because I'm shaking."

"You really are shaking. What's the matter?"

Prem held her tightly and led her to the couch in the living room and made her sit. Once they had sat, he didn't let go of his grip. She put her head on his chest.

"Now are you going to tell me what happened or not?"

She felt her shakes diminish as Prem ran his fingers through her hair.

"Your hands feel so good," she sighed.

Prem kissed her forehead. Maya felt the internal involuntary muscles of her throat in spasm. When the muscles decontracted, she swallowed and spoke.

"Will you do that again?"

When he turned his face down to kiss her forehead, she lifted her face up and received his lips on hers. The first lips in ten years, the first lips since Valérie's ten years ago. The exploration of her tongue, her lips, her gums came naturally to Prem. He ran his index finger on the smooth skin on the back of her neck as he kissed her.

When they finally drew apart, Maya felt as if she and Prem had always been kissing.

"It's finally upon us," Prem said.

"I was not sure you had that kind of interest in me."

"How could I not? But I'm old, idiosyncratic, and crabby. I'm a difficult person." Prem smiled as he played with her hands. He spoke with the slow rhythm of a lover who has all the time in the world to get to know his beloved. He touched her with the same rhythm.

"I've seen your petulant side. I know," Maya said.

"Actually I wasn't certain either until I saw your sketch of the statues on the island."

"We can go there now. We could eat dinner there."

They took a taxi to Bois de Boulogne. Maya had the driver

drop them off as close to the boat as possible. The ride across the lake lasted less than a minute. Maya held Prem's hand as he got off the boat and kept holding it.

"I can hear a peacock," Prem said.

They climbed up the path. Some fifty yards into the path they saw a peacock, his plume fanned out. They both stopped. Peahens were walking around the grass, entirely indifferent to the strutting of the male member of their clan.

"They're not too impressed," Prem whispered.

"Shh," Maya whispered, and took a quiet step toward the peacock. Prem followed.

The bird did not register their presence. They stepped even closer. The bird turned around. His saturated inky-blue neck reminded Prem of the way Krishna was always rendered in Indian temples. In the slight breeze that was blowing, the large fan of feathers with hundreds of blue-green eyes billowed. Maya had inched nearer. She extended her hand now and touched the bird's plume.

Prem noticed the beautiful bird's ugly claws. The claws and the cawing of the bird, both hideous, didn't detract from its beauty. They made the beauty vital in the way that living things were vital, heartrending in their imperfections. The bird moved away. Prem suddenly imagined Maya entirely naked, dressed in peacock feathers.

"Are we going to the statue?" he asked her.

She nodded. They held hands again and walked to the northern tip of the island. Even though Maya knew where the statues were, they seemed to appear all of a sudden. Once more the legs first caught her attention. Prem watched her as they closed in on the ensemble. He squinted at the statues. The posture of the male statue was erect, energetic, taut. But the woman, looking up to the man, reaching for him, was somehow slack.

Maya circled the statues. She peered up and down at their

faces and stepped up onto the pedestal where they were placed to look at the spaces between their bodies.

"I hadn't realized from the other side of the lake that their faces were left blank."

"They must have been commissioned for this spot. This faraway spot."

She moved away from them and came to Prem.

"What do you think?" he asked.

"They are two, not one. I was wrong. I thought that even if they were not touching, they could be one. Imbued with the same energy."

"Are you disappointed?"

"No. You're seeing them with me. That's what counts."

"Should we get dinner?" he asked.

They walked to the restaurant on the island by the boat landing. The air was fresh, and some peahens were roaming in between the patrons. The waiter seated them at a corner table and took their orders.

"How is your family?" Prem asked.

"My father is coping. He is duty bound to her, and I should admire him for it. But I want him to have joy. If he goes away even for a weekend, she stops eating. I can't help thinking that she's punishing him. But he accepts all the punishment. He smiles through it."

"How long has it been this way?"

"Too long. Four years. I used to go often to see them in the beginning, but I can't bear it. And I realized that the only thing that can get my father out of there for a few days every year is a trip to see me. So I insist he come for three days to New York around my birthday and spend time with me. Just with me."

"That's nice."

"He was very reluctant at first, but I told him it was the birthday present I wanted. And now he does it without guilt. It's the only time he lives. We go to the museum. We take a walk by the Hudson. We see a show, go to brunch, browse in bookstores."

"How old is he?"

"Fifty. He's youthful, he's gentle. He deserves to live." She had tears in her eyes.

"And you do too. Maya, I'm seventy-five. We can't be with each other."

She was momentarily stunned. *Why had she told him? Oh, why?*

The waiter took away their plates and placed dessert menus on the table. They were both silent. She got up from the table and went to the ladies' room and washed her face. For the first time since she had met Prem, she felt really confident. Up until this moment she was afraid he would leave, their contact would not last. But now there was a feeling in her belly, the kind an animal feels for its young. She could fight vehemently to the finish for him. Logic was the antithesis of everything they had in common, everything that they had shared. It was art that gave them joy, and she would be damned if he got reasonable now.

She came back to the table smiling.

"The night after our fight, I walked along the quais for a long time. I eventually found myself outside your building. I even came into the main courtyard and sat by the door to your apartment entryway. I didn't think it would have been right to ring the bell. Now it's different. I would ring the bell."

Prem imagined Maya sitting in the cold outside on the steps. The waiter interrupted them, and she ordered dessert. Then she folded the menu and looked at him again.

"You aren't going to lose me as a friend. You know that."

"Stop being ridiculous, Prem. If it doesn't work out, we'll stop."

Prem's heart fluttered at her words. It was said gently but was so entirely out of character, he knew it could only stem from desire. The reverence in her eyes had been replaced by the incandescence of a woman in love. For a moment he felt their roles reversed—he was the young object of desire, and she the older person commanding him. He blushed.

They shared the compote of wild berries that Maya had ordered and took a cab back to his flat, where Prem gave her an extra pajama set.

"I've not done this for ten years. We have to give it some time."

Maya moved close to him in bed and held his hand. His tenderness was so sweet, she could have remained in that state, just a few steps shy of passion, for a long time.

"We can give it as much time as we want," she whispered. Then she slid her hand inside his pajama top and caressed his chest as he fell asleep.

In the morning they went to the café by the carrefour for breakfast. The handsome waiter gave Maya a smile and paid her a lot of attention. Prem sipped his coffee, amused.

"My family is showing up. I need to organize the flat. They'll take the so-called office room. Since I'm not working on a new book, it's not a problem, but I have to clear it up."

"I can help you. I won't get to see you much with your family here. I might as well try to get more of you now."

Prem's grandson had looked covetously at his flannel pajamas, once remarking they were like velvet. Prem wanted to buy two identical sets, one for himself and one for Ratan. He knew Ratan would get excited when he saw that they were both wearing the same thing. The truth was that even Prem, despite his advanced years, took a secret thrill from the idea. At an expensive men's shop Maya helped Prem pick out a soft flannel set in a shade of blue that went well with his silver hair. They had the identical set in a boy's size.

Maya took stock of all the dishes in the kitchen cabinets and made sure there were enough glasses, flatware, plates, soup bowls, and side plates for a family of three to eat. Espresso cups were missing. She bought a set of four from a store on the boulevard St-

Germain. They were sleek and colorful. Each cup was painted different on the outside and the inside. The saucers were different colors entirely.

Having family over was like nothing else. Prem was not alone for a single moment after they arrived. Homi and his wife, Deepika, took the guest room, but Ratan insisted that the settee on which he was to sleep be placed in Grandpa's room.

"I promise you he won't bother me in the least," Prem had to reassure Homi a few times before Ratan could have his way.

Deepika ensured that Ratan was ready for bed in his new pajamas and kissed him. "Promise not to disturb Grandpa."

"I promise." Ratan obediently kissed his mother, got into his bed, and drew the sheets over. Minutes later, when Grandpa got into his bed, Ratan stealthily made his way to Grandpa's bed as if he were trying to hid his voyage from Grandpa himself. As soon as he was at the edge of the bed, Prem lifted his quilt to let the boy jump in. It was their secret.

Prem accepted Ratan's small thin frame in his arms and slid his pillow to share it. His heart filled with immense gratitude for being the recipient of this particular love. At the same time he had the sense of being taken back in time, of being ten years old himself. Invariably, after Ratan fell asleep, Prem lay awake in bed speaking to his dead sister. He heard every breath of their grandson for her sake, remembering the last days before her death, wondering when his own would be upon him. *Meher, I want to die like this, with this lovely boy beside me in bed. If it weren't for the fact that it would traumatize him to find me dead, I can think of no moments happier than the moments with him.*

Occasionally Ratan's size four feet kicked him. In the bedroom, as the rotating beam from the Eiffel Tower illuminated his grandson, Prem looked at Ratan's eyelids, drawn so long and relaxed they took up half his face. In the morning Ratan woke up at the same time as his grandfather. *A light sleeper like Meher and me.*

Prem pulled on his pants to go get some croissants from Poilâne, and Ratan, still in his pajamas, held his hand and accompanied him.

"Grandpa, I think I love you more than Daddy loves you."

"Why do you think that?"

"For Daddy you are his uncle. But for me you are Grandpa."

"I'm still your grandmother's brother. It's just that you've always called me Grandpa because none of the other grandparents were around when you were born."

"But it makes a difference. A grandfather is closer than an uncle."

The woman at the counter handed Ratan a small, fresh *sablé de blé.*

"One for the road," Ratan said, stepping out.

"That's a good expression."

"I wish I had your surname. That way when I win the Nobel Prize everyone will know that two people from the same family won it."

"Marie and Pierre Curie were a husband and wife who won it."

Over breakfast Prem convinced Homi to take Deepika to Versailles.

"But Ratan can be very demanding, especially in the afternoon when you want to take a nap. I think he should come with us," Homi said.

"I want to stay with Grandpa."

"And Grandpa wants him to stay," Prem said, looking at Homi.

Ratan was less distracted and more talkative in the absence of his parents, as if he understood that he mustn't tire the old man out. Prem arranged to have lunch with Pascal near his house in the fifth. He would take Ratan to the Panthéon before lunch.

Within minutes Pascal called back to say Irène was depressed. Would Prem mind if she joined them for lunch? "I wanted to ask you first because I know Ratan will be there. She's looking awful."

Prem reflected for a moment. He remembered how bad Meher had looked in her last days and the distaste he had sometimes caught on Homi's ten-year-old face at that time. And yet Homi had been a good boy, had tried to remain cheerful around his mother.

"Yes, it's okay."

"Are you sure? I know it'll make her feel better. She loves kids."

"Then we must do it."

"Your grandson is so delightful. I never gave her kids." Pascal sounded as if he were about to weep. "Remember your job is to make her feel better, *mon vieux.*"

The cab dropped them on rue Soufflot, and Prem walked with Ratan to the Place du Panthéon. Once they were in the interior, Ratan threw his head up to look at the immense ceilings. In the center Foucault's pendulum was oscillating. Prem sat Ratan on a metal barrier so that he could watch the small screen playing an English film that explained the mechanics of the pendulum.

"Some of France's greatest writers and thinkers are buried here. We're going down to see them," Prem said.

They took the narrow circular stairs. Prem descended holding on to the railing.

"Most of the people were buried elsewhere when they died, but then the State moved their remains here at different times to honor them."

"Daddy says you took care of Grandma when she was dying. He says you did more for her than his father did."

"Your dad's father was working. I had come from England

just to look after Grandma and was free all day. Let me tell you more about some of these people.

"This man here, Rousseau, said, 'Man is born free, but he is everywhere found in chains.' " How much could Prem explain to a boy of ten?

" 'Born free but found in chains,' " Ratan repeated, puckering his face.

A sign said that Rousseau was a man of nature and of truth.

"Should I win the Nobel Prize like you, or should I become the Prime Minister of India? I don't think I can do both; it'll be too much work. Daddy says no one can do both."

"What does this have to do with Rousseau?"

"I think the Prime Minister of India is not free at all. He has to welcome all the people who want to talk to him and pretend he is interested. But you seem quite free. Even in the middle of the day when you are not on holiday, you can decide to go sightseeing."

"How do you know I'm not on holiday?"

"Daddy says that just because you don't go to an office, it doesn't mean you don't work very hard. He says that writing books that win prizes takes a lot of time."

Ratan was excited by the passageway leading to the deeper crypts, the steps and archways along the way. He wove his way through the columns while Prem sat for a moment on a bench. They walked to the Curies. Some of the neighboring graves in the crypt had their doors open, and wreaths on the tombs, but the Curies' was closed. Through the trelliswork of the door, they craned their necks to see the severe chamber where Marie Curie was commemorated, and below her Pierre. In comparison to the grand tombs of France's sons Rousseau and Voltaire, these looked like the tombs of stepchildren.

"If they won the Nobel Prize, what did the others win to have better tombs?"

"Nothing. Voltaire and Rousseau were very important to the history of France and were placed here much earlier than the Curies. They only came in nineteen ninety-five. Let's see the writers."

Prem found the chamber with Dumas, Hugo, and Zola after consulting the map.

"I know Victor Hugo wrote *Les misérables*. I read it in the Bournvita Quiz Book."

"That's right. We can go after lunch with Pascal to the house where Victor Hugo used to live. He used to write while standing."

"Like you?"

"Yes. Like me."

Outside the Panthéon the sky was a clear perfect blue. The slight chill in the air enhanced the brilliant rays of the sun. The pale yellow stones of the Place du Panthéon seemed like part of a film set. Prem held Ratan's hand to cross the paved street east of the Panthéon.

"We are going to meet Pascal and Irène for lunch. She's not feeling very well, so if she doesn't speak much, don't get too scared."

"What happened to her?"

"She's got cancer."

"Grandma had cancer too."

"Irène is sad today. But Pascal and I are going to laugh and tell jokes so that she becomes happy. Pascal said she wants to see you because she loves children."

"I'll tell my airplane joke."

"Good. And you can tell them what we saw. We must try to convince her to come with us to Victor Hugo's house. She took me there the first time I came to Paris."

They descended the few steps past the church where Pascal had arranged to meet them. He and Irène were already seated on one of the sunlit *terrasses* of the Place Larue. As they approached the table, and Irène came into clearer view, Prem felt Ratan's grip tighten. Prem squeezed his hand before greeting Irène and Pascal with kisses.

"So what did you do today, young man?" Pascal pulled Ratan onto his lap. Prem took the chair beside Irène.

"We saw the Panthéon. We saw all the graves of the famous people."

"Your French is good. You pronounced *Panthéon* very well."

"I know all the famous people."

"Who are they? Tell us," Irène interjected.

Ratan looked away with embarrassment.

"Voltaire, Rousseau, Pierre et Marie Curie, André Malraux."

"Who taught you to speak like a French boy?" Pascal asked.

"This is how the guide was saying the names of the people."

"Which guide?" Prem asked surprised.

"The lady in the red dress who was talking to the tourists."

"I thought you were listening to me."

"I was listening to you and to her at the same time, Grandpa."

The adults laughed.

"You see this street?" Pascal pointed to the street sign. "It's named after Descartes. Do you know who he was?"

Ratan shook his head.

"Descartes was a great philosopher. He said, 'I think, therefore I am.' "

Ratan closed his eyes and repeated, " 'I think, therefore I am.' "

"Do you know what that means?" Pascal asked, waiting for the boy's response.

Ratan opened his eyes. "I think I like it more than"—he closed his eyes—" 'born free but found in chains.' "

"You learned a lot today. Very good. Now I have to put you back on your chair." Pascal moved Ratan to another chair.

Ratan looked at his grandfather and lifted his little finger.

"Do you want me to come with you?" Prem asked.

Ratan shook his head.

"*Mon petit*, the toilet is in the back there," Pascal said, pointing to the interior of the bar to the right of the counter.

Ratan went off. Pascal pulled out a piece of paper and wrote on it. Prem looked at Irène, who seemed rather contemplative. He thought it best not to interrupt her. *I hope Homi and Deepika don't mind that I brought Ratan along to see Irène and told him she had cancer.*

Ratan was back. Pascal handed him the paper on which he had written. "I wrote what Descartes said for you in both French and English."

"Thank you, Pascal Uncle. But I think he's wrong. In the toilet I just thought I was big like you and Grandpa, but I'm still small. So this Descartes is wrong."

"No, he means the fact that we think is proof that we exist. That's how we know we're not just in someone's dream but are real. Do you dream?"

Ratan nodded.

"Do you remember your dreams?" Irène asked suddenly.

"Yes." Ratan looked down at the table instead of at her.

Irène was wearing a tight red Gilda's Club–type turban to hide her baldness. Her thin face had lost the little bit of flesh it had once had. Her skin was pale. Her lips were dry, and the medicines had turned the corners of her mouth white.

"What did you dream last night?" Prem asked.

"I dreamed that you and I were flying in a plane," Ratan said, looking up at Prem.

"You didn't tell me this in the morning," Prem remarked in a neutral voice.

Pascal looked at Prem. The child had their total attention and not just because he was cute. None of them had any insight into his world.

"Don't you think dreams are interesting?" Pascal said. "You feel as if it's all happening and you are sure, but when you wake up you know it's a dream."

"But that's because your mind plays tricks on you. It's like an"—Ratan closed his eyes at this stage and then emitted the phrase—"optical illusion."

"Yes, just like a mirage," Irène said, smiling. Prem noticed for the first time that even her voice had aged and fallen ill. The voice corresponded to what she looked like now and not to what she had looked like earlier.

"What is a mirage?" In his eagerness to know, Ratan looked at Irène.

"Do you notice that when it gets very hot in Delhi in the summer, and you are in the car, you can see water on the road?"

"Yes. How do you know?"

"Pascal forced me to go Delhi in the middle of June one year to visit Prem. That effect of the water, that's a mirage." Irène spoke slowly. She told Ratan about the people of the desert looking for water and imagining that there were oases everywhere. She told him stories as Prem and Pascal ate their lunchtime steaks. Ratan could not be persuaded to more than nibble his sandwich, so enraptured was he by her storytelling.

"I was telling him that we should all go and see Victor Hugo's house," Prem said.

"Pascal can take you. I really shouldn't come. I'll get tired."

"But, Irène Aunty, Grandpa said you love that house. You must come with us." Ratan smiled his most angelic smile, and Prem knew then that Ratan knew that no one could ever say no to that smile. *He could be an actor. Or a writer. A* séducteur.

"I guess we can go for a short while," Irène said.

Ratan looked at his grandfather and gave him a triumphant smile.

At the Maison Victor Hugo, Irène took the initiative to guide them through the house, making sure to provide details that might be interesting to a young boy. Prem and Ratan thanked her for the tour. After his grandfather had kissed Irène on the cheek, Ratan got on his tiptoes and waited for the lady to bend down so that he could kiss her too.

"Did Grandma look like that when she died?" Ratan asked in the cab back.

"She looked weak, but she was much younger so she had more energy."

"When is Irène Aunty going to die?"

"I don't know, honey." Prem pulled Ratan close and ran his hands through his hair.

"Is Pascal Uncle very sad?"

"I think he's very sad, but he tries to hide it."

"Daddy said you tried to hide that you were sad when Grandma died."

"Does he speak a lot about Grandma's death?"

"He speaks to me about Grandma only when Mommy is not there. Mommy doesn't think a young boy should know about death. But I know all about it."

"What else did Daddy say about Grandma's death?"

"He said that Grandma never laughed as much as when you came to see her. He said that she was the bravest person he ever knew. She was braver than Rani of Jhansi and Joan of Arc. She was even braver than most men."

Prem had been too grief-stricken during Meher's death to realize how much Homi had been affected.

That night Ratan didn't make his way stealthily into Prem's bed. Instead he got under the quilt before Prem could turn off the bedside lamp. Once Prem slid down from his seated position and made himself comfortable, Ratan took Prem's large hand in his own and said, "Grandpa, I promise I'll take care of you when you get old. I'll make you laugh a lot."

At that moment Prem wanted never to die. He could have fought viciously for his life to spare this boy from the absolute loss that is death. He understood now how Meher had found energy, even on her worst days, to live rather than die, selfless even in moments of extreme pain for the sake of those she loved. Only someone graced with the total love of another person could choose pain over the permanent release from pain.

"I know you'll make me laugh."

Prem lay still, waiting for Ratan to fall asleep. He hadn't recovered from Meher's death, though he had been thirty years old at the time. What kind of person would he have been if she had died when he was ten? How had Homi coped? Should he prepare Ratan for his own death or hope he'd live long enough for the boy to be in a position to understand?

"I can't sleep, Grandpa."

"You know, I was just thinking that even though your grandma died so long ago, she's still with me. I talk to her every day."

"Daddy said that when people die, they don't go away."

"That's right. You'll know even when you win the Nobel Prize, one day when you grow up, that I am watching you and am proud of you."

"I'll try to win it when I'm young so that you're still alive. You won it only when you were seventy."

Where love made most people dreamy and distracted, Maya experienced a sense of discipline. Her emotional existence was taken care of in a single sweep, when Prem's lips first touched her mouth. In the few weeks left of the Paris Fiction Fellowship she still had most of her book to write, but it was suddenly easy. Waking at seven in the morning, she worked from eight to noon and then again from one to six.

Nadine waved at Maya late one afternoon as she was taking a small break from her work to look at the roofs. Maya asked her up for a cup of coffee.

"*Salut,*" Nadine said as she kissed Maya on the cheeks.

"How are you?"

"I just broke up with my girlfriend."

"I'm sorry. Was it difficult?"

"It was too easy."

Maya chuckled. She remembered the humidity trapped between Jean-Pierre's body and his sheets and how it had intensified that particular animal smell of his. It had been easy.

"My girlfriend asked me this week if we could live together," Nadine said. "It seemed like not such a bad idea because I did feel attached to her. But I was eating dinner with some friends yesterday and met someone."

"Did anything happen?"

"No. But I wanted something to happen. If I was living with my girlfriend, it could never happen. I think of the restrictions that the life of a couple imposes on you, and I feel suffocated." Nadine gripped her throat tightly to show just how suffocated.

"Why did nothing happen with the person you met last night?"

"I wasn't sure if she wanted it. We spoke a lot, and we laughed. She had long hands, much longer than mine." Nadine raised her hand to show Maya her own fingers.

"Yes, yours are pretty long. How old is she?"

"My age, our age. At some point when no one else at the table was listening, she told me that she liked being sodomized, and I couldn't get that out of my head. I thought of it the rest of the evening even when we talked about other things."

Maya looked at Nadine's hands again. How would she sodomize this other woman?

"At the end of the dinner I said I was delighted to have met her, but what I really wanted was to ask her to come back with me."

"I am with the *vieil écrivain,*" Maya said. "I spoke to him the day after we talked."

"Es-tu heureuse?"

Nadine drew out her question languorously, her *heureuse* saturated with a sense of luxury. It was a luxury to be so happy.

"Oui," Maya replied.

"Do you think my decision makes sense? Do I make sense?" Nadine asked anxiously.

"Your fear of losing your freedom?"

"Yes. But also that after Clara used the word *sodomy,* I can't get it out of my head."

Maya laughed.

"I'm serious. My relationship with my girlfriend has unraveled due to the force of that one word, that one idea. Isn't that how all you writers work? You take a word and spin a whole universe around it."

"I guess one could." *I can do that with the word Prem.* She broke from her reverie and asked, "Is *enculation* a word, or can one only use *enculer* in French?"

"Enculation is no word."

"I'd want to write a book in French just to make *enculation* a word."

Nadine shrugged. "That would be like saying *sodomation* in English."

"No. *Sodomation* doesn't work. *Enculation* would work."

Nadine grabbed Maya's hand and looked at it.

"All night I wanted to compare the size of her hands to mine." Nadine placed her palm against Maya's. Maya repositioned her palm, ensuring that the baselines of their palms were aligned. Their hands were the same size.

"More nerve endings from our hands and face reach our sensory cortex than from other parts of our body," Maya said. "We sense much more from hands than their surface area suggests."

"I always knew hands were important. Are you seeing your writer today?"

"No, his family is here from India."

"Do you want to go to a movie?"

Maya found her *Pariscope*, and they browsed the movie listings, eventually choosing something at the local cinema at the Place de Clichy for convenience. After the movie they went to Au Rendez-vous des Amis for a drink.

"You know, Clara doesn't live far from here."

"Why don't you call her?"

"You think so?"

"Of course."

Nadine called the long-fingered sodomy-loving Clara, who said yes.

"Do you want me to leave?"

"You have to stay! You heard what I told her on the phone, didn't you? I said I was here with an American friend who's a writer. She's also a writer."

"Go ahead—use me as bait."

Nadine smiled and fluttered her eyelashes at Maya teasingly.

Clara walked into the bar. Her skin had a fresh, tanned look. They rose from their table and kissed her in greeting. Maya eyed her hands. They were quite beautiful. She missed Prem's hands. She hadn't seen him for three full days.

Clara's phone rang. She fumbled through her purse but couldn't seem to find it.

"*Zut,*" she let out, as she tossed half her bag out onto the table in a hurry. Prem's *Sisters in the Louvre* fell out. The French version. Maya picked it up.

"*C'est lui,*" she said, holding up the book.

Nadine turned it over to read the back.

Clara was finished with the phone and organized her bag.

"She's the girl in love with the old writer. It's him," Nadine said to Clara. Then she turned to Maya. "I told her yesterday at dinner about you."

"He's really famous," Clara said.

Maya nodded and excused herself. When she came back, Nadine and Clara were holding hands. They decided not to order a second round of drinks and to head home instead.

"Are you liking *Sisters in the Louvre*?" Maya asked.

"I love it." Clara and Nadine were walking with their arms linked.

"I'm reading it for the second time, and I really love it too," Maya said.

"What kind of person is he?" Clara asked.

"He's——" Maya hesitated. "I'm blind about him. I don't know."

Clara laughed and reached out with her free hand for Maya's shoulder. As they descended the steps on rue Paul Albert, all three took their steps together, half-hopping.

Maya kissed them goodnight on the third-floor landing and climbed up the next flight. After shutting off her light, she looked out the window to see the girls making love.

In the morning she awoke with a start. She'd been waiting for Prem in her dream, and since he hadn't come back, she'd awakened. She called him.

"I was frightened so I called you. I had a bad dream."

"My grandson and I just got back with croissants. Tell me your dream."

"We were both in the shower, you were behind me. I moved my bum close to you, and you sighed. I could feel your sex. Then you went to get something. I waited. And waited. And waited. But you never came back. I got very cold standing in the shower."

"I think this means I've kept you waiting for too long. You need to feel my sex."

"Prem, I'm missing you."

"How much?"

"Very badly."

"We're eating dinner at the Café de l'Industrie on Wednesday. Do you want to join us?"

"I'd love to."

"My grandson will be there. I don't want him to think any-thing."

"Don't worry. I'll be very discreet."

Prem encouraged Homi and Deepika to leave Ratan with him daily so that they could explore Paris. One afternoon he called Valérie and asked her if she wanted to meet him with her kids so that Ratan could amuse himself. They arranged to meet at Musée Zadkine.

Valérie arrived with an enormous bag of drawing sheets and crayons. They led the kids to one of the rooms in the museum.

"Now all of you must choose one statue—it doesn't have to be the same one—and draw it." Valérie handed them each a sheet. They immediately sat down cross-legged on the floor. She opened the box of crayons and placed it near the kids.

"Now, be nice and share the crayons. Can we leave you here alone?"

They nodded.

"Come, let's go into the garden," she said, looping her arm through Prem's.

"That's a good idea. They keep busy, and we get to talk."

"He's your nephew's son?"

"Yes. How come your kids speak English?"

"They go to a bilingual school."

"And how are you doing?"

"I married a solid guy. He's not very imaginative, but he's a good father."

"Have you had the customary first affair after marriage yet?"

"I hope it never happens, but I can't say. In ten years it might, but right now I'm too busy with the kids. I still find it interesting with him. And you?"

"I followed a young woman from New York to Paris. I'm not

the same as I was ten years ago. I feel old and not a little shriveled. Desiccated." Prem laughed.

Valérie touched his face and smiled.

"You still look very good. Enough to put a sixty-year-old to shame."

"I wonder how long it can last. How long she can sustain her feelings."

"I'm sure she's much more in love with you than you think. Your work is very seductive. When I read your books, I still think of you. One can't help it."

"There are practically no erotic scenes in any of my books."

"It's your entire approach, your understanding of women, that is erotic. Do you know how much publicity you got last year when *Technolore* was translated? Every woman between twenty and sixty in the metro was gripping your novel more tightly than the handrail. One day I counted all the people on a *terrasse* in Beaubourg who were reading books; ten out of twelve were reading one of yours. *C'était hallucinant!"*

For years he'd followed Pascal's easy policy of not asking too many questions and making the most of the situation. But with Maya every bone in his body rebelled at the thought that she might be there because of his status. For his writing yes, for his status no.

"So it was my fame?"

"I asked myself that. I think Julie and I would never have approached you if you weren't famous, but it was only the initial reason. I really did love you that summer, and I fell in love only when we were in Parrain's house."

"Your abrupt departure was very difficult for me."

"It hurt me to leave that last time we saw you, but Julie's hold over me was very powerful. I couldn't say no to her for anything at that time."

"So you were in love with her."

"Oui."

Through the glass door from where they had stepped out, Prem saw Ratan's head lift up from his drawing.

"Should we check on the kids?"

"I loved being taken to a museum and being asked to draw the sculptures when I was young," Valérie said, pushing the door open.

Valérie's two kids continued drawing. Ratan was bending his head over Valérie's daughter's drawing and holding her hand in his as she applied the pencil.

Valérie clapped lightly.

The kids all held up their drawings. The renditions of Zadkine's angular abstract faces were angular and abstract, outlined in colors a lot more imaginative than the original sculptures. All three kids had drawn butterflies and flowers around the main drawing.

"Why don't you color the inside of the drawing?" Valérie suggested to Ratan, since the other two had not yet finished sketching. He nodded and got back to his sheet.

Valérie and Prem stepped out onto the porch again.

"Is it common for kids to imagine butterflies everywhere?" Prem asked.

"I think flowers and butterflies are the first things they learn to draw in school, so when they have to draw something new, they start with something they already know. It's just like a warm-up."

"Or like foreplay." Prem gave Valérie an open desirous look. She blushed.

"We liked your tenderness, Julie and I. We talked a lot about you that year."

"Is your husband tender?"

"Yes, I need it. I couldn't marry someone who was like an animal in bed. I had one lover like that. It lost its appeal very fast."

Valérie and Prem looked into the room once more. Ratan had finished. He was holding Lulu's hand again. She smiled at him. Ratan gave the little girl a kiss on the cheek.

"Maman, il est si gentil," Lulu said, looking up at her mother.

Lulu's brother continued drawing, closed up in his own world.

Valérie collected the crayons and put them into her bag. She rolled Ratan's drawing and tied it with a pretty ribbon, then handed it to him.

Back on rue d'Assas they said goodbye.

"Did you enjoy drawing?" Prem asked Ratan.

"I made the drawing as a gift to someone."

Prem waited expectantly, but Ratan didn't go on.

"Who will you give it to?" he finally asked. He would frame it and hang it next to his bed back in New Jersey.

"To Irène Aunty. Will we see her again?" Ratan asked.

Despite the fact that he was indeed touched by his grandson's kindness, Prem felt a momentary sensation of acute jealousy. He bent a little and picked Ratan up in his arms, something he barely had the strength to do for more than a few seconds.

"Grandpa, Daddy said I am too heavy for you."

Prem squeezed Ratan next to his chest and kissed him on the cheek.

"I love you, my darling boy. I love you."

He let Ratan slide down his body.

"We can ask Pascal if we can meet Irène again. I think she'll be very happy to get this gift from you."

"Yes, I think so too," Ratan said happily.

Homi and Deepika returned late from their sightseeing trip to Fontainebleau and arrived at the Café de l'Industrie after the others—Prem, Pascal, Maya, and Ratan—were already seated. Ratan was so absorbed with Maya that he waved hello to his parents without going over. Introductions were informal.

"Prem was telling me your sightseeing schedule. Versailles, Fontainebleau, and Giverny all in a week is very ambitious," Pascal said.

"And since he's been taking care of Ratan in the evenings, we even managed the Moulin Rouge one night," Deepika said.

"Do you like Paris?" Pascal looked at Homi.

"I like it. But my wife *adores* it." Homi put his arm around Deepika.

"I was asking Maya about her favorite places in Paris. She's here from New York. It's nice to see that this city still draws young talent from other parts of the world," Pascal said.

"What do you do, Maya?" Deepika asked.

"I'm writing my first novel."

"Is it set in Paris?" Homi asked.

"No. It's set in India. I already have all my notes. I'm putting it together."

"You've been to India?" Deepika asked.

"Yes, many times. Prem said you live in Delhi. Whereabouts do you live?"

"In Greater Kailash," Homi said.

"I stayed in Def Col for a few days, but I spent most of my time in the south."

"It's your turn," Ratan said, demanding Maya's attention.

"Sorry," she said, turning to him. They were playing tic-tac-toe.

"Young man, do you remember what Descartes said?" Pascal asked.

" *Je pense, donc je suis.* I think therefore I am.' " Ratan spoke with his eyes on the game.

"Where did you learn that?" Maya asked Ratan.

"Pascal Uncle wrote it for me."

"Did Pascal tell you about Pascal's bet?"

"Another Pascal? What is the bet?" Ratan was immediately curious.

"Tu penses il va comprendre?" Pascal asked from across the table.

"What did he just say?" Ratan asked Maya.

"Ask him directly," Maya said, looking at Pascal.

"I asked her if she thought you'd understand. Even I don't understand this other Pascal's bet too well." He laughed.

Maya drew rows and columns and wrote out the God-exists, God-doesn't-exist scenario for Ratan. He had no trouble with the concept.

"I like Pascal more than Descartes and Rousseau." He smiled at Maya, then whizzed off to the other end of the table to show his parents the matrix.

Homi and Deepika turned their attention to their son. Pascal asked Maya something. Maya felt Prem's hand running along her leg, then under her skirt. She momentarily forgot the question Pascal had posed. Pascal realized what was happening and waited.

Ratan now made his way to his grandfather with the paper. Prem lifted his hand from Maya's thigh.

"Sorry," said Maya to Pascal, nervously playing with her hair.

"I was asking if you have a good sense of where each chapter is going."

"I think I do, but it's my first attempt at writing a novel. I don't know if my approach is quite optimal." She wanted to tell Pascal how Prem's writing was infiltrating everywhere inside her own. Maybe he would understand.

"My method refined between my second and third novels, and since then it's not changed all that much."

"I wrote my undergraduate thesis on your work," Maya said.

"Prem never told me that."

"I may not have mentioned it," Maya said.

Pascal winked at her.

Their food arrived, and two waiters bustled about the table.

"Maya is an Indian name," Ratan said as he took his seat next to Maya again.

"My father loves India. That's why he decided to call me Maya."

"Maya is magic," Ratan informed Pascal.

"Do you like cheese? This warm cheese on my salad is the best I've ever eaten. Would you like to try some?" Maya asked Ratan.

"Yes."

She cut a toast with *crottin* in half and maneuvered it onto Ratan's plate.

"How old are you?" he asked her.

"I'm twenty-five."

"But you are friends with Grandpa, who is seventy-five."

"I am friends with you, and you are ten. And you are friends with Pascal, who is sixty-five. Aren't you?" she asked.

"Are you both friends too?" Ratan looked at Pascal and then at Maya.

"Yes, now we are," Pascal laughed.

"Oh! Let me put away this paper before it gets dirty." Ratan wiped his hands on his napkin and folded the sheet on which Maya had explained Pascal's wager.

"Was Blaise Pascal in the Panthéon too?" Pascal asked, testing the boy.

"No, I don't think he was."

"Did you remember that you passed by another church after you left the Panthéon the other day, when we had lunch with Irène?"

"Yes, I remember the church. Is he there?"

"Yes," Maya said.

"Grandpa." Ratan leaned behind Maya and tugged at Prem's arm. "Can we go to the other church next to the Panthéon to see Blaise Pascal?"

"Only if your mother will let me have you to myself one more day. I don't think she wants to see Blaise Pascal."

"Mommy, please," Ratan begged his mother at the other end of the table.

"We'll see tomorrow, darling."

"Mommy, I have to see all the *grands hommes*. Otherwise how will I become one?"

"All that will come later. Now you have to eat your dinner."

"Another ten days here, and my son will turn *français*," Homi said.

Soon Ratan got sleepy and went to sit on his mother's lap.

Deepika and Homi started planning their day, and Prem and Pascal turned to Maya.

"Miss Maya just told me she wrote a thesis on my work."

"You did?" Prem said, looking at her, surprised.

"In college. I only started reading you after I graduated," she said, turning to Prem. She took the moment to look into his eyes. To her surprise, her heart seized up.

Pascal offered to drive Prem and his family back to the sixth after dinner.

"They leave on Saturday afternoon. Do you want to come to my place at four? I'm impatient to have you in my arms," Prem whispered as they all rose from the table.

For Prem, time in constant company flew differently than when alone. Between walks with Ratan, meals, and boat rides on the Seine, Homi's trip passed in the flutter of an eye. Deepika fell in love with Paris, and Homi was thrilled to see his young wife so enthused about every lamplight and narrow twisted street.

Prem invited Pascal and Irène to dinner at his house the night before his family was to fly back to India. Deepika said she would cook an Indian meal for everyone.

"Please don't show your surprise at Irène. She's rather unwell and looks it," Prem said as they shopped at Bon Marché. Ratan had made off to the chocolate section.

"Maybe we should put Ratan to bed earlier then," Deepika suggested.

"What nonsense!" Homi immediately said.

"Uncle, please explain to him that just because there is suffering in the world, it doesn't mean my son has to constantly see it up close at the age of ten," Deepika implored.

"Deepika, he's already met Irène. He made a drawing for her. It'll be fine."

Deepika shopped silently and spent the afternoon in the kitchen sulking. Over their afternoon tea she responded to Prem in monosyllables.

"Mommy, don't be sad. We'll see Grandpa again soon," Ratan said, coming to her.

"Yes, we will," Homi said before Deepika had a chance to say anything.

"Why don't you men go for a walk so that I can cook in peace?" Deepika said.

Ratan clapped his hands and jumped. "Let's go and see that statue in the garden."

"Which one?" Prem asked.

"The dead lady in the man's arms with the big monster on top of them."

Deepika looked accusingly at Prem now.

"She's not dead. She's only sleeping," Prem said defensively.

"Yes, that one," Ratan said. He was already on his feet pulling Prem by the hand.

Homi rose from the table. He took the cups and saucers and placed them in the dishwasher in the kitchen.

"Take it easy, darling. My uncle is no fool. Ratan doesn't look in the least bit traumatized," Homi whispered to Deepika.

The three men set off to the Luxembourg Gardens.

"I am glad you could come to Paris while I'm here," Prem said.

"Deepika's had a wonderful time. Don't worry—she'll get over her mood," Homi said softly. They were both a good two feet taller than Ratan, who couldn't hear them.

"I'm not worried."

"I need to ask you something about Mom."

"What is it?"

"I can't remember how she died in the end. Was I there? I remember seeing her fall ill, and then I remember her face lit up when you arrived. Then she looked really sick again. The next I remember we were in the midst of rituals and relatives."

"We shielded you for the last few days. Meher was in mad pain for forty-eight hours, and your dad couldn't bear to watch, so he went to his brother's house with you. In the end, when she died, I was the only one there. I sat immobile holding her hand. She was so tired she couldn't even grip mine. She was too exhausted to speak. We stared into each other's eyes, and then her hand slipped. At some point I knew she was no more."

"I was in a daze for the first few years after that. Dad sent me to boarding school, and everything was new. It took all my energy just to adapt. I don't even remember seeing you during the first few years after her death."

"You did. I came to Delhi for one month each summer during your vacation so that I could see you. But I didn't stay at your dad's house."

"Didn't we go to Benares once?"

"Yes. Your dad was nice that way. He let me see you without any restrictions, though I think it was difficult for him to see me. It made him remember Meher."

"I was going through some old papers just before we came to Paris. My father's brother died recently, and my cousin came across a box marked with my father's name when he was clearing out the house. They were Dad's papers. For some reason he had stored them with his brother. I opened them, and that's when I realized that you paid for my education. Even the money I inherited after his death from the trust was yours."

What else was in the box? Had Meher ever written anything that her husband might have found? Prem had asked her on her deathbed, and she'd insisted there was no compromising information.

"It was clear you couldn't stay home with your father. He just couldn't take care of you all by himself," Prem said.

"I was never really that close to him."

Prem remained silent.

"Why have you done so much for me?" Homi asked suddenly.

Is he going to ask me if he is my son? What would Meher want?

"What sort of question is that, Homi? You are all I have. I never married and never had children. You would have done exactly the same in my shoes."

At the traffic light by rue Vaugirard, Homi grabbed Prem's hand along with Ratan's as they crossed the street and held it well after they were inside the Luxembourg Gardens. Ratan let go of his father's hand as soon as they had crossed and walked ahead of them.

"Be careful. I turned very sentimental at sixty. You'll be there in four years. You're not a young man anymore," Prem warned.

"And now at seventy-five? Are you as sentimental?"

"I'm trying to live in the present moment since there won't be many more."

"Don't talk like that."

"Let's face it. I'm getting on. Some days I'm so tired, the only thing that keeps me going is to see him grow up." They walked toward Ratan, who had stopped to watch a bee hover over a red flower.

"I don't understand why you won't just come to India and live with us. You know that nothing would make us happier. All of us. Ratan, me, and even Deepika."

Prem turned to look at Homi and brought his hand to rest on Homi's shoulder. "I just started a new chapter of my life. If it doesn't work out, I might come."

Ratan looked up at his father and grandfather. "You're both walking *so* slowly," he whined.

Then he charged forward in the direction of the statue.

"Okay, not too fast or Grandpa can't keep up," Homi said behind his son.

"Nor can you!" Prem chuckled. At moments he saw Homi for what he was, a man of fifty-six running after a ten-year-old young enough to be his grandson.

"He has your eye. Deepika and I don't notice things as much as you do."

Ratan ran down the narrow pebbled passageway, dodging the chairs by the small canal, and reached the statue.

He looked back impatiently, then loudly said, "Grandpa."

Prem brought a finger to his mouth. He was still twenty feet away. "This is Paris. No shouting here," he said when they reached the statue.

Prem wanted to wade through the water and touch the woman's legs. Had Ratan somehow inherited his extreme irrational impulses for beings of stone and metal?

"The doctor said my heart was that of a seventy-year-old man," Homi said.

"I might even be in better shape than you. You should really ask Deepika to go slow on all the *desi ghee* food she cooks."

"Did you bring the camera, Daddy? I want to take pictures."

Homi handed him the camera and looked at the woman stretched out in the man's arms. Her delta clearly visible, a cloth draped over her right leg. Ratan got busy with the photos. With a simultaneous sigh Prem and Homi sat on a chair and then laughed.

"I don't think it's just because he's my son, but I can't help thinking he is brilliant."

"I think he'll do great things. But you have to talk him out of this Nobel Prize and prime minister nonsense. That's a lot of pressure on a boy."

"I never gave him those ideas. I've never put any pressure on him—ask Deepika. It's all him. In another five years he's going to be totally beyond his mother and me."

Ratan came up behind them and startled them with a bark.

"Let me see your photos," Prem said.

Ratan handed him the digital camera.

"You'll have to show me. I can't operate it," Prem said.

Ratan turned it back on and showed his grandfather the screen. He pressed the button to move to the next photo and the next.

"Can I take a picture with it?" Prem asked, getting up from the chair. Ratan's pictures weren't bad, but he hadn't been able to capture the expression on the woman's face or the sensuous angle at which her passive body was screaming to be touched. Prem took a photo.

"Let's go—your mom is waiting for us. We should help her set the table," Prem said.

It had turned chilly, and there was no more sun. They walked back briskly.

Homi helped his wife set the table while Prem brought out wineglasses from his cabinet. He was slightly apprehensive about the evening, but when Deepika welcomed Pascal and Irène into the house, she was instantly warm. Prem greeted Irène and Pascal with kisses on the cheek. Homi and Deepika formally shook hands with the guests.

At dinner Ratan looked at Pascal and Prem and then declared, "I think sculptors are much greater than writers. Everyone can enjoy what they make. You don't have to know how to read, and you don't have to be grown up."

Before Pascal could launch into a pompous discussion on the greatness of writing, a favorite topic of his, and chop the boy's balls, Prem said, "That is absolutely true. Show Pascal the photos you took."

"Not now. After you finish eating," Deepkia said. But it was already too late—Ratan had slipped away and returned with the camera.

Prem watched Pascal's face and saw the familiar gleam in his eyes, the gleam that told him yet again why he was Prem's dearest friend.

"Il a le même regard que nous," Prem said before Pascal made a lewd comment in English that would enrage Deepkia.

"Very good. I especially like the last picture," Pascal said.

"Grandpa took that one."

"Now finish your food," Deepika said.

Ratan sat back and ate obediently. After dinner he went to his room and returned with the sketch.

"Irène Aunty, it's for you," he said, handing her the rolled piece of paper.

"Merci beaucoup, mon chéri." She lowered her head to kiss him.

Deepika seemed horrified. Before anyone else noticed, Ratan had happily given Irène a big smacking kiss on her cheek and a hug.

"Ah! Zadkine," Irène said, unrolling the drawing.

Despite the drawing's childishness the essence of Zadkine's work had been preserved. Ratan had refused to show the drawing to his parents. They stood behind Irène to look at it. After they were finished, Irène passed it to Pascal.

"But you must sign it, *mon petit,"* he said.

"Yes, Ratan. Please sign it," Irène said.

Ratan looked uncertainly at his mother.

"Come, let's go find a crayon from your set that matches the color," Deepkia said.

Ratan took the drawing from Pascal and disappeared into the guest room where his things were kept.

"Your son is such a lovely boy," Irène said to Homi.

"Thank you," Homi said formally.

"Anyone want some port?" Prem offered, rising from his chair.

They all did. Homi offered to serve them and went to the kitchen for glasses.

"How are you managing without Mademoiselle Maya?" Pascal asked.

"She's busy writing. She calls once a day."

"Did you show her the dirty stuff you wrote?"

"You remember that? Not yet. I didn't tell her about it."

"I want to read it."

"It's not for you."

"Out of literary interest."

"It is utterly out of the question."

"The one thing I've got over my biggest literary rival is about to be wiped out by that notebook of yours."

"Right!" Prem laughed.

Homi walked into the room clearing his throat to warn them he was back. He had never felt comfortable with his uncle's friends when they talked openly about such matters. His own life in Delhi was traditional and restrained, his existence consumed by his family.

"The port."

Deepika and Ratan came back with the drawing. He had written, all in block letters, *Irène Aunty, I hope you get well soon and can come to see us in India. Love, Ratan.*

"Now it's complete," Irène said, smiling.

"Now it's time for you to say goodnight to everyone and go to bed," Deepika said.

Ratan followed his mother to change into his pajamas.

"To your son," Pascal said, raising his glass of port and looking at Homi.

After the digestif Pascal and Irène said goodbye. Prem saw them off at the door and came back to the living room.

"I'm sorry I had my misgivings about this dinner, Uncle," Deepika said.

"Don't worry. It's natural."

"I'm exhausted. We should all go to bed," Homi said, getting up.

Prem changed into his pajamas and brushed his teeth. Ratan was fast asleep already. *But it's the last day. He's going to leave tomorrow.*

Prem pulled the quilt away from his bed and then lifted Ratan
and placed him on his bed. The boy was much heavier asleep and
horizontal, but Prem managed. As soon as he lay down and shut
the light off, he too fell fast asleep.

In Maya's memory, the Prem who had appeared in her dream
in the shower had replaced the real Prem. In her mind when she
thought of him, his skin was younger, softer, less blemished. Her
memory had applied the airbrush to everything except his hands. As
Maya sat with Prem on Saturday afternoon having a cup of tea in silence, she stared at him to take him in whole. Everything was just a
little different from the image she had kept alive in her mind. She
waited for the details of the real Prem to replace the ones of the
imagined Prem. His hands, however, consoled her. She remembered
them exactly as they were. The shape of his carpals and metacarpals
were imprinted with extraordinary accuracy in her head.

"You are very silent today, dear."

"I didn't see you for too long. You're just slightly different
than I remember."

"You saw me the other night when we had dinner."

"I mean alone. I couldn't really take such a good look at you
then."

"You're even more beautiful than I recall. Come here." Prem
patted the space beside him on the loveseat.

Maya walked over and sat next to him. Some sense of mod-
esty prevented her from looking at him closely where his skin was
exposed. When they caressed, and later, after dinner, as they lay in
bed, Maya removed Prem's shirt only after the room was dark. But
then, without warning, the rotating light from the Eiffel Tower
swept directly over Prem. His body turned a strange blue purple
before passing into the dark again. Maya tiptoed to the window
and drew the straw-colored curtains. Then she moved close to
Prem in bed and spooned his body. Prem felt tired. He kissed her

gently, unable to even imagine how he might make the leap of energy required of a lover. Inside his *caleçon* he could feel his member asleep. He hugged her, worried that his dick was no longer working.

"Prem, I'm happy," she whispered before falling asleep.

The next night when Maya visited Prem in his apartment, her mind had readjusted to the real Prem. They walked over to the soufflé restaurant on the Square Récamier for dinner.

"I just realized I'm leaving in five days," she said.

"Are you ready to leave?"

"Not at all. The writing is in good shape—I got a lot done trying not to miss you when your family was here—but I feel like I haven't had nearly as much of Paris as I'd like."

"For one, you should stop wasting your time with me and profit as much as possible from Paris. I'll fly back next weekend to the United States."

"I have this terrible anxiety about leaving Paris. I'm afraid things will change in New York. You live so far away. You may not want to see me as much."

"I have a proposition for you. I've been thinking."

"What have you been thinking, Mr. Rustum?"

"Ridiculous as it is for a man of seventy-five to say this, I've been thinking about *the future.*" Prem laughed self-consciously.

"I want a future. Let's move to Paris."

"At my age you don't think of *forever* and *ever.* You think of today, tomorrow, day after. And in any case, I don't think a young woman like you should have to worry about wheeling around an eighty-year-old man."

"Unless I want to," Maya said quickly.

"No, not even then."

The waiter came to their table to take away their salads. Maya had not finished hers.

"I haven't finished yet," she said.

"Sorry, mademoiselle. The soufflé waits for no one," he said, walking away. In less than a minute he was back with their soufflés and put Prem's in front of him. Maya moved her salad plate to the side, and he put hers down.

"Anyway, I don't want you forever and ever. I want you for a limited period of time. Say for five hundred hours."

"Like a lease on an apartment. Or a hotel room rented on an hourly basis."

"Exactly." Prem had been stroking her hand but withdrew it to eat his soufflé.

"Are you suggesting this for my sake or for yours?" Maya asked.

"For both of us."

"You don't trust me, is that it? You think I'm just going to up and leave?"

"I think that we'll both live it more uncompromisingly if we are doing it for a limited period of time. We can always renew the lease, if we both want to, at the end of the period."

"Is your soufflé good? Mine is heavenly."

"Try some for yourself." Prem offered a spoonful to her. The creamy gorgonzola melted in her mouth.

"So is this lease for your apartment or mine?" Maya poured some of the morel sauce they had given her over her soufflé and offered it to Prem.

"It's in my house. In suburbia."

"You're testing me!"

"Ideally I'd like you to feel you have your own room in my house. You can come and go as you like. Maybe spend the week-end or a few days in the week."

"And maximum how much time can I spend with you on the basis of this contract?"

"You're making fun of me!" Prem said. He ate more of his soufflé at a leisurely pace, not bothering to respond immediately to her question. When the waiter came by to ask if they were enjoying their meal, Prem ordered champagne.

"Maya, there's no minimum or maximum. I don't want you to get sick of me. I've got a very quiet life, and I'm too old to be going out all the time and doing the kinds of energetic things you young people do."

Maya looked at Prem's eyes as he spoke. He was just trying to make it as easy for her as possible. The vestige of rationality in Maya appreciated him for this. But Maya had not felt compelled by irrational impulses in a very long time. And with Prem she felt not just their immediacy but also felt safe in giving in to them.

"Can we keep this simple?" she asked him.

"Of course."

"Are you basically saying that I can bring two suitcases and come to your house for five hundred hours when you have returned?"

"Yes."

"Good, we're agreed then."

The waiter offered Prem and Maya a chocolate soufflé, which they shared before walking back. The César statue of the half-man half-horse at the carrefour was gleaming in the moonlight. As Maya walked over the metal grille that surrounded the statue, a gust of air blew up her skirt, making it billow like a parachute. Prem thought she would rise up and fly away.

Back in bed as they were lying in the dark, Prem said, "I have something to tell you."

"*Je t'écoute.*"

The full moon high in the sky glowed on the lower edge of Prem's bed.

"I only came to Paris because you were coming. I had not made any sure plans for the summer until I saw you."

Maya whistled.

"You didn't tell me how you found my ad online."

"Pascal said he met women by searching for his own name."

"If I'd had any idea you'd be there, I'd have been too embarrassed to write that ad. It would have been like mixing the kingdom of the gods with the kingdom of mere mortals."

"Gods? I feel more a satyr than a god."

"At the Rodin Museum that day I could not get enough of all the old man–young girl type pieces. Or the hands. I should have seen this coming that day."

"Do you remember which ones?"

"Minotaurs and centaurs corrupting young maidens. And all the hands, of God, of satan, of lovers. Hands with women contained within. There was also a Plexiglas box with a work in plaster of an old man on his knees kissing a girl's midsection."

"I know that one rather well."

"What is it called?"

"*L'homme et sa pensée.* She is his thought the way you are mine."

"Am I your thought? Am I in it? Part of it?" In the *clair de lune* he could see her upper lip trembling like a bird beating its wings when it has been caught.

Slowly, as if desire were like water at the bottom of a deep well, needing time to be drawn up, Prem started to kiss Maya with increasing passion.

"I feel like Galatea coming alive to Pygmalion's kiss," she whispered, moaning at the sensation of his flesh everywhere against her own. Prem was touching her with the same expertise with which he wrote sentences and books.

Maya came.

A few minutes later she started kissing Prem and moved her hand down his chest, and then farther down his body. He was no longer stiff. He pulled her hand up and brought her into his arms and caressed her to sleep.

The next morning Maya and Prem walked over to his usual haunt by the carrefour for their morning coffee.

"When do you want me to come over to suburbia?" Maya asked him.

"I'll send a car over to pick you up on Sunday if you like."

"I can take the bus."

"I live in the boonies, my dear. New Jersey Transit will take you four hours with changes and waiting times. The car takes just over an hour."

"Why did you move there?"

"I used to have a place in the city. So when I was looking for something outside the city, I wanted something as far away as possible. Or rather as inconvenient as possible, so that it was hard for people to find me if I didn't want to be found."

"I'm going to sort out my mail and find my friends when I get back. I'll be ready to try out the 'burbs once you are back."

"Do you have a lot of friends in New York?"

"A few. I never told you, but someone else responded to that ad before you did. He had met you the same night at a party. It was such a coincidence. He's become a friend of sorts. He's going through a rough patch. I feel like he's a kindred spirit."

"Did you sleep with him?"

"I slept in his bed. But we didn't have sex."

Maya pulled her jacket closer around her as a breeze hit them.

"What are you doing today?"

"I've still not been to the Carnavalet. I'm going to have dinner with Nadine one night. She's the neighbor. I also want to have a coffee with Jean-Pierre if possible and make some peace. I met two writers through the Paris Fiction Fellowship offices. I need to see them too."

"You better run along and start your day."

"I'm going to miss you."

"I'll give you something to keep. Something I wrote."

Maya's eyes lit up.

"We have to go back to my flat."

They paid the bill and left.

Maya grabbed Prem's hand as they walked. "Remember I told you I'd started writing?"

Prem unlocked the door to the flat. "Of course. I was too afraid to ask you questions about it after what happened the last time we discussed your writing."

"I was writing something to you, for you. It's rightfully yours."

He went to the bedroom and returned with his orange notebook.

"There is one condition—you won't read it until you get on the plane," he said.

Maya raised herself on her toes and kissed Prem on the lips when he handed her the notebook.

Despite the temptation to pick it up in her last few days in Paris as she ran around trying to stock up on French books and cheese, Maya refrained from opening Prem's notebook. She settled instead for touching its cover. She read it on the plane. Once she started reading it, she was no longer aware of the wailing babies or the unpleasant smell of mass quantities of packaged food being heated up.

Prem had missed nothing about her, the small mole on the tip of her right ear, the configuration of her teeth, her habit of walking with her right foot angled open. He had grabbed her by the elbows once and noticed that the skin on the elbows was rough; he had imagined her resting on her elbows as she thought of what to write next. The roughness of her elbows and his tenderness for the roughness had told him just how much trouble he was in. But these things came after the first half of the notebook. The half without reflection. It lacked entirely that basic element of writer's craft: observation. Prem's direct, unadulterated desires roared from every page. Maya's hands trembled. She was vaguely aware of feeling hot, of removing her sweater, and then her scarf, and then of sweating. But this registered rather dimly on her consciousness. The second time she read through the notebook on the plane, after lunch and coffee had been served, she understood more. Shapes and forms emerged from the notebook, ghosts of people, the past. Nothing concrete, just an intuition that there was a past, a rich past. Possibly an unforgiving one. At one moment Maya thought for no reason of Hegel. She remembered a teaching assistant in class saying that if they took away anything from Hegel, it should be the phrase *the end of history.* On the third reading, an hour before the plane touched down at JFK, things were clearer. The ghosts from Prem's life would live through her.

part vii

In the beginning, there was desire, which was the first seed of the mind. Sages having meditated in their hearts discovered by their wisdom the connection of the being with the non-being.

Sex is also revenge on death.

DAVID KEPESH IN PHILIP ROTH'S
THE DYING ANIMAL

Prem woke up in the morning after having slept for eleven hours. Mrs. Smith made him scrambled eggs and toast for breakfast.

"It's nice to be back home, Mrs. Smith."

"August was very humid. The whole summer was horrid. It was good you got away."

"Mrs. Smith, someone's going to be coming for dinner, and she's going to stay."

"I'll air out the guest room in that case. Will she just rest one night or more?"

"She's going to stay, Mrs. Smith."

Mrs. Smith, taken aback, looked at Prem for a second before recovering herself. "Right then, Mr. Rustum. I'll prepare the room."

"Thank you, Mrs. Smith. And for dinner, could we have something rich by way of dessert?"

"Sure, Mr. Rustum."

The tension in the house was palpable as Mrs. Smith went about the floor above. He could hear her punch the pillows and do the laundry.

Maya knew she had arrived back in New York when she was addressed variously as *Hello beautiful, Will you be mine, Wow!, Sexy,* and *Mamasita* on her way to the grocery store by men of assorted colors. The air was cold for early September, and the sky that ultraclear blue that gives New York its crystalline quality in the fall and winter months. Maya walked briskly. Her white skirt and black boots were not warm enough. For breakfast she ate a bagel. She had missed bagels. She and Johnson arranged to meet at the greasy spoon in her neighborhood for lunch. Maya wanted to see if Mrs. Nona and Costas were still alive and kicking.

The greasy spoon itself wasn't—it had undergone a drastic renovation. There were no vacant high stools by the counter and no Mrs. Nona. The prices were up—and not by fifty cents or a dollar. Fancy items with fresh basil, tamarind, and saffron were featured on the menu.

"I don't know why New York feels so amplified," she told Johnson.

"Is it New York, or is it you? Is your writing going better?"

Maya nodded.

"I saw something on the street and got it for you."

Johnson put his hand into his messenger bag and brought out a brown paper envelope. He hesitated.

"Aren't you going to give it to me?"

"I don't want you to misunderstand."

Maya reached out and opened the envelope. Three postcards of nudes fell out.

"These are like Schiele," she said.

"Exactly what I thought. Schiele did all his work before twenty-eight. He died young. It reminded me of what you had said about Rimbaud. On his deathbed Schiele said that he had already created everything he had to. He was ready to die when he was my age."

"That's not heartening at all."

"Yes and no. The woman who made these started her art only after she turned fifty."

Maya smiled. "You're telling me I have time?"

"We both do. We'll manage."

"What's her name?"

"Carolyn Weltman."

"I'm glad you're feeling optimistic."

"Prem's agent called me all of a sudden. He wanted to see the rest of the stories."

"That's fantastic! Did you send them yet?"

"Yes. He's taking me on."

"I'm so glad for you. I can't believe you took so long to tell me." Maya reached across the table and took his hand in hers.

"You haven't told me anything about the unrequited love that is more powerful than your will."

"No longer unrequited. I'd like to tell you about it, but now is not the time," Maya said, getting up. Prem's car would soon be coming to pick her up. She gave Johnson a hug when they parted.

Maya arrived in her deep pink skirt looking flushed. Oblivious of Matthew, the driver who had chauffeured him for many years, Prem took his time to kiss Maya on the mouth. Matthew looked away, smiling to himself. Mrs. Smith came out and directed the driver to carry the bags up to the guestroom.

"Maya, this is Mrs. Smith."

Maya shook hands with Mrs. Smith.

Prem held her by the shoulder, and they walked to the studio. Matthew would, no doubt, question Mrs. Smith. Prem hadn't been able to think of a way to prepare her. They hadn't had a woman spending the night in the house in at least fifteen years, maybe longer.

Maya instantly made herself comfortable. She slid from the sofa to the chair, examined the books, the high lectern on which he wrote, the stacks of translations of his books in German, Dutch, Hebrew, Japanese, Arabic, and Finnish, the framed awards and plaques honoring him.

Prem buzzed Mrs. Smith on the intercom. "We'll take our tea here, Mrs. Smith."

Then he turned to Maya. "Give her a few days. I haven't told her anything. She'll figure it out for herself."

Maya nodded. Outside the writing studio the sun cast long shadows as it glowed like a pink grapefruit on its way to sleep.

After tea Prem took Maya for a tour of the house. His bedroom was at one end of the house past the dining room, living room, and den.

"Here's our love nest," he said, shutting the door to his room.

Maya kicked off her white sandals and sat cross-legged on the bed. Facing her was a long, narrow painting some six feet in length, radiating gold.

"Is that a real Klimt?"

"It's good, isn't it? I bought it from some artists in France. It's so whole. The figures, the background tones, the material of the canvas itself, all are from a single source."

"This is the energy I felt from those statues in the Bois de Boulogne, when I saw them from across the lake." Maya extended her legs and relaxed back, staring at the picture.

At dinner Mrs. Smith produced a soup, fish, and a chocolate pudding.

"That was a delightful meal, Mrs. Smith," Prem said, wiping his mouth with his napkin after he was finished with dessert.

"Yes, thank you," Maya said formally.

"Would you like tea or coffee?"

"No, we'll make some ourselves if we want," Prem said.

"See you in the morning then," Mrs. Smith said, taking the plates away.

"Mrs. Smith, don't bother to get here before nine. Goodnight."

"Where does she sleep?" Maya asked.

"The other side of the house from the studio. It used to be a barn, but I had it redone for her with a bedroom and a kitchenette. When I told her I was leaving for the summer, she bought a huge TV. Apparently she's addicted to crime shows."

Prem put on a Prokofiev CD. They listened to it together.

"My apartment is invaded by ambient noises. I like listening to music here, because one hears only the music."

"You're going to go crazy with this life in retirement in about two days."

"Or adjust."

"I haven't given you time to settle in since you got here."

"I want to unpack. Can I come down to your room when I'm finished?"

"I'll be waiting."

"Can I leave you waiting with something? I wrote a reply to the first entry in your notebook to me."

He put out his hand.

"I'll be right back." Maya charged up the stairs, and he heard her on the floor above him. Then she came running down the stairs again with a few pages.

"Here." She placed them in his hand, which he was still holding out for her.

He watched her walk up the stairs, her skirt swaying to the rhythm of her hips, her feet navigating the steps one by one.

Edward walked to where Maya was standing and kissed her on both cheeks, gripping her shoulders.

"I'm sorry we are meeting this way."

"My name is Maya," she said.

"I know. I've already spoken to Pascal and to Prem's nephew in India. They're both trying to get on the next plane to the United States, but we're going to go ahead and cremate the body today. That's what he wanted. We'll have the ashes at the service."

"When will it be? The service?" Maya asked.

"I'll arrange it as soon as I know that Pascal and Homi have seats on the plane. Homi didn't want to wait six months to organize a major service."

Mrs. Smith handed Edward an espresso. He sipped it. Maya stared at his right hand, which held the small cup by its handle. He was holding the saucer in his left hand—he hadn't placed it on the table. He glanced up from his cup and looked at Maya. Prem had called him the previous week to tell him about Maya. The tone of his voice had been near jubilant.

"I'm writing a book for one person. You'll never see it," he'd said with the kind of triumphant tone that Edward had long associated with recalcitrant old men who refused to take their medicines, like his own father now in an old people's home.

"What is this book? As long as it's not very good, I don't care."

"It's an erotic journal, a private journal. I gave her the first chapter. I'll give her the second in a few weeks."

"Are you ever coming back to New York?"

"I'm flying in at the end of the week. She's going to move in with me."

At this Edward was alarmed. But he knew better than to say anything that would provoke Prem's stubborn streak.

"How did you meet her?"

"Through that boy who sent you that story."

"You're with *that* girl."

"Listen, I called with a purpose." Prem's tone changed.

"What is it?" Edward relaxed. He had been standing and clasping the phone. He undid his tie and opened his collar. It was hot in the office.

"I want you to call the attorney and change my will."

He's going to give her everything he has! At this thought Edward heavily fell into his large leather executive seat. *Prem has gone senile.*

"What do you want to change?"

"I want my notebooks and fan mail to go to her. Maya. Maya Stevenson."

"And?" *Was that all?*

"And what?"

"That's it?"

"No, one other thing. You can take that boy on, the boy who brought her to me."

"I can't even remember his name."

"Find it. It's important."

"But I gave you my word. I remember I promised *Not till you're dead.*" The secretary had probably thrown out the story when she sent him the formal rejection. Why did Prem want him to go through all this trouble now? What kind of sorcery was Maya up to?

Prem laughed.

"I'm never going to die now, Edward. Never. Not as long as she loves me."

Edward regretted those words *Not till you're dead*. Why had he said it that second time on the phone? And then why had he rushed about finding Johnson's fax, yelling at the intern, the secretary, and the junior agent until they had turned the office upside down for the meager dossier in which the short story had been filed? And why, oh why had he offered to represent Johnson when Prem was still alive?

"He called me from Paris to make changes in his will. I'm the executor of his estate."

Maya nodded, not quite listening.

"He's left you all his notebooks. The original longhand drafts of every book he ever wrote and the private notes that go with them. They are yours from now."

"Mine," Maya said mechanically.

"He's also left you all his correspondence. Some fifty cartons."

After the body was cremated, Edward drove Maya back to the city with a few boxes of Prem's letters that would fit in his car. He brought them up to her studio. As Edward placed the last box down on Maya's floor, he took another look at her. What had Prem said to her in the notebook? Had he seen it all coming? Edward had no choice but to talk to this girl. He had not seen Prem since the time they ate lunch at the beginning of the summer. She was his connection to Prem.

"Do you see what he did in the end? He rejected literature. He used to say his immortality lay in his work. And then he made *you* his immortality. He wrote for you. Do you know why he rejected literature? Did he speak about it in the notebook he gave you?" Edward spoke in a neutral voice, sweat streaming down his face.

"He told you about the orange notebook?"

"Not what was in it. That's why I'm asking. What was in it? It's important. You understand that? This is the life of the most important writer of our times. Of our world."

"It was personal. He didn't want me to share it with anyone."
Maya was certain of that. And since she had not a grain of doubt,
she knew that this tall, lean, samurai warrior in her studio could do
nothing to change her mind.

"The world needs to know why he rejected literature."

Edward's voice had gone thin and high like an animal howl-
ing at the moon. He had sat down on a chair at some point. Maya
was still standing.

"I don't think he rejected literature. You're misunderstanding
everything. We talked about books and art all summer, the possibility of creation, of art engendering art. He went to Normandy with
Pascal and said to me that it was crucial for a writer to talk to other
writers." Maya put a light hand on Edward's shoulder as she spoke.
She felt his breathing calm down, and with it her own muscles,
which had scrunched up at his aggression, eased.

"Why did he write only for you then?"

"Doesn't he have the right to even write love letters?" *What did
this man want from her? From Prem? Did he want to rob them of everything
they had shared?*

"He didn't call it a letter but a book. He said he gave you the
first chapter of a *book.*"

There was a misery in Edward's eyes, a yellow misery that Maya
felt directly in her spleen. But she couldn't comprehend the meaning
of all he was telling her. She slumped onto the floor cross-legged.

"Excuse me a minute." Edward got up and went to the bathroom. He washed his face and dried it on the only towel hanging
there. He could smell the girl's body on it. Had this scent kept
Prem? It was a delicate scent. *I shouldn't do this to her.*

"I am sorry, you're already so upset," he said, coming back
out. Maya was still sitting on the floor.

"Maybe you should ask Pascal. I am sure he can answer your
questions."

"I will. Please don't worry about it. Are you going to be all
right over here?" He looked around the studio.

Maya nodded and stood up. He left her standing contemplating the boxes they had deposited haphazardly on her floor. On the way down he had to lean against the elevator wall for support. He was tired. He wanted to go home and sleep in his wife's arms for a few hours to gather his forces before all the interviews, press releases, and radio and TV programs he would be needed for. It was best not to mention that notebook to anybody.

If only she had not written that letter and they had not made love as they did. Two times. If only she hadn't strained him, been so greedy to be close to him, he might still be alive.

Maya's letter to him lay in the pages of the notebook he had written to her. To avoid picking up the orange notebook, she spent the two days leading up to the service immersed in the cartons that Edward had deposited in her apartment. In the first three boxes the correspondence was all opened flat, but in the fourth box the letters were still in their envelopes, the envelopes themselves of all shapes and sizes. There was a slip of paper on top that was marked Judith Q and labeled Set III. Maya opened one at random and read it. It began:

How much longer must I wait? I know you are mine, you were meant to be mine.

Maya dipped her hand into the box and pulled out a handful of envelopes. Inside one was a peacock feather. He had told her in their first meeting that Judith Q had no Peacock's Eye but Maya did. The letter was more or less a repetition of the previous plaint. One had a pink panty with a note tacked on that said *mes culottes.* There were stubs from flights to Paris, a small stone wrapped in cotton that looked suspiciously like a diamond, and locks of hair. A cardboard reinforced envelope had photographs of a woman in her late forties; there were some wrinkles on the face, and her light brown hair was worn at a medium length. Maya discerned a slight bitterness at the edge of the mouth, but she could have imagined it. She read the letters suspended between disbelief and horror. Their tone was intimate, of the genre that began *Dear Diary* or *Dear God,* and Maya had difficulty in following the thread of the conversation. Maya learned facts pertaining to Prem's life. She learned that it was after Prem had been dropped by the French girls that he decided to permanently give up the sex nest he had maintained in Manhattan and withdraw from the city to suburbia. Scenes from times spent with Prem whizzed in Maya's head. The peacock dancing in the Bois de Boulogne. Soufflés, drums, walks.

Maya had turned down the volume of her answering machine and her ringer with the first sound of the telephone. She listened to her messages now. Jean-Pierre, Nadine, Johnson, and finally Nadine again. The last message from Nadine said to call her no matter what time of day or night—she needed to talk. Not one of them said Prem was dead. They all started and ended with *I'm sorry.* Even Johnson, who had not known, who could not possibly begin to know the history.

In the late hours of the night, Maya opened her notebooks from India and read them. They allowed her to be with Prem without the desolation of having lost him; they were from a time when he was yet alive and remote. Edward called her early in the morning to inform her that a car would pick her up for the service scheduled later that day. Both Pascal and he would speak at the service along with a scientist called Krishnan. Did she want to say anything? She declined.

Edward went to the airport himself to pick up Pascal. He saw no other possibility of them talking alone. The limo slowly wormed its way through Queens.

"Do you think he was less than himself this summer?"

"To the contrary. I've never seen him better. He had his ups and downs, but he had many, many burst of energy. Brilliant energy. Colorful energy. Joy. Explosions."

"I can't understand. The final decision to stop writing. To write for the girl."

"Oh, that! It was fantastic. I think he loved the idea and loved doing it."

"He rejected everything he stood for."

Pascal was silent. He looked out of the tinted windows of the car. It was the flip side of what he, Pascal, needed to do soon.

"You don't think so?" Edward pressed. They were nearing the Midtown Tunnel and with it the frenzy of public speaking and public relations that would be required at the funeral. Everyone would have time to contemplate Prem, to think of him one last time. But Edward would have to manage the show, always watch from the outside, make sure that what was best for Prem's legacy was happening. He would need a vacation after this. A vacation with one or two of Prem's books to bid him farewell.

"Prem held himself back all these years. He never made the final plunge with any of his girlfriends in the past thirty-five years. He had options, real choices with devoted women, but he always held back that kernel of himself to save it for his writing. Just the way I have always saved that kernel of myself for my emotional comfort, for feeling close to people, for love. We decided to reverse it in the summer. We talked about it at Mont-Saint-Michel. He had only so much time left to *live*. He chose to *live*."

"How could he think he would live without writing?"

"I don't think it was a systematic decision. But you know Prem, when something was circumscribed by time, he thought he was less free. He needed to know he was now in it with Maya, only with Maya, not with books. I don't think he asked how long he wouldn't write. What was important was the immediate future. I like to think that once I came out with a book, he wouldn't have liked me having the last word, and he'd have written another."

"And you? Your book?"

"Once Irène is gone, I am going to do what he told me to. I am going to keep the isolation and not seek release from it. I am going to write with it."

"Are you sure that was all there was to it with Prem?"

"I'm certain. He looked back on his life and said, 'What have I not done that I should have done?' And he chose to do it. By doing it he affirmed that it was not too late. Do you understand what it means when a man says; *'It's not too late?'* "

"Tell me." Edward had not seen Pascal since the previous fall. He missed hearing his accented English. His peculiar facility with language, his complete lack of embarrassment in stating things that most of his American writers would never verbalize.

"It means that I am going to keep evolving. Prem wanted to die in the midst of change, of activity. The important thing is to choose to keep moving instead of getting comfortable, settling, sedimenting. He taught me this."

Pascal's words seemed to start from somewhere deep within his huge gut and come out not from his lips but from his eyes. The eyes were burning with a hunger Edward had not seen before. An absolute, total, concentrated hunger. The greed for the prize, the desire for recognition, the craving for praise that he had often seen in Pascal had fallen away. What was left was pure will. Pure by being no longer in the service of another end but in its own service. It was Prem's will.

"You have to write your next book. I think you should drop the one you are working on about the critics and their criticism. It's not vital," Edward said softly.

"That one is almost finished. I write it in Irène's apartment while I hang around."

The car pulled up at the chapel where the funeral service was to be held. Within minutes Maya joined them.

"The ashes from the crematorium are inside. We'll take the urn with us after the service is over," Edward said to them.

"I'm going to scatter some in the Seine. He wanted that."

"Are you sure it's legal?" Edward asked Pascal.

"*Je m'en fous.* Who cares?"

Pascal turned to Maya. "Were you with him?"

"Yes, I was." She hadn't spoken to anyone since she had last seen Edward. Her mouth felt stiff as the words came out.

"Did he suffer?"

Edward turned his body fully to look at Maya.

"I think he was asleep. I was asleep," she said.

In the early hours of the morning Maya had felt the sheets rustle. And then she had felt Prem get back into bed. Maya, still half-asleep, had reached out to him.

"You wore your clothes," she whined.

"I was feeling cold. Do you want something too?"

"You. Closer."

Her warm body reached out and folded him into her arms.

"I know we're going to renew this lease," he whispered.

"Our lease will love forever." Maya was already half in a dream, pulled heavily into a deep sleep.

She woke up with a start. "Prem."

Even as she shook him, she knew something was wrong.

"Prem, say something," she said, fumbling for the light switch on her end of the bed.

The light was harsh and hurt her eyes. She tore away the cover. He was still warm but no longer breathing.

"No, you can't, Prem. Oh God!"

She told Edward and Pascal how she had awakened startled. If he had been in pain, he would have shouted or moved and she would have woken up. No, Maya was pretty sure he hadn't been in pain or she would have known—their bodies had been touching.

The sedan with Homi arrived. Edward walked to it immediately. Homi and Edward came back to them. Homi shook hands with Pascal and gave Maya a hug.

"I haven't told Ratan. I only told him that Prem was very ill. Was it a painful death?"

"Definitely not. He passed away in his sleep. Couldn't have been more beautiful," Edward stated authoritatively. Then he caught Maya's eyes and lowered his own.

By eleven, when the service was scheduled, the hall was full, and people crowded the aisles. Maya sat in front flanked by Pascal and Edward. They both gave their eulogies. Homi twisted and untwisted his hands. Maya felt as if she were not present. It was hard to focus on what was happening. The Indian scientist who spoke was nothing like Prem. He spoke with an accent that was hard to follow and said that a great man's measure was the people he had inspired.

The service was already over. All sorts of people came and shook Homi's hand. They were all four standing together one beside the other.

"I think we can go soon," Edward said, bringing the urn that had been placed on the table by the microphone.

Homi took the urn from Edward and held it close to himself, his eyes glistening.

A reporter called out to Edward.

"I'll be right back," he said, striding to the man.

"Mr. Homi Verma," a woman's voice called.

Maya and Pascal both looked at her for a second.

"Yes?" Homi said, turning to the woman. Maya looked at the woman and blinked.

"We met. Don't you remember?" she asked Homi.

Homi furrowed his eyebrows.

"Pascal, can you come here a minute?" Edward called out to Pascal.

"Sorry, I'll be right back." Pascal touched Maya's elbow before walking away.

The woman talking to Homi had lifted the cover of the jar and fished out a stainless steel spoon.

Maya looked transfixed.

"Madame, I—I—" Homi began.

"He wanted it so badly. You'll find it in his will. Unfortunately I'm flying out in a few hours." The woman spooned out some gray powder for her glass jar.

Is that all that's left of you? Maya fainted.

Judith Q walked out of the chapel as fast as possible following the commotion that accompanied Maya's having fallen to the floor. She hailed a taxi nervously and jumped in, clasping the jar against her chest. She stroked it like a baby. *Was it a felony to run off with someone's ashes?* She had taken only two spoonfuls. Once back home she placed it on a side table in front of her largest Rustum photo.

What to do with you? She demanded of the jar as she opened it to touch the fine gray ash inside. She scooped a spoon to examine it more closely against the light. All her life she had wanted Prem to complete her. Through his books he had owned her, and now finally she could put him inside her where he belonged. Own him.

When Maya came to, Edward, Homi, and Pascal were kneeling beside her, their faces peering overhead. She was on the wooden floor and a hand was on her forehead, Pascal's.

"*Ça va mieux?*" Pascal asked.

She nodded. He removed his hand and got himself up with the help of a chair.

Edward held her hand and stood up slowly, helping her up at the same time.

"Who was that woman?" Edward asked Homi.

"He stayed with her in West Indies when he wrote his book *Cricket in the Colonies.*"

"He stayed with my friend Swinn," Pascal said.

"She said he wanted to have his ashes scattered in the clear blue sea by Trinidad." Homi repeated what she'd said to him.

"Oh, no!" Maya brought her hand to her forehead and slapped it hard.

"What?" Edward was immediately beside her. He pushed her down into the nearest chair lest she faint again.

"She's Judith Q. I saw the photos last night. Her hair was brown in them."

"Dammit! If it hadn't been for that reporter, she'd never have gotten away with this," Edward said, gritting his teeth.

"*Quelle horreur!*" Pascal said. He sat down beside Maya. He recalled that Deleuze once said to be wary of being in anyone else's dreams. He had gone so far as to say that even the dreams of a young girl were devouring. At one point several years ago, when Judith Q had been writing every day to Prem, he had talked to Pascal about her and about Deleuze.

"Why don't you meet her once? There's little to lose," Pascal had said.

"I don't recognize such claims. Just because someone experiences my work directly or strongly doesn't mean they have any right over me or even over the creation."

"It's just you who has the right to be inspired by Maillol's statue of Flore, is it? The rest of us aren't allowed to appropriate what inspires us?"

"It's my art that gives me a claim over it! My interest in Maillol, in sculpture, isn't sterile. I engage with it, and that justifies my *small* personal claim over it. This woman's interest in me is barren. In principle it's everything I loathe."

Prem's utter distaste as he mouthed the word *loathe* still rang in Pascal's ears. It resonated with the timbre of Prem's voice. Was his friend really no more?

"What is she going to do with the ashes?" Homi asked.

"Sanctify them," Edward said.

Pascal looked at Homi, who seemed satisfied with the answer. How could he explain the abhorrent intrusion to them? Maya looked very despondent. Pascal decided to stay silent on the subject.

Edward nodded to them all, indicating it was time to leave.

"We're all dining at my house. I hope you'll join us," Edward said to Maya.

Maya looked uncertainly at Pascal.

"Absolument. Don't be alone, not tonight."

Maya waited until they had driven away and sat down on the steps of the chapel. In her purse she had the notebook Prem had given her. She brought it out and stared at the angles the letters made with the lines on which they were written, the curves that joined one word to another. When the words ended, Prem died. She opened her own note to him that was folded in the pages of the notebook. If she just continued writing to him, added her words to his, then he could live. Even a trace of Prem in her work could keep him alive, just the way Klimt lived in Schiele and Schiele in Weltman.

Maya's note to Prem was exactly like his to her and equally outside of the etiquette of polite conversation they had had with each other. Her writing was terse in its style but not in the range of possibilities it put forward. Maya had practically offered to replay in the five hundred hours any and all scenarios from his past, from his fiction, from someone else's fiction, from her own fiction, and from what was to become her fiction. She talked of her body in much the same way he had talked of it, as if both of them together owned her body. Yes, she would help him in the taking of her own flesh. Yes, he was wrinkled, his skin a drastic contrast to her own in texture, tautness, unblemishedness, and it was this very aesthetic incongruity of them together that would fuel their fire; that fueled her fire already. In the end, the epicenter of the human being, the teeming core of desire, aspiration, rage, tenderness, cruelty, and need was all independent of form. In the nude, as savages, giving full rein to their viciousness, their vulnerabilities, their mad minds, their crumpled egos, their writers' arrogance, their selves teetering on the edge of what was tolerable, livable as paradox, their bodies were stand-ins for every woman, every man, every sex organ, their instincts simultaneously chaste, whorish, romantic, their fusion a complete rejection of one another yet a complete consumption of one by the other. No possibility unturned. No derangement impossible. No whim to be denied.

Maya handed the letter to Prem and then joined him in his room half an hour later in her flimsy white tank. He felt like Priapus all over again on reading her and seeing her. They were silent. The pages had aroused Prem to the point that his whole body was turgid. She slid quietly into bed and put her hand into his boxers before she had even kissed him. They fucked wordlessly and urgently.

"It's nothing like I thought it would be. I always imagined sweet, slow lovemaking."

"There is no single it. There never is." Prem drew her close.

"I wasn't complaining. Both of us were in the same mood."

"Were you shocked when you read the notebook?"

"It was unexpected. I was so much kinder than you. I didn't give you anything to read on a transatlantic flight for eight hours. Do you know how difficult it is to be delirious in a closed public space?"

Prem laughed.

"I'm still hungry."

"I take it that you're not talking about food."

"No. I mean for your skin. For your touch. For all the slow deliciousness I always imagined it would be with you. Are you tired?"

"Not in the least. Let's straighten out this sheet first." Prem sat up in bed and smoothed out the sheet that covered them.

They lay in an embrace, and Prem ran his hands on Maya's chest and belly.

"Has anyone other than your sister called you Premi Prem?"

"Now you have. It's a *jeu de mot*. *Premi* in Hindi means 'lover' and *Prem* means 'love.' "

"She was your lover, wasn't she?"

"Yes. You guessed?"

"Why else would there be echoes from *Meher* in the orange notebook? I am sorry—is it painful to speak about her?"

"Not with you. She started calling me that when we were quite young, but as we got older our relationship metamorphosed into what the words suggested."

After a second of silence Maya asked, "Is Homi your son?"

Her heart beat fast, as if she were crossing a new frontier by asking the question.

"I don't know, Maya. Should I know? Should Homi know? Have I failed in the most basic task given to a man when he is born?" There was an uncertainty in Prem's voice that Maya had not heard before. She kissed him.

"The doubt kills me sometimes. Not about whether he's my son but about what the right thing is. Have I robbed him of a birthright?" he whispered.

"Oh, darling!" She pulled him into her arms.

"I don't want to doubt anymore. I don't want to doubt us," he said, overcome.

"Don't doubt us. Feel my hand, feel this, and this," Maya said, running her palms over Prem's torso and his face: touching the surface of his cheeks gently, but then squeezing sections of his neck and shoulder that felt tight.

Maya's touch was rejuvenating. He wanted it everywhere. On his feet, between his toes, on his back, the space where the back of his thighs joined up with his ass, the sides of his ribs. As she touched various parts of his body, those parts let go and forgot the abuses they had suffered. Prem himself let go.

"Turn on your stomach," she said.

Maya covered his back with light kisses and then lay herself over him, supporting herself on her elbows, afraid of putting her full weight on him.

"Am I too heavy?"

"Not at all," he said, his voice heavy with pleasure.

Maya smiled to herself in the dark.

"To think we could have entered this paradise months ago!" she said.

"I was jealous of that French fellow."

"If you'd asked me back with you after the concert, I'd have followed."

"He had his hands all over you," Prem said. He remembered those hands tapping her body like a drum. He had a sudden searing need to cover her with his own hands. He pulled her off his back and grabbed her flesh. She moaned.

"Can you feel my hands?" he asked, his voice hoarse.

She moaned again. She felt small, like a small marble encased in giant Rodin hands, protected, owned. Contained within his palms by the crisscrossing lines that marked his life and fate.

Prem stuck his thumb into Maya's mouth. And then his fingers in her sex and then his sex in her sex. His tongue in her mouth, her nose, her ears. When they finally separated, sleep invaded their bodies more or less simultaneously.

And then the sudden panic as she woke up knowing something was wrong. The hazy hours as Mrs. Smith made a series of phone calls. How she had cried beside his body pleading *You can't leave me now. Not now. We've just begun after waiting for so long.*

Maya didn't know how long she had been sitting on the steps of the chapel when a familiar voice asked, "Are you doing okay?"

It was Johnson.

"I'm sorry, Maya." He sat down beside her on the steps and

put his arm around her. "You knew him, didn't you? He was the one."

Maya looked at Johnson.

"I'm really sorry, Maya."

"Prem is dead," she finally said. The effort of saying it brought all the muscles of her face into a spasm.

"But he left all those books. The best books."

Maya rested her head on her knees. They were burning from lack of sleep and crying. She wanted to sleep inside a book. Sleep for years.

"Are you okay?"

"I saw the world through Prem's books. But then, most of all I saw everything this summer through his eyes."

"And he through yours, no less. Don't forget that."

"I want to keep seeing from his eyes. The eyes are immortal, aren't they? I want a book choked with his presence. I want to write Prem. Not about him, not about me, not about what could have been or was. But Prem himself. I want to write a book of him. There's no preposition in the language for it."

"You will, Maya."

"I feel very tired. As if I weigh a thousand pounds."

Maya closed her eyes for a second and saw Prem's face again. It had been serene. She had touched his lips with her fingers and then kissed them. Their coldness had sent a shiver in her body.

Johnson got up and gave her his hand to help her up.

"Come now. Let me get you home."

Acknowledgments

For their comments on my draft I would like to thank Claudette Buelow, Marcello Cavagna, Krzysztof Owerkowicz, and Brent Isaacs. My agent Ira Silverberg and John Siciliano at Anchor Books provided invaluable support and criticism. Lorna Owen has been a model editor. Thank you, Lorna, thank you. I am grateful to the team at Doubleday who made it happen behind the scenes.

Chérif at Fil'O'Fromage in Paris generously shared his expertise and his infectious enthusiasm on matters cheese. Cláudia Sofia drove me to Brittany and Normandy and allowed me to remain with my characters. Carine, Sylvie, and the entire Barco family have gone a long way in making me feel at home in Paris and elsewhere. For answering an assortment of questions I am grateful to Professor Emeritus Howard Lentner, Olivier Fontenay, Luis Vassy, Erkki Maillard, and Cédric Labourdette. Any errors that rest are mine. Ravi and Priti Aisola extended their kindness and hospitality on many occasions. Yann Apperry's care and attention with the French orthography in this novel has been priceless. *Merci a tous!*

Finally, heartfelt thanks to Nan Talese.

A Note About the Author

Born in New Delhi, India, ABHA DAWESAR
has written two other novels. Her most recent novel, *Babyji*, won the 2006 American
Library Association's Stonewall Award. She
is also a winner of a NYFA Fiction fellowship